The

Music Dramas of Richard Wagner

RICHARD WAGNER

THE MUSIC DRAMAS OF RICH-ARD WAGNER AND HIS FESTI-VAL THEATRE IN BAYREUTH ✄ ✄

BY ALBERT LAVIGNAC PROFESSOR OF HARMONY AT THE CONSERVATOIRE AT PARIS ✄

TRANSLATED FROM THE FRENCH
BY ESTHER SINGLETON WITH
ILLUSTRATIONS AND DIAGRAMS

HASKELL HOUSE PUBLISHERS LTD.
Publishers of Scarce Scholarly Books
NEW YORK. N. Y. 10012
1969

First Published 1898

HASKELL HOUSE PUBLISHERS LTD.
Publishers of Scarce Scholarly Books
280 LAFAYETTE STREET
NEW YORK, N. Y. 10012

Library of Congress Catalog Card Number: 68-25293

Standard Book Number 8383-0284-x

Printed in the United States of America

PREFACE

IN writing the thousand and first book on Richard
Wagner and his work, I do not pretend to accomplish anything better than has yet been done. My aim
has been something quite different, — a real practical
guide to Bayreuth for the French which will answer the
needs and satisfy the curiosity of those of our nation
who have not yet taken that little journey, which is so
easy and attractive. I have also desired to indicate in
what state of mind it should be undertaken and what
seductive preliminary studies are necessary to the complete enjoyment of the trip; finally, it has been my
desire to present the Wagnerian style in its own proper
light, by dissipating the clouds with which it has been
enveloped by certain of its commentators, who, far from
smoothing the way, have made it bristle with difficulties.
This is the sole criticism I will allow myself: they write
for Wagnerians, not for neophytes.

Of course, I have not read all that has been written
about Wagner, — one human life would not suffice for
that, and one would have to be a polyglot, — but I have
studied a very large number of important works, especially
those of *Ernst, Schuré, Chamberlain, de Brinn' Gaubast,*
the biography by *Adolphe Jullien* and that in *Grove's*
English Dictionary, *Wagner's* Letters and Autobiography,
the writings of *Wolzogen, Maurice Kufferath, Soubies,*

Malherbe, etc., all very remarkable from various points of view; and the spirit and matter of these I have endeavoured to condense. But my most precious documents are those I myself collected on the spot, and among them are many which are now printed for the first time; for these I am indebted to the kindness of Herr A. von Gross, the head of the *Bühnenfestspiel;* my learned friend, J. B. Weckerlin, librarian of the Conservatoire, has greatly facilitated my researches for others; and I have laid under contribution the inexhaustible archives of M. Lascoux, one of the first and most enthusiastic Wagnerians, and the erudition of my friend, Vincent d'Indy, from one of whose letters I have not scrupled to borrow whole paragraphs.

To all of these kind collaborateurs I here offer my most heartfelt gratitude. I also owe thanks to my pupil, Paul Jumel, who has aided me in classifying the notes and in correcting the proofs.

A. L.

PARIS, 1897.

CONTENTS

ILLUSTRATIONS

The
Music Dramas of Richard Wagner

CHAPTER I

LIFE IN BAYREUTH

"O ye who dwell . . . on the shore
sacred to the virgin goddess of the
golden shafts . . . where the Greeks
meet in famous council . . . soon
shall the glorious voice of the flute
go up for you again, resounding with
no harsh strain of grief, but with such
music as the lyre maketh to the
gods!" — SOPHOCLES.

BAYREUTH, as is witnessed by the beauty of many
of its monuments and the width of its streets,
had its period of splendour when it was the residence of
the Margraves during the seventeenth and the first half
of the eighteenth century. It has now again become a
fine provincial town, quiet and easy-going; life should
be peaceful and comfortable there, to judge from several
imposing private hotels which are almost palatial, the
smart houses which line the aristocratic quarters, and the
fine theatre, whose interior, a veritable marvel of the " ro-
coco " style, attests past grandeur. This theatre, which
keeps a respectful silence when its celebrated and over-
powering neighbour begins to speak, offers all the sweetness of Italian music, of *opéra comique*, and even of
operettas to the inhabitants of Bayreuth, who seem to

ɪ

welcome with interest *Les Dragons de Villars*, *Lucia di Lammermoor*, and *La Fille de Mme. Angot*.

But it is on the approach of the performances in the Festival-Theatre that the town is to be seen departing from its accustomed calm and adorning itself to welcome its guests, who become more numerous each season.

A full month in advance the performers, coming from all parts of Germany, and even from abroad, to co-operate in the great work, begin to animate the usually silent streets with their presence, gathering in the inns, and from morning to night dotting the road leading to the theatre, to which they are called by the numerous rehearsals.

The hotels make their toilette; private houses, destined also to entertain strangers, are put in their best order: nothing is too good, according to the idea of these kind and hospitable people, for the expected lodgers. The housekeeper, who has cleaned her house from top to bottom with scrupulous care, in honour of her visitors deprives herself of all her ornaments to decorate their rooms lavishly, adding garlands and bunches of artificial flowers. She selects the finest embroidered sheets from her chests, and provokingly puts covers, which are always too narrow, on them by means of a complicated system of buttons. The first night or two we are a little out of our bearings, but we quickly grow accustomed to this strange fashion and soon come to sleep peacefully under the benevolent eyes of the host's family portraits, among which a bust of Wagner and a lithograph of Franz Liszt are always found.

During this period of preparation and work, it is especially in the neighbourhood of the Festival-Theatre that activity is concentrated. The artists have not always the time, after the morning rehearsal, to go back

VIEW OF BAYREUTH FROM FESTIVAL-THEATRE

to the town at the lunch hour, and often take their meal
in the spacious restaurant, which is near by, and which
is also smartened up and festooned with the Bavarian
colours to receive in a few days the numerous guests to
whom it will serve the most varied *menus* of a good French
cuisine. In the meanwhile, it supplies the *personnel* of the
theatre with a very comfortable dinner (in Germany they
dine at one o'clock), for the modest sum of one mark.
There is nothing more amusing than these groups in
which Siegfried is seen fraternizing with Mime, and Parsifal in no wise terrified by the presence of the Flower-
maidens. At a table set in the open air, and always
surrounded by a family group, dines Hans Richter, who,
with his sandy beard, large-brimmed hat, and short velvet
coat, would be recognized among a thousand.

But the hour strikes; it is time to get back to work:
the large break drawn by two white horses, well-known
to the inhabitants of Bayreuth, arrives, and, after describing a skilful curve, sets down before the porch of the
Theatre the inspirer and oracle of all this little world,
Frau Wagner, the valiant custodian of the traditions and
wishes of the Master, whose activity never forsakes her
and who is present at all the rehearsals, watching over
the smallest details. Here is also Herr von Gross, who
seconds Frau Wagner's efforts with his wide knowledge
of affairs and enlightened devotion.

We next direct our steps to the hall where the door
is shut, conscientiously guarded by an old servant of
Wahnfried. The silence lasts until nightfall and is only
broken by occasional pedestrians, inhabitants of the town,
who sometimes stroll as far as this to enjoy the view and
the splendid sunsets which are to be seen from the ter-
raced gardens adjoining the Theatre.

The ordinary rehearsals are strictly private; but to the

general rehearsals of each work, which take place just before the opening of the season, Frau Wagner invites her friends in Bayreuth (who have no seats at the series, which are all reserved for strangers), and also the families of her faithful auxiliaries, the artists.

It would be impossible, moreover, to judge of the desired sonorous effects if these final rehearsals took place in an empty hall; the presence of the spectators very sensibly improves its acoustics.

FESTIVAL-THEATRE, BAYREUTH

The date fixed months before for the first performance at last arrives: every one is at his post, armed and ready; the town is adorned with flags, and, let it be said in passing, there is no fear of missing the French colours from among the flags of all nationalities, which will at once reassure those people who are doubtful — if any remain — of their kind reception by the Bavarians.

In a few hours Bayreuth is full of the animation of its great days. People very limited with regard to time

often arrive at the last moment; but that is a bad plan,
and we cannot too strongly advise those who can do it
to reserve at least half a day for rest, during which they
may familiarize themselves with the very special moral
atmosphere of this little district, before they climb the
leafy road which leads to the theatre.   People do not go
there as they go to the Opéra in Paris, or in any other
city, taking with them their cares of yesterday and their
worldly indifference.   Or, at least, they should not go
thus, for it would be voluntarily depriving themselves of
one of the most intense artistic emotions it is possible to
experience, if they entered the hall of the Festival-
Theatre at Bayreuth without being sympathetically at-
tuned to what they have come to hear.   Unfortunately
that is what often happens now that the Wagnerian
pilgrimage has become as fashionable as it is to go to
Spa, or to Monte Carlo.   I know perfectly well that it
is impossible to make all the spectators pass an examination before permitting them to enter the hall, or to make
sure that, either by their musical education or by the
intelligent interest which they take in matters of art,
they are worthy to enter into the sanctuary; but it must
be confessed that it is painful to hear the absurd remarks
which show how unworthy is a certain portion of the
public that now frequents Bayreuth.   I have heard one
woman ask who was the author of the piece to be given
the next day; and another rejoiced that they were going
to perform *Sigurd* (*!*), which she liked so much.   Her
companion, an enlightened musician, to whom she made
this astonishing remark, set himself respectfully, though
greatly distressed, to correct her grave error, and began to
sketch for her the subject of the Tetralogy, which, indeed,
interested her very much, for she had not the least notion
of it, when, darkness enveloping the hall and the grum-

blings of the admirable prelude to the first act of *Die Walküre* being heard, it was necessary to interrupt this education, alas! so tardily begun.

More than an hour before the time fixed for the play a long line of carriages forms to bring the public to the theatre. These carriages, too few for the number of rich amateurs, are taken by assault; it is well to engage them in advance if you do not wish to go on foot, which you can do in a delightful walk of about twenty minutes along the shady lanes parallel with the principal avenue. The landaus and victorias, somewhat out of date and made to be drawn by two horses, have never more than one, harnessed to the right side of the shaft (as horses are scarce), which produces the most comic effect.

If you are among the first to arrive, you have ample leisure to examine the new-comers and to notice that the toilettes have singularly gained in elegance during the past years. Formerly every one was contented with a simple travelling costume; then, little by little, the standard rose, and if tourists' costumes are seen now, they are in the minority. I speak here principally of the ladies, who display bright and fresh toilettes. The sole annoying point for them is the hat, which they will not consent to leave with the attendants during the acts, when it is strictly forbidden to keep it on the head. They resign themselves, then, to holding it on their lap, which is scarcely comfortable.

This moment of waiting in the open air and daylight, 'for the performance begins at four o'clock (*Rheingold*, which begins at five o'clock, is an exception), is perfectly charming. The situation of the Theatre, admirably chosen by Wagner, commanding a smiling country with the town in the foreground and the woods and meadows of green Franconia for the horizon, is absolutely enchanting. However, it must not rain; for the building, so well arranged for everything else, only offers under its exterior galleries which are open to every wind, a poor shelter, where at such times the public huddles under umbrellas streaming with rain. But, doubtless, God protects the spectators of Bayreuth, for it is generally fine, and you can stay outside till the last moment.

Now let us go into the hall and make its acquaintance while it is still brightly illuminated.

You enter it in the simplest way: no black-coated gentlemen are seated behind a desk. One *employé* only is found at each of the numerous entrances to see that you have not mistaken your door, and tears off the coupon of the performance for that day. You will come back again after each *entr'acte* without any one troubling about you.

The hall, which we will describe later in detail, before the curtain rises gives one the impression of an aviary in full activity; every one is moving about, more or less excited, talking with his neighbour, exchanging his impressions, or relating his previous visits to this musical city; then you search the distant rows for friends, or simply for the well-known faces of those whom you know to be attending the same series as yourself.

During this time the gallery reserved for the crowned heads, and which is called the Royal Boxes, fills. Frau Wagner's seats are filling in their turn. Her aristocratic profile is visible; she seats herself in the front row with her delightful daughters, and Siegfried Wagner, the living image of his father, joins them when his duties do not call him to the orchestra or upon the stage. However, the last call of the trumpets (see Chapter V.) sounds outside and the rare late arrivals come in. Suddenly

darkness envelops the hall and there is perfect silence.
I should like it better if people were silent from the very
first. It seems to me that all this agitation is a bad
preparation for what is to come; but it cannot be
prevented.

The eye can distinguish nothing at first, then it gradually gets accustomed to the feeble light produced by
some lamps near the ceiling.

From this moment one might hear a pin drop; every
one concentrates his thoughts, and every heart beats
with emotion. Then amidst the luminous and golden
haze which rises from the depths of the " mystic abyss,"
mount, warm, vibrant, and velvety, the incomparable
harmonies unknown elsewhere, which, taking possession
of your whole being, transport you to a world of dreams.
The curtain opens in the middle and masses itself
on each side of the stage, exposing to view scenery
which, as a rule, is very beautiful. Criticism, which
never gives up its rights, disapproves of many things,
though almost always wrongly in our opinion; but let
us set that question aside (as well as the performance,
which will be fully dealt with hereafter) to recall our
impressions at the end of the act, when, the last chord
having sounded, we start from our ecstasy to go and
breathe the pure air outside.

Let us state in passing that the atmosphere of the
hall, thanks probably to an ingenious system of ventilation, has never seemed mephitic to us, like the majority of theatres we know; on returning we do not
experience that asphyxiating sensation that is usually so
disagreeable.

Nothing could be more delicious or more restful
than these *entr'actes* passed in the open air, nor could
anything be gayer; we find many people there, we hear

French spoken on all sides, and we have the feeling of
being at home, as on coming out of the Conservatoire,
or the Lamoureux or Colonne concerts. The memory
of our " absent country " does not come into our minds
with any sadness.

Usually at the end of the performance people go to
supper in one of the large restaurants immediately adjoining the theatre. There is a third, a little higher up
and a little more isolated, where those who like to prolong their meditations will find a calm, quiet, and
comfortable retreat.

It is prudent to engage a table in advance at the large
restaurant, for without doing so we risk a very late
supper. The *cuisine* there is excellent. We can either
select a very choice *menu*, for which we shall have to
pay accordingly ; or we can satisfy ourselves for a very
reasonable price. The artists often meet there, and
when after the performance one who has greatly delighted the public enters, it is not rare to see everybody
spontaneously rise to give him a warm and noisy ovation. And this so much the more willingly because they
never appear on the stage to receive the plaudits of their
admirers. This is a custom which Wagner established
from the first. At first it was even strictly prohibited
to applaud at the end of the work, and the performances of the *Ring*, which during the first year formed
the programme of the Festivals, ended in a respectful
and affecting silence, which certainly agreed better with
the poignant impression left by the admirable final scene
than noisy demonstrations ; however, several regrettable
infractions of the rule took place, the enthusiasm mani-
festing itself in the usual way, which was against
Wagner's wish, and which he had much trouble in
repressing. It has always remained the tradition not

to applaud *Parsifal*, but for the other works the public
has had its way : it is not possible to prevent the
bravos from breaking out at the end of the performance.   The public even took it into its head, in 1896,
at the end of the first series, to call for Richter, who had
conducted the Tetralogy in a masterly manner.   For more
than a quarter of an hour frantic applause and shouts,
enough to bring the house down, were heard on every

MARKET PLACE

side; but the noble and modest artist, faithful to the
established rule, did not yield to the general wish, and
remained obstinately invisible; he even avoided showing
himself at supper where he doubtless feared a renewal of
the demonstrations.   A similar scene recurred over Mottl
eight days later.   He had literally electrified his audience
by his admirable conducting of the orchestra; but, being just as retiring as his rival, he kept out of sight
with the same modesty.   And when Siegfried Wagner's

turn came to conduct his father's work, he also respectfully conformed to the tradition, notwithstanding the
sympathetic recalls of the entire audience.

The mornings pass quickly in Bayreuth; while waiting
for the Theatre to open we visit the town and the monuments, which, to tell the truth, have only a secondary
interest; but it is charming to lounge about there.

THE NEW CASTLE

The local guides will tell the reader that he must see
the ancient castle, where there is a tower, to the top of
which you can drive in a carriage (as in the Château
d'Amboise), and from which a beautiful view is to be
had of the surrounding country, gay, smiling, and fertile; the new castle also, which contains a collection
of indifferent pictures; they also point out the statues of
kings, writers, and pedagogues which adorn the squares,
and tell him the number of churches he should visit, enu-
merating, meanwhile, the tombs of the Margraves which
they contain.   The conscientious tourist will certainly

not neglect to make this round in detail.   Others, on
the contrary, maintaining that they have come solely on
a musical pilgrimage, do not *wish* to know anything else
than the road leading to the Festival-Theatre.

Many people employ their mornings in reading over
the score which they will hear in the evening, or the
poem, and these are not the worst employed.   You can
procure a passable piano at a large price, but you must
be a millionaire to hire a grand piano!   In every street
are heard harmonious chords, and from numerous open
windows float the well-known *Leit-motive.*

The loungers, to rest their minds, content themselves
with quiet walks through the streets and with visits to
the book-shops, where are to be seen the classic collection of portraits of the Master, the photographs of the
principal artists, and a lithograph representing an " Evening at Wahnfried."   Formerly there were also shops
for " souvenirs of Bayreuth," which offered all possible
extravagances and were really amusing.   At that time
announcements like the following might be seen :

---

*Latest
Novelty.*   **Souvenir of Bayreuth.**   *Latest
Novelty.*

*A very pretty box, decorated with scenes from the operas
of Richard Wagner, and containing* Spiced Bread *of
an exquisite flavour, highly recommended to all visitors
to the Festivals.*

Choice Selection.

Cuff Buttons *and* Scarf Pins, *with the* Portrait *of our great Master,* Richard Wagner.

But they have now become more quiet, and this year you would have much trouble to find foulards with the Festival-Theatre printed in two colours, and shirt-fronts embroidered in *Leit-motive*.

The lunch-hour comes quickly; then, according to our purse or our tastes, we go either to one of the fine and famous restaurants which are found in the principal streets and in all the large hotels (there we can meet with the stars and the principal people of the Theatre), or to the more picturesque and characteristic inns, such as Vogl or Sammt, where the artists and the old inhabitants of Bayreuth often meet after the performances.

Here in the open air we can try the excellent beer of the country, served in a mug of extraordinary height and capacity, surmounted by a pewter lid, which is as embarrassing to novices as the long-necked vase was to the fox in the fable. For these mugs you pay the astonishing price of fifteen *pfennige*. With this Bavarian beer it is not unfitting to take an *omelette aux confitures*, or those delicious *Pfannkuchen*, of which only the German *cuisine* has the secret, or a dish of sausages and sauerkraut. Let not delicate palates exclaim at this: what seems gross at home often becomes delicious when served in its proper surroundings. The buffet at the station also offers those who would lunch a resource of which one rarely thinks; there you are well treated, and served more quickly than elsewhere.

Let it be said here that, contrary to the accepted idea, the trip to Bayreuth does not necessarily mean an excessive expenditure, and is within the reach of moderate purses. Thinking how profitable and instructive it might be for musical students, or even for young amateurs of limited means, to be able to attend these model performances, we have studied the plan of this journey from an economical standpoint, even setting ourselves, with this end in view, to try the restaurants of different grades which seemed acceptable to us; and we have calculated that a young man who does not mind travelling second class, and taking twenty-four hours on the journey to Nuremberg, will spend on the railway, going and returning, very nearly one hundred and thirty francs (the return ticket is 121fr. 25c.). Let us allow him about forty francs for extras and restaurants during the two days that he spends *en route*, going and returning; this makes one hundred and seventy francs. It is possible to live very comfortably in Bayreuth for a dozen francs a day, room and meals. It now remains to see how many performances he wants to attend, and to remember that the price of a single seat is twenty-five francs. Admitting that he attends four, which up to the present time [1] has constituted the longest series, we shall arrive at the conclusion, without being great mathematicians, that he can pay for everything during six days' absence with three hundred and fifty francs. It is certain that he must not indulge himself in any follies, or even useless expenses, that he must be content with a simple valise to avoid the expenses of baggage (nothing is carried free in Germany), that he will make use of his own legs in his excursions, and that he will not bring back a present for each member of his family. But, on the other hand, what profound, indelible memories he will return with, and what a precious lesson he will have gained!

He who intends to travel comfortably, and without denying himself anything, must expect to spend from five hundred to six hundred francs.

[1] For the first time in 1897 there were five works represented, the Tetralogy and *Parsifal*.

During the days of rest which separate the performances, or in the mornings, it is pleasant to make some
of the excursions which the environs offer.

You can go to Berneck; the trip is about two
hours in a carriage; it shows you a picturesque corner
in the smiling valley of the Œlsnitz; the little town is
beautifully situated on the rock in a wild and mountainous country; it makes a delightful walk.

THE ERMITAGE

There is also the Ermitage, whose beautiful park
and celebrated elm-grove merit more attention than the
horrible structure of the castle, encrusted from top to
bottom with shell-work and cut pebbles.   Let us mention, however, a very graceful colonnade in hemicycle,
also the basins in which they will make different jets of
water play in your honour, recalling the far distant ones
of Versailles.

The Fantaisie, the park of which is open to the
public, is a private estate, which is almost always rented

during the season to some distinguished visitor. From the terrace of the castle there is a lovely and melancholy view, which reminds you of certain compositions of Gustave Doré.

All of these places are naturally provided with restaurants where you can lunch; here are to be found our neighbours of yesterday and to-morrow, as well as the artists, who come with their families to rest after their interesting but severe labours. Sympathetic relations are quickly established, and you cannot resist the pleasure of seizing their hand, even if you do not know them, and congratulating them on their intelligent interpretation. You can express yourself in French, if you do not speak German; such things are understood in all languages. In my opinion, one of the charms in the life in Bayreuth is this frequent meeting with the artists, whose lives are so often full of interesting particulars.

You also have the chance of seeing them at Wahnfried, if good fortune gives you any right of introduction there.

Frau Wagner, triumphing over all the fatigues caused by her arduous occupation, every week during the season gives entertainments, to which she invites her personal friends and a small number of the happy elect. As precious as any other memories are those passed in the house of the Master, which is still so full of him, and amongst those who have known and been with him.

How can we describe the exceptional charm of the mistress of the house, and the exquisite affability with which she receives the most modest, as well as the most authoritative, admirers of Wagner? We, for our part, are profoundly touched by it, as well as with her gracious and very particular courtesy to the French.

Frau Wagner is admirably seconded in her rôle by her son and by her very charming daughters, who rival each other in the amiable reception of their guests.

At these receptions the interpreters from the Theatre are often heard, and sometimes foreign artists, marvellously accompanied by Herr Mottl, who, not contenting himself with being a great orchestral conductor, is also a pianist of the highest order.

The large central hall in the villa, where they have the music, is ornamented with a very handsome bust of Wagner, and statues of his principal heroes : the Flying Dutchman, Tannhäuser, Lohengrin, Walter von Stolzing, and Hans Sachs. A frieze *en grisaille* represents the principal scenes of the Tetralogy. The superb library adjoining this hall proves, by the number and selection of its volumes, the rare erudition, as well as the eclecticism of him who formed it. Here, also, among a profusion of objects of art and precious souvenirs, we admire interesting portraits of the Master and his wife.

The villa is situated in a fine park at the end of Richard Wagner street, originally named *Rennweg*, one of the principal arteries of the town. It is built in the style of a Roman villa, and in front, above the entrance door, is an allegorical fresco representing Wotan and his two ravens, with Tragedy and Music on either side, and with them stands the young Siegfried, the " *chef-d'œuvre* of the future." Beneath it an inscription reads : " Here where my imagination has found peace, this house shall be called by me the peace of imagination." [1]

---

[1] The German words are : " Hier wo mein Wähnen Frieden fand, Wahnfried sei dieses Haus von mir benannt." The figures of the fresco are portraits : Wotan represents Betz ; Tragedy, Mme. Schroeder-Devrient ; Music, Cosima Wagner ; and Siegfried, Siegfried Wagner. — E. S.

It is in the grounds of this estate, in a spot selected by himself, that the Master sleeps his last sleep, near those who loved him so much and who only live to venerate and glorify his memory.   On Sunday morning, accomplishing a pious pilgrimage, you can pass through the gate, which is then open, to the severe and bare tomb overlooking the city's recreation ground, a beautiful park planted with ancient trees.

WAHNFRIED

Not far away in the Bayreuth cemetery, the Abbé Liszt reposes in a chapel, still encumbered with offerings of sorrow from his numerous worshippers.   Death surprised him in 1886, during the performances at Bayreuth, whither he had come, already ill, to visit his daughter and to bring once again the homage of his affectionate admiration for the work of the friend whom he had been one of the first to understand, and whom he had never ceased to console and comfort in the painful road to glory.

When we read Wagner's correspondence and biographies, and take into consideration his struggles, the innumerable difficulties encountered on the way, the ill-will, the unintelligent fetters which retarded for so many years the expansion of his labours (which did not go so far as to make him doubt his own genius — he felt it working in him too powerfully to be able to mistake it — but sufficiently to make him doubt if he would ever be allowed to spread his wings), when we recall all this bitterness, all this sadness, and when we now see the work standing full of life, increasing every day, and gathering around it so many faithful devotees in this town of Bayreuth, almost unknown hitherto, and to-day bearing inscribed forevermore in letters of gold this glorious name which serves it as a luminous aureole, when we see these thousands of pilgrims coming from all parts of the world to bring the tribute of their enthusiastic cult, and lastly, when we remember that all this is the result of the will and of the greatness of one human brain, we remain silent, pensive, and filled with admiration for that prodigious intellect and that matchless organization, whose equal cannot be found among the annals of the past.

CHAPTER II

BIOGRAPHY

> " It was necessary that he should suf-
> fer, for he was a man of genius."
>   H. HEINE.

R ICHARD WAGNER, born in Leipzig, May 22,
1813, was the son of *Carl Friedrich Wilhelm
Wagner*, a police-officer raised to the rank of chief of
police by Davoust during the French occupation, and of
Johanna Rosina Bertz, who died in 1848.

Several of Richard Wagner's eight brothers and sisters
embraced the theatrical career: *Albert*, who was the
father of *Johanna Jachmann*, a celebrated singer; *Johanna Rosalie*, wife of *Oswald Marbach*, who was a distinguished actress; and *Clara Wilhelmine*, who was also
a talented singer.

After the battle of Leipzig an epidemic carried off the
father of the family, who left his widow in a precarious
condition. She was married again in 1815 to Ludwig
Geyer, an actor, minor dramatist, and portrait-painter.
Geyer took his wife and her children to Dresden, where
an engagement called him; he conceived a deep affection
for the little Richard (who loved him like a father), and
wanted to make a painter of him. But the child showed
little aptitude for drawing, and manifested, on the other
hand, a marked inclination for music. Wagner himself
relates that the day before his stepfather's death in 1821,
having played on the piano some pieces which his sisters

had taught him, he heard the dying man in the next
room say in a weak voice: " Will he have the gift of
music ? "

From his earliest years Wagner had an absolute passion
for Weber; he knew *Der Freischütz* by heart, and hid
himself to watch its composer, who frequently came to
see Mme. Geyer, whose great intelligence made her a
favourite with artists.

From the beginning of his studies in the *Kreutzschule*
of Dresden he showed a strong taste for literature, as
well as a manifest facility for versification.   Æschylus,
Sophocles, and Shakespeare, strongly excited his admiration, and under their influence he planned a great drama
in which the forty-two characters all died in the course
of the play, so that in order to finish his fifth act he had
to bring them back as spectres.

In 1827 he had been taken from the *Kreutzschule*,
where he had reached the third grade, and placed in the
Nicolaïschule in Leipzig, in the fourth, which completely
discouraged him.   He became a very bad pupil, and
neglected his studies to devote himself exclusively to his
drama.   During this period he heard at the *Gewandhaus
Concerts* for the first time Beethoven's Symphonies and
Egmont, which made a deep impression upon him.   In
his enthusiasm he wanted to write music for his wonderful drama, and diligently set to work, to the great distress
of his family who did not believe in his vocation.   However, he insisted to such a degree that he succeeded in
getting music lessons with an organist named Müller.
Fearing nothing, he wrote an overture for full orchestra,
which he managed to have performed.   " This," he
says, " was the culminating point of my absurdities.
What I did, above all things, wrong was a roll *fortissimo*

upon the kettle-drums, which returned regularly every four bars throughout the composition. The surprise which the public experienced changed first to unconcealed ill-humour, and then into laughter which greatly mortified me !"

WAGNER'S BIRTHPLACE IN LEIPZIG

Then come the troubles of July, 1830, when young Richard turns his thoughts solely to revolutionary politics, and, entering into them with might and main, he abandons all his studies, including music. He, however, enters the University of Leipzig to follow the courses of æsthetics and philosophy, but gives himself up to the extravagances of student life. Luckily, this soon disgusts him, and he feels the need of returning to his work. He has the good fortune to find in the excellent Theodor Weinlig a remarkable professor, who knows how to gain his confidence, and induces him to make a thorough study of fugue and counterpoint. He learns to know and appreciate Mozart, and composes a Polonaise and Sonata, awkward imitations of the styles of Beethoven and Schubert, which he dedicates to his master Weinlig. These two compositions were published at Breitkopf and Härtel's, where they are still to be had. His lessons only lasted six months, for he profited by them to a remarkable extent, and thus " acquired," as he himself has said, " independence in his method of writing."

He left in 1832 for Vienna, where he found French music and *pots-pourris* the fashion. On his way back he stopped at Prague and managed to have several of his compositions played there, among others a symphony. There he wrote the poem and the first number of an opera, *Die Hochzeit*, in which the deplorable influence of the bad French school is felt, and which he tore up the following year because the subject was displeasing to his sister Rosalie.

His career as a musician really begins in 1833. He goes to Würzburg to be with his brother Albert, a distinguished singer, and, whilst fulfilling the duties of chorusmaster in the theatre of the town, he composes, after one of Gozzi's fables, the libretto and music of a romantic opera, *Die Feen*, which contained many good things, and was manifestly inspired by Beethoven and Weber. Fragments were performed at the theatre of Würzburg, but it was never staged. The manuscript afterwards became the property of the King of Bavaria.

It was in 1834 that Wagner for the first time heard Mme. Schroeder-Devrient, whose dramatic talent exercised such powerful influence upon his genius in making him comprehend what wonderful effects might be produced by an intimate union of poetry and music. Long afterwards in his career he said of her: " Every time I compose a character, it is she whom I see."

It was also at this period that he began to write his opera *Das Liebesverbot* (also entitled *La Novice de Palermo*), which he finished in 1836, when he was director of a theatre in Magdeburg. One single representation of this work (in which he entirely abandoned his first models to follow the reigning French and Italian schools), was given at very short notice the same winter before the company of the theatre had been licensed; after having caused its author a thousand vexations, it was never repeated.

On leaving Magdeburg, the artist, financially embarrassed, went to Berlin, and then to Königsberg, where he passed a sterile year, and composed only an overture, *Rule Britannia*. In Königsberg he married Minna Planer, to whom he had been engaged a year before in Magdeburg; but he had been forced to postpone his marriage for want of money to provide a home.

In 1837 he obtained the post of musical director in the theatre at Riga. He there wrote many pieces, and began an opera which he abandoned, because he perceived with annoyance that he was on the highway to produce music "*à la Adam*."

He then felt the need of applying himself to some important work in which he could give full play to the artistic faculties which he felt developing within him.

He set to work with ardour, and when he left Riga in
1839, the two first acts of *Rienzi* were finished.   The
hope of seeing this work represented on a large stage,
determined him to go to Paris.

He embarked for London with his wife and his dog,
a Great Dane named Robber.

It was during this terrible voyage, which lasted three
weeks, during which the ship sought refuge in one of
the fjords of Norway, that Wagner heard the legend of
The Flying Dutchman from the lips of the sailors.   The
deep impression produced upon him by this battle with
the wild elements, when he faced death more than once,
ripened his genius and had a strong influence upon him.

After a short stay in London, he landed at Boulogne,
where he remained four weeks.   There he made the
acquaintance of Meyerbeer, who listened with great
interest to the two acts of *Rienzi* and gave him letters of
introduction to Léon Pillet, director of the Opéra,
Schlesinger, editor and proprietor of the *Gazette Musicale*,
and several other persons.   The young composer arrived
in Paris buoyed with hopes which soon dissolved into thin
air : Meyerbeer, being constantly absent from the capital
at this period, could not render effective the benevolent
support which he had promised.   The Théâtre de la
Renaissance, on the point of producing his opera, *La
Défense d'Aimer*, unluckily failed, and the director of the
Opéra, to whom he timidly proposed his *Rienzi*, wrapped
up a formal refusal with meaningless polite phrases.   On
the whole, performances on our principal stage were not
so good as he had anticipated, and the Italian singers,
who were so much the fashion there at that time, dis-
gusted him with Italian music.

On the other hand, he took an immense interest in
hearing Beethoven's Symphonies at the Concerts of the

Conservatoire, then conducted by Habeneck; the Ninth especially excited his admiration to the highest degree; he, in fact, preferred it to all the others.

In the meantime, his pecuniary resources were failing; he had left the Rue de la Tonnellerie to establish himself in a newly-furnished apartment in the Rue du Helder: it was there that he experienced all the agonies of poverty. Wagner had to accept an order to write the music for a vaudeville, *La Descente de la Courtille*. The preliminary sketch was pronounced unplayable by the actors. He then tried in vain to secure an engagement in the chorus of a small boulevard theatre; but he was refused on account of his lack of voice.

He then wrote the music to Heine's *Die beide Grenadiere*, and three melodies to the words of Ronsard and Victor Hugo; for these he obtained some little money.

At this period he finished a masterly overture, *Faust*, which was not played until fifteen years later, and in which the influence of Beethoven is again distinctly felt.

Finding himself, by the failure of all his plans, master of his own time, he returned to *Rienzi*, which was destined for the theatre at Dresden, where his name was not unknown and where Mme. Devrient and the celebrated tenor, Tichatschek, were then singing. He ended his work in November and sent it to Dresden, where it was immediately accepted. It was represented there in 1841.

It was at this period, 1840, that Meyerbeer, during a trip to Paris, induced him to enter into relations again with Léon Pillet, the director of the Opéra, to whom he submitted the sketches of his poem, *The Flying Dutchman*, since called in France *Le vaisseau fantôme*, partly borrowed from the legend heard on his sea-voyage and

partly from H. Heine's *Salon*. The theme pleased Pillet
so much that he proposed to buy it and let some one
else set it to music. Wagner at once positively refused,
intending to renew the subject at some future time, when
Meyerbeer, who was again absent, would be able to lend
his aid; and in order to obtain the pecuniary relief in
which he stood so greatly in need, he wrote several articles for the *Gazette Musicale*, among others *Une visite à
Beethoven* and *La fin d'un musicien allemand à Paris*,
which were quite successful. To increase his resources,
he also made transcriptions for the piano of *La Favorita,
L' Elisire d' Amore, La reine de Chypre,* and *Le Guitta-
reo,* and arranged a number of operas for the piano and
for the cornet-à-piston.

The winter of 1841 is passed in battling with poverty.
In the spring, learning that his idea for *The Flying
Dutchman* has been divulged to an author who is at
work upon it, he decides to part with the French rights.
With the modest sum obtained for it (500 francs), he
retires to Meudon, and, returning to the subject of which
he has been dispossessed, he begins to treat it in German
verse. It is not without strong misgivings that, having
procured a piano, he asks himself if he is still capable of
writing after having been so long banished from all
musical atmosphere by difficulties of a sordid nature.
At length he finds to his joy that he can compose better
than ever, and in seven weeks he finishes the three
acts, both poetry and music, of his work. The overture alone is retarded by fresh pecuniary embarrassments.
During this time he has been negotiating with Munich and
Leipzig about this score, which is refused on the grounds
that it would not please German taste. He had, however, kept his fellow-countrymen in mind while writing
it. But finally, thanks to Meyerbeer's intervention, it is

accepted in principle by the Royal Theatre of Berlin.
It was not performed there until January, 1844.

The prospect of having his two last works given in
Germany decides him to leave Paris, where he has suffered so greatly and in so many ways, but which, on
the whole, has not been without value to him, and in
which city he has formed, as he himself says, many
treasured and lasting friendships.

He therefore leaves with his wife in the spring of
1842, happy and moved even to tears at returning to his
German fatherland, to which he vows eternal fidelity.

Rienzi was mounted with great magnificence and performed at Dresden in October, 1842, with the aid of
Mme. Devrient and Tichatschek ; it was an enormous
success. At the close of the first representation, which
lasted from six o'clock to midnight, the author proposed
cuts to which the artists were opposed, for they did not
want to sacrifice a single note of their rôles. Two
other representations took place before a crowded house,
and when, at the end of the third, the conductor, Res-
séguier, courteously handed the bâton to the young
composer, the enthusiasm of the public became delirious.

Encouraged by this success, which surpassed their
hopes, the directors of the Dresden theatre hastened to
mount *The Flying Dutchman*, which was represented
in 1843. Mme. Schroeder-Devrient filled the rôle of
Senta. But the public, expecting an opera in the
style of *Rienzi*, was slightly disappointed, or surprised,
rather. The work was none the less appreciated by
musicians of authority. Spohr and Schumann praised it
highly ; it was given with success at Riga and Cassel,
and the following year MM. Bötticher and Tzschiesche
and Mlle. Marx interpreted it in Berlin.

The qualities of conductor which Wagner exhibited

in directing *Rienzi,* brought him the post of *Hofkapell-meister* in Dresden at the beginning of 1843. He had hesitated to present himself at the competition for this post; but it would mean independence for him, permitting him to devote himself to his labours freed from all material cares. He decided to run the risk, and triumphed over all his competitors by conducting his venerated master's *Euryanthe* in a masterly manner.

He inaugurated his new duties by conducting the works of Berlioz, who was then making a tour in Germany, and who has shown in his *Mémoires* his appreciation of the zeal and devotion which Wagner gave to this matter. On the other hand, the French composer gives only very faint praise to *Rienzi* and *The Flying Dutchman,* which he had the opportunity of hearing.

During the seven years in which Wagner filled this important post (1843–1849), he mounted successively *Euryanthe, Der Freischütz, Don Giovanni, Die Zauberflöte, La Clemenza di Tito, Fidelio, La Vestale, Midsummer Night's Dream, Armida,* etc.

. The presence of Spontini, who came to Dresden at Wagner's instigation to conduct *La Vestale,* was fertile in instructive experiences for the young composer. The exactions of the old master in the presence of the orchestra caused him much embarrassment, but his patience carried him through triumphantly. He never ceased to show great deference to the author of *La Vestale,* who became very fond of him, and, on leaving, amicably gave him this singular advice: " When I heard your *Rienzi,* I said: ' This is a man of genius; but he has already *done more than he can !* ' Listen to me, and henceforth *give up* dramatic composition ! "

At first Wagner had hoped to change many things around him and to raise the artistic level of Dresden;

but he met with so much opposition and prejudice that he soon abandoned his projects of reform. He, however, kept to the study of Beethoven's Ninth Symphony with great tenacity, and, having succeeded in communicating his enthusiasm to his musicians, he gave a marvellous performance of it which was a veritable revelation to his *dilettante* public. It is said that two of his future disciples and collaborateurs, Hans von Bülow and Hans Richter, took part in this concert.

In the midst of his numerous occupations he found time to write a cantata, *Das Liebesmahl der Apostel,* which was given in 1843 in the Church of Our Lady, the remarkable qualities of which passed entirely unnoticed. His principal work at this period was the composition of his opera, *Tannhäuser.*

During the last weeks of his stay in France, the idea had first come to him whilst reading the legends of *Tannhäuser* and *Lohengrin* by the old minnesinger Wolfram von Eschenbach, and he was attracted by the thought of what might be made of the song-contests at the Wartburg. From this time forward, abandoning the scarcely-outlined sketch of a poem on *Manfred,* he broke away, once for all, from historical subjects, which chained him with a thousand fetters, in order henceforth to treat subjects of a purely human interest, which alone seemed to justify the simultaneous use of poetry and musical language.

In 1844 he had been appointed head of a committee formed in Dresden to bring over the remains of Weber, who died in London in 1826. For this occasion he composed a *Funeral March* on two *motive* of *Euryanthe,* and a chorus for male voices, which produced an excellent effect.

Under the influence of these ceremonies, in which his

feelings were so deeply concerned, he completed the music of *Tannhäuser* in 1845 (not as it is now played, for he afterwards altered it very materially : for instance, more has been made of the scene of the Venusberg ; he also extended the last scene of the third act).

The Dresden theatre hastened to mount the work with magnificent decorations and *mise en scène;* but, like *The Flying Dutchman*, it did not appeal to the taste of the public, who had hoped to see the composer return to that species of composition which had brought him such success with *Rienzi,* and the seventh performance was reached only with great difficulty. The rôle of *Tann-häuser* was sung by Tichatschek, and it fatigued him. From a sense of duty Mme. Devrient had accepted the rôle of Venus, though persuaded that she could make nothing of it. The character of Elizabeth was given to a *débutante, Johanna Wagner*, the author's niece.

The failure of *Tannhäuser* was a great blow to Wagner, who had flattered himself that he would win over the public without sacrificing anything on his side. He wrote : " A feeling of complete isolation took possession of me. It was not my vanity ; I had deceived myself with my eyes open, and now I was quite stunned by it. I had only one thought : to bring the public to understand and to share in my views, and to accomplish its artistic education."

Musicians were no more indulgent to him than the public. Mendelssohn, Spohr, and Schumann sharply criticised the work, whilst recognising that here and there it contained some good things. Schumann even went so far as to write on this subject in 1853 : " It is the empty and unpleasing music of an amateur ! " Spohr, at the same period, acknowledges, however, that " the opera contains certain new and fine things, which at first I did not like, and to which I became accustomed on repeated hearings."

The following year, 1846, was full of many new cares of all kinds for Wagner ; the publication of his operas *Rienzi*, *The Flying Dutchman*, and *Tannhäuser* led him into disastrous financial complications ; then at this epoch he plunged into politics and made many enemies ; the press became more and more severe on him and influenced the directors of the theatre, who refused to play his works, regarding him as eccentric and difficult to get on with.

Then, retiring for a time from political agitation, he took up again with energy his new work *Lohengrin*, barely outlined in 1845, the subject of which, like that of *Tannhäuser*, had been taken from Wolfram von Eschenbach. He worked at it, fully realising that he was going farther away than ever from the prevailing taste of the public, at that time solely infatuated with Donizetti's operas. Moreover, so much of his time was taken up by the Dresden theatre, that the completion or the work was indefinitely postponed, and the only portion which can be referred to this period is the finale of the first act, performed in September, 1848, for the anniversary of the inauguration of the royal chapel.

As soon as the score of *Lohengrin* was finished, Wagner thought of writing a drama on *Jesus von Nazareth*, but he abandoned the idea (though he used its mystical theme in after years in another form), and vacillated for the last time between an historical subject, *Friedrich Rothbart*, and a purely mythical one, *Siegfried*, the germs of which he found in the old poem of the *Nibelungen* and in the Scandinavian Eddas.

He chose the myth, and thenceforth worked on the poem of *Siegfrieds Tod;* but his work was suspended

3

during the political troubles which then broke out in Germany.

He elaborated a complete plan of reforms which tended towards nothing else than an entire revolution of musical affairs in Saxony.

At this period he became connected with August Rœckel and with the revolutionist, Bakounine, who rapidly gained great influence over him. Throwing himself with his habitual ardour into militant politics, at a club of which he was a member he made many imprudent speeches which gave great offence in high quarters as coming from a *Kapellmeister* of the Court!

Justly fearing trouble in Dresden, he went to Weimar to join Liszt, who was then actively directing the rehearsals of *Tannhäuser*, and with whom he had close relations, notwithstanding the aversion which he had vowed in his youth to the *virtuosi* in general, and to Liszt in particular. But his peace was immediately disturbed by an order for his arrest: he was marked out as a dangerous agitator! Liszt quickly obtained a passport for him under a fictitious name, and he had to leave his country in great haste. His exile, which thus began, was to last for twelve years.

First he directed his steps to Paris, where he hoped to get his works represented. But what theatre would be disposed to mount a tragedy at such a time? He also tried to publish a series of articles upon artistic and revolutionary subjects, in which he would elaborate the thoughts which were working in his brain. But his proposition was very coldly received by the editor of the *Journal des Débats*, to whom he applied. Seeing that there was nothing for him in Paris, he left in June, 1849, for Zürich, where his wife joined him, and where he found many of his friends, political refugees like himself.

The life of an exile was not hard for him; he became a citizen of Zürich, and soon met with enlightened and sympathetic people who surrounded him with an atmosphere of intelligence and devotion. This was one of the most profitable and productive periods of his life. In this calm retreat, where he entirely recovered himself, his genius, soaring with each new production, at length found its definite form and attained its highest expression. From his first work conceived in exile, to the last, *Tristan*, he marches with a giant's stride. He has, at last, found his true path, and henceforth has nothing to do but continue in it.

Feeling the need of making his political and socialist theories known and leaving musical composition alone for a time, he successively published several articles : *Die Kunst und die Revolution* and *Das Kunstwerk der Zukunft*. At last, in 1850, in the *Neue Zeitschrift für Musik* of Leipzig, there appeared an article entitled *Das Judenthum in der Musik*, signed *Freigedank*, but in this every one rightly recognized Wagner's style and ideas. This article had a varied reception, and was violently condemned by his enemies, who accused him of black ingratitude to Meyerbeer, his protector in France as well as Germany, who was especially singled out by him in this virulent essay, which quickly agitated the musical world.

These labours not sufficing for the Master's activity, he, at the same time, composed a drama entitled *Wieland der Schmiedt*, intended for the Paris Opéra, notwithstanding the discouraging receptions which he had there met with on several occasions. At Liszt's advice he sent it in early in 1850, and the fresh refusal which followed produced a nervous illness.

During the same year Wagner finding among his

sketches *Lohengrin*, which he had almost forgotten, he submitted it to Liszt who was then in Weimar. Liszt hastened to mount it at the festival of Goethe's anniversary. The work made a great impression, although after the first representation, the author, much against his will, had to authorize several cuts.

The critics, who had been invited from every quarter, were generally favourable to it, and it is from this epoch that Wagner's fame in Germany really dates. *Lohengrin* was played with success in many towns during the following years.

In a letter to his friend Rœckel, about 1851, Wagner says that his fame is increasing in a surprising manner, but that he does not owe it to a comprehension of the true spirit of his works, for the artists, like the public, only see his effeminate side, appreciating neither the majesty nor the mighty passion of the dramas. Two years later, writing to the same friend, he rejoices " at having no longer to work solely for money. Whatever I undertake here (Zürich), I shall never make pay (a life which I should never be able to lead elsewhere without resources), for to follow art for money is exactly what would alienate me forever from art, for that is, moreover, the very thing that provokes so many errors on the subject of the essence of artistic work."

At Zürich he conducted several symphony concerts in the theatre of the city assisted by his two young pupils, Karl Ritter and Hans von Bülow, and applied himself to his work on the *Nibelungen*. At first he intended to treat only of the *Death of Siegfried* (which became at a later period *Die Götterdämmerung*), then afterwards, for the sake of making the drama clear, he was led to write successively *Siegfried*, then *Die Walküre*, and finally *Das Rheingold*, the Prologue to these three parts. In 1852, his poems being finished, he gave a first reading of them all (except the Prologue), on three evenings just before Christmas at the house of his friend Wille, at Mariafeld, near Zürich.   Frau Wille relates in this connection that on the last of these evenings, she, being called to the side of one of her children who was ill, had to leave the room for a moment, and that Wagner, offended at this breach of etiquette, bestowed the name of Fricka [1] upon her when she returned.   Although essentially kind-hearted, his nervous nature often made him irritable.

When over-excited, he would preferably use the French language.

He commenced the music to his Tetralogy in 1853, beginning with the Prologue.

He himself relates that during a sleepless night at Spezia, while on a trip to Italy, he formed a clear plan of the music for *Das Rheingold*, and, not wishing to write it on Italian soil, he hastily returned to Zürich, where he set to work.   In May, 1854, *Das Rheingold* was finished. He wrote the music of *Die Walküre* in the winter of 1854–1855, and the first two acts of *Siegfried* in 1857. Then followed a long interruption.   He set aside the Tetralogy for *Tristan*, which, at this period, was more in unison with his state of mind.

While applying himself to this colossal work, Wagner had engaged in many other occupations.   He had mounted *Tannhäuser* in Zürich, and, in the course of a long visit which Liszt paid him, he organized a concert at Saint-Gall, in which he conducted the *Symphony Eroica* and Liszt directed his symphonic poems of *Orpheus* and *Les Préludes*.

At this period he had an offer to give some concerts

---

[1] In the Tetralogy Fricka is the goddess of marriage, with a disagreeable character.

in America, but he declared that he was " not disposed to
go about as a concert-pedlar, even for a fabulous sum."

However, in January, 1855, he consented, " more out
of curiosity and to see what people there are doing," to
direct eight concerts of the " Philharmonic Society " in
London. He then formed very cordial relations with
Berlioz, who was at the same time conducting the
orchestral concerts of the " New Philharmonic Society."
A correspondence was established between them when
Wagner returned to Switzerland.

Prince Albert greatly appreciated the music of the
German master, although the latter was very discreet in
introducing it into his programmes. After hearing the
overture to *Tannhäuser*, which excited general enthusiasm, the Royal family summoned the author to their
box to receive their congratulations. The English press,
however, was hard upon him. Among other things it is
said they reproached him with conducting Beethoven's
Symphonies from memory. Wagner, therefore, to please
his audience, appeared at the next concert with a score;
the public was perfectly satisfied, and claimed that the
execution was much better ; but what was the indignation of every one, when, later, it was seen that the score
was that of *Il Barbiere di Siviglia*, and that it was upside
down on the desk !

Wagner wrote to his friend Rœckel : " If anything
could increase my scorn of the world, it would be my
expedition to London. Let me only briefly say that I
am paying dearly for the foolishness of which I was
guilty in accepting this engagement, attracted as I was
by a silly curiosity, in spite of my former experiences."

During his stay in London, the Master gave Klindworth the task of arranging his scores for the piano.

It was after his return from England that, although

suffering from frequent attacks of facial erysipelas, he finished the instrumentation of *Die Walküre*; and then, frightened at the amount of work which remained to complete *Der Ring des Nibelungen*, which he could see no possibility of getting represented on any stage, and wanting to write a work which would have some chance of being easily performed, he diligently set to work upon his poem of *Tristan*.

The little select circle in Zürich, which the Master loved to frequent, included Wille, Gottfried Semper, and the poet Hedwig, a fervent disciple and worshipper of Schopenhauer. He drew Wagner's attention to the works of this philosopher, which made a great impression upon him. It was under the influence of these ideas, as well as of the state of his own mind at that time, that Wagner wrote his new drama, which he finished in 1859.

It was first proposed to produce it at Karlsruhe, where the rôle of Tristan should be given to Schnorr, a young tenor of the greatest talent, who had sworn an undying devotion to Wagner's music. But the Master only knew the singer by hearsay, and hesitated to accept as an interpreter a person afflicted with excessive corpulence, fearing that he would make a ridiculous effect upon the stage. He relates in his Souvenirs that, being in Karlsruhe in 1852 when Schnorr was singing *Lohengrin* there, and never having seen him, he went to hear him incognito, and was so much impressed by the unusual intelligence displayed by the artist from the very first notes of his rôle, and being affected very much as he had been in his youth by Mme. Schroeder-Devrient, he immediately wrote and invited Schnorr to visit him. Schnorr, accompanied by his wife, then spent several weeks at Biberich with the Master and Hans von Bülow, who had joined them. Schnorr worked on the *Ring*, and even

more on *Tristan*, which afterwards became one of his
finest parts.

Wagner's hopes of having *Tristan* represented at
Karlsruhe were speedily shattered, notwithstanding the
sympathetic interest displayed by the Grand Duke of
Baden. He neither obtained the permission to reside
definitely in the Baden dominions, nor to return to Germany as he so much desired.

Turning his eyes again towards Paris, he arrived there
in September, 1859, with the hope of gaining a hearing
for his work; but he soon had to give up his idea of confiding it to German interpreters. He also counted on
French versions of *Tannhäuser* and *Lohengrin*. M. Car-
valho, the director of the Théâtre Lyrique, had some
thought of mounting *Tannhäuser*. He even called one
evening in the Rue Matignon to see the composer, who
played the work to him, but could not manage to make
him understand its interest.

The Master, who, notwithstanding his increasing successes in Germany, was hardly better known in Paris
than when he arrived there the first time, then determined,
as a means of presenting himself to the Parisian public
and of introducing his music, to give some concerts,
which he immediately organized in the Salle Ventadour.
The rehearsals were held in the Salle Beethoven, Passage
de l'Opéra. Hans von Bülow conducted the choruses,
which were chiefly composed of German amateurs.
The programme included the overture to *The Flying
Dutchman*, several excerpts from *Tannhäuser* and *Lohengrin*, and the prelude to *Tristan*.

Wagner attained his end and attracted the attention
of the *dilettante* world, but the financial results of the
first three concerts were small; therefore, after finding
a deficit of 6000 francs, he did not accept the offer

which was made to him by the Maréchal Magnan on the part of the Tuileries for a fourth concert in the Salle de l'Opéra. He gave two concerts in Brussels, which were not more fortunate in a pecuniary sense.

Very naturally he was beginning to feel much discouraged, when an intelligent patronage brought him unexpected support. Mme. de Metternich and several members of the German colony in Paris so strongly interested Napoleon III. in his favour that that sovereign, usually indifferent to musical matters, gave orders to mount *Tannhäuser* at the Opéra. At first the Master was not enchanted at this news, for he had reason to fear the public (greatly prejudiced by a hostile press), before whom he was going to produce his work ; however, the management showed itself so generous on the question of *mise en scène*, so eager to grant the author all the rehearsals he desired and all the artists he wanted (the German tenor, Niemann, who had a good French accent, was expressly engaged for the rôle of Tannhäuser), that Wagner took heart, and showed himself quite willing to make any revisions that were demanded and which he thought reasonable ; in particular, this is how the scene of the Venusberg came to be extended.

A few weeks before the first performance, he had thought it incumbent on him to explain his ideas on the musical drama, ideas so new to the *dilettante* world of Paris, and which he had already developed several years before in his article entitled " *Opéra et Drame.*" He therefore published a long, explicit, and interesting " *Lettre sur la Musique,*" which may be considered as the Wagnerian profession of faith. [1] But his enemies,

---

[1] This letter, addressed to M. Frédéric Villot, and followed by four *poëmes d'opéra : Le vaisseau fantôme, Tannhäuser, Lohengrin,* and *Tristan et Iseult,* is published by A. Durand et fils, 4 Place de la Madeleine.

who were exceedingly bitter against him and incapable
of comprehending the artistic sincerity and exalted views
of this mind so devoted to the true and beautiful, only
saw in it the presumption of an unlimited conceit.

Is it necessary to recall here the incidents which are
still fresh in every memory : the exactions of the manager, who, to please his subscribers, wanted a ballet in
the very middle of the action ; the author's natural resistance, and the cabal led by the members of an influ-
ential club and a few journalists, who worked so well
and successfully that, despite the very evident sympathy
of the Emperor and his Court, despite the marked interest of the majority of the public, the work failed at its
third representation ?

How many are there among the survivors of that unintelligent coterie, who, while still failing to understand
the genius of the Master, now go into raptures when
they hear the duet of *Tristan* or the prelude to *Parsifal?*
But at that time it was not fashionable to appreciate
Wagner ; and the great artist, refusing with dignity to
impose his work any longer on a public incapable of
being interested by it, withdrew his score and returned
to Germany, which had, meanwhile, been opened to him
by the successful efforts of his devoted protectors.

How can we be surprised if Wagner subsequently
harboured some bitterness against a public whose favour
he had sought so often, who had at first received him
with ignorant indifference, very galling to a genius conscious of his own worth, and who had finally treated
him with an inhospitable harshness, very nearly approaching brutality ?   Let us say, in passing, that Wagner, notwithstanding the popular legend which has formed and
which has so long kept us from knowing and admiring
his work in our country, was never guilty of the mali-

cious sallies against France which have been attributed
to him. Those who wish to be convinced have only to
read his letter to M. Monod; let them also examine his
skit called *Une Capitulation*, for which he has been so
much condemned; they may find it a dull and dubious
kind of wit, but they will see that it was only a joke, a
jest in bad taste, directed as much against his own
countrymen as against ours. Moreover, he did not
write it for publication, and consequently had no intention of offending us. It was not printed until many
years after the war, and then in German.

In order to understand it, we must also take into
account the character of the Master, singularly fiery
and carried as readily to an excess of impetuous gaiety
when his good-humoured wit spared no one, as to
melancholy moods in which he despaired of everything
and was profoundly unhappy. In this connection let
us cite M. Monod's interesting analysis: "He exer-
cises an irresistible ascendency over all who approach
him, not only by his musical genius, the originality
of his mind, and his varied knowledge, but above
all by his strength of temperament and will, which
shines through his entire personality. In his presence
there is a feeling as though some force of nature were at
work and were breaking loose with almost irresponsible
violence. When we know him intimately we find him
sometimes, in unrestrained gaiety, giving vent to a torrent
of jokes and laughter, — sometimes furious, respecting
in his attacks neither titles, nor powers, nor friendships, always obeying the irresistible impulse of the
moment, and we end by not reproaching him too severely
for the lack of taste, tact, and delicacy of which he has
been guilty; we are tempted, if Jews, to pardon his
brochure on *Judaisme dans la musique;* if French, his

buffoonery on *La capitulation de Paris*; if German, all
the insults with which he has overwhelmed Germany;
just as we pardon Voltaire, *La Pucelle* and certain letters
to Frederick II.; Shakespeare, certain jests and sonnets;
Goethe, certain pieces of ridicule; and Victor Hugo,
certain discourses. We must take him as he is, full of
defects, perhaps because he is full of genius, but incontestably a remarkable man, one of the greatest and most
extraordinary our century has produced."

Mme. Judith Gautier, who was a constant guest at
Triebschen,[1] and had vowed an undying admiration for
the Master, also says: "We must recognise that the
character of Richard Wagner contains violent moods and
many asperities, which often cause him to be misunder-
stood, but only by those who judge by appearances.
Nervous and impressionable to excess, his feelings always
run to extremes; a small trouble with him almost
becomes despair, the least irritation has the appearance
of fury. This marvellous organisation, so exquisitely
sensitive, is in a constant state of tremour; we even
wonder how he can restrain himself at all. One day of
trouble ages him ten years; but when joy returns the
next day, he is younger than ever. He is extremely
prodigal of his strength. Always sincere, entirely devot-
ing himself to so many things, and, moreover, of a very
versatile mind, his opinions and ideas, always positive at
first, are by no means irrevocable; no one is ever more
willing than he to acknowledge an error; but the first
heat must be allowed to pass. By the freedom and
vehemence of his words, it often happens that he unintentionally wounds his best friends; always in extremes,
he goes beyond all bounds, and is unconscious of the

[1] Wagner's house on the Lake of the Quatre Cantons, facing
Lucerne.

pain he causes.   Many people, wounded in their vanity, go away without saying anything of the hurt which rankles, and they thus lose a precious friendship; whilst, if they had cried out that they had been hurt, they would have seen the Master so full of sincere regret, and he would have tried with such earnest efforts to console them, that their love for him would have increased."

To complete these two portraits, let us add one drawn in a recent publication by M. Emile Ollivier, the brother-in-law of Richard Wagner: "The double aspect of this powerful personality was shown in his face; the upper part beautiful with a vast ideality and lighted with eyes which were reflective, deep, severe, gentle, or malicious according to circumstances; the lower part wry and sarcastic; a mouth cold, calculating, and pursed-up, was cut slantingly into the face beneath an imperious nose, above a chin which projected like the menace of a conquering will."

Wagner in 1861 entered his own country with a constantly increasing desire to have *Tristan* represented; but, notwithstanding the renown which he had acquired during these last years, augmented by his much-talked-of defeat in Paris, which gained for him a newly-awakened sympathy among his compatriots, no manager cared to mount his work.   The Grand Duke of Baden, after having shown himself well-disposed toward the work, lost interest in it, and at Vienna, where rehearsals were in progress, it was abandoned at the fifty-seventh one, on the pretext that the strength of the tenor, Ander, had given out.

The years which followed were among the most troublous ones of the Master's life.   Everything conspired to distress him : the great disappointment caused by the ill-luck of *Tristan*, and the isolation of his life, for his hearth was now deserted and his household broken up; his wife, a good and devoted creature, but of the earth earthy, was not able to comprehend his genius, and thus there were constant disagreements, which finally ended in a separation.

Several years later, malevolent reports about Wagner were circulated on this subject: he was accused of leaving his wife without resources, but a few days before her death she herself wrote to contradict these calumnies, attesting, on the contrary, that her husband had always furnished her with quite sufficient remittances.

Fresh pecuniary embarrassments pursued him, for his operas brought him very little money, in accordance with the usual arrangements in Germany between theatres and authors. At last, however, he had the satisfaction of seeing *Lohengrin* represented in Vienna in the month of May. It was then that he began to write the poem and to work on the score of *Die Meistersinger*, the first sketch of which he had committed to paper in 1845, immediately after the completion of *Tannhäuser*, to which he wished to make a comic pendant.

The poem of *Die Meistersinger* was finished in Paris during a short stay that Wagner made there in 1862, and was immediately published by the house of Schott in Mayence, which had already negotiated with the Master for *Der Ring des Nibelungen*. But the music, with which he began to occupy himself from this moment, was not finished until 1867.

The whole year 1863 was employed by Wagner in travelling through Germany and Russia and giving concerts which somewhat repaired the state of his finances. The Grand Duchess Hélène, who was an intelligent musician and a passionate admirer of his works, greatly contributed to his success in Russia.

On his programmes figured Beethoven's Symphonies
and some fragments of the *Meistersinger* and the *Ring*.
He also performed in Vienna, with very great success,
the overture to *Freischütz* as it was originally written
by Weber, and as it is never given. On his return
from his visit to Russia, Wagner established himself in
Penzig, in the environs of Vienna, where he lived
quietly with his two servants and his faithful dog.
(Wagner always had a passionate love for animals. He
says: "I am more and more deeply moved at our relations with animals, which are so horribly maltreated and
tortured by us; I am happy above all to be able to-day
to indulge without shame the strong compassion which
I have at all times felt for them, and to be no longer
forced to have recourse to sophisms to try to palliate the
wickedness of man on this question.") Indispensable
measures of economy compelled him to abandon this
abode; he went to ask shelter of his friends in Zürich,
with the intention of finishing his *Meistersinger* there.

As for the Tetralogy, at this time he had totally abandoned the hope of ever seeing it represented (the ideal theatre, which his dreams had pictured long ago and which
he believed would never exist, was needed for that), and
had published the poem in 1853 as a literary work, without taking any further trouble to complete the music.

It was in 1864, that, having drunk deeply of every
kind of bitterness, having at last arrived at the lowest
depths of discouragement and feeling he could no longer
struggle against it, there came into his life that unheard-
of and unhoped-for patronage, which, changing the cur-
rent of his destiny as with the touch of a wand, permitted
him to take a new flight, henceforth freed from all the
miserable fetters in which his genius had so long been
struggling.

The young Louis II. of Bavaria, who had become king at the age of nineteen on the death of his uncle Maximilian II., an ardent and passionate admirer of the Master, whose works he had studied to the exclusion of all others, fifteen days after his accession hastened to call the great artist to his side, and, by removing all difficulties of a sordid and material nature from his path, enabled him to finish his abandoned *Nibelungen* and to have his other works magnificently represented.

He relates this event on the same day, May 4, 1864, to his friend, Mme. Wille at Zurich in these words: " You know that the young King of Bavaria has sent for me; I have been presented to him to-day. Unfortunately he is so handsome, so intelligent, so enthusiastic, and so great, that I fear lest in this vulgar world his life should fade away like a fugitive and heavenly dream. He loves me with the ardour and fervour of first love; he knows and understands all that concerns me. He wishes to have me live near him always, that I may work and rest and have my works represented; he wishes to give me everything I need; he wants me to finish the *Nibelungen*, and to have it represented exactly as I desire. He comprehends it all seriously and literally, just as you and I do when we are talking together. All pecuniary burdens are lifted from me; I shall have everything I need, on the sole condition that I stay by his side. What do you say to that? What have you to say about it? Is it not unheard-of? Can it be anything but a dream?"

Wagner's first care, in gratitude to the king, was to become a naturalized Bavarian and to compose a military march, *Huldigungsmarsch*, in honour of his sovereign; then, at the request of his royal friend, he elaborated a plan for a national school of music to be established in

Munich; but this project was never put into execution, on account of the ill-will of the musicians of that city. In the year 1864 he had *The Flying Dutchman* performed in the capital of Bavaria, and conducted concerts composed entirely of his own works; but the Bavarians, already discontented and uneasy at the extraordinary favour shown to the composer, whose influence over the king they feared, would not go to hear them, and the room remained almost empty. However, his royal patron, not troubling himself about these hostile manifestations, now actively turned his thoughts to the erection of the theatre dreamed of by Wagner, studying the plans with Gottfried Semper, the Master's friend. Then, by paying a forfeit to the manager of the theatre in Dresden, he made Schnorr and his wife come to sing *Tristan*. He took advantage of the presence of this incomparable interpreter to have a splendid and unique performance of *Tannhäuser*.

The rehearsals for *Tristan* were directed with the greatest authority by Hans von Bülow, the Master's disciple and friend, who, by Wagner's influence, was at this time appointed pianist to the king of Bavaria. The performance, which took place in 1865, was superb. Wagner now knew the deep and intense satisfaction of hearing his work given according to his dreams and desires. Schnorr interpreted the rôle of Tristan with such intelligence and intensity of emotion that Wagner, stirred to the depths of his soul, declared, after the fourth representation, that he never wished another, and refused to let his friend exhaust himself with such superhuman efforts. Schnorr, who, during the third act on the last evening, had contracted rheumatism, caused by the draughts of the stage, died fifteen days afterwards in Dresden, and thus deprived the Master's works of their best interpreter.

Meanwhile, the cabal organized against the king's protégé became very threatening, and the sovereign was forced, on November 30th, 1865, to send the great artist away for a time to calm people's minds. However, it seems certain that he had no influence over the king with regard to politics; whenever he broached that subject (he himself has told us), the king stared into vacancy and began to whistle. What the people had more reason to fear was the excessive expenditure into which he led the sovereign.

Wagner, whose nervous system was very much run down and needed rest, took a short trip to the south of France and Switzerland, and settled at Triebschen, near Lucerne. For all that, the King did not abandon his protégé, and came to see him in the strictest incognito.

The Master took advantage of this period of rest to write articles in the paper of his old friend, August Rœckel: he published a brochure on *Deutscher Kunst und Deutsche Politik*, and finished his score of *Die Meistersinger*. It was at this time that Hans von Bülow introduced to the Master a young musician of great ability, Hans Richter, who acted as his faithful and devoted secretary, and afterwards became one of his most wonderful aids at the performances in Munich and Bayreuth.

The first representation of *Die Meistersinger* took place in Munich in June, 1868. Wagner had confided the rehearsals of his work to his friend Bülow, who acquitted himself of his task with the most intelligent devotion. Nevertheless, the Master was able to be present at the last rehearsals and at the six performances, which gained an enthusiastic success.

He then applied himself diligently to the composition of the music of the *Ring*, which he had abandoned in 1857 in the middle of the second act of *Siegfried*. He finished

Siegfried in 1869, and the first act of *Götterdämmerung* in 1870; but the whole work was not finished until 1874. There was thus a lapse of twenty-two years between the first draft and the completion of the Tetralogy. It is true that *Tristan* and *Die Meistersinger* come in the interval.

In 1870, Wagner, having been freed five years previously by the death of his first wife, married Mme. Hans von Bülow, the daughter of his friend, Liszt.

The following year she presented him with a son, whom he called Siegfried, the name of his favourite hero. On the occasion of the christening of the child, who had Mme. Judith Gautier for his godmother, a delightful family *fête* was held at Triebschen : in the garden of the villa the Master had hidden a little select orchestra conducted by Hans Richter, which, at the moment that Mme. Wagner appeared on the porch, began to play a delicious piece composed by the happy father on an old German cradle-song and four *Leit-motive*, which are woven together in the third act of *Siegfried ; Peace, Sleep, Siegfried Treasure of the World*, and *The Decision to Love*. This piece was published in 1877 under the name of the *Siegfried-Idyll*.

King Louis II., impatient to hear *Rheingold*, demanded a performance of it in Munich, notwithstanding the difficulties of *mise en scène* and representation which arose. The result was disappointing, and the work, incomprehensible to a public unprepared for it, was coldly received. The following year *Die Walküre* was much more successful; but these performances only served to increase the desire of both the Master and his royal patron to build a special theatre in which the entire Tetralogy could be given.

After having published his two studies, *Ueber das Diri-*

giren and *Beethoven*, Wagner travelled through the country looking for the most suitable site for his theatre.

The Master's life during the years which followed, so intimately bound up with the history of the Theatre of Bayreuth, will be traced at the end of this chapter. Let us say, however, that in 1875 Wagner had the satisfaction of hearing *Tannhäuser* and *Lohengrin* performed in Vienna in their entirety. He himself directed the rehearsals. *Tristan* was also given with equal success in Berlin in 1876. In 1877 the series of concerts which he consented to direct in London alternately with his *collaborateur*, Hans Richter, resulted in many marks of sympathy from the royal family, and an enthusiastic reception by the London public, who also highly appreciated his talented lieutenant. He had his *Kaisermarsch* performed with success, and some fragments of all his works. But the pecuniary result was not very brilliant, nor did it correspond to the efforts made.

In 1877 Wagner had written the poem of *Parsifal*, borrowed from the legend of the Grail as sung by the old *trouvères*, the first idea of which had come into his mind in 1852 in Zürich when he was projecting his *Jesus von Nazareth*. He took this new poem to London, and read it to a small circle of friends in the house of Mr. Edward Dannreuther, his friend and faithful historiographer (from whose remarkable biographical study many points have been taken for this brief sketch of the Master's life). He composed the music for the first two acts of *Parsifal* in the course of the year 1878; the Prelude was performed at an entertainment of intimate friends in Bayreuth at Christmas; and he finished the third act in 1879.

Considerations of health (he suffered cruelly from a painful erysipelas), forced him to pass his winters in

Italy, and at Palermo, in 1882, he finished the orchestration of this work, which he felt would be his last.

The Festival-Theatre, which had been closed since 1876, was opened so that *Parsifal* might be represented.

VENDRAMIN—CALERGI PALACE, VENICE, WHERE WAGNER DIED

The sixteen performances which were given went marvellously and had the greatest success. On the last evening the Master gave himself the pleasure of taking the bâton from the hands of the distinguished director, Hermann Levi, and conducted the work himself.

A new series of performances took place in the following year; they greatly fatigued the Master, who in the
course of the rehearsals on one occasion had a serious
attack of strangulation. An affection of the heart, which
the doctor concealed from him, was slowly undermining
him. He went to Venice with his wife and family early
in the winter of 1882–1883 and established himself in
the Vendramin-Calergi Palace, one of the most splendid
Venetian residences on the Grand Canal.

It was there that a fatal attack suddenly carried him
off on February 13, 1883, at the moment when, leaving
the piano, where he had just been playing and singing
the first scene of *Rheingold*, he was about to take his daily
outing in his gondola.

The body was borne with great pomp to Bayreuth,
where his friends and admirers buried him in a solemn
and impressive manner. He was accompanied to his
last resting-place by the solemn and majestic notes of
Siegfried's Funeral March.

Now he rests under a simple stone without any inscription, guarded by his faithful dog, Russ, buried under
a neighbouring hillock, and among the very shadows of his
villa, Wahnfried, not far from that Theatre which seems
to be at once the symbol and the fruit of his aspiration,
that Theatre which was the work of his whole life, and
over which the pilgrim who comes to Bayreuth feels the
spirit of his colossal genius still brooding.

HISTORY OF THE THEATRE

The idea of building a model theatre, specially intended for the performance of his great dramas and expressly constructed with this end in view, had been
working in Wagner's mind long before he was enabled
to put it into execution.

As early as 1836 in a *Communication à mes amis*, we find Wagner declaring that henceforth he will write no more *pièces de répertoire*, and that he has a great desire to see his works represented in " one fixed place and under special conditions."

In 1853, after the success of his concerts in Zürich, he had already conceived the idea of establishing a theatre in Switzerland, of temporary construction but appropriate to all his needs, where he could have all of his works, including the Tetralogy of the *Ring*, represented *for a year*, as we find in a letter dated Zürich, June 8, 1853, and addressed to his friend, Rœckel, a political prisoner at Waldheim, who was then an exile like himself.

Later in 1862, in the preface to *Der Ring des Nibelungen*, still more clearly he expresses the wish to construct a new theatre for holding theatrical festivals, and there he announces the idea that private co-operation would be needed, and, above all, the distinguished patronage of a sovereign : a curious presentiment, for two years afterwards, in 1864, the accession of King Louis II. to the throne of Bavaria, at the age of nineteen, crowned his wishes. From 1865 to 1870 *Tristan, Die Meistersinger, Das Rheingold*, and *Die Walküre* were performed in Munich. Then the construction of a Festival-Theatre was decided on in principle; the King wanted it in Munich ; Wagner did not.

However, in 1867, his very talented friend, the architect, Gottfried Semper, had been commissioned by King Louis II. to make drawings carrying out Wagner's ideas; but Semper only understood magnificent proportions and noble and imposing forms; he therefore produced a plan of such magnitude that the king himself was alarmed at the exorbitant expenditure into which he would be drawn, — an expenditure far above the resources of the royal treasury.

Wagner then had to recognize that, notwithstanding all his prestige, the king's support was still insufficient, and, to gain his end, he made up his mind to address himself to the entire German nation, by playing upon its artistic pride.

It was in the month of May, 1871, that, after having travelled through and examined many places, he visited for the first time the pretty little town of Bayreuth, which captivated him at first sight. He then took counsel with good friends and practical men, particularly MM. Feustel and Gross, who obtained from the municipality a free grant of the land necessary for the erection of the Theatre and his house,[1] and it was on the 9th of November of the same year that in Mr. Feustel's house, situated near the station between the Hirschenstrasse and the Mittelstrasse, a house henceforth historic, it was decided that the Festival-Theatre should be built in Bayreuth, and nowhere else.

The architect Semper was again commissioned to prepare definite plans. Nothing but the money was wanting, and the estimated cost was 1,125,000 francs.

But Wagner was not a man to be discouraged by such a small thing. At that time, through all artistic Germany, nothing was talked of but his writings and manifestos; his concerts attracted crowded audiences, and the performances of his last works had obtained the most brilliant success. Wagnerian societies were formed; he profited from this effervescence, and, at the advice, it is said, of one of his most enthusiastic admirers, the pianist Tausig, he issued 1,000 shares at 1,125 francs each, by which

---

[1] The town has had no cause to repent of this intelligent and artistic bounty ; it reaps its reward from the visitors who are attracted by the Festivals. They have caused a veritable resurrection for it.

means the original subscriber acquired the right of attending the three complete series of the Tetralogy of four evenings each. The shares might be divided into three, each third admitting the holder to one series.

The council of administration had for its president Friedrich Feustel, the rich banker of Southern Germany, and was composed of Adolphe Gross; Theodor Muncker, of Bayreuth; Emil Heckel, of Mannheim; and Friedrich Schoen, of Worms.

One of these, Herr Heckel, had founded in Mannheim the first Wagnerian association, and had gained the conviction that many people, finding it impossible to spend 1,125 francs, would, nevertheless, be willing to come to the aid of the work according to their means. Therefore the council of administration, becoming the committee of patronage, encouraged and instigated the formation of Wagnerian societies, not only in Germany, but throughout the world, in France, Russia, Holland, Belgium, Sweden, England, Italy, Egypt, and the United States, whose mission was to collect subscriptions, no matter how small they might be, for the triple representation of *Der Ring des Nibelungen :* the one end in view was the threefold performance of the Tetralogy.

Hardly had one-third of the total sum necessary been collected, when they proceeded to the laying of the foundation stone of the Festival-Theatre, which was performed with great solemnity by Wagner himself. This took place May 22, 1872 (on the sixty-ninth anniversary of Wagner's birth).

On this occasion a concert was given in the fine hall of the old Margraves of Bayreuth; the *Kaisermarsch* was played and Beethoven's Ninth Symphony, with some additions, which were perhaps not quite respectful ; but this is a detail.

More than four hundred German artists, singers as well as instrumentalists, gathered at this imposing ceremony, at the end of which Wagner addressed a veritable proclamation to this little world of artists.

The work was immediately begun under the direction of the architects Runkwitz and Brückwald, but money was lacking and subscriptions ceased to arrive; without a moment's hesitation, Wagner travelled through Germany giving concerts in the large cities, which brought him about two hundred and fifty thousand francs, a concert in Pesth with Liszt, and several in Vienna; and, furthermore, he accepted the order to compose a Festival-March for the opening of the Universal Exposition in Philadelphia in 1876, which paid him twenty-five thousand francs; all this went to the Bayreuth fund, but it would have still been insufficient without fresh generosity on the part of Louis II., who advanced the sum that was wanting, reserving the right to reimburse himself when the shares were finally sold.

It is thus only after forty years of struggles and incessant efforts that Wagner saw the realization of the colossal project which had been germinating in his mind since 1836, and perhaps before. This is a fine lesson of perseverance and a good subject for meditation for those who are too easily discouraged.

The first rehearsals lasted two full months, July and August, 1875, and were renewed in 1876, from the 3rd of June to the 6th of July; then only it was that the success of the enterprise might be definitely regarded as certain, and the dates of the general rehearsals and the performances were fixed; then also for the first time was seen the comforting spectacle of convinced artists, abandoning their lucrative employment, or sacrificing their vacation to enroll themselves under the banner of the New Art, and thus setting the example of that spirit of abnegation and that sacrifice of all personal pretension which have remained, and should remain, characteristic of the artist at Bayreuth.

The general rehearsals were to begin on the 6th of August. On the 5th the King of Bavaria, that almost miraculous patron, had arrived, being anxious to be present at every one of them. He would have liked to be the only person present; but after the beginning of the first rehearsal he had to give up this selfish wish (the emptiness of the theatre interfered with the tone effects); and, with the best grace, he consented that the doors should be opened to everybody. A general scramble followed which necessitated the intervention of the police. This incident suggested to the management the idea of charging admission for the remaining rehearsals, which resulted in the unexpected receipt of about 24,000 francs.

The three representations of the Tetralogy took place, as had been announced : the first from the 13th to the 16th of August; the second from the 20th to the 23rd; the third from the 27th to the 30th ; each of which began on a Sunday and ended on a Wednesday, and was separated from the following by three days of rest, a tradition which has been preserved at Bayreuth ever since.

But if the artistic success was great, it was otherwise with the financial result, for the total deficit was 187,500 francs (150,000 marks), the expenses having been much greater than had been anticipated. This deficit could not in any way affect the subscribers, who had filled their engagements, and it fell entirely upon Wagner. This fresh disaster had to be repaired. Wagner left for London in the spring of 1877, to give a series of concerts, which was always a trouble to him; moreover, he allowed an impresario, whose name has escaped me, to take possession of the scenery of the Tetralogy and hawk it about from city to city; this scenery was very beautiful, and it must have been heart-breaking for him to abandon it in this way.[1] All this did not suffice; the generosity of the young King of Bavaria and several of the original founders had to intervene, and at length Wagner found himself free from his embarrassments, with the satisfaction, thanks to his tenacious perseverance, of having loyally accomplished, without losing heart, the dream of his life, the creation of the Festival-Theatre, and the complete representation of his Tetralogy.

But for six years, until 1882, it was impossible to open the Theatre for want of money, despite the excellent management of the council of administration.

During his life Wagner saw his Theatre open only three times: in 1876 for the inauguration, then in 1882, and in 1883.

Since his death, performances have taken place there eight times: in 1884, 1886, 1888, 1889, 1891, 1892, 1894, and 1896,[2] under the active and indefatigable administration of Herr von Gross, Wagner's testamentary executor and the tutor of his son. Frau Wagner has, so far, never deducted the slightest amount from the receipts, for she regards this Theatre not as a money-making enterprise, but as a work exclusively for art. When a surplus is left over from one year it is reserved for the expenses of the next season and to cover improvements and the renewing of material, as well as the maintenance of the Theatre.

[1] He had intended only to lend them. But they were totally lost, and when the Tetralogy was revived in 1896, it was necessary to make new scenery, as well as costumes and accessories.

[2] Again in 1897.

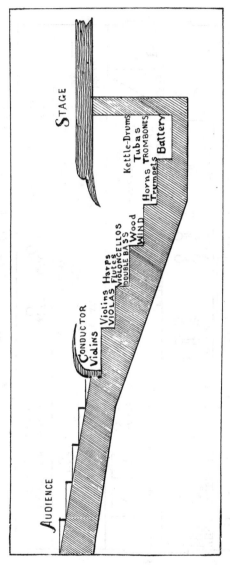

Section of Orchestra

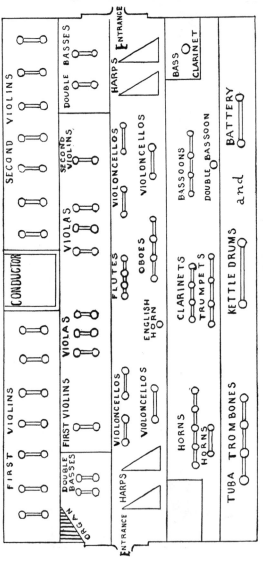

Arrangement of the Orchestra

The hall of this model theatre contains 1,344 seats, arranged in a fan-shaped amphitheatre in a rectangular building. Each stall consists of a large folding cane-seat, without support for the arms. Because of their fan-shaped arrangement, the number of seats is not the same on each row; the first contains only thirty-two, and the thirtieth has fifty-two; the chairs are placed alternately in each row, so that every one is interfered with as little as possible by those in front, and a good view may be had from every point.   However, it is certain that the best places, for seeing as well as hearing, are in the centre of the 4th, 5th, 6th, 7th, and 8th rows.

Behind this amphitheatre, and consequently at the very back of the hall, there is a row of nine boxes, known under the general name of Royal Boxes; these seats are reserved for Royalties and for Frau Wagner's invited guests. Although I believe that the public may sometimes get them at a price, yet officially they are not at the public disposal, which is not a matter for regret, for they are so far away that you are better off elsewhere.

Finally, above the Royal Boxes there is another large gallery containing two hundred seats, for which the *personnel* of the theatre have orders. There you can hear marvellously well, but you have a bad view and it is very warm. Altogether the hall contains about 1,500 spectators.

There is no ticket-office; the entrances and exits are ten side doors, five on the right and five on the left, opening directly from the outside, and each giving access to a certain number of rows.

The lighting consists of a double row of incandescent electric lamps; the lower row, midway up the columns

which surround the hall, is entirely extinguished one
minute before the beginning of each act; the other,
quite close to the roof, is simply turned down; there is
then almost total darkness.

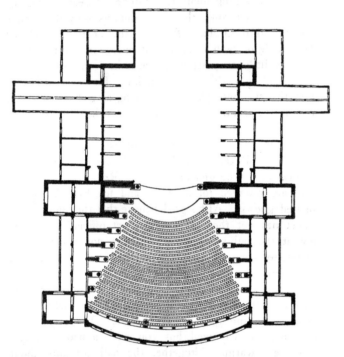

THE HALL, THE ORCHESTRA, AND THE STAGE

The ventilation is perfect; it is never too warm, and
yet a draught is never felt.

The orchestra, which is made invisible by means of
a double screen, which partly covers it, is arranged upon
steps, which are a continuation of those of the spectators, and descend a long way under the stage as into a

kind of cave, which has received the name of the
" mysterious space," or the " mystic abyss." There
the instruments are grouped by families, exactly as at
large symphony concerts, except that things are reversed,
the conductor and violins being above, and the noisy
instruments below at the back; moreover, the first
violins are to the right, and the second to the left; it is
simply an ordinary orchestra reversed.

The space reserved for the stage and the artists'
rooms is a little larger than the hall; the curtain divides
the building almost into two equal parts with regard to
its length. The stage is very deep, perhaps unnecessarily so, for the whole of it is never used, and the back
serves as a kind of store-room for properties. There
is nothing unique about the interior arrangements of
the Theatre; it is almost the same as what you find in
all well-equipped theatres; the height of the roof and
the depth under the stage are sufficient to allow of an
entire scene being raised or lowered, and it may also be
made to disappear on either side. The artists' dressing-
rooms are spacious, but extremely simple.

A little room serves as a *foyer* for the instrumentalists
to tune their instruments in, as this is not allowed in
the orchestra, where silence is enforced.

There is no *foyer* for the public; the neighbouring
country takes its place when it is fine, as it generally is
in July and August; in case of bad weather, people take
refuge in one of the café-restaurants which have been
established in the vicinity since 1876, and still exist.
On the same floor with the Royal Boxes in the little
annex built in 1882, there are three fine rooms, one
of which is furnished as a dining-room, with a buffet,
which serves as a *foyer* for privileged guests; these
rooms are also used for partial rehearsals, but the public

is not admitted. Finally, above, on the gallery floor, in a long room in the form of a lobby, the innumerable wreaths sent from all parts of the world on the occasion of Wagner's funeral are piously preserved on the walls; there also may be seen, under a protecting glass, the slate on which he was accustomed to write the hours for the next rehearsal, and which still bears his last order. In the adjoining room the already voluminous archives are kept.

The exterior of the edifice is not at all remarkable. It is a large building of red brick, with projecting beams, and a base of free-stone, with very little of the artistic in its appearance; its best point is the little court in the form of a *loggia*, added afterwards, with a balcony, containing the reception-rooms; but it is entirely without architectural pretension; it was planned solely with the view to its practical use and its interior arrangement, and this end is well attained.

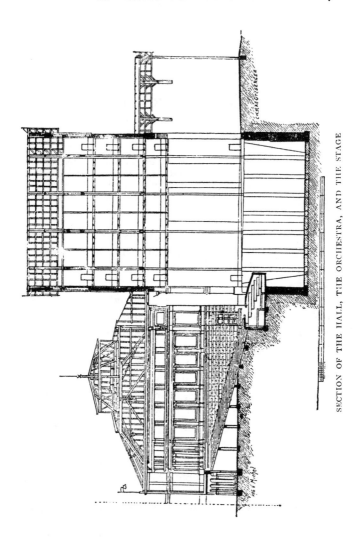

SECTION OF THE HALL, THE ORCHESTRA, AND THE STAGE

CHAPTER III

ANALYSIS OF THE POEMS [1]

> " Perfect art, art which pretends to re-
> veal the entire man, always demands
> these three modes of expression :
> gesture, music, poetry." — RICHARD
> WAGNER.

WE are no longer — and, thank Heaven, we have not been for a long time — in the period when Wagner was debated and stood in need of champions; if a few rare detractors (sour or paradoxical spirits) still exist, they are now a *quantité négligeable*, and need not trouble us at all. Therefore it seems to me absolutely out of place (and I am anxious to say this at the outset of this study of Wagner's style) to lavish upon him praises which he does not need, or to refute the criticisms which he has had to endure, but which nobody now ventures to utter. It is not, therefore, from lukewarmness, as I explain here once for all, that I abstain from eulogies which can never equal my admiration, but from a sentiment of profound respect, like that which keeps people from applauding *Parsifal*. Before this colossal genius and his gigantic work we must bow with uncovered heads, but remain mute, since silence is in some cases the highest and most eloquent form of veneration. If Wagner

---

[1] Those who wish thoroughly to study Wagner's powerful dramatic art cannot consult works more seriously written and sincere than those of Ernst, Kufferath, and Houston Stewart Chamberlain.

were still alive, I think that no one would venture to ask to be presented to him to compliment him on his talents. We look at the sun and watch it in its course, but we never think of congratulating it upon its power, nor of thinking that its glory would in any way be augmented by the addition of our mite of personal appreciation. This is why I shall systematically abstain from all expressions of admiration, confining myself, in this respect, to silent contemplation, which seems to me the only respectful attitude.

At present, then, everybody admires Wagner, but in different ways and in various degrees, according to the extent of each individual's intellectual culture, his previous studies, and his special initiation. It is these degrees and shades of individual admiration that I should first like to define and clearly distinguish.

First, there is the admirer of Wagner *exclusively*, for whom no one existed before him and no one can come after him. This extravagance, honourable as it may be, seems to me exaggerated and excessive, and, I would even say, somewhat wanting in respect to the Master of Bayreuth, who had his own passionate enthusiasms which he did not conceal; it seems to me that one may, and should, admit at least those for whom he himself professed unbounded admiration: Sophocles, Æschylus, Shakespeare, Goethe, Bach, Beethoven, and Weber. Now, it is difficult to admit Bach without giving some attention to certain of his predecessors, if it were only Palestrina, Monteverde, Heinrich Schütz, and his contemporary Handel; we can scarcely separate Beethoven from Mozart and Haydn, from whom he is derived; it is impossible to recognize Weber's worth whilst scorning the works of Mendelssohn, Schubert, and Schumann, whose scores still adorn the splendid library of Wahnfried, as they enriched the mind of its illustrious founder.

Wagner's sympathies for Bellini and other Italian masters are not less certain; he acknowledges them, and we can find indisputable traces of them in the melodic structure of his work.

Now, all these masters, and many others, long before Wagner's advent raised the question regarding his musical progenitors, were of themselves powerful geniuses, and it is a very false idea to believe that you elevate him in abasing those whose works prepared his triumphal way by providing him with the necessary elements. Mont Blanc would not appear higher if you levelled the neighbouring mountains; on the contrary, it is by ascending their peaks that its full majesty is best revealed. The fanatical, exclusive Wagnerian reminds me of an Alpine-climber who would deny the existence of Buet or the Jungfrau, believing, in all good faith, that by so doing he will increase the unassailable prestige of the highest peak in Europe.

I will go still farther : I believe that in order to be justified in boasting that we really and thoroughly understand Wagner, we must be convinced that we understand (I say *understand* in the sense of *appreciating* — I do not say *admire*) everything which worthily preceded him in the evolution of the art. And he who pretends to understand *only* Wagner, who impertinently rejects the works of our great contemporaries as unworthy of his attention, thinking that by so doing he confers upon himself a mark of high musical intelligence, proves only one thing, — that he understands nothing whatever.

Then there is the *rational* admirer, he whose admiration is based on the study and analysis of the classics by whose immemorial efforts has been progressively raised the edifice of German Art, which was already superb when Wagner (a classic himself, since he combines all styles in his prodigious personality) arose to bring it its great and glorious crown.

This is the thorough and erudite admirer; he appreciates the purely musical beauties of J. S. Bach; he sees the feeling for expressive declamation developing in Gluck; he penetrates into the philosophical depths of Beethoven's style, and notes that the entirely modern science of orchestration begins with him; he marks how Weber and Schumann are drawn into the romantic movement and idealism; and when he finds united in Wagner all these elements, and others besides, all carried to a higher perfection and put to the service of a dramatist, great among the greatest, he has the right to say that he admires because he understands what there is to admire. Of the beauties of every kind that abound in Wagner's work, not one is hidden from him, all are revealed so much the more abundantly in that he has a deeper knowledge of their origin, and his only trouble is to know what to admire the most; for Wagner, when he pleases, is as pure in his writing as Bach; his declamation is even more expressive than Gluck's, and truer; his orchestral effects, in their richness and variety, surpass even the prodigious orchestration of Beethoven, Weber, and Mendelssohn; he is just as poetic and not so obscure as Schumann; and, finally, he has excelled every one of those whom he has taken as a model. Moreover, above all hovers, like the dove of the Grail, the breath of his personal inspiration, the individual characteristic note of his genius; whence it follows that whilst we are able to establish with certainty the chief lines of his artistic genealogy, it is impossible to confound him with any of his predecessors, and that each of his pages is as though sealed with his seal, with the indelible mark of his incommensurable genius.

There is also the *intuitive* admirer, who is musically ignorant, but endowed with an exquisitely sensitive temperament which serves him instead of erudition. I would not dare to say he understands, but he feels. It is another thing, and yet it is the same thing.

What first captivates him is the stately and imposing character of the art displayed; little by little he grasps the details by means of frequent and repeated hearings, and more especially by the aid of the poetry; for, even if he is ignorant of the music, he is far from being illiterate; little by little the assimilation of the *Leit-motive* with analogous situations also strikes him, attracts his attention, and fills him with emotion; he constantly finds himself trying to sing them, and never quite succeeds; the instrumentation affects him by its pomp and inexhaustible richness of colour, without his troubling to learn how it is done; he gladly resigns himself to all these influences, he submits to the mastery of the great German Art, but he is incapable of explaining the cause of his emotion to a third person, or sometimes even to himself; when he attempts it he falters, but he is sincerely and profoundly moved.

This admirer, whose instinctive admiration is the most flattering of all, is, perhaps, the most sympathetic, but he is not the most happy: for he is more of an artist at heart, and he suffers more from the want of the technical instruction which would allow him to comprehend and to analyze what he feels so strongly.

Finally, there is the *partial* admirer, he who makes reservations, who thinks the beginning of the second act of *Lohengrin* too dark; who complains of the interminable monologues of Wotan or Gurnemanz, and who would like the duets between Tristan and Isolde or Kurwenal to be cut, whilst still recognizing, in other places, beauties which delight and transport him.

This one is an admirer in the first degree of initiation; and if he is sincere, if he has not the obstinacy to cling to his first impression, he will gradually see his horizon widen. If he is a musician, the simplest thing for him is to study the scores carefully and without prejudice, paying especial attention to the declamation; [1] if he belongs to the class of intuitive amateurs, it is by reading and analyzing the poetry as well as by repeated hearings that he will arrive at the same result. It may take a long time, but he will come to it; for Wagner is not one to be liked by halves, and if anything of his is not admired, it is because it is not understood.

I once experimented with myself in a way which I do not regret, but which I would not repeat for anything in the world, because it is most distressing. The series of performances which I was to attend consisted of *Parsifal*, the *Meistersinger*, *Tristan and Isolde*, and again *Parsifal*. I had devoted several weeks to a deep study of *Parsifal*, so that there could be no surprises in store for me; I knew the *Meistersinger*, which was also in the series, pretty well; but (and this is the important part of my experience) *I had not read a single note of " Tristan and Isolde*," a few fragments of which I only knew from poor performances.

Now this is what happened; the two days of *Parsifal* were for me two days of the most pure and never-to-be-forgotten happiness; I was actually living among the

---

1 Be it understood, I speak here of the German score, and more particularly of the orchestral score. If one does not know enough German to understand Wagner's very difficult poetry, it is easy to obtain a literal translation.

Knights of the Grail, and I seemed to be in a dream as I strolled outside between the acts smoking cigarettes; the scenic illusion was as complete as possible and the happy impression it left upon me will never be effaced from my memory. I was more highly amused at the buffooneries (although somewhat coarse) of the *Meistersinger* than I had ever been at the Palais Royal; at the same time I was profoundly moved by the tender kindness of Sachs and his touching spirit of self-sacrifice. But as for *Tristan*, I understood nothing at all, nothing, nothing, absolutely nothing. Is that clear?

It takes a certain amount of courage to confess these things, especially when one has subsequently succeeded in penetrating the innumerable beauties of *Tristan and Isolde*; but I wish my sad example to be of service to others, and therefore it is necessary to relate it.

We must not go to Bayreuth, then, without first having made a serious preparatory study of the works which we are going to hear, and this study is just as necessary for the poetry as for the music. The more it is prolonged and intelligently conducted, the more pleasure we may promise ourselves from it.

I need scarcely say that I do not place in any class of admirers those unfortunate victims of snobbishness who go to Bayreuth because it is the fashion, or to show off their clothes, or to pose as intimate friends of the Wagner family, and get Herr Ernst to explain the work during the *entr'actes*. The symptoms of their disease — alas! incurable — are exceedingly simple; it is sufficient to sit down to the piano and improvise some utterly meaningless strains which you dignify with the name of *Leitmotive*; they immediately go into raptures. But this experiment is not without some danger; if by chance they find you out, you may suffer for it.

It is not for these that I write, nor for the rational admirer, whom I have nothing to teach; but for those who admire intuitively or with reservations; they alone will find advantage in being guided and in profiting from the experience of another, so as to direct their own researches with a certain method, — the only way of not missing anything.

It is expedient first to examine the general structure and the chief outlines of the work.

All Wagner's great works are divided into three acts; [1] I have not met anywhere with the reason which led him to adopt this evidently intentional division, but it seems to me that such a division is less fatiguing than that in four or five acts; I prefer two long *entr'actes* to four short ones; besides, this division is admirably adapted to each of the subjects treated by Wagner, as may be seen by reading the poems, or the brief analyses which follow.

The acts themselves are not divided into separate numbers, as in the opera, but into mutually connected scenes, without any break in the action, so that, in many cases, it would be difficult to decide exactly at what phrase one ends and another begins. With the exception of this method of weaving everything together into a permanent orchestral web, this division of the musical drama is not an innovation of Wagner's. He only amplified the form, and gave to it, as it were, the force of a law, after the lack of uniformity in the drama which prevailed at the beginning of this century.

Almost all the musicians of the 17th and 18th centuries, and especially the French, always divided their dramatic works into scenes, following in that respect the usage of the tragedy in verse.

---

[1] With the exception of *Rienzi*, which has five acts, and follows, moreover, the form of opera.

In the majority of these scenes were introduced, it is true, airs for one, two, or three voices, even purely instrumental airs; but in the musical works of this period many scenes exist in which the course of the action is treated without any *air* properly so-called (the air being, then, only a reflection of the situation).

To quote only one example from one of the most beautiful and best-known lyrical tragedies of the 18th century, let us take the second act of Rameau's *Dardanus*. We find:

SCENE I. — An orchestral prelude linked to a very melodic strain by Isménor, which, properly speaking, is neither an air nor what the ancients called the accompanied recitative.

Without any interruption there follows: SCENE II. — Dialogue between Isménor and Dardanus. This dialogue contains a passage of twenty-four bars called *air*, because the musical phrase occurs in a regular manner, but which has nothing in common with the type of *air* used later; then the dialogue continues and is linked to a second *air* of only eight bars, which, in truth, is only a continuation of the dialogue, and can no more be regarded as an air as we have since come to understand it, than Gurnemanz's melodic phrase in the " Spell of Good Friday."

SCENE III. — The great incantation of Isménor and his " ministers," broken with symphonic airs accompanying a pantomime and very melodic solos (notably the famous solo, with double-bass accompaniments), is in very truth a *dramatic scene*, and not a musically constructed air. This scene is continued on the arrival of Antenor by a very stirring dialogue between Antenor and Dardanus as Isménor.

SCENE IV. — Dardanus and Iphise, containing an *air*, or rather a melodic phrase by Iphise, of forty bars,

more like our operatic airs on account of its arrangement,
major and minor, andante and allegro; then the dialogue
continues, and ends on the recognition of Dardanus by
Iphise, an action which closes the act, as was usual at
that time; but, in fact, during this entire act the composer only occupies himself with the *progress of the dramatic action*, and with the musical expression demanded
by the incidents of this action, without interrupting the
dialogue, except very briefly as the episodes occur. Without considering here the part played by the accompanying music, this is exactly the structure of the Wagnerian
scenes, and this form is not at all peculiar to Rameau;
we find it in all the composers of the last two centuries,
before virtuosity destroyed interest in the part recited (at
that time the most important part of the action) and gave
an exaggerated importance to the air part (sonata or con-
certo for the voice), an intrusion of the symphonic form
into the construction of the drama, which gave rise
to the whole of the system of opera existing before
Wagner.

We must not think, then, that this constitutes what
has been called the Wagnerian *reform*, — a wrong word,
since it is not here so much a question of modifications
or improvements made to a form already existing, as a
new conception of the work of art itself. It is far more vast
and profound. That is one of the things which Wagner
had most trouble in making people understand; and
among his most fervent and passionate admirers there are
a good number who do not yet comprehend it.

It is not possible in a work of such modest dimen-
sions as this to enter into a thorough discussion of this
question which, has been so often disputed: Which was
greater in Wagner, — the poet or the musician, the
composer or the dramatist?

We cannot, however, entirely neglect it, without danger of leaving too many things in obscurity.

In order to establish a kind of neutral ground between those who wish to regard Wagner especially as a dramatic poet, and those, more numerous, who prefer to admire him as a musician, let us obviate the difficulty by the introduction of a third term, and say : Wagner was above all else a *profound philosopher*, whose thought assumed in turn, with equal facility, the poetic or the musical form; and it is thus that he must be regarded to perfectly understand him in his two aspects.

The ancient philosophers were often at the same time mathematicians, astronomers, poets, musicians, and, at need, legislators. They possessed, then, very striking capacities, which were only various manifestations of their very high intelligence and of their genius. Now, Wagner's genius, exclusively directed from his earliest youth towards one sole end, the extension and exaltation of dramatic power, was confronted with two modes of expression, music and poetry, each as energetic and each as incomplete as the other, and he foresaw that by combining them in one single art he would be able to carry them to their utmost power.

The whole effort of his life, his undeviating advance through all struggles, his fixity of purpose, and the unity of his works, are evidences of this conviction, inspired by which a character so opinionated as his would not allow itself to be turned from the straight line to the goal so obstinately sought.

The New Art, which he created, he himself says is derived from the ancient Greek theatre. Now, among the Greeks, we find united under the one name of music three arts, which at present we consider distinct : poetry, already in its splendour; music, at that time

quite rudimentary; and dancing, which we must consider as mimetic; the same individuals who formed the
chorus used to sing rhythmical words and dance at the
same time. This combination constituted the art of
the Muses — Music — which was then a complex art,
if it ever was one. And we have never heard it said
that in those days, as in ours, there was ever any question of collaboration between a poet, musician, and
dancing-master; tragedy sprang complete, fully armed,
from the brain of one single author, who was a philosopher, poet, and musician.

Such is Wagner also, a complete dramatic genius,
sufficient in himself, and holding, as his innate principle,
that the highest tragic power can only be attained by
the intimate and perpetual union of music and poetry
aided by gesture, each one keeping to its own sphere of
action and exhibiting its highest powers, without inter-
fering with the other.

This requires some explanation; for it will be said
that music has been set to words in all ages. This is
why for a time Wagner believed that the opera form
might correspond to his *desideratum*; in fact, at least
since Gluck, we find in opera a certain agreement between words and notes, tone and speech, verse and
melodic sentiment; but it is incontestable that the stage-
setting, whilst being an indispensable canvas for the
composer as a point of departure, becomes a secondary
matter, and when it comes to the performance the spectator's interest is concentrated almost entirely upon the
music. This, then, is not the intimate union dreamed
of, since the dramatic is absorbed by the purely musical
part, and the librettist himself is forced to cast his literary work in conventional forms, simply for the sake of
the music. On the other hand, there are cases when

we feel that the introduction of music is almost superfluous, that it adds nothing to the action, the prosaic and
sordid character of which could easily dispense with the
form of verse even.

Can it be that there are some subjects not adapted to
music and the modes of expression peculiar to it?

It is here, between the musician and poet, that the
philosopher intervenes, and this is how he resolves the
question: "Everything in a dramatic subject which
appeals to the reason alone can only be expressed by
words; but, in proportion as the emotion increases, the
need of another mode of expression makes itself felt
more and more, and there comes a moment when the
language of music is the only one capable of adequate
expression. This peremptorily decides the class of subjects suitable to the poet-musician, which are subjects of
a purely human [1] order, freed from all conventions, and
from every element having no signification except as an
historic form."   (RICHARD WAGNER, 1858.)

This, then, settles the first essential point, to know
what subject to choose.

Henceforward Wagner will accept no more historical
subjects, like *Rienzi*, nor legendary ones, like *The Flying
Dutchman*; he will mount the steps of Montsalvat, or
those equally mysterious ones of Walhalla, and will dwell
apart on those heights where reason and reasoning have
no longer the right to intervene. There, in fact, emotion
and music reign supreme, and fancy may soar at will.

---

[1] "What Wagner calls 'purely human basis' is that which
also constitutes the essence of humanity; that which soars above
all superficial differences of time, place, and climate, above all
historical and other conditions, in one word all that directly proceeds from the divine source."
                    H. S. CHAMBERLAIN,
               Das Drama Richard Wagners (Leipzig, 1892);
                    French Translation (Paris, 1894).

This question of the choice of subject is, then, of the first importance, and the Wagnerian drama can only move in the regions of mysticism, of the supernatural, of mythology, or of the purely legendary, as in *Tristan and Isolde*. He does not derogate from this law in treating the subject of the *Meistersinger*, which, under its appearance of levity, conceals a real drama of sacrifice and abnegation, which drama passes in Sachs's mind, and for that reason belongs to the domain of emotional music.

We already see here, then, that the musician, by this very conception, is indissolubly united with the dramatist, and that it would be useless, even idle, to try to establish a priority in favour of either one or the other, because, in truth, they are but one, and it cannot be otherwise.

Precision of speech and the still more penetrating accent of musical tones seemed to him both equally necessary to the expression of his mighty ideas, which it would have been impossible to convey in all their fulness and splendour by one of these two means alone. To these also must be added gesture, the stage-business; for Wagner, unlike his German predecessors who were essentially symphonists, always kept the *stage* in his mind. He wrote his poems with the idea in view of setting them to music, and, doubtless, he would have been ill at ease if he had had to work upon the libretto of another, but this he never attempted.[1] His great and incomparable power lies in the fact that he unites in himself all the elements necessary for the *complete production* of the work of dramatic art as he conceived it, impressive and emotional in the highest degree, which work stands veritably complete as a whole, and for that reason it is so much the more moving and fascinating.

[1] His very remarkable melodies on the poems of Victor Hugo, Ronsard, and Heinrich Heine are not in the same category.

He wrote his poems long before the music; but whilst writing them he must have foreshadowed the music; in some measure it must even have been hovering around his poetic conception, or have been latent in it; without its vivifying agency these very poems would have been incomplete; we should feel in them the lack of something higher, something more elevated, which could only be the music, and which, perhaps unconsciously even, presided at their conception.

At this point, where the power of spoken language ends, there begins the province of music, which alone is capable of portraying or provoking states of mind, and there also, where words become insufficient, Wagner the poet calls to his aid Wagner the musician.

We must not regard him as a poet who knows how to set his verse to music, nor as a composer who writes his own poems; but as a complete genius, a philosopher, and a great thinker, who has two languages at his command, two means of making himself understood by his fellow-men, poetry and music, which, being united, form but one language with an absolutely matchless intensity of expression. By means of poetry Wagner reveals to us the outward man, who speaks and acts; by means of music, he enables us to penetrate into the secret thoughts of the inner man; with music also he raises us above terrestrial humanity and transports us into the supernatural regions of the ideal.

The equilibrium to be established between these two forms of the dramatico-musical language was the object of much thought and groping in the dark on Wagner's part. He constantly sought it, even in his first works, though there unconsciously; in *Tannhäuser* and *Lohengrin* he comes considerably nearer; and the equilibrium is complete and perfect in all his last works, *Tristan*, the

Meistersinger, the Tetralogy, and in *Parsifal*, which finally appears as the masterpiece *par excellence* of the new and complex art which he laboured to create; there the fusion is complete, the composer and the dramatist are at last one, and emotion attains its highest power.

It would seem, then, that the most natural way of analyzing works of such unity would be to deal with the music and the poetry at the same time, since they are inseparable and indissoluble.

But after a trial, I recognized that this plan, although attractive, was totally lacking in clearness. I therefore regretfully abandoned it, and I am first going to relate the poems here, deferring to a future chapter that which treats specially of the music.

Concerning the poems, my one desire is to succeed in presenting them in their true aspect, which in the main is always simple, following the action step by step, without neglecting any details necessary to the complete comprehension of the drama; but I shall systematically abstain from commentary, digression, and superfluous annotation, the work being there to explain itself in all parts which are intended to be understood, the other parts often have a domain of their own in the mysterious clouds with which it has pleased the Master to veil them. It would seem to me almost to be going against his wishes should I try to let in a factitious light where he desires obscurity, and the spectator whom I desire to guide would gain nothing from it, since by so doing I should deprive him of one of the most intellectual pleasures reserved for him, that of penetrating for himself into the hidden essence of the drama.

However, the musical side cannot be completely separated from the poetic.

At the beginning of each analysis of a poem I place

a synthetic table of the entire work, which I think I ought to explain, as it is drawn up in a new way.

The first column contains *the names of the characters in the exact order of their appearance on the stage*, particularizing each voice; it also, in a few words, describes them and their genealogy when it is needed; the other columns, of variable number, show, act by act, tableau by tableau, and scene by scene, the successive appearances of the same characters.

We are thus enabled, at a glance, to see the personality of the character, the quality of his voice, the relative importance of his rôle, the scenes in which he appears, the number of actors on the stage at any given moment, the introduction of the choruses and the kinds of voices of which they are composed, besides the great divisions of the work, etc.[1]

TANNHÄUSER; or THE TOURNAMENT OF THE SINGERS AT THE WARTBURG

Act I.

SCENE I.—The stage represents the Venusberg, or subterranean realm of Venus (near Eisenach). In the background of the grotto, sparkling under a rosy light, a blue lake extends as far as the eye can reach.

In its waters sirens and naiads are sporting; on the shores and hillocks amorous lovers are grouped; and nymphs and bacchantes are dancing with wild abandon. In the foreground, to the left, upon a magnificent dais, is a sumptuous lounge on which Venus lies. At her feet, with his head upon her lap is Tannhäuser.

---

[1] In all the tableaux the sign □ indicates a silent character; the actor is on the stage, but does not speak.

TANNHÄUSER

CHARACTERS in the order of their first entrance.	Act I — Tab.1 Sc.1	Tab.2 Sc.2	Sc.3	Sc.4	Act II Sc.1	Sc.2	Sc.3	Sc.4	Sc.5	Act III Sc.1	Sc.2	Sc.3	Sc.4	Sc.5
Sirens (*Chorus:* sopr., contr.).	■													
Venus (sopr.). Goddess of beauty, who has enthralled Tannhäuser and brought him into her realm.	□	■											■	■
Tannhäuser (tenor). Poet-knight and singer, loves Elizabeth whom he has abandoned for Venus.	□	■	■	■		■		■				■	■	■
A Young Shepherd (sopr.). (Episode.)			■											
Old Pilgrims (*Chorus:* ten., bass.).			■							■				■
The Landgrave Hermann (bass). Prince of Thuringia, Lord of the Wartburg, Elizabeth's uncle.				■			■	■	■					
Walter (tenor). Poet-knight and singer.				■				■						■
Biterolf (barytone). Poet-knight and singer.				■					■					■
Wolfram (barytone). Poet-knight and singer, loves Elizabeth at a distance.				■		■			■	■	■	■	■	■
Henry (tenor). Poet-knight and singer.				■				■						■
Reinmar (bass). Poet-knight and singer.				■				■						■
Elizabeth (sopr.). Niece to the Landgrave Hermann, loves Tannhäuser.					■	■	■		■	■				
The People (*Chorus:* sopr., ten., basses).								■	■					
4 Pages (sopr., contr.).								■						
Nobles (*Chorus:* tenors, basses).								■						
Young Pilgrims (*Chorus:* sopr., contr.).								■						■

The sirens invite the inhabitants of the voluptuous empire to intoxicate themselves with the delights of love; the dances grow ever more animated, then they gradually cease as the couples withdraw, and the mists, which now mount and gather in the background, obscure all the figures but those of Venus and Tannhäuser in the foreground.

SCENE II.—The knight, apparently waking from a dream, passes his hand across his brow, as if trying to dispel his vision; he thinks he hears the bells of his native country, which he left, alas! so long ago. In vain his goddess endeavours to calm him; memories of the wonders of earth, of the starry firmament, of the emerald meadows, of the radiant Spring haunt him; he regrets these things and longs for them again. Venus reminds him of the sorrows that he endured upon that earth and contrasts them with the joys which are his in her companionship. She bids him take his harp and sing of love, the love which has conquered for him the Goddess of Beauty.

Resolutely seizing the instrument, he celebrates the enervating ecstasies of voluptuousness which the goddess, whilst making him the equal of the gods, has lavished upon him so generously; but his song ends with a cry of lassitude; he no longer delights in intoxication, and asks that he may depart forever. In vain the enchantress, with alternate menace and entreaty, tries to hold him. Twice again he sings the hymn in which he extols the beauty of his queen and the enchantments of her empires, vowing to sing them forever; but his desire to see fresh Nature and her verdant woods becomes more and more imperative; he implores the goddess to let him go.

A prey to violent rage, she finally consents, threatening him with all the sorrows of that earth which he wishes to see again so ardently, also praying in her spite that he may bitterly regret the life which she has made so sweet to him and which she now closes to him forever; then, with a sudden revulsion, she again tries to keep him, renewing her seductive witchery.

The knight's aspirations turn only to repentance, to death; and, animated by an ever-increasing exaltation, with an impulsive fervour, he calls on the aid of the Virgin Mary.

His prayer, heard without doubt by the divine protectress, breaks the spell which has kept him enthralled. A terrific crash is heard: the realm of pleasure suddenly disappears, and the freed sinner finds himself in the beautiful valley which is dominated, on the right, by the Wartburg.

SCENE III.—In the distance, at the back, is the Hörselberg, the entrance to the realm of the damned. On the left, a road descends among the trees and rocks to the front of the stage; to the right is a mountain road, and half way up, a shrine of the Virgin.

In the woods to the left herd-bells are tinkling; a shepherd, seated on a high rock, sings and celebrates the Spring which is just budding, and then plays upon his pipe. Meantime, in the distance, a chorus of men's voices has been heard coming down the mountain. These are old pilgrims going to Rome to obtain expiation for their sins, and singing praises to Jesus and the Virgin, whose heavenly help they implore. They slowly cross the stage, still singing, and disappear; the shepherd waves his hat to them as they pass and begs to be remembered in their prayers.

Tannhäuser, who during this scene has remained standing, motionless, in a deep and silent ecstasy, now falls upon his knees, praying in his turn to that God against whom he has so greatly offended; he mingles his ardent prayer with the pilgrims' chant, which grows fainter until gradually lost in the distance, whilst far-away church-bells are heard in the valley. Tears choke the voice of the sinner; he weeps bitterly over his sins and makes a vow to expiate them by neglecting repose and seeking suffering.

Scene IV. — In this attitude of sorrowful humility he is found by the Landgrave and his minstrel knights, who issue from the woods on their return from the chase. Wolfram, one of his former companions, recognizes him; yes, it is certainly the knight, Heinrich Tannhäuser, who so often and victoriously took part in the poetical contests of the Wartburg, and who disappeared mysteriously seven years ago.

All give him cordial welcome, and press him with questions, to which he responds evasively. His friends, happy at having found him again, wish to keep him with them; he protests, secretly faithful to his vow; but Wolfram pronounces a name which has an invincible power over him: it is that of Elizabeth, the Landgrave's niece, a chaste and pure maiden who secretly loves Tannhäuser, and who, since his disappearance, has languished in silence and desolation, absenting herself from the gatherings which she formerly adorned with her presence.

Tannhäuser, much affected, allows himself to be persuaded, and, joining his companions in a cheerful song, asks to be conducted to the gentle being for whom he feels a returning love. The Landgrave winds his horn and collects his huntsmen, who mount their steeds, and the procession joyfully ascends the road to the Wartburg.

Act II.

Scene I. — The stage represents the hall of the singers at the Wartburg. Through the large windows at the back the court-yard of the castle is visible, and beyond the open country stretches till lost in the distance. Elizabeth, animated and joyous, enters the hall which she has so long deserted, and which she salutes with delight, feeling new life return at the approach of her heart's choice.

Scene II. — He is not slow in coming, accompanied by his loyal companion, Wolfram, who halts at the entrance of the hall, while Tannhäuser impetuously casts himself at the feet of the princess. Greatly moved, she raises him and demands whence he comes. — From a distant country, which he has already forgotten, he replies, and from which only by a miracle he has made his escape. — She is radiant at this, but checks herself in confusion, whilst revealing, with a grace tinged with exquisite modesty, the secret of her virgin heart.

Tannhäuser gives thanks to the God of Love who has permitted him, by the aid of his melodies, to find the way to this pure soul. Elizabeth joins her hymn of happiness to that of her knight, while Wolfram, who has loved the maiden with a secret and profound tenderness, sadly witnesses the destruction of his own hopes.

Scene III. — As the two knights withdraw together, the Landgrave enters, happy to see his niece's return to gaiety and life ; he begs to be taken into her confidence, but the young woman, much moved, only half confides in him, and he respects her secret : the contest which is in preparation will, perhaps, bring about its revelation.

Scene IV. — The knights, holding their noble ladies by the hand, and led by pages, first salute their host, the

Landgrave, Prince of Thuringia, and then range themselves upon the raised seats facing the dais covered by a
canopy which the Landgrave and his niece proceed to
occupy.

SCENE V. — The singers, for whom stools have been
reserved in front of the assembly, enter in their turn, and
bow with grace and dignity. Tannhäuser is at one end
and Wolfram at the other.

The Prince then rises, and recalls for their inspiration
the tournaments of song which have previously taken
place in this hall and the glorious crowns for which his
knights contested when they were fighting victoriously
for the majesty of the German Empire.

But what the Landgrave proposes to celebrate on this
happy occasion is the return of the gallant poet who has
been so long absented from the Wartburg by a mysterious destiny. Perhaps his songs will reveal his Odyssey.
And the generous Prince ends by proposing the definition
of Love as the subject of the tournament, inviting the
victor boldly to solicit the highest and most precious reward, which his niece Elizabeth will be as happy to grant
as he himself.

The knights and ladies applaud his decision, and four
pages advance to collect the names of the candidates in
a golden cup, to determine the order of singing.

The name of Wolfram von Eschenbach is the first
one drawn. While Tannhäuser, leaning on his harp,
seems lost in a reverie, the knight rises and describes
his conception of Love. He understands it as pure,
ethereal, and respectful, and compares it to a beautiful
spring of limpid water which he would fear to disturb by
his approach. The mere sight of it fills his soul with inexpressible delight, and he would rather shed the last
drop of his heart's blood than sully it with his touch.

His song ended, he receives the warm approbation of the assemblage. But Tannhäuser rises quickly to combat this definition of Love, which certainly is not his; he conceives of the passion as less ideal, and under a more material, more carnal form. Elizabeth, who in her innocence blindly accepts Tannhäuser's point of view, makes a movement to applaud, but checks herself before the grave and cold manner of the assembly. Walter von der Vogelweide, and after him Biterolf, take part in the debate, expressing the same ideas as Wolfram; Tannhäuser responds with vivacity and increasing heat, defending his theories of pagan Love, full of voluptuousness and enjoyment, which he contrasts with the pure and respectful ecstasy celebrated by the other knights. The discussion becomes embittered: swords leap from their scabbards; the Landgrave makes heroic efforts to quell the tumult; Wolfram calls for Heaven's assistance to make virtue triumphant by his song; but Tannhäuser, at the height of his exaltation and madness, evokes the memory of past delights and of the goddess to whom he owed them, and invites those who are ignorant of these passionate ardours to repair to the Venusberg, where they shall be revealed!

A cry of horror bursts from every throat at this unholy invocation; all draw aside from this cursed one, escaped from the realm of Venus, who dares to defile them with his presence. Elizabeth, with a wild gesture, alone remains in her place, leaning against her chair.

The Landgrave and his knights consort to punish the reprobate, who stands motionless in a mental ecstasy. They rush upon him with drawn swords, but Elizabeth throws herself before them, making a rampart of her body for the guilty man. — What are they going to do? What harm has he done them? By plunging the sinner in the abyss of death at the moment when his soul is under the influence of an evil spell, will they condemn him without mercy to eternal punishment? Have they the right to be his judges? — She, his pure betrothed, so sad and so cruelly undeceived, offers herself to God as an expiatory victim; she, suffering for the criminal, will implore Heaven to send the sinner the repentance and faith necessary for his redemption.

Tannhäuser, who little by little has recovered from his frenzy and has heard Elizabeth's prayer, falls to earth, overcome by sorrow and remorse. Touched by the generous supplication of the tender-hearted princess, the Landgrave and his knights sheathe their swords; the Landgrave then induces him, whose soul is charged with so heavy a crime, to go to seek pardon in Rome with a band of young pilgrims, who are now just gathering from all parts of Thuringia to undertake the holy journey. If he returns absolved by the Sovereign Pontiff, they will also forget his sin. All present unite with the Landgrave in promising forgetfulness of his crime in that event. Pious hymns are now heard in the distance: they come from the band of young pilgrims already on the march to the Holy City. Every one listens with emotion; and Tannhäuser, now sustained by divine hope, rushes with intense enthusiasm into the train of repentant sinners.

Act III.

Scene I. — The landscape is the same as that shown at the end of Act I., but with an autumnal dress. The day is at its decline; on the mountain Elizabeth is seen prostrate, fervently praying at the feet of the Virgin. Wolfram descends through the woods at the left and stops as he sees her; he contemplates the saintly creature, who prays to Heaven day and night for him who has so cruelly betrayed her. Already, thinks Wolfram, the autumn approaches when the pilgrims are to return. Will he be among the elect who have received absolution for their sins?

Absorbed in reflection, he continues his descent, when in the distance an approaching chorus of old pilgrims is heard; he again halts. Elizabeth has heard their hymns; she beseeches the hosts of Heaven to assist her in this moment of anguish, and rises to watch the pious travellers as they pass praising the Lord and his mercies vouchsafed to them.

Elizabeth looks anxiously for Tannhäuser among the saintly company; not seeing him, she kneels in an attitude of sorrowful resignation, while the procession recedes; and, in an ardent invocation to the Mother of God, she blames herself for the profane desires and earthly thoughts which formerly occupied her heart, and beseeches the Divine Consolatress to reclaim her and open to her the abode of the blessed, where she can more effectually pray for him who still bears the burden of his guilt. Her inspired countenance is raised towards the sky; she rises slowly, and when Wolfram, who has been regarding her with profound emotion, approaches and asks permission to accompany her, she makes him understand by an affectionate and grateful gesture that the road that she must take is that which leads to Heaven, and no one may follow her. She walks slowly along the road leading towards the castle.

Scene II. — Wolfram sadly watches her departure, then, being alone, he seizes his harp, and, after a prelude, begins a song full of poetic melancholy, in which he apostrophizes the lovely evening star whose pure rays illume the dark night shrouding the valley and reveal the path to the perplexed traveller. To this serene star he confides her who is about to leave the earth forever and enter the abode of the blessed.

SCENE III. — During his song, night has fallen; a pilgrim, exhausted with fatigue, with ragged clothes and emaciated face, appears, leaning painfully upon his staff; it is Tannhäuser, in whom Wolfram recognizes with consternation the still unpardoned sinner. How dare he show his face in this country?

Tannhäuser, with a sinister manner, asks of him the way to the Venusberg, which he once knew so well but which he cannot find now. At these words Wolfram is terror-stricken; his old companion, then, has not been to Rome to sue for divine grace?

Tannhäuser's anger blazes forth, and in a recital of poignant despair, he retraces the progress of his unhappy voyage, his humility, his desire for mortification which caused him to multiply the trials and difficulties of the way; then his arrival in Rome, his great hope at the sight of the Pontiff who promised redemption to all the penitents, and finally the breaking up of his whole being when, with a broken heart, having confessed his past crimes, he saw himself, the only one among thousands of pilgrims, pitilessly repulsed by God's representative — the Sovereign Pontiff — who pronounced him forever accursed, and predicted for him the sufferings of an infernal furnace in which hope would no more blossom for him than his pilgrim's staff would ever again put forth green leaves.

At that moment, so extreme was his despair that he fell almost lifeless to the ground; but now, having somewhat recovered, he can measure the extent of his misery; only one thing is left to him, and to this he is hastening with the eagerness of despair: his shall be

Venus, his the corrupting enchantment of her ardent delights.

SCENE IV. — In vain Wolfram tries to arrest the unholy invocation on the lips of the unhappy man and take him away with him : Venus has heard his call, and she hastens to him. A light cloud floats into the valley, delicious perfumes are borne on the air, through the rosy mists are seen the seductive dances of the nymphs, and soon a brilliant light reveals the goddess reclining upon her couch. She calls the enraptured Tannhäuser to her side, reminding him of the myriad joys which await him anew within her realm. Wolfram struggles desperately in his attempt to tear his friend from these fatal seductions ; but Tannhäuser resists all the knight's virtuous exhortations. In another moment his soul will be lost, Venus is about to seize her prey, once for all, when, for the second time, the name of Elizabeth, that angel of purity, pronounced by Wolfram, produces its blessed effect. On hearing it, Tannhäuser stands motionless, as if struck by lightning.

SCENE V. — At this moment a chorus of men in the distance proclaims the end of the pious martyr's sufferings. Her soul, freed henceforth from earthly sorrows, has taken its radiant flight to the celestial sphere, where she intercedes for the pilgrim at the foot of the throne of God.

Venus, recognizing at last that she is defeated, disappears with all her magical attendants.

Down the valley descends the long train of nobles, accompanying the Landgrave, then follow the pilgrims carrying on a litter the body of the young saint and chanting a sacred dirge. At a sign from Wolfram they set down the mortal remains of Elizabeth in the centre of the stage ; Tannhäuser falls by its side, invoking the

heavenly aid of the blessed Elizabeth, and dies, overwhelmed with grief and repentance.

At this moment the young pilgrims advance, carrying
the cross, which is bursting into leaf and covered with
flowers, a miraculous manifestation of divine pardon,
and all present, deeply affected, sing an Alleluia in gratitude to Him who, taking pity on the sufferings of the
sinner and heeding the prayers of his gentle protectress,
has granted His supreme mercy to the guilty one.

LOHENGRIN

Act I.

Scene I. — The action is placed in the 10th century
in Brabant; the first scene passes on the banks of the
Scheldt, near Antwerp. In the middle distance, on the
left, is an enormous ancient oak, behind which runs the
river, describing a curve of such extent that its windings
are visible a second time in the background.

At the rising of the curtain, the Emperor of Germany,
Henry the Fowler, is sitting under an oak, surrounded
by the Counts of Saxony and Thuringia and the nobles
who form the King's Ban. Facing them are the nobles
and people of Brabant, headed by Frederick von Telramund and his wife, Ortrude.

The herald-at-arms, advancing, sounds the King's
call and demands the submission of his Brabançon
subjects; all swear fealty. King Henry then rises and
describes the situation of Germany to his vassals: he
recalls his sanguinary struggles with the Hungarians,
the frequent invasions from the east, and the nine years'
truce which he has obtained and employed in fortifying
the frontiers and in drilling his armies; but now that the

LOHENGRIN

CHARACTERS in the order of their first entrance.	ACT I.			ACT II.					ACT III. Tab. I.	Tab. II.	
SCENES:	1	2	3	1	2	3	4	5	1	2	3
Herald-at-Arms (bass). Appearing most frequently escorted by 4 trumpeters sounding the King's call.	■	■	■	..	..	■					
The Brabançon Knights (*Chorus:* tenors, basses).	■	■	■	..	..	■	■	■	■	..	■
King Henry (bass). King of Germany. Historical character: Henry the Fowler, Emperor of Germany.	■	■	■	..	..	..	■	■		..	■
The Saxon Knights (*Chorus:* tenors, basses).	■	■	■	..	..	■	■	■	■	..	■
Frederick of Telramund (baryt.). Brabançon count. Once Elsa's betrothed. Husband of Ortrude; through ambition becomes traitor to honour, and the accuser of the innocent Elsa.	■	■	■	■	■	■	■	■	■	..	□
Ortrude (mez. sopr.). Wife of Frederick; daughter of Ratbold, King of the Frisians; in default of Elsa and her brother, heiress to the crown of Brabant. Sorceress, sacrifices to pagan gods. Frederick's evil genius.	□	■	■	■	■	..	■	■		..	■
Elsa of Brabant (sopr.). Daughter and heiress of the Duke of Brabant, falsely accused by Frederick and Ortrude of the murder of her young brother. Marries Lohengrin.	..	■	■	..	■	..	■	■	..	■	■
Maidens (*Chorus:* sopr. contr.). Elsa's attendants.	..	■	■	..	..	..	■	■	..	..	■
Lohengrin (tenor). Knight of the Grail; son of Parsifal; champion of Elsa, whom he marries. He is proclaimed Protector of Brabant.	..	..	■	..	..	..	■	■	..	■	■
4 Brabançon Noblemen (2 ten.. 2 basses). Conspire with Frederick against Lohengrin.	..	..	..	..	..	■					
4 Pages (2 sopr., 2 contr.).	..	..	..	..	..	■					
Pages (*Chorus:* sopr., contr.).	..	..	..	..	..	..			■	■	■

7

time has expired, the enemy, having refused all concilia-
tion, is again advancing threateningly and the sovereign
is organizing a universal enrolment of his people to
repulse his adversaries and force them to respect the
German Empire, which they will then no longer think
of insulting.

But on his arrival in this province, what was his grief
to hear of the discords to which it is a prey! What
has happened, and why is it without a prince and given
up to intestine war? The sovereign questions Frederick
von Telramund on this subject and invites the virtuous
knight to reply without circumlocution.

Frederick, promising to give his King and sovereign a
true account, describes the events which have occurred
as follows: The old Duke of Brabant at his death left
two children; a daughter, Elsa, and a young prince,
Godfrey, the heir to his throne, whose education had
been confided to his faithful knight, Telramund. What
was the grief of the latter one day on learning that the
young prince, whilst walking out with his sister, had disappeared without leaving any trace behind! Struck with
horror at the thought of the crime which Elsa alone
could have perpetrated, Frederick hastened to renounce
the hand of the maiden who had been promised to himself and to marry Ortrude; now, he demands justice
against the odious criminal, at the same time reminding
King Henry that he is the direct heir to Brabant by his
relationship to the old Duke and also by Ortrude, his
wife, who is also of the princely blood.

All present, moved by the knight's accusation, try to
defend Elsa; the King himself doubts her crime; but
the implacable Frederick explains the dark designs of the
maiden, by saying that in her heart she has a secret love
which she would be more free to indulge if she became

sovereign mistress of Brabant in the place of her brother whom she has assassinated.

Henry then decides to have the accused one brought to trial without delay. He invokes the aid of God, so that he may be enlightened with the wisdom of the Most High in this solemn moment.

Scene II. — Elsa advances slowly, with a grave and sad air, followed by her train of women ; her gentle and sympathetic looks gain all hearts ; the sovereign asks her if she is willing to accept him as a judge, and if she knows of what crime she is accused. What has she to say in her defence ? — To all these questions she only replies by gestures of resignation ; then, with a far-away look in her eyes, she softly murmurs the name of her brother. The curiosity of every one is excited by this strange behaviour, and the King asks her to explain herself. Elsa, as though speaking to herself and plunged into a kind of ecstasy, recalls the day when, overwhelmed with sorrow, she addressed an ardent supplication to God, and fell into a deep sleep ; in this sleep a knight clothed in shining armour appeared to her, sent by Heaven to protect her. It is he whom she awaits ; he will be her defender and will make her innocence clear.

Seeing the gentle creature dreaming thus, the King cannot believe in her guilt ; Frederick, however, persists in his rôle of accuser, and, the better to gain their attention, he recalls his past valour, defying any one who is willing to take Elsa's part to fight with him. All the nobles challenge him. Henry, not knowing how to decide, calls on the judgment of God, and asks Elsa whom she will choose for her champion ; she again repeats that, relying on the protection of God, she awaits the knight who is to fight for her, and on whom she will bestow her heart and crown, in reward for his devotion.

The King orders the trumpets to be sounded to the
four cardinal points, and orders the combat to be proclaimed; but a dismal silence is the only response.
Elsa, falling at the feet of the King, entreats him to
order a repetition of the call, which her knight may not
have heard in his distant retreat.   Henry grants her request, and the trumpets sound once again.   Elsa, in an
ardent prayer to the Most High, implores him not to
abandon her.

Suddenly, those spectators who are nearest to the
bank see in the distance on the river a boat drawn by a
swan and bearing a knight, standing erect, clothed in
silver armour.   They call to all the assembly; every one
cries a miracle, and all are lost in wonder; meanwhile
the swan continues to advance, following the winding of
the river, and the frail bark soon brings the voyager
to the bank.   The King looks on from his seat; Elsa
gazes enraptured; Frederick is a prey to the most intense astonishment; and Ortrude, whose face is marked
with a malevolent and anxious expression, angrily glances
at Elsa and at the mysterious arrival.

SCENE III.—The knight, on leaving his boat, leans
towards the swan, and, bidding it a touching farewell,
tells it to return to the distant country whence they
come; the swan takes the boat back in the direction
traversed and majestically sails away up the river.   The
mysterious stranger sadly follows it with his eyes; then,
when it is lost to sight, he advances towards King Henry,
and, respectfully saluting him, announces that he has
come, sent by God, to defend the innocent maiden who
is unjustly accused of the blackest of crimes.   Then,
addressing Elsa, who since his arrival has followed him
with her eyes without moving from her place and in a
kind of ecstasy, he asks her if she is willing to entrust

him with the care of defending her honour and if she
has confidence in his arm to fight against her enemy.
Elsa, who has been roused from her silent contemplation
by these words, and who casts herself at his feet to express
her ardent gratitude, answers in the affirmative; he then
begs her to consent to become his wife when he has
victoriously defended her; if she will grant him this happiness, he will crave one more favour, — which is that she
shall never seek to know, either by persuasion or by
strategy, either his name or whence he came. He
vehemently insists upon this important stipulation, and,
when the maiden has made him the formal promise
never to attempt to penetrate the mystery which surrounds his coming, never to ask his name nor his origin,
he presses her tenderly to his heart before the eyes of the
King and the delighted populace.

Then he confides his betrothed to the King, loudly
proclaiming her innocence, and calls the Count of Telramund to the combat, of which God shall be the judge.

Frederick betrays great agitation; his followers, now
convinced of the injustice of his cause, persuade him to
decline the combat; but, fearing to appear a coward if he
withdraws, he meets his adversary's challenge with an
answering defiance. The King then appoints three
witnesses for each champion, whom the herald-at-arms
soon sets face to face, after having instructed them in the
conditions of the combat. The two knights engage,
and, after several skilful passes, the stranger strikes
Frederick to the ground at the mercy of his sword;
with one blow he might run him through; but, considering the proof sufficiently convincing as it is, he grants
him his life, and, turning towards the gracious sovereign,
he receives the radiant and agitated Elsa from his hands.
All present share in the joy of the conqueror; the

knights and nobles press into the lists, and, while Frederick crawls painfully along the ground grieving over his lost honour and Ortrude pursues the elect of God with her malevolent mutterings, the Saxon nobles raise the conqueror on his own shield ; and the Brabançons, placing Elsa on the King's shield which they cover with their mantles, carry the betrothed pair off the stage in triumph, amid the songs of joy and the enthusiastic shouts of the entire wondering assembly.

ACT II.

SCENE I. — The stage represents the inner court of the castle of Antwerp. At the back is the Palace, where the knights live, the windows of which are all brilliantly lighted ; to the left, the porch of the church, and, further back, the gate which leads into the town ; to the left, the Kemenate, or women's quarters, which is reached by a flight of steps leading to a kind of balcony.

As the curtain rises, two people in sombre and miserable garments are sitting on the steps of the church. They are the knight Telramund and his wife. Frederick breaks out into imprecations against his companion : why has he no weapon left to strike her and rid himself forever of her odious presence ! It was she who led him into this combat and made him lose his honour ; she who, lying and calumniating, affirmed she had seen from afar Elsa accomplish her crime in the forest ; she, again, who formerly induced him to renounce the hand of the maiden to sue for an alliance with her, Ortrude, who pretended, as the last scion of the race of Ratbold, that she would soon be called to reign over Brabant !

Ortrude scarcely replies to this flood of reproaches, and lays the shame of his defeat upon Frederick; why did he not oppose his adversary with rage such as this! — he could then soon have vanquished the self-styled *protégé* of God! But, however that may be, says she, everything may yet be repaired; for the occult sciences which she has studied have revealed to her what she has to do and will supply her with the means: if Telramund will only allow her to act, she will answer for her success. First of all, they must trick Elsa and instil into her heart a leaven of curiosity with regard to her husband's past. If they can manage to make her break her promise and question him regarding his origin, and make him divulge it to her, the charm which protects the mysterious knight will be broken. In order to force the hero to reveal himself, it will suffice to accuse him of having deceived the tribunal by the aid of sorcery. If these means fail, there is still another: if, during the combat, Frederick had succeeded in giving the body of his adversary the slightest wound, the protecting charm would equally have ceased to defend him. He must therefore challenge him again and endeavour to wound him slightly, for, however light the scratch may be, it will suffice to break the spell.

Hearing these perfidious words, Frederick, in his hatred, takes fresh courage and swears to his wife that he will second her in her dark designs.

SCENE II. — At this moment Elsa, clothed in white, comes out to lean on the balcony of the Kemenate to dream of her happiness. Her two enemies are still on the steps of the church, but the darkness prevents her from seeing them.

Ortrude comes under the balcony, and, calling with an humble and lamentable voice, makes herself known

to Elsa; she implores her pity. What has she done to
be so cruelly stricken? She asks herself in vain. Is
it because she has married him whom Elsa had so disdainfully repulsed? Why has she incurred such dis-
grace? And, continuing her hypocritical speech, she
excites the pity of the gentle Elsa, who, moved at her
great misfortunes, promises to protect her and restore
her to favour.

Whilst the maiden leaves the balcony to come to her,
Ortrude, seeing her victim already in her power, offers
up a wild prayer to the pagan gods, Wotan and Freïa,
to whom she sacrifices in secret, but she resumes her
supplicating attitude on the return of Elsa, who raises
her kindly, promising that she will plead her cause with
the husband who is about to lead her to the altar; she
will see that her friend and *protégée*, in magnificent
attire, shall accompany the nuptial train.

Ortrude, feigning the liveliest gratitude, says she
wishes to prove it by giving her some good advice —
Elsa must not trust this mysterious husband to whom
she is going to be united; one day, perhaps, he will
depart as he came, deserting his too confiding companion. Elsa, troubled by Ortrude's words, answers that
she cannot doubt him whom she loves, and spurns these
insinuations; but Ortrude's perfidious machinations will
germinate, nevertheless. Ortrude enters the Palace with
her victim, whilst Frederick, remaining before the
church, unperceived, but having heard everything, hurls
his curses at the gentle creature.

SCENE III. — Day is just breaking. It soon becomes
broad daylight; the soldiers sound the reveille and answer each other from tower to tower. The servants,
coming out of the Castle, go to the fountain to draw
water, the porter opens the massive gate, and people

begin to stir about. Four trumpeters appear at the entrance of the Palace and sound the King's call; the nobles and knights come into the court-yard, and salute each other and converse.

The herald-at-arms appears, and proclaims that, by the King's will, Frederick is banished from the empire for having falsely appealed to the judgment of God; furthermore, he threatens with the same fate whoever shall afford him asylum or protection. Then, after another flourish of trumpets, he declares, still in the name of the King, that the stranger sent by God on whom Elsa has bestowed her hand, in accepting the crown, declines the title of Duke, for which he intends to substitute that of Protector of Brabant, and invites his new subjects to prepare without delay for the battles in which, accompanying the King on his martial expeditions, they will reap a new harvest of glory.

The people, who have attentively followed the proclamation of the herald-at-arms, concur in the King's sentiments with regard to Telramund as well as his enthusiasm for the unknown knight, and joyfully approve of his warlike projects; but, while the crowd talks with animation, in the front of the stage a group of four nobles forms, who are discontented with the actions of the Protector and jealous of his new authority. Seeing that they are evilly disposed towards his enemy, Frederick approaches them craftily, and in a few words tells them of the plan of the combat into which he is going to enter against the stranger.

The nuptial train advances, and Frederick has only time to conceal himself behind the nobles, who hide him from the view of those present.

SCENE IV. — Elsa appears in the middle of the train arrayed in her bridal robes. Ortrude follows her, also richly apparelled; but, at the moment when her benefactress is about to mount the steps of the church, her anger blazes out, and, quickly placing herself between Elsa and the door of the church, she declares she will not any longer remain in the second place, and that she will reconquer her station, which a false judgment caused her to lose. Who is he, this unknown, who has surprised the confidence of all to the detriment of a knight unanimously esteemed until now? Can he prove his nobility? Can he tell his origin, and from what country he comes? If he has forbidden her whom he is espousing to question him upon this subject, it is doubtless because he has grave reasons for keeping his secret. Elsa tries in vain to stop this torrent of malevolence; Ortrude does not cease until the King's train is seen approaching.

SCENE V. — The monarch, only having heard the disturbance from afar, demands the cause of it, and the bridegroom, thus learning the blackness of Ortrude's heart, sternly drives her away. After this brief incident the procession again forms and is about to enter the church, when Frederick in his turn stops its progress, and, despite the throng which wishes to ward him off, approaches the King and presents the accusation which he has prepared against his adversary: he formally declares him guilty of having suddenly surprised the public confidence at the moment of the combat, and says that he wants to know at least the name and origin of him who has robbed him of his honour. The King and the whole assembly anxiously await the reply of the knight, who, whilst defending himself from all charge of disloyalty, refuses to reveal his origin to Telramund. There is only one person to whom he will reply if she asks it, and that is Elsa, who, although greatly troubled, will yet not put the fatal question; but it is evident that her heart is disquieted to its very depths, for the venom is producing its effect. The King and the Brabançon nobles, for their own part, have no doubt of the perfect honour of the Protector of Brabant; all the sympathies of the sovereign as well as of the people are on his side. In the meanwhile, Frederick and Ortrude apart watch their victim, Elsa, and trace on her features the dangerous thoughts to which their perfidy has given rise in her heart. Whilst the sovereign utters many noble words of confidence to his *protégé*, the traitor stealthily approaches the anxious and frightened Elsa ; he counsels her, in order to attach her husband to her eternally and to render herself mistress of the charm which will bind him forever, to consent to accept his (Frederick's) support. He tells her that this very night he will be near the nuptial chamber, ready to answer her first call. Elsa's lover, surprising this odious aside, advances threateningly towards his enemy, whose dark schemes he divines. He drives him away, and asks Elsa, for the last time, if she has sufficient confidence in him never to seek to know his origin; on her passionate reply in the affirmative, he leads her to the altar, accompanied with the good wishes of the whole people. The bells peal, the organ is heard in the church, and the bride, who at the moment of entering has encountered the menacing gaze of Ortrude, passes through the door leaning in terror against her husband.

Act III.

Scene I. — The first scene takes us into the richly decorated nuptial chamber. On the right, near a large window open to the gardens, is a very low bed. On the left, is a door leading to the other apartments. At the back is another door through which enters the procession accompanying the newly-married pair, — Elsa

surrounded by her women, and the Protector escorted by
the King and nobles.

The lords and ladies sing a chorus, offering their good
wishes to the young couple, and then the King presents
Elsa to her husband; pages next relieve the knight of
the rich mantle which covered his shoulders, whilst
Elsa's women also take off the garment which covered
her nuptial robe; then all present, after saluting the
bridal pair, depart, continuing their songs, which die away
gradually in the distance.

SCENE II. — Elsa, overcome with sweet emotion, falls
into the arms of her lover, who leads her to the couch,
where he holds her in a tender embrace. He murmurs
words of love in her ear, and she replies with ardour;
before they had met, their hearts had already known and
understood each other. Had she not already in a dream
seen him on whom she had called in her distress to defend her? And at this appeal from afar had he not
hastened to her, being led by the invincible power of
Love?

He then passionately utters the name of his well-beloved, who in turn deplores her inability to pronounce
the name of the husband to whom she has given herself
entirely; why will he not consent to reveal it to her now,
when no indiscreet ear can overhear them? He feigns
not to understand her words, and, tenderly embracing
her, he draws her to the window to inhale the intoxicating perfumes which rise from the flowers. But Elsa,
possessed by the fatal idea which was suggested by
Ortrude and Frederick, repeats her question, and becomes more insistent; in vain her husband begs her to
have that absolute confidence in him which he had in
her, when, without any proof, he believed in her innocence and vouched for it. Elsa insists; the knight,

to calm her, assures her that she has nothing to fear regarding his origin, which is even more exalted than that of the King, and that the region whence he comes is glorious and splendid.

These words only excite in Elsa a fever of curiosity, which soon becomes a veritable delirium; she thinks she sees the swan coming to deprive her of her hero, and at the height of agony and frenzy, she plainly puts the fatal questions which she has taken an oath never to ask. Even at the forfeit of her life, she wants to learn the name of her husband, and to know who he is and whence he comes.

Hardly has she uttered these words, which he vainly tries to arrest on her lips, when Frederick and the four Brabançon nobles who accompany him burst into the room brandishing their weapons. Elsa, recovering herself, rushes for her knight's sword, which he has laid on the couch, and gives it to him; he springs at Frederick and with a single blow stretches him dead at his feet. The traitor's companions, in terror, fall at the feet of the hero, whilst Elsa, overcome, faints in the arms of her husband, who sadly gazes upon her. He then orders the four nobles to carry the body of Telramund to the King's tribunal; then, calling Elsa's women, he orders them to robe their mistress and to lead her before the sovereign, in whose presence he will answer to the iniquitous questions which she has had the fatal imprudence to ask him.

A curtain veils the whole scene. Trumpets and martial flourishes are heard.

Scene III.—When the curtain rises, the scene again shows the course of the Scheldt, the place where the boat landed, the meadow and the oak; the same setting as the first act.

The Brabançon nobles, who have gathered to fight under the royal banner, defile past, one after the other, followed by their esquires and standard-bearers; the counts hail the arrival of King Henry, who thanks them for their noble ardour. The arrival of the Protector of Brabant is alone awaited; but suddenly exclamations of terror are heard at the sight of the four nobles bearing the corpse of Telramund on a bier. Elsa follows, pale and trembling, and the King, who has advanced to meet her, asking her the cause of her trouble, leads her to an elevated seat prepared for her, and returns to his place under the oak.

The knight then appears, clothed in his silver mail; he advances alone and without escort; his face is marked with deep sadness, and he replies to the sovereign's gracious welcome by expressing the grief he feels at not being able to lead his troops to battle. He has only come to this assembly to fulfil certain painful duties; first, to justify himself for an act to which he was forced in defence of his own life; and he relates the plot by which he nearly fell a victim to Telramund. Was he in the right in killing his enemy, and will his sovereign pardon him? Henry reassures him on the legality of his act and turns with horror from the corpse of the traitor exposed to his view.

Then the hero, continuing his sad task, loudly and before everybody accuses the woman he loves of having broken the promise she solemnly made in this very place, and renewed many times. Blinded by the perfidious counsels of his enemies, she has foolishly broken her oath, and, since she exacts it, it shall be here, in the presence of all, that he will reveal the redoubtable secret, the revelation of which can only be made at the cost of the happiness of both.

In a far and mysterious country, on a peak pure of all profane contact, is situated, in the heart of a magnificent castle, a temple which has no equal in any other country. In this temple is kept a precious vessel, which was formerly brought there by a legion of angels, and which, in its sacred shrine, may only have for its guardians knights of the purest and noblest nature. This vessel is endowed with a divine and miraculous power, which is renewed once a year by a dove, descending from the celestial regions; this vessel is the Holy Grail.

Whoever is elected its guardian receives by that very fact a supernatural power, but on the express condition that he shall not allow his secret to be penetrated by any human being; for, if his quality is once known, if he remains among mankind, he will be deprived of his power and influence; so that what obliged the hero so rigorously to conceal his origin was that he is one of the servants of the Grail. His father, Parsifal,[1] is the prince of these knights, to which glorious band he, Lohengrin, belongs.

At this name, now pronounced for the first time, the entire assembly is moved with respectful awe; Elsa is utterly overcome with her emotion, and Lohengrin, taking her in his arms, bids her a tender and sorrowful farewell. In vain the wretched woman, now understanding the magnitude of her fault, tries to keep her beloved husband, and offers to make amends for her unfortunate curiosity by the hardest means of expiation; in vain also the sovereign and the warriors pray the knight to remain to lead their arms. Lohengrin must go. He has already offended by his protracted absence from the

---

[1] Like the Templars, the Knights of the Holy Grail took the vow of chastity and celibacy. Only their Grand Master, their Priest-King, was excepted, in order to perpetuate the dynasty.

Grail; but, before going, he wishes to leave a consolatory promise with the monarch who has received him
with such noble confidence, and he announces that
German soil shall never have to submit to the shame of
a barbarian invasion.   Henry's vassals owe this boon to
the purity of their sovereign.

Suddenly a clamour is heard in the direction of the
river-bank.   It is caused by those who see the swan
bringing again the boat, empty this time, as it had done
before, when it brought the knight.   Lohengrin goes
to it, and sadly gazes upon it, telling it how grieved he
is to see it again under such painful circumstances, when
he had thought to see it one day under happier skies,
free and liberated from the charm which now holds it in
bonds.   The by-standers do not catch the meaning of
his words.

Turning again to Elsa, Lohengrin, in great grief, tells
her how he had hoped one day to restore that brother
whom she thought lost forever.   He is deprived of this
pleasure since he is going away; but if Godfrey is ever
restored to her affection, she is to give him, in the name
of the lost knight, this horn, which will be invaluable to
him in the hour of danger; this sword, which will
render him invincible; and this ring, which will remind
him of the champion of the defenceless.   He kisses
Elsa's brow, and she falls fainting into the arms of her
women; he then walks towards the boat, whilst all
present manifest deep sorrow.

At this moment Ortrude appears, giving every sign of
brutal joy; addressing Elsa she reveals that the mysterious swan that is taking the beloved hero away forever
is no other than Godfrey himself, whom she has thus
transformed by witchcraft, and who will now be irrevocably lost; she adds that if Lohengrin had remained,

he would have had the power to deliver the youth and restore the heir of Brabant to his sister's affection.

Lohengrin, who was about to embark, halts, on hearing this fresh revelation of Ortrude's atrocity. He falls on his knees on the river-bank and lifts up a fervent and silent prayer to Heaven. A white dove is then seen hovering above the boat; it is the dove of the Grail. Lohengrin approaches the swan and takes off the chain which attaches it to the boat; the swan dives and disappears, and in its stead there appears a youth whom all present recognize as Godfrey, the young Duke of Brabant.

Lohengrin then springs into the boat, whose course is immediately directed by the dove.

As they recede in the distance, Elsa, in a transport of fugitive joy, receives her brother in her arms, and then falls back fainting, seeing that her lover has left her forever. Ortrude, recognizing that her sorceries have been baffled, drags herself away in a dying condition, and expires with rage, whilst the nobles, happy at the deliverance of their young lord, gather about him with manifestations of enthusiastic delight.

TRISTAN UND ISOLDE

Isolde, Princess of Ireland, was the affianced bride of Sir Morold, an Irish knight, who went to war in Cornwall and met his death in a combat with Tristan, the nephew of King Mark. The ungenerous adversary, in cruel irony, sent the head of his victim to the princess, who discovered in the deep wound a splinter of steel, left by the murderer's weapon.

But, in the struggle, Tristan has himself been hurt by Morold's poisoned blade, and his wound will not heal;

8

TRISTAN UND ISOLDE

CHARACTERS in the order of their first entrance.	ACT I.					ACT II.			ACT III.		
SCENES :	1	2	3	4	5	1	2	3	1	2	3
A Young Sailor (tenor). (Episode.)	invis. ■	■									
Isolde (sopr.). Princess, somewhat of a sorceress, daughter of the sovereigns of Ireland; was betrothed to Morold, whom Tristan has killed; becomes the wife of King Mark. Loves Tristan, at first in secret.	■	■	■	■	■	■	■	..	..	■	■
Brangäne (sopr.). Isolde's attendant and devoted confidant.	■	■	■	■	■	■	■	..	..		■
Kurwenal (bass). Squire; an old and faithful servant, devotedly attached to Tristan.	∴	■	..	■	■	..	..	..	■	■	.. ■
Tristan (tenor). Knight of Breton origin; nephew of King Mark, defender of the throne of Cornwall. Loves Isolde, at first in secret.	..	■	..	..	■	..	■	■	■	■	■
The Sailors (*Chorus:* tenors, basses).	(invisible.) .. ■	■	..	■							
Knights, Esquires, Men-at-Arms (*Chorus:* tenors, basses).	..	■	..	..	■						
Melot (tenor). One of King Mark's knights. Tristan's treacherous friend. Loves Isolde in secret and takes revenge upon her.	..	..	..	..	..	..	..	■	..	..	■
King Mark (bass). A generous prince. King of Cornwall, Tristan's uncle, and Isolde's husband.	..	..	..	..	..	..	..	■	..	..	■
A Shepherd (tenor). (Episode.)	..	..	..	..	..	..	..	..	■	..	■
A Pilot (bass).	..	..	..	..	..	..	..	..	..	..	■

he then remembers that the young Irish princess possesses the secret of some precious balms which alone can cure his hurt, and he determines to go to her and request the aid of her knowledge.

In a dying condition, he takes ship for Ireland, and, presenting himself incognito to Isolde under the name of Tantris, he implores her assistance. The young princess, moved by the sufferings of the dying man, devotedly tends him; but one day the truth is unexpectedly revealed : her lover must have received his death-blow from the sword of Tantris, for its blade contains a notch which corresponds exactly to the fragment of steel found in Morold's wound.

Isolde indignantly brandishes the weapon over the head of the impostor : she is about to strike the fatal blow, when their eyes meet. Tristan's glance is supplicating, and Isolde has mercy on him. She conceals from every one the secret that she has discovered ; and Tristan shall return to his home, safe and well, and relieve the princess of his hated presence. The knight departs, after many protestations of his gratitude and devotion ; but, oh treason ! he soon returns under his true name of Tristan, and accompanied by a brilliant retinue, to demand the hand of the maiden for his uncle, King Mark. Isolde's parents accept this alliance for their daughter, who in obedience must depart for the realm of her future husband under the knight's escort.

But in secret she grieves bitterly : for she believes that she is loved by this hero whom she has saved and who has so unworthily betrayed her; and without acknowledging it even to herself, she loves him, despite the blood-stained past which rises as a barrier between them.

Such is the condition of affairs when the curtain rises for the first act.

We will only sketch this, and the two others, briefly, and with bold outlines. In the poem of *Tristan* the situations are simple and the episodes not numerous. The whole interest of the drama lies in the various emotions of the hero and heroine. How can we explain them without weakening the intense feeling called forth by the representation? Will it not be better to leave every one to appreciate and feel it according to his own nature, than to destroy its bloom by unnecessarily insisting upon details which are purely psychological?

ACT I.

SCENE I. — Isolde is aboard the ship which is bringing her to Cornwall; a tent made of rich tapestries has been erected on the deck and is completely closed at the back. The princess is lying on a couch; a melancholy song, which a sailor is singing from the mast above, wounds and troubles her, and she gives way to her despair when she learns from her attendant, Brangäne, that land has been sighted and that the voyage is nearly over.

SCENE II. — She sends her companion with an order for Tristan to appear before her; from the beginning of the voyage he has persistently avoided her, thus forgetting the deference which he owes to his sovereign. Brangäne carries her mistress's order to the knight, who, although greatly moved on hearing the name Isolde spoken, nevertheless recovers himself and respectfully, but firmly, refuses to leave the helm of the ship confided to his care.

SCENE III. — Brangäne reports the knight's reply to her mistress, and Isolde, now giving full rein to her bitterness, reveals something of her secret to her companion, and tells her of the earnest care which she formerly be-

stowed upon Tristan, who has so ill rewarded her compassion for him.   Hiding the true cause of her grief, she
revolts against the idea of becoming the bride of the
King of Cornwall, whom she considers unworthy to be
united with one whose brow may wear the royal circlet
of Ireland.

Brangäne tries in vain to calm her and to justify the
conduct of Tristan, who, according to her ideas, has
brilliantly paid his debt of gratitude by obtaining for her
the gift of so beautiful a kingdom as that of Cornwall.
Isolde is thoughtful, and, talking to herself, deplores that
she is condemned to the torture of living forever beside
an accomplished being whom she cannot inspire with
love.   She is thinking of Tristan; but Brangäne, mis-
interpreting her words, advises her, if she fears that King
Mark may not love her as much as she desires, to have
recourse to the wonderful philtres which her mother, the
Queen of Ireland, gave her at parting.   Among these is
one which is infallible in subjecting all who drink it to
the power of love.   Isolde with dark resolve accepts her
attendant's counsel and makes her bring the precious
coffer containing the magic potions.   But it is not the
love-philtre that she chooses; she wants one still more
potent, and selects a flask filled with the elixir of death:
this she will induce Tristan to quaff.

SCENE IV. — Haste is imperative, for they are near-
ing land : even now they see the flag of rejoicing
floating above the battlements of the royal castle.
Kurwenal, Tristan's faithful squire, comes to announce
that they are entering port.   Isolde then sends to ask
Tristan for one moment's conversation, and orders the
terrified Brangäne to pour out the fatal draught in a cup.
In vain her distracted attendant tries to turn her from
her fatal purpose; Isolde imperiously commands; she

makes a violent effort to appear calm on the arrival of
Tristan, who respectfully presents himself before her.

SCENE V. — For a long time they look at each other
in silence; at last Isolde, after reproaching him for
having persistently neglected her during the voyage,
reminds him that there is a debt of blood between them
which she has not forgotten : she has not yet pardoned
the murder of her lover; and since no man has come
forward to avenge his death, it is she who must punish
the guilty one. Tristan listens, pale and sombre; he
hands her his sword and is ready to die.

But no, says Isolde to him, she has no right to deprive the King of his most faithful supporter, the one to
whom he owes both title and crown ; and, since she has
already spared the life of Morold's murderer, she must
pardon him again. Let him therefore quaff the cup of
reconciliation and forgetfulness. Whilst the sailors have
been raising their cries of joy at the approach of land,
Brangäne, trembling all over, has been preparing the
fatal philtre. Isolde snatches the cup from her hands
and gives it to Tristan.

Tristan has divined Isolde's fell design, but resolutely receives the draught which will deliver him from
the griefs with which his heart also is overwhelmed ; he
raises it to his lips and drinks; but Isolde immediately
snatches away the cup, drinks it to the dregs, and throws
it away.

Overcome with intense emotion, they gaze at each
other in ecstasy ; in the crisis of that supreme moment,
their eyes make no attempt to hide the secret which
consumes their hearts ; at last they fall into each other's
arms and remain locked in a long embrace, whilst Brangäne, distractedly hovering about them, tries to measure
the magnitude of her intentional mistake : for the elixir

of death she has substituted the love-potion! The two lovers, absorbed in each other, are unconscious of everything around them; they scarcely notice the bustle which tells of their arrival in port. Mechanically Isolde submits to be clothed with the royal mantle; Brangäne, to recall her to her ordinary senses, now despairingly confesses how she dared to make the fatal substitution. Tristan and Isolde look at each other in wild distress; Isolde falls fainting in the arms of her servant, whilst the entire crew joyously hails the arrival of the King on board the ship.

ACT II.

SCENE I. — The threshold of Isolde's dwelling, with steps leading down into the park planted with large trees, over which reigns a clear and radiant summer night. A lighted torch is placed beside the door. In the distance hunting-horns are heard growing gradually fainter, to which Brangäne, standing on the steps, lends an attentive ear. Isolde, in great agitation, issues from her apartment and interrogates her attendant. She impatiently awaits the moment when the royal hunt shall be far enough away from the palace for her to give the signal which will bring Tristan to her feet; but Brangäne implores her to be prudent: she has a suspicion that a trap has been set for the two lovers, and in particular suspects Melot, who, from the very hour when the King boarded the ship to receive his bride, suspiciously eyed the agitation of Tristan and Isolde, and must have discovered the cause of the trouble which reigned in their hearts. Ever since then he has played the spy, and this nocturnal chase, undertaken at his suggestion, probably covers some perfidious snare. Despite the protestations of the Queen, who has a blind faith in the fidelity of

Melot, Tristan's friend and confidant, Brangäne laments
the disobedience which led her to substitute the love-
philtre for the death-potion; far better would have been
a fatal and sudden end than these cruel agonies. She
bitterly accuses herself of all the evils which may fall
upon her mistress.

No, replies the latter, Brangäne is not to be blamed.
The goddess Minne [1] is responsible for all: she it is to
whom life and death are subject; she has transformed
hatred into love; Isolde is henceforth her vassal, and
will blindly submit to her decrees.

Notwithstanding Brangäne's prudent counsels, Isolde
seizes the torch and extinguishes it on the ground: this
is the appointed signal for Tristan. Brangäne turns away
in consternation and slowly mounts the steps leading to
the tower.

Isolde peers down the avenue, trying to pierce the
darkness; at last her gestures show that she sees her
lover; her emotion is at its height.

SCENE II.—Tristan enters impetuously; they passionately rush into each other's arms; their hearts over-
flow with love and rapture; they curse the light of day,
which has always antagonized their happiness: was it
not day that led Tristan to Ireland to demand Isolde for
King Mark? Was it not also day, which, shedding a
false light on the knight, caused him to be hated by her
who now cherishes him with her whole heart? Ah, why
cannot these lovers shroud themselves forever in the
sweet twilight of night and death that should indissolubly
unite their souls and their destinies! They sit upon a
flowery bank and remain locked in a long embrace, calling for death which they so ardently desire.

---

[1] Minne personifies love. She is the protectress of lovers.

Absorbed in this ecstasy, they take no heed of the flying hours and lose all count of time. Brangäne, who is
keeping watch above, warns them that the dreaded day
is breaking and bringing danger with it. Twice, while
engrossed with each other, she breaks in upon them;
then suddenly gives a piercing cry of alarm, and, at the
same moment, the brave and devoted Kurwenal rushes in
backwards, brandishing his sword.

SCENE III.—Behind him Melot and King Mark, followed by several courtiers, press tumultuously forward
and halt before the couple, intently regarding them with
various expressions. Brangäne has run to her mistress,
who has turned away and before whom Tristan with an
instinctive movement, has spread his mantle to shield her
from the gaze of the intruders.

Melot boasts to the King, who stands stupefied with
grief, of the great service he has rendered him, and for
which the King has not had the grace to thank him.
He is too deeply distressed at the terrible discovery he
has just made. This Tristan, whom he regarded as the
soul of honour and virtue, who was the hope of his de-
clining years, for whose sake, until now, he had refused
to take a second wife, since the death of the first, so as
to leave him his sole heir, — it is he, this perfidious
nephew, who brought him the marvellous beauty whom,
in his adoration, the generous King has respected as if he
were her father; he it is, who, after having made his heart
more sensitive to grief by the possession of this treasure,
ends by giving him this mortal wound, and pours into
his soul the cruel poison of suspicion against her whom
he loves best in all the world. Why has he cast him
into this hell from which nothing can again release him?

Tristan, who has listened to the reproaches of this
noble prince with ever-increasing sorrow, casts a look

of deep pity upon him; his secret he cannot tell; none shall ever learn it. Then, turning to Isolde, who looks at him with yearning eyes, he tells her that he will set out for that dreary country where his mother gave birth to him in sorrow and death. There his well-beloved may find an asylum, if she wishes to follow him to his sad retreat. Isolde replies that nothing shall prevent her from following him, he has only to show her the way; her lover softly kisses her brow; but at this point, Melot, boiling with rage, draws his sword and attacks Tristan, who places himself on guard. Their swords cross, and Tristan sinks, wounded by his enemy. He falls into Kurwenal's arms, as Isolde throws herself, weeping, upon his breast.

ACT III.

SCENE I.—The scene represents the wild and desolate garden of Tristan's old manor, Karéol, situated in Brittany, upon an eminence beside the sea. Far away the horizon line is visible above the walls, which are half in ruins and covered with vegetation. At the back is the gate of a feudal castle with loop-holes. In the centre of the stage, under the shadow of a lime-tree, is the bed on which Tristan lies.

The unfortunate man is dying of the wound which the traitor Melot gave him; his faithful Kurwenal has brought him in a bark here, to the domain of his ancestors, in a dying condition, and battles with death for him, impatiently awaiting the arrival of Isolde, for whom he has despatched a faithful servant to Cornwall. A shepherd, who has been placed on the look-out at the top of the cliff to signal the coming of the ship that is bringing Isolde the moment it appears on the horizon, plays upon his pipe a sad and plaintive melody, which will be changed for joyful notes when the longed-for sail appears in the offing.

At the raising of the curtain, he has left his post of observation for a moment, and has come to inquire for particulars about his master; what mysterious and fatal adventure has brought him to this sad state? Kurwenal refuses to reply, and sends him back again to watch the lonely horizon, on which no vessel is yet visible. The shepherd resumes his melancholy music, whose rhythms rouse the sufferer from his deadly torpor. At first he does not recognize his surroundings; the good Kurwenal helps him to collect his thoughts; but the sole idea that his mind clearly grasps is that of Isolde. His love again takes complete possession of him, he calls distractedly for his well-beloved, and life burns with temporary strength when his faithful servant promises him the early arrival of his adored one. In his fever he sees all his sad life pass before his eyes; his unhappy youth, his unlucky voyage to Ireland, and the fateful potion — the manifest cause of all his misfortunes. His excitement constantly increases, but his strength fails him, and he falls back fainting. The frightened Kurwenal revives him with difficulty. Why does not the ship arrive and bring joy and healing?

Scene II. — Suddenly a joyous melody is heard; it is the signal agreed on to announce the good news. Kurwenal, who, at Tristan's request, has mounted to the top of the tower, already sees the flag of joyfulness fluttering among the sails. Isolde is coming; the ship has passed the dreaded headland and is entering the port. The dearly-beloved makes signals, she springs to shore, and Kurwenal goes to welcome her, leaving Tristan a prey to the greatest excitement. The wounded man, thinking that he can henceforth defy death, springs to meet his love; but he has over-estimated his strength: it fails him, and he falls dying into the arms of his adored one.

Death, once invoked with such ardour, has at last heard the call; night, the blessed adversary of hostile day, shrouds him in her veil. Kneeling beside him, Isolde gently winds her arms around him and entreats him to let her cure his deep wound, and to live if only for an hour; but, seeing him forever deaf to her voice, she falls dying upon the body of him she has so dearly loved.

SCENE III. — Kurwenal, mute with grief, has been present at this heart-rending scene; his glance never wanders from Tristan. At this moment a clash of arms is heard; the shepherd runs in to announce that a second ship has just entered port. Great confusion follows; Kurwenal, thinking this a hostile invasion on the part of King Mark, rushes upon Melot, who is one of the first to enter, and kills him. He is, himself, mortally wounded in the fight, and returns to die beside the body of his beloved master. And yet what a mistake he made! The noble and magnanimous King, informed too late, alas! by Brangäne of the disastrous effects of the philtre, and convinced that Fate was alone to blame for the treachery of the two beings whom he so dearly loved, had come to bring them his pardon and to unite them forever. He gently reproaches Isolde for not having confided in him; he has been so happy at discovering the innocence of his dearest friend! The unhappy woman does not understand; with wild eyes she gazes on the mortal remains of Tristan, but her soul is already taking its flight, and, transfigured by the kind hand of death, she expires in her faithful Brangäne's arms.

King Mark blesses the dead amidst the deep emotion of all present.

DIE MEISTERSINGER

CHARACTERS in the order of their first entrance.	ACT I.			ACT II.							ACT III. Tab. 1.				Tab. 2.
SCENES:	1	2	3	1	2	3	4	5	6	7	1	2	3	4	5
The Congregation of the Faithful (*Chorus:* sopr., contr., ten., basses).	■														
Walter von Stolzing (tenor). Young Franconian knight, poet, and musician of talent; lover of Eva, whose hand he obtains by triumphing at the contest of the Meistersinger.	■	■	■					■	■	■		■		■	■
Eva (sopr.). Pogner's daughter; the precious reward promised to the victor in the contest. Loves Walter.	■					■			■	■	■	□		■	■
Magdalene (sopr.). Eva's nurse, confidante, and servant; engaged to the young apprentice, David.	■				■	■		■	■	■	■			■	■
David (tenor). Sachs's pupil and apprentice; Magdalene's lover.	■	■	■	■	■	■			■	■	■		■	■	■
The Apprentices (*Chorus:* contr., ten.). Band of students, always disposed to mischief; pupils of the masters of the different guilds of the town of Nuremberg.		■	■	■						■					■
Pogner (bass). Goldsmith; citizen of Nuremberg and Meistersinger. Father of Eva, whom he has offered as a prize in the contest.				■		■			■	■					■
Beckmesser (baryt.). Town clerk; an absurd and disagreeable character, pedantic and jealous. Meistersinger and marker of the corporation. Aspires to Eva's hand.				■					■	■		■		■	■
Hans Sachs (bass). Shoemaker and popular poet. Meistersinger; character of extreme kindness, a gentle and tender philosopher, and the protector of the loves of Walter and Eva, whom he wishes to unite.				■		■	■	■	■	■	■	■	■	■	■
Vogelgesang (tenor). Furrier. Member of the Corporation of the Meistersinger.				■					■	■					■
Nachtigal (bass). Tinsmith. " " " "				■					■	■					■
Kothner (bass). Baker. " " " "				■					■	■					■
Ortel (bass). Soapmaker. " " " "				■					■	■					■
Zorn (tenor). Pewterer. " " " "				■						■					■
Moser (tenor). Tailor. " " " "				■					■	■					■
Eisslinger (tenor). Grocer. " " " "				■					■	■					■
Foltz (bass). Brazier. " " " "				■					■	■					■
Schwartz (bass). Stocking-weaver. " " " "				■					■	■					■
The Night-Watchman (bass). A comic character (episode).									■	■					■
Neighbours (*Chorus:* sopr.).										■					■
Companions (*Chorus:* ten., basses).										■					■
Old Citizens (*Chorus:* basses).										■					■
The Shoemakers (*Chorus:* ten., basses).															■
The Tailors (*Chorus:* ten., basses).															■
The Bakers (*Chorus:* ten., basses).															■
Populace (*Chorus:* sopr., contr., ten., basses).															■

DIE MEISTERSINGER

I think it well to give a less detailed analysis of the poem of *Die Meistersinger* than of the dramas, because, even at the first hearing, there is much less on which the spectator needs to be informed.

It is a comedy full of wit and tender emotion; and if ignorance of the German language prevents our comprehension of the numerous jests and witticisms, yet the gay and light-hearted character of the music and the suggestive gestures of the actors make it almost as easy to understand as if it were merely a pantomime.

The essential thing is to form a clear idea of the principal characters: Sachs is the type of kindness, uprightness and good sense; Beckmesser, his antithesis, is the ridiculous and malicious pedant; Pogner thinks it a sublime idea to set his daughter up for competition; David is a gay companion; Magdalene a fine servant; and Walter and Eva are lovers of a highly poetic nature.

The Meistersinger are not in the least grotesque in themselves, because of their serious conviction: they are good and honest citizens who have appointed themselves conservators of the art of singing, and are very rigid with regard to the observance of traditional rules, from which they will not allow any deviation.

All their names are strictly historic, as is evident from a document published at Altdorf in 1697, by J. Christopher Wagenseil; we also learn from it that the meeting of the Meistersinger took place after the noonday service in the church of Saint Katharine, which is now closed. The odd names of the various modes and the rules of tablature also appear in the same work, which is extremely scarce.

But there were four markers; Wagner had to combine them into one to form the mirth-provoking and ill-
natured character of Beckmesser, around whom the
whole play revolves.

Act I.

Scene I. — The action takes place in Nuremberg, at
the beginning of the 16th century. The first scene
occurs in the church of Saint Katharine ; the scenery
shows the church viewed from one side with only the
last seats visible of the nave, which runs towards the
left.

The worshippers are just finishing the chanting of a
psalm. Two women, sitting in the last row, have
attracted the attention of a young noble, the knight
Walter von Stolzing, who, leaning against a pillar, cannot take his eyes off the younger of them, Eva, the
daughter of Veit Pogner, goldsmith and citizen of
Nuremberg.

Walter makes a mute but eloquent appeal to the
maiden, who timidly responds with a discreet, but somewhat confused gesture.

The service ended, the church slowly empties, and
the knight approaches the woman he loves. The innocent maiden, notwithstanding her guilelessness, would
not be sorry to manage a *tête-à-tête* with the handsome
knight ; with a charming ingenuousness she pretends to
have left her fichu in her seat in the church, and sends
her nurse to fetch it. Meanwhile Walter begs her to
decide his fate and pronounce the word which will
encourage his hopes; since his arrival in Nuremberg,
where he was received with such cordial hospitality by
Pogner, Eva's father, he has loved the maiden, and
aspires to be her betrothed, if perchance she is free.

Meantime the nurse has returned, and, to prolong the conversation, Eva again sends her in search of a brooch, which has probably fallen on the way. The *tête-à-tête* continues as the two lovers could wish, for Magdalene, in her turn, has forgotten her psalter and goes away a third time. When she returns and sees the knight, she gratefully thanks him for having taken care of Eva in her absence and invites him to come and see Master Pogner again. Was he not well received on his arrival in Nuremberg, that they do not see him any more? But the young man deplores that fatal visit to the goldsmith's house, for since he first saw Eva he has known no rest. The nurse cries out at this declaration, made in a loud voice in the open church, as being likely to compromise Eva; she wants to go, but Eva detains her: she does not know how to answer Walter's question if she is betrothed, and desires her companion to answer for her. Magdalene, disturbed for a moment by the sight of her lover, the apprentice David, who comes out of the sacristy, then explains to Walter that Eva is promised — without exactly being so: the goldsmith, Pogner, has determined to offer his daughter as a reward to the victor in the competition which is about to be held by the Meistersinger of Nuremberg. No one, therefore, yet knows the happy man, whom, moreover, Eva will be free to refuse if he is displeasing to her.

The maiden relies particularly upon this last point of her nurse's story, and whilst Walter, strongly excited, strides up and down, she tells her that she positively must have the knight. At first sight she felt she belonged to him; besides is he not like David? — "Like David?" cries the nurse in amazement, thinking of her own lover. — "Yes," replies Eva; "King David; not the one we see on the banner of the Meistersinger, but the David painted by Dürer and represented by the artist with the sword by his side, the sling in his hand, and his head with an aureole of golden curls." An amusing passage of complicated cross-purposes.

The name David, repeated several times, attracts the attention of that Apprentice, who is going and coming, making preparations for the meeting which will shortly take place in the sacred edifice itself. At this meeting for the presentation of candidates, the Apprentice who does not fail in the rules of tablature is to receive his freedom and to be appointed a Master. The knight therefore comes just at the right time, replies Magdalene. She confides the young noble to David's care to be initiated. The latter is Hans Sachs's pupil, in singing as in shoemaking, and he has long been studying in hopes of one day obtaining the Mastership : he, therefore, will give the knight complete instructions regarding the difficulties to be conquered for the morrow's meeting, and also for the preparatory test, which will take place immediately. The two women then go home.

Scene II. — The first thing necessary, David explains, is to mount the first step and to obtain letters of freedom. But the degree of Meistersinger is not to be gained so easily. There are several grades to conquer first. He must recognize and sing the tones and melodies without hesitation in order to become a *singer*. And David, in a long enumeration, recites to Walter all the titles, sometimes burlesque ones, of the modes with which he must familiarize himself: the short, the long, the slow, the fragrant hawthorn, the tortoise, the cinnamon stalk, the calf, the frog, the faithful pelican, etc. Then he must compose words adapted to one of the well-known modes ; and this will entitle him to the grade of *poet*.

Lastly comes the third and most formidable test : the

composition of a complete work, *poem and music*, in which the judge cannot allow more than seven infractions of the established rules.   If Walter triumphs over the last difficulty, all honour to him; he will receive the victor's crown of flowers and will be proclaimed Meistersinger.

The Apprentices, who during this whole scene have not ceased, whilst getting the place ready, to torment and interrupt David, have finally brought into the centre of the stage a platform surrounded by black curtains; then they place a chair, a desk, and a slate to which a piece of chalk is suspended at the end of a string.   They join David in wishing the candidate good luck, jesting with him, and dancing around him; then they respectfully retire on seeing the Meistersinger arrive one after the other.

SCENE III. — Beckmesser, one of the members of the corporation, a ridiculous and crabbed character, accompanies Veit Pogner, and is insisting on his granting him the hand of Eva, for whom he has a great desire, but whose love he does not think he possesses.   The goldsmith promises him his good will, without, however, binding himself to anything, which does not satisfy the grotesque personage, who is uneasy regarding the success of his suit; he therefore regards every fresh face with hostility and eyes Walter malevolently as the young knight approaches Pogner, who is astonished to see him at the assembly, and tells him that he wishes to undergo the trial and have himself immediately received as a member of the company.   Pogner, on the contrary, is delighted with this idea and promises the knight his cordial support.

The assembly is now complete, Hans Sachs having just arrived; one of the Meistersinger calls the roll,

9

which affords occasion in the German text for a series
of more or less witty jokes and jests, the sense of which
is lost in translation.

Pogner then begins to speak, reminding them of the
importance of the festival which is to bring them together
on the morrow, Saint John's Day. There will be prizes
for the victors in the Song-Contest, and Pogner himself,
being anxious to refute the charge of avarice, which is
made against the citizens throughout Germany, and wishing to prove that he places nothing above art, has decided that what he will offer as a prize to the conqueror
shall be his most precious treasure, his only daughter,
Eva, with all that she possesses. Only one restriction
accompanies this offer: Eva will be free to refuse the
conqueror if he is not pleasing to her; but she will,
nevertheless, not be allowed to choose a husband outside
of the corporation of the Meistersinger.

This speech of Pogner's occasions much discussion,
accompanied by noisy acclamations from the Apprentices,
who are happy at any uproarious manifestations. Some
approve the goldsmith, others criticise his idea: amongst
the latter is Beckmesser, who, thinking himself sure of
victory, recognizes how unfavourably this last condition
will affect him. Hans Sachs proposes to add the popular
voice to the judgment of the Meistersinger, feeling certain in his simple good sense that it will give good advice and find itself naturally in accord with the maiden's
feelings; the Apprentices noisily applaud this motion,
but several of the Meistersinger oppose the idea, as they
are unwilling to let the common people join in their affairs. The goldsmith, having explained to Sachs how
many complications would be caused by this new clause,
he abandons it with his characteristic good-nature. A
little skirmish then occurs between the cobbler and Beck-

messer; the latter, having undertaken to ridicule the excellent Hans, hears him say that *they are both too old* to
aspire to the hand of the maiden, which greatly annoys
that grotesque person.

At last the excitement calms down, and Pogner presents the young knight, whose nobility and honourable
character he guarantees, to his colleagues, telling them
he asks to undergo the test for the Mastership. Beckmesser, anxious to create difficulties for him whose
rivalry he foresees, tries to adjourn the examination; but
the Meistersinger outvote him and prepare to hear the
candidate, first asking him the name of the teacher who
gave him the precious lessons.

Walter says he has studied poetry in the silence of the
long winter evenings, by reading over a hundred times
the ponderous tome of one of the most celebrated Minnesinger of Germany; and therefore this old master
taught him the art of poetry. As for music, he learnt
that in listening to the birds singing in the woods, when
early in the year Nature, freed from her frosts, awakes
at the balmy breath of spring.

At these words, the discussion is renewed. Some,
headed by Beckmesser, who has been sneering all the
while the knight has been speaking, declare Walter's
pretensions absurd; others, with larger ideas of art, such
as Vogelsang, Pogner, and Sachs, form a better opinion
of the young candidate, and induce the corporation
to hear him. Walter accepts the examination, and,
to gain the precious reward to which he aspires, he will
attempt to express in poetry and melody the memories of
his childhood; he will sing under the inspiration of the
Love in which he has placed all his hopes. Beckmesser
is appointed marker: he is shut up in the chair surrounded by curtains, which the Apprentices brought in

a while ago, to write down the aspirant's mistakes on the
slate; he installs himself in his tribunal, after having
wished his rival good luck, accompanying this wish with
an ironical and malicious grimace.

Walter collects his thoughts for a moment, while one
of the Meistersinger, Kothner, who has made one of
the Apprentices bring him a large placard hanging
against the wall, reads to him the rules of tablature
which he will have to observe if he wishes to be received;
he then gets up into the seat reserved for the candidates,
and, after having evoked the gracious image of Eva to
give him courage, he sings the first strophe of his musical poem, which is a hymn to Nature, to Spring, and
to Love.

While he is singing the first couplet, Beckmesser is
heard stirring about in his box, angrily marking the mistakes on his slate.   The knight, disturbed for a moment,
recovers himself and continues the second strophe, but
the town-clerk, without giving him time to begin the
third, opens the curtains and announces with a rasping
voice that the number of errors allowed is already far
exceeded, that he has failed and must retire.   He then
shows the assembly the slate so thickly scored with big
chalk marks that every one bursts out laughing.   The
discussion then recommences more vehemently than
ever; the jealous town-clerk, now triumphant, harangues
his companions, mocking the young knight's unfortunate
efforts, and rallying to his side all the old Meistersinger,
who are slaves to routine, and cannot understand what
fresh poetry breathes in Walter's song; on the other
hand, the knight's partisans, Pogner and Sachs, defend
the new form which he has adopted; Sachs claims for
his *protégé* the right of, at least, being heard to the end;
according to their rules he has the right of completing

his trial; and, besides, adds the poet-cobbler, is it just
that he should be judged by one who is his rival in
love? At these words Beckmesser's rage is beyond
all bounds. In vain Pogner tries to calm the general
uproar: the majority of the Meistersinger side against
Walter, who is greatly disheartened, and whose only
defender is the benevolent Sachs, whose artistic soul
sympathizes with that of the young man.

Beckmesser renews his campaign of abuse with fresh
bitterness; they all take his part, and, in the midst of a
general tumult, Walter, again taking his place, begins his
third and last strophe, in which in the heat of despera-
tion, he caustically criticises his persecutors.

The good Sachs admires the knight's courageous attitude; but it only serves still further to increase the dis-
pleasure of the obstinate townsmen, who unanimously
decide that he has failed, failed without appeal. They
all excitedly disperse. The Apprentices, mingling with
the Meistersinger, add still more to the confusion and
disorder. They again form a wild ring around the
marker's box, and try to bring Sachs into their dance; he
is left alone and makes an expressive gesture, eloquent
of his discomfiture and discouragement. Then they all
disperse.

ACT II.

SCENE I. — The stage represents a street scene in
Nuremberg, intersected in the middle by a narrow lane.
The corner which it forms on the right is occupied by
Pogner's house, a rich citizen's dwelling, which is
approached by several steps; above the steps is an arched
doorway with stone seats. In the front of the house is
a lime-tree surrounded by shrubs, and under the lime-tree
is a bench. The corner on the left is formed by the

more modest dwelling of Hans Sachs; the door of his
cobbler's shop is horizontally divided in two parts, it
opens directly into the street, and is shaded by a thick
elder-tree.   On the side towards the lane the house has
two windows, the first of which belongs to the shop, and
the second to the room of the Apprentice David.

The act passes during a beautiful summer evening;
the night is slowly falling.   David and other Apprentices
are putting up the shutters of their masters' shops, whilst
singing and celebrating in advance the festival of Saint
John, which will take place on the morrow.   The
scamps are teasing their comrade David by trying to imitate the voice of Magdalene, who noiselessly issues from
the goldsmith's house, with a basket on her arm, and in
a low voice calls her lover, for whom she has some dainties, but whom she first wants to ask for news of the
song-examination which occurred in the morning.   Did
the knight come victorious out of the trial?   At David's
reply in the negative, she quickly snatches away the basket, into which he is already diving: there is no reward
for the bringer of bad news; and she re-enters the house
showing her disappointment by her expressive gestures.
The Apprentices, who have watched the scene from a
distance, approach their abashed comrade, congratulating
him on his good fortune in marrying an old maid, and dance
around him; David, in a rage, is trying to thrash them
all, when Sachs, coming out of his shop, asks the reason
of all this noise and sends the pugnacious youth to his
room, telling him he shall go to bed without having his
singing-lesson, as a punishment for his riotous conduct.
Whilst they go in together, the Apprentices disperse,
and Eva appears at the corner of the street leaning on her
father's arm, returning from a walk.

SCENE II. — Pogner, who is secretly preoccupied with

to-morrow's contest and with his daughter's fate, would like to talk with his friend Sachs, and looks through the crack in his shutters to see if the cobbler is still awake; the maiden, also anxious, but without wishing to show it, keeps silence. She is vaguely hoping that she may have a visit this evening from him whom she loves, and of whom she has heard no news since the morning; she therefore lends an idle ear to the conversation of her father, who is trying to interest her in the coming contest, of which she is to be the heroine; she insists on leaving the bench on which they are sitting and entering the house.

Pogner goes in first, and the maiden, standing on the threshold, rapidly exchanges a few words in a low voice with the nurse who has been awaiting her. She learns from Magdalene of the knight's failure and makes up her mind to go secretly, after supper, to her old friend Sachs to ask him for fuller information. Magdalene has another message for her from Beckmesser; but that is of no importance: Eva takes no notice of it and enters the house in her turn.

Scene III. — Sachs, after having reproved his Apprentice for his turbulence, orders him to set his bench and stool near the door, and then sends him to bed. As for himself, he sits down, intending to get on with his work; but hardly is he alone, when he falls into a reverie in spite of himself; he leaves his work and, leaning with his elbows on the lower part of the door, he gives rein to his thoughts, which return to the morning's trial: What poetry there was in that song, although it was constructed in defiance of all established rules! How new and full of freshness was that hymn of Spring! How evidently it rose from the soul of an artist, and how entirely it has captured the heart of the good Sachs!

SCENE IV. — While he thus meditates, Eva, who has
come out of her house, has approached the shop door,
looking in every direction to see if she has been noticed;
she wishes her old friend good-evening, and, sitting down
near him on the stone bench, she tries to lead the conversation to the subject which fills her heart: the contest
of the morrow, the prize of which is to be herself. —
Who will take part in the contest? she asks. The poet-
cobbler, who has the necessary rank to enter the trial;
has he no idea of competing? — She questions him in a
round-about way, but is quickly reassured: the excellent
Sachs loves her as a child, he has known her from her
birth, but he would not take such a young girl for his
wife: that would be folly on his part; besides has he not
been married and been the father of a family already?
And he rejects the idea upon which Eva insists, and
which is, perhaps, a little nearer to his heart than he
would care to acknowledge to himself. — Then is it not
his intention to favour Beckmesser? — No, again replies
the worthy man, who sees perfectly well what she is
driving at; and when, after more beating about the bush,
she at last speaks of the morning's examination, asking
who were present; whilst thinking of the love freshly
awakened in this young heart which he cherishes unknown to himself and which will never be his, he cannot help feeling a moment's sadness, and despite his
kindheartedness, he takes a half-malicious pleasure in
criticising the song Walter composed, saying that the
young knight, with his new and strange ideas, will never
succeed in producing anything, and may at once give up
all hope of gaining the rank of Master.

At these words, Eva cannot restrain her annoyance;
she rises quickly, saying that if Walter cannot find grace
in the eyes of the dry-as-dust pedants of Nuremberg, he

will certainly be appreciated elsewhere by hearts which are warm, ardent, and progressive. Then, without waiting any longer, she goes away with Magdalene, who has come to call her in a low voice.

The good Sachs, who has learnt from his young friend's manner what he wished to know, watches her with a pensive glance as she goes away in anger, and generously vows to protect her innocent love-affair with all his power. He then shuts the upper wing of his door, which only reveals a narrow slit of light, whilst the two women, standing aside together, argue in low tones. Magdalene tries to make Eva go in, as her father has called her several times; but the maiden has decided to await the knight in the street, for he cannot fail to come, and she is determined to talk with him. The nurse then gives her Beckmesser's message : that ridiculous suitor asks his beautiful lady to give a hearing to the song which he has prepared for to-morrow's competition, and which he is coming to sing with a lute accompaniment under her window this very evening to submit it to her approbation. Eva, wishing to get rid of him, sends Magdalene to take her place on the balcony, to the great affliction of the latter, who fears to excite David's jealousy by so doing. But Eva will not listen to her; she pushes her companion into the house, where Pogner is still calling for her, and in spite of Magdalene, who tries to drag her in with her, remains on the threshold, listening to footsteps which without doubt herald the longed-for approach of Walter.

SCENE V. — It is, in fact, the young knight coming down the lane. Eva runs to meet him, and, in a state of exaltation, declares that, whatever happens, she will choose him against all the world as her companion and husband. Walter, still upset and indignant at the morning's failure, tells his beloved how contemptuously those antiquated Meistersinger received him, — him who, filled with courage and fortified with his love, had submitted to their examination. Therefore, since he sees perfectly well that he can never acquire that title, which according to the goldsmith's will is the indispensable condition of obtaining Eva's hand, one sole resource remains for them if they wish to belong to each other, and that is to fly together, and so gain their liberty. In a fever of excitement, he fancies he still hears the raillery of the Meistersinger pursuing him and proclaiming their pretensions to his dear one; fiercely he lays his hand upon the hilt of his sword: but the distant noise which he heard was only the horn of the night-watchman, who is making his rounds and inviting the inhabitants of the town to rest. The two lovers have only just time to conceal themselves from sight: Eva disappears into the interior of the house with Magdalene, who has come back to look for her, and Walter hides himself behind the lime-tree, while Sachs, who has overheard the conversation, opens his door a little wider and lowers his lamp, so as to continue his observation without being perceived, determining to watch over the two imprudent young people and prevent their committing any folly.

The watchman goes on his way, and Walter leaves his retreat, anxiously awaiting Eva's return. She soon appears, muffled in her nurse's clothes, which she has taken the better to conceal herself. She is already pointing out to her lover the road by which they must fly, when Sachs, who is lying in wait inside his shop, suddenly turns upon them the light of his lamp, shining through his wide open door.

SCENE VI. — The two fugitives, thus fully illumined,

do not know what to do : to follow along the street is to
risk meeting the watchman; to go down the lane under
the cobbler's eyes is impossible.   Walter then wants to
extinguish the lamp of the troublesome neighbour, but is
astonished to learn that it is no other than Sachs who so
well defended him that morning, and who, as Eva tells
him, now decries him like all the others.

In addition, a fresh difficulty now presents itself under
the ungraceful form of Beckmesser, who is coming to
give his serenade.   The knight's irritation is redoubled
on recognizing his declared enemy ; but Eva calms
him by assuring him that the ridiculous person shall not
long remain there, and will go away as soon as his song
is sung.   She draws her lover towards the bench, and
they both hide behind the bushes.

Sachs, who on Beckmesser's arrival had turned down
the lamp again, directs its light into the street at the
moment when the town-clerk is beginning to tune his
lute to sing, and, sitting down to his bench, he sings a
popular song with all his might, whilst loudly hammering
upon his last.   The grotesque Beckmesser, in a rage,
nevertheless tries to put a good face on the matter, and
begins to talk to Sachs to induce him to be quiet and let
him sing in his turn ; but the malicious cobbler will not
lend himself to his scheme ; he pretends that he thinks
Beckmesser has come to hasten the delivery of a pair of
shoes, and sets busily to work, redoubling his noise.
The song he selects is intended to exasperate the ugly
town-clerk, whose rage increases in an amusing manner,
and to warn Walter and Eva that a friend is acquainted
with their doings and will find a way to balk their hot-
headed plans.   The maiden is greatly worried at this,
and has all the trouble in the world to calm the knight's
irritation, when, by a happy diversion, Eva's window

softly opens, and indistinctly reveals a female form, which is none other than Magdalene dressed in the clothes of her mistress.   This trick played on his presumptuous rival amuses Walter, who now follows the scene with interest.   Beckmesser, thinking himself in the presence of his loved one, is anxious to warble his melody to her; so he pretends that he has come to sing to Sachs to get his opinion; but the crafty Hans denies any competence in the matter and applies himself noisily to the town-clerk's shoes, which seem to absorb his whole interest.   Beckmesser insists and flies into a passion; Sachs, with apparent simplicity, imperturbably continues his teasing, and obstinately refuses to leave his noisy work.   The situation is prolonged in the most comic way; the town-clerk is on thorns: suppose Eva should grow impatient and leave the window!   At last they come to some sort of an agreement: Beckmesser, conquered by the stupid tenacity of the cobbler, consents with a sigh to be judged by Hans, who, nevertheless, will not relinquish his dear shoes and will mark the poet's faults by driving the nails into the soles with blows of his hammer.   The singer then places himself well in view of Eva's window, which is wide open, and, after having played a prelude on his lute, which, in his fury, he has tuned falsely, begins his first couplet, which is soon interrupted by one and then by two, and then three blows.   He turns round furiously, but noiselessly, to this new marker, who stops him at every moment by remarks on his verses, and ends by tranquilly advising him to begin his song again.   In this song he celebrates the day which will soon break, the competition which is going to take place, and the beautiful maiden who will be the prize.   In proportion as his song proceeds, the strokes of Sachs's hammer are redoubled, accelerated, and increased a thousandfold. At each stroke, Beckmesser makes a significant grimace, and, in an attempt to drown them, he sings louder and louder, thus giving his song, which he meant to be languorous and expressive, a roaring, jerking, and altogether ridiculous rendering. Sachs then asks him, in a perfectly serious way, if he has finished his song: as for him, Sachs, he has ended his work, thanks to the numerous faults he has had to mark; then, giving him in two words his opinion, which is anything but flattering, of the poetical work, he bursts out laughing in his face and turns his back on him. Then Beckmesser, who is exasperated, but will not desist, continues to sing under the window of his charmer, although the latter has retired with a gesture of disapprobation; he bellows at the top of his voice in such shrill tones and makes such a noise that the neighbours are awakened, and begin to show themselves at the windows. David appears with the others, and, thinking that it is Magdalene who is being serenaded, he springs into the street with a cudgel in his hand, and, rushing at the town-clerk he breaks his lute and administers a drubbing which continues for the rest of the scene. The inhabitants of the quarter then come down into the street half dressed, and, trying to separate the two combatants, start quarrelling among themselves. The Apprentices run from all directions, delighted to increase the tumult, then follow the weavers, curriers, butchers, potters, etc.; the Meistersinger and the citizens, attracted by the noise, arrive in their turn; every one is fighting with his neighbour: the women join in on recognizing their husbands and their brothers; the brawl is at its height, the tumult is general, every one is shouting excitedly, nothing but bleeding noses and black eyes are visible on every side. Magdalene has come down from her window to make

David let go of Beckmesser, whom he is still thrashing; but Pogner, who thinks she is Eva, whose clothes she is still wearing, orders her to come into the house again and keep quiet, then he descends to the ground floor, and appears on the threshold of his door.   Since the tumult began, Eva and Walter have remained concealed under the lime-tree full of anxiety; but, profiting by the general uproar, they are again thinking of flight; followed by his companion, the knight, sword in hand, advances to make a way for himself through the crowd under cover of the night, for the cobbler's lamp no longer illuminates the scene; but Sachs, who has not ceased to watch the lovers, comes out to make David relinquish his hold, sending him rolling into the shop with a kick, while Beckmesser limps away as fast as possible.   Sachs then advances into the middle of the street and pushes Eva towards her house, where the goldsmith, believing her to be Magdalene, receives her and quickly closes the door behind them; Hans then seizes Walter by the arm, draws him into the shop, and shuts the door.   At this moment some of the belligerents have the idea of calming the others by sousing them with water, crying " Fire!"   The rout then begins; next is heard in the distance the horn of the watchman, who is slowly approaching; the citizens, guilders, and Apprentices take fright, disperse in the twinkling of an eye, and disappear into their houses, quickly shutting the doors and windows, so that when the watchman arrives to invite the inhabitants to rest, the quarter has resumed its accustomed calm; the good man, thinking he must have been dreaming when he heard the distant echoes of the fight, rubs his eyes and finds only a city sleeping in the luminous beauty of the moon, which has just risen.

Act III.

SCENE I. — We are now introduced into Sachs's shop.
At the back is the street door with the upper part open.
To the left is a window with pots of flowers, and looking on to the lane; upon the right a door opens into a
small room.

The cobbler is sitting in a large armchair near the
window, illumined by the rays of the morning sun; he
is absorbed in reading a large folio volume which he
holds on his knees, and does not notice the arrival of his
Apprentice, who puts his head in cautiously from the
street and looks around the room, then, seeing that he is
not noticed, enters on tiptoe and gently sets down behind the bench a basket which he has on his arm.   He
examines its contents with great interest, and successively takes out flowers and ribbons, and then a cake and
a sausage, which he begins to eat, when, at the noise
which Sachs makes by turning over a leaf, he starts and
quickly hides his treasures.   Then, fearing his master's
anger for his turbulent conduct of the past night, he
begins to justify himself in a flood of words which Sachs,
being still absorbed in his reading, does not hear.   David,
full of his subject, continues to plead his cause with an
ardour that is touching and comical at the same time,
while occasionally casting an expressive and anxious
glance on his provisions, which cause him considerable
uneasiness.   The kind poet at last shuts his book, and
slowly rousing from his reverie, is greatly astonished at
seeing David on his knees, quite overcome by fear and
anxiously looking at him.   Sachs, noticing the flowers
and ribbons, begins, to David's great delight, to talk
quietly, and without any display of anger, of the festival
which is in preparation, and makes his pupil recite for

his lesson the verses on Saint John. The youth, in his confusion, sings the words to the air of Beckmesser's absurd serenade, then at Sachs's sign of astonishment, he takes up the proper air of his song, the subject of which is the baptism of a Nuremberg infant, who was taken to the banks of the Jordan and called Johannes in Latin, or Hans in German; this transition leads the singer to give his master the good wishes for the day, while eagerly offering him the flowers and dainties in his basket; he ends with the wish that Sachs, being triumphant at the competition and obtaining Eva's hand, may thus adorn his house with a gracious face which will bring new gaiety into it. The worthy man replies gently, but with some reserve, keeping to himself his secret thoughts, which are sad with the renunciation of a happiness within his vision, but one which, with his courageous good sense, he has never acknowledged even to himself, and sends David away to make himself ready for the festival which is about to begin. David, quite touched, and happy at having escaped a reprimand, respectfully kisses his master's hand and goes to his room, while the poet-philosopher resumes the thread of his thoughts, still holding the folio on his knees. He meditates profoundly on human nature, which, alas, is so prompt at ill deeds and quarrels. How small a thing suffices to let loose human passions and make men clash together! What made these placid inhabitants of Nuremberg so enraged last night? An unknown cause, most certainly puerile, set them at one another: the exhalations of a flowering lime-tree, the malicious prompting of some kobold, or, perhaps, the heaviness of the air on that Eve of Saint John? This thought of Saint John, which suddenly occurs, reminds him that on this day he has a task to accomplish. He must manœuvre very skilfully and use every means to forward the happiness of the youthful pair whose love-affair he has taken under his protection.

Scene II. — At this moment the door of the little room opens to admit Walter, who stands still for a moment looking at Sachs; the latter turns round and lets the folio fall from his knees to the floor.

Walter, who has received most cordial hospitality from his host, has passed under his roof a comfortable and refreshing night, during which he has had a dream of the most ideal beauty. Hans then suggests that he shall take this dream as the basis of his competition-song; for he wants to see him make the venture, notwithstanding his failure of yesterday. He must not feel resentful against these good honest people, who may have been mistaken in all sincerity, and may, moreover, have been somewhat troubled by the novel and unrestrained form of the song which he gave them. Sachs most certainly does not despair of seeing his *protégé* succeed; had it been otherwise, would he not have been the first to favour the flight and union of the two lovers? Come, let Walter get to work quickly and compose a beautiful Master-song.

"But first, what is meant by a Master-song?" replies the knight; "what is the use of these strict rules which they insist on imposing upon everybody? Can genius accommodate itself thus to fetters which impede its flight?"

"In the spring-time of life," the good Sachs replies, "when all the ardour and sap of youth are flowing in the heart and brain, genius can certainly do without rules, and often succeeds in producing a beautiful and strong work without their aid; but when time and life, with its train of sorrows, have frozen this ardour and

dashed this enthusiasm, he who is no longer guided by
enthusiasm and youthful illusions will never be able to
create anything if he does not seek the support of science;
those who have taken the trouble to formulate and group
these rules have been precisely men tried by the hardships
of life and who have felt the need of such an aid." And
Sachs, after a melancholy allusion to his own state of
mind, ends by recommending the young knight to begin
his work without delay, — to relate his dream, which shall
serve as a basis for the subject, and his master will teach
him how to make it accord with the rules of the Meistersinger, so that they may approve and crown it.

Walter, collecting his memories, sings the first strophe,
describing a wondrous garden full of the sweetest odours
and displayed before his eyes in the clear light of a brilliant dawn.

" Very good indeed," says Sachs, telling him immediately to compose the second strophe, so that the parallel
may be completed.   Walter continues, in a second
couplet, to describe the enchanted garden, then, at his
teacher's instructions, he adds the conclusion, in which
he sings of a radiant beauty who appears to his dazzled
eyes and leads him toward the tree of life.   Sachs,
moved with the poetry of the first *Bar*,[1] invites the young
poet to compose a second, into which Walter again puts
all his heart.   A third one is wanted; but the knight
will easily be able to compose that at the time of the
contest; he must now go and put on his festival robes,

---

[1] " Every Meistersinger Song or *Bar* has a regular measure. . . .
A *Bar* most frequently consists of various strophes. . . . A strophe
is usually composed of two *Stollen* which are sung to the same melody.   A *Stoll* is composed of a certain number of verses; the end
of which is indicated by a cross.   Then comes the *Abgesang* (the
envoy); it also consists of a certain number of verses, which, however, are sung to another melody." — WAGENSEIL (1697).

for the solemn moment approaches. Sachs, full of confidence about the happy issue of the trial which his *protégé* will undergo, opens the door for him with an air of great deference, and makes him pass out first.

SCENE III. — Beckmesser then appears at the window, and, seeing nobody, ventures in. He is in gala dress, but his movements are painful, as he still feels the beating that David gave him the evening before. He limps, rubs his limbs, and seems furious; he angrily gesticulates as he looks at Pogner's house and Eva's window, then he walks to and fro, and suddenly stops, noticing on the bench the paper on which Sachs has just taken down Walter's composition. He inquisitively reads it, and his anger breaks out, for he thinks the cobbler has composed this poetical essay on his own account. Then he quickly hides the paper in his pocket, as he hears the door opening; it is Hans coming in, also in full dress, and who, appearing pleasantly surprised with his visit, asks him, in a tone of malicious interest, how he likes the shoes which were finished and delivered the night before. Alas! the soles, which served as a target for the blows of the improvised marker, are very thin, and scarcely protect their owner from the pebbles in the road; but it is not that which troubles him. The town-clerk tells Sachs that he now sees clearly through his game, and some day he will pay back his treacherous pleasantry of last night, a pleasantry intended to ruin him in the beautiful Eva's eyes, besides furthering the cobbler's own ambitious plans with her, of whose person and wealth he is equally covetous. Sachs in vain protests his innocence and the absence of any intentions with regard to the maiden; the town-clerk refuses to believe it, and, thinking to confound him, draws from his pocket the paper on which the sketch of Walter's composition is written

and shows it to him. The cobbler jeers at the mean
fellow for the indelicate conduct he has just been guilty
of in stealing this poetic essay; and, to prove to him
what little store he sets on this scrap of paper, he gives
it to him. Beckmesser is surprised and delighted at pos-
sessing a poem by Sachs to make use of in the song-
contest. What a god-send! He immediately alters his
behaviour towards the man he has just been insulting so
violently, and, after having assured himself that the poem
is really given to him for his own property and that
Sachs will never claim its authorship, he becomes good-
humoured, fawning, and flattering, and goes away, still
limping, but triumphant, persuaded that his own musical
talent united with Sachs's composition, will easily gain
for him the prize he desires and which no rival will be
able to dispute with him. Sachs looks after him with a
smiling glance, thinking that the indiscreet action of this
low and vile nature will be a wonderful help to his plans.

SCENE IV. — Scarcely has Beckmesser departed when
the pretty little Eva, looking exquisite in her white
betrothal dress, appears at the shop-door; she has come
under the pretext of showing her old friend the shoes he
made which she pretends do not fit, and hurt her. The
good Sachs understands her ruse perfectly well; but pretends not to notice it, nor her stifled cry of joy as Walter
appears on the threshold in brilliant costume. Walter is
filled with ecstasy before the blonde beauty who meets
his vision. Sachs turns his back, seeming to be absorbed
in examining the little shoe; to remedy it, he takes it off
and goes to the bench as if he has not noticed anything,
philosophizing as he works. He says what pleasure it
would be, if some one would sing some verses while he
works; he heard some pretty ones just now, and would
like to know the rest! Walter, who understands his

allusion, begins to sing the third bar of his Prize-song, which, like the others, treats of his love and devotion. Sachs, who has been at work the whole time, now brings her shoes to Eva, who has been standing motionless in ecstasy. She then understands what has happened; moved by this poetic music, by the delicate kindness of her noble friend, and by his devotion to their cause, and overcome with emotion, she falls sobbing into Sachs's arms, and presses him to her heart, while Walter, also approaches and clasps the hand of the worthy man who has done so much for him. Hans, to conceal the emotion, which is also affecting him, makes jesting remarks about his difficult business as a cobbler, and as a confidant of maidens who are seeking husbands; then, to leave the two lovers alone, he pretends to be going to look for David; but Eva detains him. She wants to tell him of all the gratitude with which her heart is overflowing and all the affection she feels for him, — an affection which would have led her to choose him for her husband, if another still stronger love had not come into her heart. The kind Sachs waves aside this thought: if he had harboured it for an instant, the sad story of Tristan and Isolde and King Mark would have served him as an example and kept him from indulging such a rash dream. He will not dwell on these dangerous thoughts, and quickly calls Magdalene, who in festal array is hovering about the house, and then David, also gaily dressed, and proposes to have a baptism of the new *mode*, which owes its birth to the poetic imagination of the young knight. He declares himself godfather, Eva godmother, and David witness; but, as an Apprentice cannot be called to such a dignified office, he at once confers on him the grade of Companion, and to the great joy of the young man, he gives him the accolade in the form of a vigorous box on the ear. Then he offers to his godson all his best wishes for success, which he would have liked to weave into a joyous song, if his poor heart, which is somewhat bruised by all the struggles it has lately passed through, had left him the power to do so.

Eva and Walter unite their voices and their wishes for a success which would overwhelm them with happiness. David and Magdalene, happy at seeing their own love-affair in such a flourishing condition, thanks to the rank to which the new Companion has just been raised, join in the general rejoicing.

Whilst Eva returns to her father to accompany him to the meadow where the contest is to be held, and David puts up the shutters of Sachs's shop, the orchestra breaks into a joyous air, which is resolved into a march rhythm, and the curtain rapidly falls.

SCENE V. — When it rises again, the stage represents the meadow through which the Pegnitz winds; and in the distance the town of Nuremberg is visible; the landscape is enlivened by booths where refreshments are sold and by continual going and coming of boats, which land on the river-bank the citizens and their families in holiday attire. On the right, a platform, already adorned on three sides with the corporation banners, is prepared and provided with seats. The Apprentices of the Meistersinger in their holiday clothes, perform the duties of ushers to the new arrivals; among the corporations which they conduct to their places are: the Shoemakers who sing a couplet in honour of Saint Crispin, who stole leather to make shoes for the poor; then, preceded by fifers and the makers of toy musical instruments, come the Tailors, who proclaim in a joyous song the bravery and stratagem of one of their order, who managed to save the city from the attack of the enemy by dressing himself in the skin of a goat. The Bakers follow the Tailors, vaunting the utility of their calling, without which people would die of hunger; but they are interrupted by the arrival of a boat, decorated with flags and filled with dainty little peasants; the Companions and Apprentices run to meet them and help them land; the latter are the more successful with the new-comers, and, to deprive the Companions of their company, they take them away and begin to waltz with them. David, who is one of the joyous band, puts his arm around a pretty girl and begins to dance with great spirit, but is terrified for a moment by his comrades' menacing talk of Magdalene's arrival.

Finally, the Companions, who have been watching at the landing-place, signal the approach of the Meistersinger. Every one precipitately deserts his partner; David, on taking leave of his, gives her an enthusiastic kiss, and they all range themselves on the bank to let the Meistersinger pass between their ranks; the latter march in procession to the platform, having at their head Kothner, bearing the banner, and Pogner, holding Eva by the hand. The maiden is followed by her friends, also richly dressed, and by Magdalene. The people joyfully salute the learned corporation, and wave their hats as it passes. Eva and her father occupy the seats of honour on the platform; Kothner sets up the banner of the Meistersinger; and the Apprentices call for silence.

Sachs then advances to address the throng; but the people, at the sight of their beloved poet, who knows so well how to sing of their sufferings and their hopes, break out afresh in enthusiastic exclamations, and, with a touching spontaneousness, sing a beautiful song of Hans's composition, which is fast in the memory as in the heart of every one of them. Sachs, who during the singing has been lost in deep reverie, is touched, and, facing his fellow-citizens, thanks them for their welcome. Then, addressing the Meistersinger, he reminds them how elevated is the object of the competition which is about to open and how precious is the prize reserved for the victor. He asks that every poet may have the right to present himself freely and unconditionally, provided he can prove a stainless past, which will be a sure guarantee of happiness for the adorable being who will constitute so high a recompense. Pogner warmly thanks his friend who has been good enough to be the exact interpreter of his sentiments; then Sachs designates Beckmesser as the first to make the trial; for some time the latter has been secretly trying to learn by heart the poetry he stole at the cobbler's, and, not succeeding, is wiping his brow and giving every sign of the most comic despair.

He leaves the platform of the Meistersinger and climbs as well as he can upon the grassy hillock, which is to serve as a rostrum for the competitors, maliciously helped by the Apprentices, who make fun of him, tripping and upsetting him, laughing in their sleeves. The people, on the appearance of this ungraceful personage, express their astonishment and jest half audibly while the candidate, after having made a very consequential bow to Eva, begins the theme of his serenade, adapting to it the words of the stolen manuscript; but his memory fails him, he becomes confused, loses the train of his ideas, and begins to deliver a flood of incoherent words, which make a most ridiculous and extraordinary hotch-potch.

The crowd in astonishment begins to whisper; but he does not lose either his assurance or his presumption, and persists more than ever, confounding, interchanging, and perverting all the words of the poetry, thus forming extravagant phrases; the whispering of the people increases, and at last ends in a wild outburst of laughter. At this mockery the town-clerk turns furiously towards Sachs and denounces him before everybody as a rascal and a traitor who is the author of this grotesque work. Hans calmly picks up the leaves which Beckmesser has torn up and thrown on the ground, and, declaring that he has nothing whatever to do with this poetry, indicates Walter as its real author; at the same time he calls upon the young knight to prove his statement by singing to the words of this poem the melody which was composed to accompany it. He passes the manuscript to the Meistersinger, and Walter, walking with a deliberate step to the hillock, commences his song, which consists of three strophes.

The first of these strophes describes the wondrous garden, brilliant in the morning light, in which appeared to him the woman he loves, his Eva, who embodies for him all the delights of Paradise. The second sings the pure waters and the sacred fount towards which his Muse, sent from Parnassus, has guided him ; finally, the third exalts at the same time both love and poetry, since his inspirer, the Muse with the divine face, appeared to him under the form of his beloved, and the sweet image of Eva is inseparably connected in his soul with the first manifestation of genius, which was entirely due to her inspiration.

The Meistersinger, deeply touched, listen with delight ; the people begin freely to manifest their admiration for the young poet, and, without awaiting the decision of the tribunal, enthusiastically proclaim his victory. The Meistersinger then sanction the judgment of the crowd and award the prize to Walter amid general joy. Eva, who from the very beginning has listened with ecstasy to her lover's song, advances, radiant, to the edge of the platform and places on the brow of the victor, who kneels before her, a crown of myrtle and laurel; then she leads him to her father, before whom they both bow themselves and who raises his hands to bless them.

The crowd applauds Hans, who has so judiciously comprehended and defended the poet, despised yesterday and now admired; but the good Sachs's task is not yet quite finished. The young victor, who is not at all anxious for the Mastership which Pogner wishes to confer on him, scorns to be enrolled in the body of the Meistersinger, and refuses the chain ornamented with the image of King David, which forms the insignia of the order. Hans explains to him how ungrateful he would be to behave thus towards those men who have just awarded him the prize which is so precious to his happiness; he also reminds him of their great merit in preserving intact the noble traditions of German art, and ends by uttering a warm panegyric on the national genius and art, which he thinks are menaced by the vicissitudes through which the Empire is passing, and which he recommends to the patriotism and fidelity of all.

At these words, the acclamations of the people break out again, more enthusiastically than ever; Eva takes the crown from Walter's head and places it on Sachs's; the two lovers vie with each other in doing him honour, whilst Pogner bends the knee in homage before him. There is a general clapping of hands, hats are waved, and the curtain falls upon a veritable apotheosis of the popular poet, whom the Meistersinger with universal consent seem to point out to every one as their chief.

It is easy to see in the subject of the *Meistersinger* a sort of gay and humorous pendant to the poem of *Tannhäuser*, and this, moreover, was in Wagner's mind.

THE TETRALOGY OF THE RING OF THE NIBELUNG

CHARACTERS in the order of their first entrance.	RHEIN-GOLD	DIE WALKÜRE			SIEGFRIED			GÖTTERDÄMMERUNG			
		ACT I.	ACT II.	ACT III.	ACT I.	ACT II.	ACT III.	PROLOGUE	ACT I.	ACT III.	ACT III.
SCENES:	1 2 3 4	1 2 3	1 2 3 4 5	1 2 3	1 2 3	1 2 3	1 2 3		1 2 3	1 2 3 4 5	1 2 3

DAS RHEINGOLD

The Rhine-Daughters. { Woglinde (sopr.), Wellgunde (mezzo), Flosshilde (contr.). } Nymphs or Nixies, guardians of the Rhine-gold.

Alberich (baryt.). Hideous gnome. King of the Dark Elves or Nibelungs, a race of dwarfs and skilful smiths inhabiting caverns.

Fricka (mezzo). Goddess of marriage, wife of Wotan, childless; sister to Freïa, Donner, and Froh.

Wotan [the Wanderer] (bass). King of the gods, father of the nine Walkyries, whose mother is Erda. Father also of Siegmund and Sieglinde.

Freïa (sopr.). Goddess of Plenty and Love. Sister to Fricka, Donner, and Froh.

Fasolt (2d bass). One of the Giants ordered by Wotan to build Walhalla, the Palace of the gods.

Fafner [the Dragon] (bass). Another Giant, who, in *Siegfried*, is transformed into a Dragon.

Froh (tenor). God of Joy. Brother to Donner, Fricka, and Freïa.

Donner (baryt.). God of Thunder. Brother to Fricka, Freïa, and Froh.

Loge (tenor). God of Fire and Flames, and also of craft and falsehood, wily and mischievous.

Mime (tenor). Dwarf or Nibelung, smith, foster-father of Siegfried, whom he hates, and who kills him.

Erda (contr.). Goddess of Wisdom and of the Earth. Mother of the Norns and the Walkyries whose father is Wotan.

DIE WALKÜRE

Siegmund (tenor). Son of Wotan (under the name of Wälse), brother and husband to Sieglinde, and father of Siegfried.

Sieglinde (sopr.). Daughter of Wotan (under the name of Wälse), wife to Hunding and afterwards to Siegmund, her brother. Mother of Siegfried.

Hunding (bass). First husband to Sieglinde, who hates him, for she was sold to him.

Brünnhilde (sopr.). Eldest of the Walkyries, daughter of Wotan and Erda, wife to Siegfried, and then, by treachery, to Gunther.

The Walkyries. { Helmwige, Gerhilde (sopr.). Waltraute (mezzo). Ortlinde, Siegrune, Rosweisse (mez.). Grimgerde, Schwertleite (contr.). } Warrior-virgins, daughters of Wotan and Erda and sisters to Brünnhilde.

SIEGFRIED

Siegfried (tenor). Son of Siegmund and Sieglinde, grandson of Wotan (Wälse), husband to Brünnhilde, then, by treachery, to Gutrune (sister to Gunther).

The Bird (sopr.). A prophetic and mysterious character.

GÖTTERDÄMMERUNG

The Norns. { 1st Norn (contr.). 2d Norn (mez.). 3d Norn (sopr.) } Daughters of the Earth, who spin the Destiny of the gods, as also of human beings, and predict the future.

Gunther (2d bass). Son of Gibich and Grimhilde, brother to Gutrune; half-brother to Hagen; husband, by treachery, to Brünnhilde.

Hagen (bass). Son of the dwarf Alberich and Grimhilde (seduced by the gnome's gold), and half-brother to Gunther and Gutrune.

Gutrune (sopr.). Daughter of Gibich and Grimhilde; sister to Gunther, half-brother to Hagen; wife, by treachery, to Siegfried.

THE TETRALOGY OF THE RING OF THE NIBELUNG

The *Tetralogy*,[1] or more properly, *The Trilogy of the Ring of the Nibelung* (*Der Ring des Nibelungen*), a festival-play with a prologue : *Rhine-gold* (*Das Rheingold*), *The Walkyrie* (*Die Walküre*), and *The Dusk of the Gods* (*Die Götterdämmerung*), has been drawn from the Scandinavian Eddas and the old epic of the Nibelungenlied, but considerably remodelled, modified, and amplified by the marvellous art of Wagner's mighty genius.

The four dramas, which form the complete *Ring*, develop many changes of fortune, brought about by the curse which the Nibelung Alberich has laid upon the power-endowing Ring, forged by him from the Rhinegold which he stole from the Rhine-maidens (Undines), and which, in turn, Wotan has wrested from him. Through many vicissitudes the cursed Ring brings destruction on all who possess it ; the series of catastrophes which it occasions result in the final ruin of the race of gods, and only comes to an end when the last victim, Brünnhilde, who returns to the purifying waters of the Rhine its stolen treasure, at last delivers the world from the terrible anathema.

The characters in the following table belong to Scandinavian mythology, but they are often modified, sometimes, indeed, changed by the caprice of the author.

We must accept them here, not according to tradition, but according to the conception of Wagner's poem, and with the character that he attributes to each.

---

[1] The proper title is *Trilogy with Prologue*, but custom has established the use of the word *Tetralogy*.

The fact is, they belong neither to Northern mythology, nor to that of the Rhine; but to Wagnerian mythology, exactly as the religion of the Grail, which we have met with in *Lohengrin* and we shall again find in *Parsifal*, does not belong to the Christian religion but to a special cult which Wagner himself originated with the aid of various legends which he altered and versified.

DAS RHEINGOLD

SCENE I. — The action of the first scene of this prologue takes place in the depths of the Rhine, among green and limpid waters, rocks, and caverns.

The three Undines, or Nixies, Daughters of the Rhine, frolic in the waters whilst guarding the precious treasure of pure gold, which their father has confided to their care.

Alberich, the most crafty, avaricious, and hideous of the Nibelungs, a species of gnomes, or repulsive dwarfs, inhabiting the black realm of Nibelheim, in the bowels of the earth, has glided into the watery dwelling, and, full of voluptuous desire, wants to seduce the nymphs. In turn they entice him with deceitful promises, and then mock at him; but by their babbling they reveal the mystery of the treasure which they guard : the Rhine-gold, forged into a Ring by the bold being who succeeds in becoming its possessor, will confer upon him an unlimited power over the whole universe, for he will be even mightier than the gods themselves, but only on the hard and fast condition of renouncing love forever.

The gnome, furious at the mocking refusals of the Undines, is inspired with fresh covetousness by their imprudent words, — the craving for gold and dominion ; he scales the rock on which glitters the treasure, and, despite the lamentations of the three Nixies, seizes it, after having made a formal renunciation of love ; he will be the one to forge the enchanted Ring and hold supreme power. He departs with a burst of sinister and triumphant laughter.

The river, no longer illuminated by its glittering treasure, is shrouded in thick gloom, into which the Undines disappear in pursuit of the rapacious elf.[1] Dark waves flowing in from all sides spread over the whole scene, and then gradually become calm and clear; they are succeeded by a heavy fog, which clears away, and, illuminated by the breaking day, a rocky country appears, intersected in the background by a vale through which flows the invisible Rhine. Far away, on the summit of a high mountain, stands a castle, with numberless pinnacles glittering in the rays of the rising sun.

SCENE II. — Wotan and his wife, Fricka, reposing on a hillock, awake and contemplate the structure, which the giants, Fasolt and Fafner, have just completed according to the god's orders. The reward promised for this work by the Master of the Universe, at the instigation of the mischievous god, Loge, is to be Freïa, goddess of youth, love, and beauty, sister of Fricka and of the gods, Froh and Donner; but Fricka is alarmed at the imminent approach of the day of reckoning, for now the giants will come to claim their due ; she reproaches Wotan for the inconsiderate bargain that he has made, and for building the palace, which she, nevertheless, had desired, hoping thereby to keep her inconstant spouse more often at her side.

Wotan promises her that he will not abandon Freïa,

---

[1] The elves, or alfs, are of two kinds : sometimes superior and beautiful, — light elves ; sometimes inferior — the dark elves — "blacker than pitch." Alberich was a dark elf.

who enters in tears, pursued by Fafner and Fasolt. She
calls her brothers, the gods, to her aid ; a dispute
ensues between them and the giants, and threatens to
become serious when Loge appears, whom Wotan has
sent all over the world in search of some compensation
to offer to the builders in exchange for the radiant goddess. But Loge has found nothing which any one would
be likely to prefer to woman and youth. One single
creature, the dwarf Alberich, has renounced these precious
possessions for the gold which bestows power, and he
has cursed love. Loge tells of the robbery of this treasure by the gnome and the lamentations of the daughters
of the river, who implore the assistance of the chief of
the gods. The avarice of the giants is excited at this
account ; they hold a long consultation, and propose to
exchange Freïa for the Rhine-gold. They make Wotan
promise to get it for them, and they bear away the goddess as a hostage, reserving the right to keep her if the
treasure is not promptly forthcoming. Hardly have they
taken Freïa away when the gods begin to fall into de-
crepitude, for she alone knows how to cultivate the
golden apples,[1] which supplied them with eternal youth.
Wotan then resolves to descend into the gloomy kingdom of the elves and to gain the Ring, not to restore it
to the Nixies, but to use it for the ransom of the goddess.
Accompanied by Loge, he penetrates the rocks into the
bowels of the earth to search for Nibelhcim.

SCENE III. — A thick vapour rises from the crevice
through which they pass (brimstone fault), and obscures
the scene with opaque clouds which finally envelop it in

---

[1] Only Loge preserves his vitality, for, as he is but a secondary
god, he does not partake of the regenerating food. It is his inferiority, as we shall see in the course of the drama, that leads him to
separate his cause from that of the other gods.

total darkness. As the vapours clear away, a rocky subterranean cavern is seen; to the right, a passage ascends to the surface of the earth; to the left, in the cavern is a forge with flickering flames and wreaths of rosy smoke.

This is the realm of the dark elves, where Alberich, thanks to the magic Ring which he has forged from the Rhine-gold, rules over the other Nibelungs, and makes them dig in the depths of the earth to extract its hidden wealth. He has forced one of them, Mime, a skilful smith, to forge for him the links of an enchanted helmet, the "Tarnhelm," which will render him invisible. Mime maliciously wants to keep his work for himself; but Alberich, by means of the talisman, makes himself invisible to his slave and beats him unmercifully. Wotan and Loge, who descend from the opening of the cave, hear the cries of the sufferer. They make him describe his troubles and the work which he is forced to do, and promise him assistance. At this moment a long line of Nibelungs is seen defiling past the cavern, bent double under the weight of ingots and treasure mined by Alberich's orders; the latter abuses his brothers and drives them before him with a whip; but when he perceives the two intruders, he turns his fury against them, warning them, as he recognizes them, of the revengeful plans which he has formed against their race, now that he has sovereign power. The outraged Wotan raises his lance against the audacious elf; but the more shrewd and politic Loge arrests the action of the angry god, and, addressing the dwarf, congratulates him upon his omnipotence, which, however, he calls into question. Piqued, and anxious to exhibit his powers, Alberich, by the aid of his magic casque, transforms himself first into a frightful dragon and then into a loathsome toad; Wotan and Loge can then easily capture him by setting their foot on him. They have him at their mercy; they seize him by the throat and carry their prisoner, foaming with rage, to the surface of the earth.

SCENE IV.—Vapours fill the cavern as before; and, when they are dissipated, the second scene is reproduced, but the background is veiled in mists. Wotan and Loge, issuing from the chasm, drag with them the dwarf, mad with anger. It is now their turn to mock him. They first force him to deliver up the treasure which he has amassed, and which, at his magic words, the Nibelungs bring from the depths of the earth; next, despite his protestations, they require the enchanted helmet forged by Mime; and finally, notwithstanding his senseless resistance and the insults which he hurls at them in his exasperation, they make him relinquish the Ring, which he wanted to keep as his last resource. Alberich, whose anger is now beyond all bounds, sees himself deprived of the talisman by Wotan; but with a fierce and sinister imprecation, he immediately calls down a terrible curse on him who is robbing him of his treasure: "Henceforth may its charm bring death to whosoever wears it; . . . may he who possesses it be torn by anguish, and he who does not possess it be consumed with envy; . . . may no one profit by it, but may it light the thief to his throat; . . . may the villain become a slave to fear; . . . may the master of the Ring become its servant; . . . and may this endure until the Nibelung recovers possession of the treasure which is now wrested from him!"

Having uttered these terrible words, he disappears in the cleft of the rock. Wotan, who attaches no importance to the malediction, quietly slips the Ring upon his finger, and thoughtfully contemplates it.

The giants now come in, on the right, for the treasure which they are to receive in exchange for Freïa. At the approach of the goddess the other divinities feel their youth and vigour returning, and joyfully welcome her; but Fasolt damps their enthusiasm by claiming the promised ransom. He takes his spear and Fafner's, sets them up, and demands that between them treasure shall be heaped up, like a curtain, till he can no longer see the enchantress whom he loves and whose loss he so much regrets. He and his companion pile up the treasure, including the magic helm, but through an aperture Freïa's sweet bright eyes are still visible. However, all the precious treasure is now gathered together, and there now only remains the Ring by which the aperture may be closed; this the giants vehemently demand. Wotan refuses; a dispute arises, and they are about to carry off the goddess forever, when the air darkens and the divinity Erda, the ancient spirit of the earth, the mother of the three Norns who spin the cord of Destiny, — Erda, who knows all things and dreams of the future, — appears in the depths of a grotto among the rocks faintly illumined with a pale light. She already foresees the gloomy end of the gods, and begs Wotan to give up the marvellous but cursed Ring. Wotan, astonished at her words, questions her: he wishes to know more, and darts towards the mysterious cave to force her to explain; but the prophetess has already vanished; and the god then falls into profound meditation, and at last makes a decisive resolution and throws the Ring upon the pile. The giants immediately begin to wrangle over it, thus being the first to experience the effects of the curse which the Nibelung has laid upon it: they come to blows, and Fafner, with a brutal stroke, stretches Fasolt dead at his feet. Fafner thus remains the sole possessor of the cursed Ring and the treasures; he calmly collects them in a large sack which he has brought with him, and disappears, dragging it after him, without casting even a glance at his brother's corpse. The gods are mute with horror; the sky darkens, and a gloomy cloud gathers.

Donner, the god of storm, in order to restore the serenity of the sky, calls all the clouds to him and disappears in a shower; the thunder growls, the lightning flashes, then the vapours break away and reveal a wonderful rainbow, made in a marvellously short time by Froh out of the tempest, to serve as a bridge by which to gain the inaccessible castle. Wotan, after having picked up a sword forgotten by Fafner, and which formed a part of his treasure, invites the gods to enter with him into Walhalla, for which he has paid an accursed price; but he foresees the struggle that he will have to maintain against the powers of darkness. The wily Loge, who is also filled with the same presentiments as Wotan, thinks about separating his cause from that of the other gods and raising his own fortune on the ruin of theirs.

From the depths of the valley the Rhine-Daughters are heard wailing for their lost treasure; the gods answer them with pitiless laughter, and proceed along the luminous path which lies before them.

The curtain closes slowly.

DIE WALKÜRE

ACT I.

SCENE I.—The action passes in a large rustic cabin built around an enormous ash, whose roots extend over the ground and whose mighty branches pierce the roof. In the trunk of the tree is visible the hilt of a sword, the entire blade of which is buried, and its handle is indistinct in the shadow. In the foreground, on the right, is a hearth, before which is a heap of skins forming a kind of couch. At the foot of the tree, which occupies the whole centre of the stage, are a rustic table and stools. Behind the hearth, steps lead to a store-room. On the left are steps leading to a room.

The storm is howling outside, the cabin is deserted.

The door at the back is roughly opened and admits an unarmed warrior, with his clothes in disorder, and looking quite exhausted; everything about him proclaims the fugitive. After examining the deserted room, he sinks on the furs before the hearth, and, giving way to weariness, is soon asleep.

The mistress of the rustic dwelling, Sieglinde, comes in, and, seeing in astonishment the stranger, she awakes him and inquires into his condition with solicitude; she gives him drink, and learns that, tracked by his enemies and betrayed by his weapons, which broke in his hand, he had to seek safety in flight. He accepts the mead which Sieglinde pours out for him, and which, according to custom, he asks her to taste first, but he wants to leave her hospitable shelter without delay, because he brings misfortune wherever he stays. Alas! she answers, sadness has long been a dweller in this house; he will not bring it; and she begs him to await the return of her husband, Hunding, who will soon come back from the chase.

SCENE II.—They earnestly gaze upon each other with a constantly growing interest, when suddenly the master of the hut is heard outside; he appears upon the threshold, surprised at the presence of the stranger, and looks at Sieglinde with a questioning glance. Having received her explanations, he asks his guest to tell him his story, and makes him sit down at the table with them. One thing strikes him as the stranger talks, and that is the strange resemblance that there is between his wife and the new-comer.

The latter then tells of his life, which seems to be devoted to misfortune. His infancy had been spent happily with his father, who was named Wälse (the Wolf), his mother, and a twin sister. But one day, on his return with his father from the chase, he found their dwelling reduced to ashes and his mother slain; as for his young sister, no trace had ever been found of her. The authors of this crime were the Neidungs, sons of Hatred and Envy. From that moment, his father and he had wandered in the forest until the day when the old man, tracked in his turn by enemies, had disappeared.

As for himself, ceaselessly hunted by destiny, which has gained for him the name of Wehwalt (the Cause of Misfortune), repulsed by every one, and weaponless, he has just experienced a final defeat in an attempt to liberate a defenceless maiden whose relations were going to give her up to a hated lover; the woman he protected was killed before his eyes, whilst he, overwhelmed by numbers, was forced to give up the fight.

From the first words of this story, to which Sieglinde has been listening with deep emotion, Hunding recognizes in the fugitive an enemy of his race whom he has just been called upon to fight by his own people. He, nevertheless, grants him hospitality for that night, but at break of day he will provoke him to the combat without mercy. He retires with threats and orders his wife to follow him, after having prepared his evening draught. Sieglinde, absorbed in her thoughts, goes to a cupboard for spices which she mingles in her lord's drink, then, as she departs, she casts a long and tender look at the stranger and seems to point out to him the trunk of the ash in which the sword is imbedded. Hunding, surprising this glance, orders her to go to her room, where he is heard shutting himself in with her.

SCENE III.—The scene is now illumined by the dying fire on the hearth, which, as it expires, casts its light on the hilt of the sword and makes it gleam in the shadows. The warrior, without noticing it, anxiously asks himself if he will find the sword which his father promised him of old for his defence in his supreme need : then his thoughts take another course; he thinks with delight of Sieglinde's beauty and of the deep feeling which she has awakened in his heart.—Is the ray which lights up the tree the radiance left there by the bright glances of his beloved ? But the fire is expiring; it is almost total darkness, and Sieglinde, clad in white, stealthily leaves her room and advances towards her guest.

She has given her husband an opiate draught in order to gain an opportunity to converse with him whose sight has captured her heart. She tells him that on the day of her sad nuptials with Hunding, to whom she had been sold by brigands, an old man, draped in a large mantle and wearing a wide hat concealing one of his eyes, had entered the hut, terrifying every one but her, who felt in this old man a protector and recognized in him the features of a beloved father. Driving a sword up to the hilt into the trunk of the ash, he promised that that steel should belong to the hero who succeeded in drawing it from its living sheath. So far no one has succeeded, despite numerous attempts, but Sieglinde feels that the conqueror will be the friend whom fate has sent her, — he who will have power to heal the wounds in her heart, and to whom, in a passionate outburst, she promises the gift of her own person. The son of Wälse ardently embraces her; they gaze upon each other with intoxication, when the door of the hut opens, moved by an invisible hand, and reveals the forest bathed in the soft atmosphere of a radiant night and flooded with the white moonlight which casts its luminous beams on the two lovers, who are thus able to gaze upon each other in delight. "Who went out?" murmurs Sieglinde in fear. —No one, but some one came in; it is sweet Spring, Spring who comes to sing its epithalamium to them and to celebrate the Love which blossoms deep in their hearts.

Looking more closely at her beloved, Sieglinde thinks she has seen him at some former time; their memories are awakened together. That piercing glance, which they both possess, is the distinctive mark of the heroic race of the Wälsungs; they are children of the same father, and Siegmund must be the name of the hero for whom Wälse destined the mighty sword. For him also is reserved the task of delivering Sieglinde from the hateful yoke that keeps her in bondage. Siegmund, in an ecstasy of enthusiasm, springs toward the ash, and, seizing the sword by the hilt, tears it out with irresistible force, calling it Nothung, the weapon promised for his distress. Sieglinde, in a delirium of joy and love, throws herself into the arms of her lover.

The curtain quickly closes.

Act II.

Scene I. — The scene represents a mountainous, savage, and arid country; on the right, a road cut in the rock leads to a kind of stony platform. Under this ledge is a grotto. In the centre of the stage there is a narrow passage with a chaos of rocks in the background; then, to the left is another heap of rocks from which a road rises, turning and leading to the rocks in the background.

Wotan charges his favourite daughter, the virgin warrior, Brünnhilde, with the fate of Siegmund, whom he wishes to be victorious in his fight with Hunding. The Walkyrie departs, happy with the mission intrusted to her, uttering her war-cry and announcing to her father the approach of the goddess Fricka, who arrives in a chariot drawn by two rams; she has come to combat her husband's resolution.

The guilty love of Siegmund and Sieglinde outrages her, the guardian of the sacred ties of marriage and of the family, and she claims the victory for Hunding, the wronged husband, who has placed his defence in her hands. In vain the god upholds the cause of those who love one another and whom he considers.free to follow the dictates of their love; in vain he explains to the goddess the imperative reasons he has in preserving Siegmund to accomplish that course of action which will save the gods from extreme peril: the goddess, already wounded a hundred times by the infidelities of her volatile husband, has been willing to put up with the presence of the Walkyries, his illegitimate daughters, who, at least, are respectful of her authority; but if the god persists in protecting this criminal couple, a living testimony to his amours with a mortal, when, under the name of Wälse, he wandered in the forests, that is something she will not tolerate.

Wotan, deep down in his heart, is forced to recognize the justice of his companion's words. Does she not represent the established order and the wisdom of affairs, and did he not once pay for his precious conquest by the loss of one of his eyes, when he wished to drink at the source of wisdom?

After a violent struggle with himself, he takes the oath Fricka demands, and remains a prey to a deep grief, while the goddess departs, strong in the promise she has gained, and he calls Brünnhilde to give her fresh instructions.

SCENE II. — The Walkyrie, disquieted at Fricka's triumphant look, hastily approaches her father, whom she finds much cast down by the attack he has just suffered and the oath he has been forced to make. Grieved at the distress of her beloved father, she casts away her arms and shield, and falls down before him in an attitude eloquent of trust and affection; she begs him to unburden his heart to her. He then confides in his favourite child, who is the mightiest expression of his will and of his most intimate thought. Before her he, diving into the deepest recesses of his heart, reviews the faults which have led to this result: the ambition which took possession of his heart when the ardour of legitimate love died down within him; the obligations he contracted in his greed for power and at the advice of the crafty Loge to render the other gods subservient; and the robbery of the Ring, which has brought upon him the implacable hatred of the Nibelung Alberich. This Ring should have been restored to the depths of the Rhine to bring to an end all the dangers which it has excited, but Wotan used it in payment for the castle Walhalla, which the giants built, and it is now the property of Fafner, who guards it with jealous care deep in his cave.

In his distress, the god wanted to consult Erda, who had already on one occasion given him salutary advice; he compelled her to tell him all her thoughts; then, seducing her by means of a love-philtre, he made her the mother of the nine warrior-virgins, Brünnhilde and her sisters, of whom he wished to make use as the instruments of his safety: the Walkyries have received from him the mission of bringing to Walhalla all heroes who die on the field of battle, and thus peopling the kingdom of Wotan with intrepid defenders in preparation for the day when Alberich's army will threateningly advance against him. But all these precautions will be vain if the gnome can again possess himself of the cursed Ring; this must be prevented at all costs, and yet Wotan cannot deprive Fafner of what he formerly gave him. Only one being can accomplish that task: this must be a hero free and independent, who will do the work involuntarily, and without having received the mission. The god had chosen his son, Siegmund, to be this hero; for long years he has prepared him for this act of redemption: he has wandered with him in the forests, stimulating him to temerity; he has armed him with an invincible sword: but what now avails all this care, since Fricka has compelled her husband to bow to her wishes?

Wotan's fury and despair break out at the thought of abandoning him whom he loves and wished to protect, and, in his desolation, he curses his own sovereignty and wishes the gods may come to an end. He can foresee that end; Erda has announced it for the day when a son shall be born to Alberich: now this child is on the way, he is about to come into the world; and Wotan, in the heat of his anger, bequeaths to him the torments and fatal splendours of divinity.

In vain does Brünnhilde plead the cause of Siegmund, whom she knows her father loves; she will act in accordance with the god's secret wishes, notwithstanding his oath; but Wotan is immovable; he bitterly enjoins her to obey Fricka; and, threatening the Walkyrie with chastisement if she attempts to transgress his orders, he departs into the mountains.

Brünnhilde, terrified, sadly gathers up her arms and takes her way to the grotto where rests her horse, Grane, at the same time watching Siegmund and Sieglinde, who are ascending the ravine.

Scene III. — Sieglinde, deaf to the words of love which Siegmund is murmuring in her ear, is beseeching him to flee without delay ; she no longer wishes to give herself to him she loves after having belonged by force to a hated master.

The distant sounds of the horn and hounds make her tremble ; her lover will not be able to fight so many adversaries, and his sword will be powerless to defend him. Mad with grief and agony, hearing the enemy coming nearer, in her hallucination she thinks she sees her lover become the prey of the furious dogs, and, uttering a piercing cry, she falls fainting. Siegmund carefully places her on the ground, and, kissing her brow, he sits down upon a hillock and rests her beloved head on his knees.

Scene IV. — Meanwhile Brünnhilde advances, gravely leading her noble charger. She appears to the warrior and announces that he is destined to perish in the coming combat ; she comes only to heroes who are devoted to a glorious death : he must prepare to follow her to Walhalla. Siegmund in contempt of death asks her if in the abode of the gods he will find his beloved Sieglinde again. — No, answers Brünnhilde, the Walkyries will pour out the mead for him ; Sieglinde must still remain upon this earth. — The warrior then refuses the joys of the enchanted abode if he may not share them with his beloved companion ; he will fight Hunding without fear, thanks to the invincible weapon, of the success of which he has been assured by his father; but if the latter now withdraws his protection, if he must die, let Hella [1] take him: he does not wish to share the fate of the immortals, and before dying he will kill his betrothed, so that no other being shall touch her living. He draws his sword and is about to transpierce the still fainting Sieglinde; in vain does Brünnhilde reveal to him that in striking his companion he will destroy two lives, for Sieglinde bears within her a pledge of his love; even then he is going to give the fatal blow, when the Walkyrie, touched with compassion by such fidelity, stays his arm, and, granting him her support and assistance in the hour of combat, promises to meet him on the field of battle, and departs with Grane. Siegmund, transfigured with happiness, follows her with his eyes as she goes.

SCENE V. — He gently places the sleeping Sieglinde on a stone seat, and hastens in the direction of the enemy, amid heavy storm-clouds which form and darken all the background of the scene. The martial trumpetings of the pursuer come nearer and nearer.

Sieglinde, in her dream, recalls her memories of childhood: she again sees the fatal fire which consumed her home and dispersed her relations, then she is suddenly awakened by the noise of the thunder rolling on every side; from the rocks, at the back, which are canopied with clouds, are heard the voices of the two combatants, Siegmund and Hunding, defying each other. Sieglinde tries to run to separate them, but she is blinded by the lightning, and totters. Then Brünnhilde is seen in the air above Siegmund, shielding him and encouraging him with her voice; he is about to give Hunding a

[1] Hella personifies common death: to her belong those who perish otherwise than in battle.

mortal blow, when Wotan, appearing in turn in a blaze
of fire, extends his spear between the two foes; at its
contact, Siegmund's sword breaks, and Hunding is able
to plunge his weapon into his heart.   Darkness over-
spreads the scene; and Brünnhilde is scarcely visible as
she raises the inanimate Sieglinde and places her on her
charger to carry her off.   At this moment the cloud
parts and discloses Hunding withdrawing his sword from
Siegmund's body.   Wotan despairingly gazes on the
body of his son, and darts so terrible a look at Hunding
that he falls, stricken, at his feet; then the god lets
loose his furious rage on the rebellious daughter who has
dared to disobey him, and starts in pursuit to punish
her.

The curtain closes rapidly.

ACT III.

SCENE I. — The stage represents a rocky plateau at
the top of the mountain.   Some fir-woods contribute a
meagre verdure to the place; in the distance, separated
from the foreground by wide valleys, are other peaks,
which, in the first scenes, are hidden by fogs driven by
the wind and constantly rising from the hollows.   On the
right is a rocky eminence, up which is a kind of stairway;
in the centre of the stage is a bare block which serves
as a post of observation over the valley.   On the left
are several footpaths leading to the plateau; at the back,
a pine, much larger than its fellows, spreads its wide
arms above its mighty roots.

Four of the Walkyries, Gerhilde, Ortlinde, Waltraute,
and Schwertleite, armed from head to foot, have stationed
themselves in observation on the summit of the rocks on
the right; they utter their war-cry to call their sisters,
who, with the exception of Brünnhilde, arrive, one by

one, riding through the air in swift clouds, and having attached to their saddles the bodies of warriors who have died as heroes and who are destined for Walhalla. The newcomers, Helmwige, Siegrune, Grimgerde, and Rossweisse, pasture their horses, which are still animated with the ardour of the fight, whilst awaiting the tardy Brünnhilde, who soon appears, breathless and mounted on her noble horse, Grane, and with a living woman, Sieglinde, on the croup.

In answer to her sisters' questions, she tells them that she is fleeing from the anger of Wotan, whom she has dared to disobey and who is pursuing her in fierce anger. She beseeches them to help her save her *protégée*; but the Walkyries are unwilling to draw down upon themselves the anger of the god, and refuse. Sieglinde, in despair at having survived her lover, reproaches Brünnhilde for having robbed her of death and adjures her to plunge her sword into her heart; but Brünnhilde tells her that she bears a Wälsung in her bosom, that she must live to preserve the life of that son, who will soon be born and who will be a valiant hero. Sieglinde, at first terrified and then seized with a great joy, now wishes to live at all costs; by the advice of the Walkyries, and for the sake of saving her child, she will take refuge alone in the forest which extends toward the east and where dwells Fafner, the jealous guardian of the fatal treasure. Wotan never bends his steps in that direction; she will therefore be safe in that retreat.

But they must make haste, for the storm, which is the precursor of Wotan's arrival, is coming nearer and nearer; lightnings play among the clouds, and Waltraute soon signals the arrival of the Father of the Gods.

Brünnhilde hastens the flight of the unfortunate woman, exhorting her courageously to support the rude life which she is going to lead in solitude, and promises her that the child she bears within her shall be a hero, supreme above all. His name shall be Siegfried, and his mother must arm him with his father's sword, which is none other than the Sword of the Gods, shattered by Wotan himself in the fatal combat, the fragments of which the Walkyrie has carefully collected, and now confides them to Sieglinde. The fugitive blesses Brünnhilde for her tender care and darts into the forest in the direction of the retreat designated.

During this last scene the storm has redoubled in intensity.

SCENE II.—Amid the rollings of the thunder Wotan's voice is heard grumbling and chiding; Brünnhilde can flee no further; pale and distracted, she tries to hide herself among her sisters; they vainly seek to conceal her from the eyes of her father, who, consumed with terrible anger, calls the culprit. The virgin then separates herself from the group of Walkyries, and, with a respectful but firm and heroic attitude, comes to submit to the will of her judge. He then breaks out into a storm of reproaches against this daughter who was formerly the dearest of all, whom he delighted to entrust with the most glorious missions, who was the child of his heart, and who now, a rebel, has dared to brave him. She has sealed her own fate : he exiles her from Walhalla, disowns her, and deprives her forever of her divine nature. He will leave her defenceless, asleep by the wayside, and the first passer-by who wakes her may make her his slave; she shall spin flax in subjection to a mortal, and shall be the laughing-stock of all.

The other Walkyries utter cries of despair, vainly trying to move their father, who threatens them with the same fate if they attempt to defend the rebel. They go away with wild cries of distress, and are soon seen on their horses in the distance, disappearing among the clouds.

The tempest, which has been raging the whole time, now gradually abates ; the masses of vapour are dissipated, and a serene night succeeds the uproar and enfolds the landscape.

SCENE III. — Brünnhilde, who has been prostrated at the feet of the god, raises her head and tries to meet her father's eye to implore his forgiveness. She beseeches him to regard her fault with more leniency : is her crime of such an infamous nature as to merit so degrading and cruel a penalty ? At first he had commanded her to uphold and bring about the triumph of the Wälsung; it was only under the duresse of a forced promise that he deprived his son of his protection ; but she, Brünnhilde, the child of his heart, thought she would act in accordance with his inner thoughts and secret desires by helping Siegmund at any cost. — No, replies Wotan, she should not have arrogated to herself the right of acting as he would personally have been so willing to do had it not been for the fatal oath exacted by Fricka ; at the very moment when her father, tortured by destiny, was dreaming in despair of annihilating himself once for all, she should not have yielded to the sweet pleasure of hearkening to her own tender compassion ; the god persists in his harsh judgment : he banishes her forever from his presence, and, since she has of her own will allowed herself to be swayed by love, she shall henceforth be the slave of love.

The unfortunate Walkyrie entreats her father to consider that, although he deprives her of her Walhalla life, she formerly formed a part of his divine being, and that he would be dishonouring himself to give her up to the first comer, perchance a coward. A new hero, adven-

turous and brave, is about to be born to the race of the
Wälsungs ; let him be her saviour and her master ! —
At the reiterated refusal of the god, she prays him at
least to permit a terrible barrier to be raised around her
during her fatal sleep, in order that none but a mortal to
whom fear is unknown may, in triumphing over the
danger, achieve the conquest.   The god, at last, touched
by the heroic courage of his unfortunate child, feels his
paternal heart melt before a spirit so proud under distress ; he consents to accede to her last wish : around
her he will raise a burning barrier, whose devouring
flames will frighten away the timid, and which the
desired hero will alone be able to pass ; then, raising
her, he holds her to his heart in a long embrace, saying
many tender farewell words. — These lips, which so
joyously sang the glory of heroes, must be silent ; these
luminous eyes, which he has so often fondly kissed and
whose glance has so often comforted him in hours of
sadness, must be closed forever for the unfortunate god,
and may only open for the happy mortal who will succeed in gaining her. — With a supreme kiss, he takes
away her divinity and closes her eyelids.   Brünnhilde,
overcome with drowsiness, slowly falls asleep ; he then
takes her to a mossy bank shaded by a wide-branched fir,
in the shelter of which he lays her inanimate form.   He
gazes upon her with emotion, then he closes her casque,
sets her lance beside her as a sign of authority, and
covers her with her long steel Walkyrie shield.

Then, striking the rock three times with his spear, he
evokes Loge, the god of fire.   A flame springs up,
increases in volume, and soon surrounds the rock with a
fear-inspiring and magnificent belt of fire, forming an inaccessible rampart around the sleeping virgin.

The curtain closes very slowly.

SIEGFRIED

Act I.

Scene I. — The scenery shows a large cavern in the midst of the forest, in which Mime has established his dwelling and forge. At the back, on the right, there are large natural openings through which is visible the verdure of the sunlit woods. On the right, in the foreground, is a bed covered with skins of animals; in the middle distance, on the left, are the hearth and bellows of the forge, from which the smoke escapes by a vast natural chimney. In the foreground is a cupboard in which the gnome keeps his food. Thick cinders lie over everything.

Mime, with growls and curses, is forging a new sword for Siegfried, who takes a malicious pleasure in constantly breaking the blades which the dwarf gives him.

Ah! why can he not succeed in uniting the fragments of Nothung, Siegmund's weapon! In the youth's hands it would easily triumph over Fafner, who, transformed into a dragon, is still the guardian of the magic Ring. Siegfried could gain possession of the talisman, which, in his turn, Mime could wrest from him; but all efforts are vain! The fragments of the mysterious sword will not unite in his hands! He spitefully continues to strike the anvil, whilst talking to himself.

Siegfried in forest dress, with a silver horn on a chain, appears, joyously leading a bear with a rope, having captured it in the forest, and sets it at the terrified Mime. He rallies him on his cowardice, and then, freeing the bear, which disappears into the forest, he claims the sword which he had ordered the Nibelung to make him, and breaks it on the anvil at the first attempt as he has done with all the others.   His conversation already testifies how little affection and esteem he has for the dwarf; and Mime vainly recapitulates all the troubles and all the care he has taken of him from his birth.   Siegfried goes and lies down on the couch, and contemptuously kicks to the ground the food which the dwarf brings him; he mocks him and asks himself how it is that, feeling such an aversion for this miserable gnome, he still returns here every day after his ramblings in the forest. — His foster-father replies that, despite his whims, this proves that Mime is dear to his heart. — But Siegfried laughs at this idea; he puts fresh questions to the dwarf and refuses to believe that this squinting and hideous abortion can be the author of his existence, as the knave is trying to persuade him.   He urges him to tell him who were his real parents : Mime tries to avoid answering, and finally, being compelled by the irritated youth, confesses that he is the son of an unhappy fugitive, who, overwhelmed with grief and agony, one day sought refuge in the forest and died in giving birth to him.   Siegfried shows great emotion at this story. The crafty dwarf repeatedly returns to the enumeration of all the benefits he has bestowed upon the child whom the poor dying Sieglinde had confided to his care, but the impetuous youth unceremoniously interrupts him and forces him to tell him the rest of his story.   Little by little he learns that, before expiring, his mother gave him his name of Siegfried, and that his father had been slain in a combat, leaving him as his only heritage the fragments of a sword which had broken in the last fight, and which are still preserved by the Nibelung.   At this revelation Siegfried flies into a passion; he orders the dwarf to weld together the fragments of his father's sword, with which he will leave the forest, free and joyous, to travel

over the world; he must have this sword immediately:
he demands that Mime shall forge it without any delay,
and springs out of the cave after having threatened the
dwarf, who, on being left alone, is in a state of despair:
he no more knows how to manage the rebel steel than
to keep him whose unconscious arm, in accordance with
his dark machinations, is to conquer for him the treasure
that he covets and that is so well guarded by the terrible
dragon.

SCENE II. — While he gives way to these discouraging reflections, there comes into the cavern a stranger,
heavily muffled in a dark cloak and having on his head a
large hat which conceals part of his face. This stranger,
who is none other than the god Wotan, refuses to reveal
his identity to Mime; he styles himself the Wanderer,
and asks to be allowed to rest after the fatigues of the
journey. Despite his grudging reception by the dwarf,
who sees in him a spy whose presence frightens and dis-
turbs him, the god enters, and, sitting down at the
hearth, tells his host that often while wandering over the
face of the earth he pays the hospitality he receives by
wise counsels which he gives to those who desire to
question him, and he offers to forfeit his head if Mime
in questioning him does not learn from his answers
something which is important for him to know. The
dwarf, to get rid of him, accepts the gage, and asks him
three questions, which the Wanderer promises to solve:
" Who are the people living in the bowels of the earth? "
first asks Mime. — " They are the Nibelungs, whom
their chief Alberich subjugated, thanks to the power of
the magic Ring," the stranger replies. — " What race
lives on the surface of the earth? " — " The race of the
giants, whose princes, Fasolt and Fafner, acquired the
treasures of the Rhine and the cursed Ring. Fafner killed

his brother, and now, transformed into a dragon, guards this treasure." — Mime, who is deeply interested in the Wanderer, again asks him : " Who are the inhabitants of the cloudy heights ? " — " They are the luminous elves who dwell in Walhalla, and their chief, Wotan, has conquered the universe by virtue of his lance, on which are graved the sacred runes."

At the conclusion of these words, the stranger strikes the ground with his staff, and a roll of thunder is heard, which makes Mime start from his reverie. The dwarf being satisfied with the answers he has received, now wants to get rid of the Wanderer, in whom he has at length recognized the Father of the Gods ; but the latter questions him in his turn, holding his head as a forfeit if he does not answer his questions : " What race is persecuted by Wotan despite the love he bears them ? " — " The Wälsungs," replies Mime, who rapidly sketches their history. — " What sword is intended, according to the dark designs of a Nibelung, to slay Fafner, by the agency of Siegfried, and make the dwarf master of the Ring ? " — " Nothung," cries Mime, carried away by the interest he takes in the question. — Finally, " Who is the skilful smith who will succeed in reuniting the wondrous fragments of the blade ? "

At these words, Mime trembles with fright ; the question reawakens all his anxieties, and the Wanderer, laughing at his emotion, tells him that only he who knows no fear will be able to triumph over the difficulty. The dwarf has not succeeded in answering the last question ; his life, therefore, is forfeit to the stranger, who goes away into the forest, bequeathing the gnome's head to him who has never known fear.

SCENE III.—On being left alone, Mime sinks down behind the anvil ; that fear which he ought never to

have felt, if he wants to forge the steel successfully,
takes complete possession of him; in his delirium he
already thinks he sees the dragon, the terrible Fafner,
approaching; he trembles in every limb, utters loud
cries, and rolls on the ground.

Siegfried, on his return from his expedition into the
forest, finds him in this condition. He again asks for
the sword; but the dwarf now knows that he himself
cannot forge it, and then understands that this youth,
who has never known what fear is, is the one to whom
the Wanderer bequeathed his head on departing. To
escape this peril, it is necessary, cost what it may, to
terrify this bold heart, and, with this idea, he tells Siegfried that, according to his mother's wish, he cannot
leave these solitudes without first having learnt fear.
To excite it he draws a moving picture of the forest
when darkness is falling upon it, when vague murmurs
mingle with the savage cries of the wild beasts. Siegfried is well acquainted with this mysterious hour, but
it has never yet disturbed his heart in any way. Mime
then speaks to him of the terrible dragon, Fafner, who
strangles and devours all who attempt to approach him,
whose retreat, Neidhöhle, the cavern of envy, is at the
extremity of the forest.

The dwarf's tale only serves to awaken the curiosity
of the ardent youth; he wants to go to seek fear before
the monster's retreat; he wants to set out, but not without being armed with Nothung, and he calls upon Mime,
for the last time, to forge it for him. At the fresh pro-
crastinations of the wily gnome, who knows he cannot
perform the task, Siegfried snatches the pieces of the
sword from his hands, and sets eagerly to work to reduce
the metal to filings and afterwards to forge it. In
honour of the cherished weapon, he sings a joyous song,

which alternates with the malevolent imprecations of the
elf, who feels all his anxieties returning, now that his
dark schemes are melting away.

The dwarf, however, will make a last effort for
success; he will let the bold youth conquer the dragon
with his wondrous sword, and then, when he is exhausted with the combat, Mime will present him with an
enchanted draught, a few drops of which will plunge
him into a deep sleep and leave him defenceless. Then
the Nibelung will only have to pursue his way to the
cave where he will easily be able to seize the treasure
which he has so long and ardently coveted. Already he
sees himself in possession of the Ring of the omnipotent
charm, and tastes in advance long draughts of the intoxicating pleasures of sovereign power. He takes from
the cupboard the ingredients necessary for his infernal
concoction and begins to mix it on the other end of the
hearth of the forge.

Meanwhile, Siegfried, still gaily singing, has finished
the forging of his marvellous weapon; he tempers it,
and then tries it on the anvil, which this time he easily
cleaves with a powerful blow. The dwarf, whose meditations are thus rudely interrupted, starts and falls to the
ground overwhelmed with terror, while the youth joyously and triumphantly brandishes his sword.

Act II.

Scene I. — The action takes place in the forest, before the cavern in which the drowsy Fafner is guarding
his treasure. On the right, in the foreground, are thick
reeds; in the centre, an enormous lime-tree with mighty
limbs, and roots which form a kind of natural seat. In
the middle distance, which is partly elevated, toward the
left, half hidden by a mass of rocks, is the opening to

the dragon's den. A wall of rugged rocks forms the background. A dark night reigns over the whole scene.

Alberich is anxiously keeping watch outside the Neidhöhle, the retreat of the monster whose treasure he still hopes to gain, when, accompanied by a storm-wind, and suddenly illuminated by a moonbeam which pierces the clouds, the Wanderer arrives.

The elf, furious at the presence of his enemy, breaks out into threatenings and insults against the god, whom he suspects of desiring to help Siegfried in his struggle with the monster. But Wotan, who has come to see and not to act, being firmly resolved not in any way to protect the hero whose race he has been compelled to abandon, answers Alberich that the only person he has to fear is Mime. Mime alone desires the Ring, of whose magic power the youth is entirely ignorant. As for Wotan himself, he disdains it. To support his words, he proposes to the Nibelung the idea of warning the monster of the danger which threatens him and offering to save his life in exchange for the Talisman. The dragon, Fafner, awakened from his heavy sleep, declines their proposition : he is not willing to give up his useless power. The god, laughing at the dwarf's discomfiture, departs in the ragings of the storm, advising him to behave in a conciliatory way towards his brother Mime.

The Nibelung, following him with a malevolent glance, renews his imprecations, swearing to pursue his conquest and one day to crush the detested race of the gods. He hides himself in a cleft in the rocks; day begins to break.

Scene II. — Mime and Siegfried arrive, Siegfried armed with the sword. Siegfried sits down under the big lime-tree, his companion faces him, and attempts to terrify him by pointing out the retreat which yawns a few paces from them, and depicting the horrible monster, the denizen of that cavern, who seizes all who have the imprudence to approach him in his terrible jaws and covers them with a venomous froth which consumes the flesh of his victims, or crushes and suffocates them in the coils of his long tail.

Siegfried, who is unmoved at his words, promises himself to plunge Nothung into the monster's heart; and when Mime insists and persists that he will feel fear on finding himself face to face with the dragon, he becomes impatient and forces him to go away, threatening him in his turn with the frightful beast.

Being now alone and awaiting the combat, Siegfried joyfully thinks that he is now going to leave forever this odious dwarf who is so hateful to him; he also thinks with deep tenderness of that mother whom he would have loved so dearly and whose caresses he has never known. He takes a delight in thinking of her as beautiful and gentle, with eyes clear and brilliant as those of a gazelle. He sighs and becomes meditative, then his dreaming is interrupted by the murmurs of the forest, which come from every direction and fill his soul with a mysterious poetry; and by the joyous song of a bird perched above his head, whose language he regrets not being able to understand; perhaps it would speak to him of that dear mother? He wishes to imitate its warbling and cuts a reed with his sword to make a pipe; but he can only draw harsh sounds from this primitive instrument, and, casting it away in disgust, he takes up his silver horn instead, and on it he sounds a joyous call. Hitherto, when he has called thus on the forest for a dear companion, he has only found the bear and the wolf; what will come now?

So saying, Siegfried turns and finds himself in the pres-

ence of Fafner, who, in the form of a hideous reptile,
has advanced to the middle of the stage, and utters a
loud roar. The youth laughs at the sight of him, and
is not in the least afraid of the monster's menacing
words; he rallies him on his delicate little teeth, and,
drawing his sword, he resolutely places himself before
him. The dragon vainly attempts to spurt his deadly
venom upon him and enfold him with his tail so as to
crush him : the young hero foils his attempts, and, profiting from an instant in which his enemy turns round, he
plunges Nothung into his heart. The dying Fafner
admires the courage of the youth who has dared to brave
him; he tells him what personality he concealed under
this hideous form, and his last words are of useful counsel to Siegfried, who must guard against the dark designs
of him who brought him here; then he rolls over on the
ground, lifeless. At the moment when Siegfried withdraws his sword from the monster's breast, his hand is
covered with the burning blood which gushes from the
wound; he involuntarily lifts his fingers to his lips to
get rid of the blood, and then for a few moments he
stands in thought. Suddenly his attention is attracted by
the bird's song, the meaning of which he now seems to
comprehend. Has such a prodigy been wrought by his
having tasted of the blood ? The bird, in a language he
can understand, advises him to go into the cavern and
take possession of the Tarnhelm and the Ring, the
power of which it reveals to him. The hero thanks
his gracious protector and disappears in the depths of the
cave.

Scene III. — Whilst he is exploring it, Mime issues
from his hiding-place, and, not seeing Siegfried, is about
to enter the cavern, when Alberich, also leaving his retreat, bars his passage. A heated discussion then arises

between the two dwarfs concerning the coveted treasure.
Mime ends by proposing to share it with his brother,
but the latter rejects the offer with disdain : he offers
him the Ring and will keep the Tarnhelm for himself,
cunningly calculating that it will be easy later to wrest
the Ring from his brother by the aid of the enchanted
casque.   Alberich contemptuously refuses ;   and   the
quarrel grows very bitter, each one swearing that the
treasure shall belong to him entirely.   They disappear
among the trees and rocks, giving place to Siegfried,
whom they are enraged to see come out of the cavern
earnestly gazing at the magic helmet and the Ring.
He halts under the tree, asking himself of what use will
be these treasures, which he would not have gathered
save for the advice of the bird, whose whole meaning he
did not exactly grasp : they will only serve to remind
him of his victory in which he had no knowledge of
fear.

Through the silence the murmurs of the forest are
again heard, increasing and flooding with a glorious symphony the soul of the youth, who, now in complete communion with the mysterious voices of Nature, plainly
perceives the sublime and hidden meaning of it all.   The
bird's song is again heard instructing him regarding
Mime's treachery : Siegfried will only have to listen attentively to the gnome's words to understand their real
signification.   In fact, the crafty dwarf again advances,
meditating the treachery which will assure him the victory he has so long coveted ; his language betrays him
despite himself, and his words exactly mirror the black
feelings in his heart, although he tries to make them
affectionate and reassuring : he has always hated the
child who was confided to his care, but he wanted to
make him his instrument for gaining the treasure ; he

now offers him a poisoned draught, under the pretext of refreshing him, and when his victim is extended on the ground with his limbs stiff in death, he will at last seize the talisman, the object of his ardent desire. Siegfried, indignant at the odious schemes of the scoundrel, lays him dead at his feet with a pass of his sword; then he raises the body and casts it disdainfully into the cavern, before which he rolls the body of the dragon; they shall thus unite in guarding the riches heaped up in the cave.

Wearied by all his exploits, the hero lies down at the foot of the tree; the melodies of the forest are again heard and he asks his pretty companion, the bird, to sing again. Cannot the friend who has already given him such valuable counsel continue to guide him, him, so lonely in the world and so hungry for the affections to which his heart has so long been a stranger? The wondrous bird then tells him that on a solitary rock, surrounded by flames which jealously guard her, sleeps the loveliest of women; she there awaits the lover who will brave the fire to gain her; Brünnhilde is her name; she will only belong to a hero whose soul has never been accessible to fear.

Siegfried, whose heart is unconscious of all fear, recognizes himself as the chosen one who is to triumph. Delighted, in a state of exaltation, and intoxicated with desire, he springs to the conquest of her who is to be his; the bird, to show the way, hovers above him, and the hero follows the way indicated with joyous cries.

Act III.

Scene I. — The scenery shows a narrow defile in a savage, bare, and rocky country. A crypt-like cave, the dark mouth of which is visible, is cut into the mountain,

which rises to a point in the middle distance. On the
left is a path among the wilderness of rocks; the landscape is shrouded in semi-obscurity.

The Wanderer has halted at the entrance of the crypt,
in which reposes in her eternal sleep Erda, the ancient
spirit of the earth. He evokes her, and, by the power
of his spell, forces her to awake. He wants to question her, for she is the wisdom of the world; no mystery is hidden from her, and the god is anxious to share
her knowledge.

The prophetess slowly emerges from her mysterious
retreat, enveloped in a weird light; her hair and her
gleaming robes seem covered with hoar-frost. She has
with difficulty been aroused by the influence of the spell
from her profound slumber, but she knows nothing : all
her knowledge abandons her when she awakes; she cannot answer Wotan, and advises him to apply to the
Norns, who spin and weave all the knowledge of their
eternal mother into the thread of the destinies. But
what the god seeks is not to know the future : he would
modify it. Why, then, does he not question the child
of his desire, the far-seeing Brünnhilde ? asks the Vala.[1]
Then Wotan informs her of the punishment which he
has had to inflict on the rebel virgin. Can he still consult her now that he has deprived her of her divinity ?
The goddess sinks into profound meditation; her
thoughts trouble her since she has awoke; she is not
willing to counsel him whose actions she blames, who,
after having ordered the Walkyrie to act in a certain
way, punishes her for having done so; who alternately
shackles justice and puts it in force and who perjures
himself in order to keep his oaths; besides, she has no

[1] Vala is the name which the Scandinavians gave to their
prophetesses.

power to change the immutable law of what is to be. She asks to be freed from the spell and to return to her eternal sleep.   Wotan, not being able to get anything from her, will allow her to descend into her dark retreat. Let destiny be accomplished : he will no longer struggle against ruin ; what he formerly decided he will now perform with joy; and the world, which in his anger he had devoted to the hatred of the Nibelung, he will now leave to the son of the Wälsungs ; the hero, who, free from all fear, has succeeded in conquering the magic Ring, is going to awake Brünnhilde, and the fallen daughter of the gods shall accomplish knowingly the act of liberation which will set the world free ; it is she who shall return to the Rhine the cursed gold which has caused such great misfortunes ; it is she also who, enveloping Walhalla in a tremendous conflagration, shall bring about the end of the gods.   Wotan then breaks the spell which holds the prophetess ; she disappears into the vault, which is again plunged in darkness ; the tempest dies away, and the Wanderer silently awaits Siegfried's arrival.

Dawn begins to break over the scene ; the guardian bird comes flying in, then, suddenly frightened at the sight of the two ravens which always accompany the Master of the World, it disappears in full flight.

Siegfried joyously advances, following the way which the bird has indicated.

SCENE II. — A dialogue commences between Siegfried and Wotan, who asks him questions, and to whom he tells the story of his exploit with the dragon, of the wondrous sword in his hand, and the sweet conquest which he aspires to make.

These words momentarily revive in the god's heart the agony of the coming events which he faced just now with a firm will; for the last time he is tempted to intervene, and endeavours to oppose the progress of the young hero. Siegfried wants at any cost to follow the road which the bird pointed out before it fled from the presence of Wotan's ravens; he becomes angry with this importunate stranger who wants to bar his way, and declares that if he opposes him he will deprive him of his remaining eye; but the Wanderer, despising the bold youth's rage and saying that he is the guardian of the rock where Brünnhilde sleeps, threatens with its flames the audacious mortal who would pass beyond, and he angrily bars the way with his lance. Siegfried, whose impatience is at white heat, draws his sword and strikes Wotan's spear, breaking it into fragments. There is a clap of thunder; the whole scene is filled with a sea of flame; and the god, finding himself vanquished, gives place to his young and impetuous antagonist, and disappears in the general commotion.

The conquering Siegfried, now joyfully sounds his horn and springs through the flames which are extending on the mountain; the sound of his horn, growing more and more distant, proves that he is scaling the rocks; then the flames abate, the clouds of smoke disappear, and reveal under an azure sky the rock on which Brünnhilde is sleeping.

The scenery is the same as in the third act of *Die Walküre*.

Scene III. — Siegfried, who has ceased sounding his horn, looks around him in amazement. He perceives the noble steed sleeping in the shadow of the fir, and then the shining steel armour which glitters in the sun; he approaches and sees an armed warrior asleep with the head enclosed in a helmet. He gently detaches the helmet to make the sleeper more comfortable. Magnificent tresses escape from it. Siegfried stands still in astonishment and admiration. He now wants to take off the stifling cuirass and with the edge of his sword he carefully cuts the thongs which hold the armour together: he is amazed and agitated at the sight of the graceful form of a woman enveloped in a flowing white garment. Suddenly his heart is greatly troubled and seized with a mortal agony, and in his emotion he calls on the memory of his mother. Is this fear which at length he feels? Was it reserved for this adorable being to inspire him with terror? To awaken the maiden he presses a long kiss upon her lips; Brünnhilde then opens her eyes, and they gaze upon one another with delight.

The Walkyrie slowly raises herself and addresses a solemn hymn to the sun's light, from whose beams she has so long been banished. Who has awakened her from her interminable sleep? Siegfried with emotion tells her his name, blessing the mother who bore him and the earth which nourished him, to permit him to see the dawn of this happy day.

Brünnhilde joins her song of joy and gratitude to that of Siegfried, Siegfried the well-beloved, who, even before his birth, was the object of her love and care.

These strange words mislead the young hero : is not this his mother whom he thought lost forever, and who is now found? — No, answers the virgin, smiling, his mother has not been restored to him, but he has near him her who has always loved and fought for him, for, although unconsciously, it was her love that led her formerly to transgress Wotan's commands, and that drew upon her the long expiation on the rock and exile from Walhalla. At these thoughts, she becomes sad ; she resists the hero's ardent caresses and wishes to get back her divine virginity and her immortal nature ; she regretfully contem-

plates the brilliant steel of her cuirass and the shining
armour which formerly shielded her chaste body from the
eyes of the profane; she calls upon her old wisdom and
god-like vision, and is terrified to find that she is inspired
with them no longer; her knowledge is departed and
darkness obscures her thoughts : the daughter of the gods
has become a simple woman.

But at the same time earthly love wells up in her
heart and fills her whole being; in vain she still tries to
struggle with herself and repulse the ardour of Siegfried,
who beseeches her to be his; love is too strong.   Brünnhilde is intoxicated with it.   She will abandon the cause
of the gods.   Let them all perish, that old and decrepit
race; let Walhalla be destroyed; let the Burg crumble
into dust; let the eternals come to an end ! . . .

Norns, unravel the rope of the destinies of the gods !
Let the dusk of the gods begin : the virgin will only live
now for the love of Siegfried, her treasure, her star, her
all. . . .

In uncontrollable emotion she throws herself into the
arms of her lover, who receives her with ecstasy.

DIE GÖTTERDÄMMERUNG

PROLOGUE. — The stage, as in the third act of *Die
Walküre*, represents Brünnhilde's rock, but the whole
scene is enveloped in blackest night.   In the distance
only is there a faint reflection of flames.

The three Norns, draped in long flowing robes, are
weaving the golden cord of Destiny, which they pass to
each other in turn.   The first and oldest is seated on the
left, under the fir; the second is lying at the entrance of
the grotto on the right; and the third, the youngest of
the three, is seated at the foot of the rock which com-

mands the valley. The first Norn points out to her sisters the light which Loge ceaselessly maintains around Brünnhilde's rock, and she tells them to sing and to weave. She ties the golden cord to one of the branches of the fir, and calls to mind that formerly it was a joy for her to accomplish her task in the shelter of the mighty branches of the world-ash, at the foot of which was a fresh spring whence wisdom was gained. One day Wotan came to the limpid water to drink there, and made the sacred payment of the sacrifice of one of his eyes; then he tore off one of the strongest limbs of the tree to make a battle-lance for himself. But from that moment the ash began to wither, its foliage became yellow and fell; in the course of many centuries the trunk perished, and, at the same time, the spring dried up. What happened then? — And the Norn, throwing the cord to her second sister, invites her to speak in her turn. — Wotan, replies the Sibyl, graved on his lance the runes of the treaties which constituted his power; he saw, fateful omen! his weapon shattered when he opposed a young hero; then he gathered together the warriors of Walhalla and made them destroy the world-ash. What happened afterwards? the Norn asks her youngest sister, throwing the cord to her. With it the heroes formed a colossal pyre around the abode of the eternals, and Wotan is sitting in silence in the midst of the august assembly of the gods. If the wood, on taking fire, consumes the magnificent Burg, that will be the end of the masters of the world. Wotan enslaved the crafty Loge and stationed him in bright flames around Brünnhilde's rock; then he plunged the splinters of his broken weapon into the heart of the flaming god. What happened then? — The cord, which the Norns are weaving, begins to part, the sharp edge of the rock is cutting it; it is the anathema of Alberich, the spoiler of the Rhine-gold, which is bearing its fatal fruit; at last the cable breaks in the middle and with it departs the prophetic power of the three sisters, who rise in terror; they precipitately gather up the ends, and tying themselves together, they sink into the depths of the earth to seek Erda, their eternal mother.

Day has been slowly breaking; it now shines in all its brilliance, and Siegfried is seen approaching, armed as a warrior, with Brünnhilde accompanying him, holding her noble horse, Grane, by the bridle.

The lovers, who have already tasted many days of radiant happiness, exchange oaths of fidelity. Brünnhilde has instructed her husband in the sacred runes which the gods have taught her; she has given him all her knowledge, asking nothing in return but his constancy and love; she is encouraging him to new exploits. Siegfried, who is about to depart, after having given her renewed assurances of his love, presents her, as a gage of his fidelity, with the Ring, taken from Fafner, which is only valuable as a visible sign of the virtues which he had to display in order to conquer it.

Brünnhilde is delighted, and gives him in exchange Grane, the noble companion, which of old bore her so often on her warlike exploits. In the midst of the combat, may the superb charger recall Brünnhilde to her husband's memory.

They separate after a last embrace; Siegfried goes down the mountain, leading his steed; Brünnhilde long and lovingly gazes after him, and in the distance is heard the joyous echo of the hero's horn.

Act I.

Scene 1. — The scenery shows the palace of the Gibichungs on the banks of the Rhine. The great hall, with large openings at the back, is on the level of the river-bank; the whole width of the river is visible. On the right, half-way up the stage is a table with chairs around it. To the left and right are entrances into private apartments.

Gunther and his sister Gutrune, of the family of the Gibichungs, are talking with Hagen, the son of their mother, Grimhilde, and are extolling the wisdom of this brother, who has always given them good counsel.

Hagen — who has inherited and carries on the dark schemes of his father Alberich (who still cherishes the idea of regaining the Ring which Wotan wrested from him) — informed of Siegfried's valiant exploits and his love for the Walkyrie, but carefully concealing this knowledge, counsels his brother and sister, who are ignorant of these facts, to strengthen their dynasty by powerful alliances: for Gunther he desires Brünnhilde, the virgin who is sleeping on an inaccessible rock, protected by a sea of flames; it is not reserved for Gunther to overcome this terrible obstacle: the only one who can accomplish the heroic act, is Siegfried, the last scion of the Wälsungs, who conquered Fafner and took possession of the treasure of the Nibelungs.

He it is whom Hagen has selected for the daughter of the Gibichungs. He will readily yield to Gunther the fruits of his victory if his heart is enslaved by the charms of Gutrune, and in this she can aid by making the hero drink a certain enchanted potion, which will render his mind oblivious of his past oaths and make him the slave of her who shall administer the philtre.

The brother and sister enthusiastically adopt Hagen's plan, and, for the fulfilment of their wishes, impatiently await him whose wanderings may at any moment lead him into their vicinity.

SCENE II. — The sound of the horn is heard in the direction of the Rhine at that very moment, announcing Siegfried's arrival. Hagen perceives the young warrior skilfully propelling a boat containing himself and Grane. Gunther goes down to the bank to receive him, and Gutrune, after having contemplated the hero from afar, retires to her own apartments in evident agitation.

Siegfried lands with his horse and asks the two men which is Gunther, whose fame has reached him, and to whom he wishes to offer the choice of combat or his friendship. Gunther tells his name and answers his guest with oaths of alliance and fidelity. Hagen, who has taken charge of Grane and led him away by the bridle, returns and questions him about the riches of the Nibelungs, which he knows he possesses; but the hero, despising these useless treasures, has left them in the dragon's den; he has brought away nothing but this helmet suspended to his belt, the magic power of which Hagen tells him without making much impression on him. He possesses one other object which belonged to the conquered treasure, — a Ring, which he has given to a noble woman, as a gage of his fealty. Hagen then calls Gutrune, who enters, bringing a cup which she offers Siegfried in sign of welcome.

The latter bows to her and at the moment of emptying the cup is absorbed in tender and touching memories of Brünnhilde, vowing, from the bottom of his heart, never to forget their true and burning love.

He drinks, and returns the horn to the confused and agitated Gutrune; but, under the charm of the philtre, passion suddenly kindles in his eyes as he looks at the maiden ; he tells her of the feeling which has just taken complete possession of him, and immediately asks Gunther to give him his sister.   Gutrune, remorseful at thus taking the hero's affection by force, makes a sign that she is unworthy of him, and leaves the hall with tottering steps.   Siegfried watches her departure with a fascinated gaze, and then asks his friend about himself.   Has he already selected a wife ?

Gunther replies by telling him of the difficulty he would have in winning her whom he loves, Brünnhilde, who is imprisoned with flames on a solitary rock.   Siegfried, at the sound of this name so dearly loved, is now only struck with a vague reminiscence, which is immediately effaced ; the philtre continues to do its work ; he undertakes this conquest for Gunther, on the sole condition that he shall receive Gutrune as a reward.

With the help of the Tarnhelm he will take the form of Gunther and will bring back the promised bride.   They bind themselves by a solemn oath never to betray their alliance, and cement the pact by drinking in turn out of the same horn, after having first mingled a few drops of blood in the draught.   Hagen, who has kept apart and refused to take any part in this fraternal pledge, giving his bastard origin as a pretext, breaks the horn with a stroke of his sword, while Gutrune, disturbed and agitated, comes to aid the departure of the warriors ; he meditates with bitter irony, on the fact that these two gallants, led astray, one by his perfidious counsels, the other by his odious sorcery, are both at work to build up the fortune of the humble son of the Nibelung.

A superb curtain is drawn across the front of the scene and hides it ; when it rises, the Walkyrie's rock is seen, as in the prologue.

SCENE III. — Brünnhilde, silent and pensive, is sitting at the entrance of the grotto, looking at the Ring which Siegfried gave her, and covering it with passionate kisses. She hears in the distance a sound which was formerly familiar, — the gallop of an aerial horse ; she listens, and, in delight, springs to meet Waltraute, her sister, who is coming to seek her in her retreat, and whose troubled expression she does not notice; is her loved companion at last bringing her the pardon from the too severe god ? Wotan must have softened towards the guilty one, since he allowed the devouring fire to protect her in her sleep and permitted happiness to grow out of her very chastisement; she now belongs to a hero whose love inflames her with pride and who has made her the happiest of wives.

Waltraute, who does not share her sister's joy, has come to her full of agony, despite Wotan's prohibition, to entreat her to save Walhalla from the misfortune which threatens it. Since having exiled the child of his heart, the Lord of Battles, in distress and discouragement, has not ceased to go about the world as a solitary Wanderer : one day he returned from his idle roamings, holding his shattered lance in his hand ; silent and sombre, with a gesture he ordered his heroes to cut down the world-ash, and with it to make a vast pyre around the abode of the eternals ; then he convoked the Council of the Gods ; and since then, sullen and motionless, he sits enthroned among them and the heroes, sorrowfully contemplating his baffled weapon ; vainly his daughters, the warrior-maidens, try to comfort him ; he remains deaf to their prayers, awaiting his two ravens, which he has sent away, and which, alas ! do not return to bring him any reassuring news.

Once only, touched by the caresses of his daughter, Waltraute, his eyes dimmed at the recollection of Brünnhilde, and he uttered these words: "If she were to restore the cursed Ring to the Daughters of the Rhine, the gods and the world would be saved." Then Waltraute furtively left the house of mourning, to come to beg her sister to perform this act of redemption.

At these words, Brünnhilde rebels. What! sacrifice Siegfried's Ring, the sacred pledge of their love, more precious to her than the whole race of the gods and the glory of the eternals? She will never consent to that, though the splendours of Walhalla crumble away this moment; and she lets her sister depart in despair, bearing her immutable decision.

Waltraute, in utter despair, hastens to her father's palace, accompanied by a storm-cloud flashing with lightning; night has fallen, and the flame encircling the rock shines with an unusual brilliance.

The sound of Siegfried's horn is heard in the distance. Brünnhilde, in delight, springs to meet him, but recoils in terror at the appearance of an unknown warrior; it is her husband, who, still under the influence of the fatal philtre which blinds his soul and by virtue of the power of the helm, presents himself to her under the form of Gunther, in whose name he wants to capture her. The unfortunate woman, overcome with horror, struggles in vain, calling upon Wotan in her distress, believing that she is again suffering from his anger. She vainly invokes the power of the Ring; her strength fails her. Siegfried throws her down, and, snatching away the Ring, he places it on his own finger, declaring her Gunther's bride, and forces her to enter the grotto, into which he follows her; but, faithful to the word which he gave to his ally, he will preserve her untouched for the son of the Gibichung. To this he calls his sword, Nothung, to witness.

Act II.

Scene I. — A long and beautiful stretch of the Rhine is visible, forming, on the left, a sharp turn, just before the palace of the Gibichungs, which is seen in pro-file in the extreme right foreground. From the escarped and rocky banks of the river, in the right centre, rises a road, beside which are a row of sacrificial stones, the first two dedicated to Fricka and Donner, and the third, larger than the others, consecrated to Wotan.

It is dark night. Hagen, armed and sitting motion-less at the door of the palace which he is guarding, seems to be asleep, although his eyes are open. His father, Alberich, sitting in front of him, is prompting his dreams, and, speaking to him in a low voice, excites him to the struggle in which he is engaged to reconquer the Ring from Wotan, the cursed: already the god has met his master among his own blood; a Wälsung has shat-tered his spear, the instrument of his power, and the god, disarmed and brought to naught, sees with anguish the approaching end of himself, and Walhalla. If Hagen is willing to help the elf who was the author of his being, he can gain the sovereignty of the gods for his own advantage. The Ring, which must be gained at all costs, is in Siegfried's possession; but the hero, not knowing its power, or despising it, by that very fact escapes the imprecation attached to the possession of the talisman; he must be tricked, then, and it must be done quickly, lest, counselled by the noble woman with whom the magic Ring is deposited, he may have time to restore to the Rhine-Daughters the treasure which they so in-sistently demand, and which, in that case, would be irrevocably lost to the Nibelungs.

Scene II. — Hagen, still dreaming, swears to his

father that he will succeed in gaining possession of the Ring. Alberich disappears, entreating his son to keep his promise. A thick cloud covers Hagen; day begins to break in the direction of the Rhine, and the sun rises, being reflected in the river, and shining on the arrival of Siegfried, who, transported by the power of his magic helm, arrives from the rock where he has captured Brünnhilde for Gunther, to announce the good news to the daughter of the Gibichungs.

Gutrune is delighted, and makes her lover relate his new exploit, joyfully learning that Gunther, having by a cunning subterfuge received his bride from his hands, is on the way with her to the palace of his fathers.

Scene III. — Preparations must be hastened for the reception of the new couple; Hagen, from a high point of observation, now calls together his brother's vassals with the sound of a horn; they run to arms, asking what danger threatens their lord and master; but Hagen reassures them : they are only called together to welcome the bride he has gained by Siegfried's aid, and to prepare the sacrifices to the gods who have been propitious to them. Let them immolate a strong bull on Wotan's altar; a boar for Froh; a goat for Donner; and let them consecrate a gentle ewe to Fricka, so that she may grant the bridal pair a happy marriage.

The vassals, carried away by the gay words of Hagen, who is usually sombre and savage, rejoice, and vow to protect their future mistress.

Scene IV. — The bark bringing Gunther and Brünnhilde has landed. The warrior steps out of it with his sad bride, who allows herself to be led with pale face and downcast eyes. He presents her to his vassals, who joyously welcome her, then to Gutrune and her future husband.

Brünnhilde, at the sight of Siegfried, is dumb with
astonishment and stands still, looking fixedly at him; he
calmly meets the unfortunate woman's glance in entire
unconsciousness of all that is passing in her mind; she
is on the point of fainting, and Siegfried calmly supports
her; she sees the Ring on the perjured man's finger;
then she violently starts away from him and asks how
the Ring, which Gunther took away from her and which
he said was the pledge of their union, is in the possession
of another.   The son of the Gibichungs is troubled, and
does not know what to reply.   Siegfried, lost in reverie
at the sight of the Ring, only remembers that he formerly won it in his fight with the dragon and freely says
so.   Hagen joins in the discussion, pretends that he
suspects the Wälsung of treachery, and goads Brünnhilde to revenge; the latter, wild with grief and revolt,
proclaims Siegfried a rogue and a villain; she accuses
the gods of all the evils which are crushing her, and
repulses Gunther when he tries to calm her, renouncing
him as her husband and pointing to the son of Wälse as
him to whom she is given body and soul.

The excitement is at its height; Siegfried is anxious
to exculpate himself of such treachery; and all summon
him to declare under oath that he has not broken his
plighted word and that in Brünnhilde he has respected
Gunther's bride.   He solemnly affirms it on the weapon
which Hagen presents to him : may hè perish by this
very weapon if he has forfeited his honour.

SCENE V. — Brünnhilde strides forward with rage and
indignation, and, by the sharp and pointed steel, calls
down vengeance on the traitor and perjurer, and as
Siegfried departs, careless of her threats and thinking of
nothing but his new love, whom he draws with him into
the palace, the unfortunate creature, a prey to the most

terrible grief, agonizingly asks herself of what cruel sorcery she has been the victim, — who has brought upon
her such misfortune, — and how can she sever her hateful bonds, now that she has lost her divine knowledge.
Hagen then approaches the poor abandoned woman, and
offers her the aid of his arm to avenge her; but at this
proposition she gives a bitter laugh; has not she herself
taken care to render the hero invulnerable? and, moreover, would not his bravery paralyze whosoever would
measure himself against him? Hagen recognizes his
inferiority in such a struggle, but may there not be some
secret means of vanquishing the guilty one?

Brünnhilde then tells him that only one point is vulnerable; knowing well that he would never turn his
back upon the enemy, she did not include that in her
enchantments: if Hagen can strike him between the
shoulders, he will be able to give him a mortal wound
there. The wretch promises to profit from this precious advice, and imparts his plan to Gunther, who has
been standing apart, absorbed in his thoughts and overwhelmed by the accusation of cowardice which his
wife has brought against him. Gunther shudders at the
thought of betraying him whom he has taken for his
brother-in-arms; but Hagen tries to still his scruples:
he reminds him in an undertone what power will result
to him from this act, since it will make him master of
the Ring. Gunther still hesitates, thinking of Gutrune's
grief. That name rouses all Brünnhilde's jealous hatred:
that woman, who must have robbed her of her husband
by a charm, must be chastised in her love; and Brünnhilde adds her entreaties to those of Hagen. Siegfried,
then, shall die, Gunther acquiesces; the hunt which
will take place to-morrow will furnish a pretext for his
death: a boar shall be said to have attacked him.

While they are weaving this dark plot, Siegfried and Gutrune, accompanied by their nuptial-train, appear with their heads adorned with flowers and leaves. They invite their brother and sister to imitate them, and while Gunther, taking Brünnhilde's hand, follows the joyous party, Hagen, remaining behind, invokes the assistance of his father Alberich, the malevolent elf, and swears to himself that he will soon possess the much-coveted Ring.

Act III.

Scene I. — The stage represents a lovely landscape on the banks of the Rhine; the azure waters, pent between rocky banks, show the Undines sporting in their transparent waves. In the foreground there is a kind of strand; on the right, a path rises among the rocks and leads to the summit of the bank.

Woglinde, Wellgunde, and Flosshilde, the three Rhine-Daughters, whilst sporting in the waves, are lamenting the loss of their gold, whose pure brilliance formerly illumined the river-bed, which is now plunged in darkness and sadness. If the possessor of the treasure would only consent to restore it to them!

Just then the distant sound of the horn tells them that the hero is coming their way. They are diving down to take counsel together, when Siegfried, fully armed, appears on the bank, having lost his way while following the game.

The Undines reappear and accost him, offering to help him recover the bear, which has escaped him, if, in exchange, he will give them the golden Ring which is on his finger.

He refuses the Nixies' proposal. What! give up a treasure which he gained at the cost of a terrible combat with the dragon, Fafner? Never! They jeer at

him, mocking his avarice and his dread, — he so handsome and so strong, — of being beaten by his wife if
she should notice the absence of the Ring, and they
again disappear in the waves. Siegfried, disturbed by
their raillery, almost decides to offer them the treasure
by which he sets such little store; he calls them back;
but the three sisters, who have concerted together, are
now grave and earnest, and counsel him to keep the
Ring till he understands the malediction which is associated with it; then he will joyfully yield it to them.
They know many fatal things concerning Siegfried's
life — his cursed Ring, made out of the Rhine-gold, by
virtue of the anathema of him who forged it devotes to
misfortune whosoever shall become its possessor.   He
shall perish, even as Fafner perished, unless he returns
it to the depths of the river; its waves alone will have
power to annul the malediction, that malediction which
the Norns have woven into the cord of destiny.   Siegfried will not allow himself to be moved by what he considers vain threats; he does not give any credence to the
story of the nymphs, and he will brave the alarming
prophecies of the Norns, whose cord, if the occasion
arises, Nothung will be able to sever.   They say this
Ring assures him the empire of the world: well, he will
willingly give it to the graceful Nixies, if they, in exchange, will give him love and all its sweet ecstasies, —
for life without love, he values it no more than this
(saying these words, he takes up a clod of earth and
casts it far from him); but threats will never induce
him to yield, for fear is unknown to him.

The Undines, finding him deaf to their exhortations,
give up the attempt to convince a madman who had not
the sense to retain and appreciate the most precious blessing that ever fell to his lot, the love of the Walkyrie, and is

even ignorant that he has trifled away his happiness, whilst he is set upon keeping the talisman which dooms him to death. But, happily for them, this very day his heritage will pass into the hands of a noble woman, who, unlike him, will listen to their prayers and do what is right. They will hasten to meet her. Siegfried follows them with smiling eyes, admiring their graceful movements.

SCENE II. — Hunting horns are heard in the distance, gradually coming nearer; the young hunter joyously answers on his silver horn. Gunther and Hagen descend the bank with their suite. The menials prepare the meal, while the huntsmen stretch themselves on the earth and begin to talk and drink. Siegfried, confessing that his chase has come to nothing, carelessly relates his meeting with the sisters, who have predicted his death for that very day. Gunther is uneasy, and furtively looks at Hagen, who asks Siegfried to tell them of the time when it is said he was able to talk with the birds. But the hero has long ceased to understand their warblings, to which he now prefers a woman's sweet words. Gunther joins Hagen in insisting on hearing about that adventure. Siegfried then tells of his childhood in the forest with Mime, the cunning gnome, whose dark schemes he baffled, his combat with Fafner by the aid of Nothung, his valiant sword, the conquest of the treasure, and the wise counsel of the wondrous bird. When the hero has arrived at this point of his story, Hagen secretly mingles with his drink a philtre, which reawakens his sleeping memories; Siegfried, now in full possession of all his faculties, to the profound astonishment of Gunther, who listens with an ever-increasing emotion, relates his victorious quest to deliver Brünnhilde, and the delightful reward which awaited him as the price of his valour.

Gunther, in amazement, seems as if he begins to understand. At this moment, two ravens, issuing from a neighbouring grove, come and wheel above the head of Siegfried, who turns to look at them ; Hagen profits by this moment to spring upon him whom in his hatred he has trapped in such a cowardly manner, and plunges his spear between his shoulders. Gunther springs up in horror to ward off the murderer's arm, but alas! too late. Siegfried raises his shield to crush the traitor, but his strength fails, and he falls to the earth, whilst his cowardly assassin tranquilly moves away and gains the top of the bank. Before expiring, Siegfried is still able to send a last farewell to the beloved one whom he is still unconscious of having betrayed, and the radiant memory of whom softens his last sufferings. Her beloved image comes to enrapture his dying moments.

The vassals place the hero's body on a litter of boughs. The funeral procession is formed. Gunther first follows the corpse, giving every sign of the deepest grief. The moonbeams light up the mournful march, and mists rise from the face of the Rhine and envelop the whole scene. When they are finally dissipated, the stage shows again the great hall in the palace of the Gibichungs, this time in darkness. Only the river in the background is illuminated by the brilliant moonlight.

Scene III. — Gutrune comes out of the silent and sleeping palace, anxiously awaiting the return of her husband and her brother; she is troubled with dark presentiments. Brünnhilde's wild and sinister laugh has interrupted her sleep. Was it she whom she saw in the distance going towards the river? She finds, indeed, that Brünnhilde has left her apartments and she is on the point of re-entering her own room when she hears Hagen's voice, which turns her cold with fear. The huntsmen have returned : why, then, does she not hear the ringing sound of Siegfried's horn ? She asks Hagen, who at first tells her that her husband is returning and she must prepare to greet him, and then brutally informs her that the hero will never again joyously wind his horn, for he has met his death in a struggle with a furious wild-boar.

The funeral procession arrives at that moment and the whole crowd of servants press in, bearing lights and torches. The huntsmen, with Gunther in their midst, set the corpse down in the centre of the hall. There is general consternation. The unhappy Gutrune falls fainting at the sight of the lifeless body of him she loved. Gunther tries to raise her; but, recovering herself, she repulses her brother with horror, accusing him of having assassinated her husband. Gunther exculpates himself, and then reveals Hagen's crime, cursing him and calling down misery and agony upon his head. The traitor impudently comes forward and proclaims aloud his odious act; he demands as a right of spoil the Ring which glitters on the hero's finger. Gunther forbids him to touch Gutrune's heritage. Hagen threatens him; they both draw, and Gunther, pierced by his brother's sword, falls dead at his feet. The assassin then wishes to seize the Ring, and throws himself upon Siegfried's body to take it; but the hand of the corpse lifts itself in a threatening manner, clutching the Ring in its fingers. There is general horror. Gutrune and her women utter piercing shrieks.

Brünnhilde, then appearing at the back of the stage, advances calmly and solemnly, commanding the noise to cease. She, the woman abandoned and betrayed by all, comes to avenge the hero, whose death will never be deplored as it deserves.

Gutrune breaks out in reproaches, accusing her of having drawn all these misfortunes upon their house; but Brünnhilde, with noble dignity, imposes silence upon her, reminding her that she (Brünnhilde) is the lawful wife, whom alone Siegfried has ever loved and to whom he had sworn eternal fidelity.   Gutrune then, in an agony of despair, understands what an odious part Hagen has made her play in counselling her to make use of the cursed philtre, and, calling down curses upon the villain, she falls on Gunther's body, utterly overwhelmed with grief.   Hagen, with a glance of defiance, stands apart in sombre reflection.

Brünnhilde, after having gazed long and sadly on Siegfried's face, solemnly orders the servants to build on the river bank a pyre to receive the hero's corpse; then she sends for Grane, her faithful and noble steed, which she wishes to share in the sacred honours which are reserved for valorous warriors.

While the vassals are piling up the wood, which the women dress with tapestries and flowers, Brünnhilde again sinks into contemplation of her beloved, the purest of the pure, the loyalest heart of all, who, however, betrayed and abandoned her, the only woman he loved. How came that to be?   O Wotan, inexorable god, who to repair his own sin did not fear to devote his daughter to this extreme distress by thus sacrificing him whom she loved!   How grievously she had learnt, by the excess of her misfortunes, what it was necessary for her to know! Now she sees, she knows, she understands everything, but at the cost of what suffering!

She sees sailing above her the two black messengers of the Father of Battles: let them return to Walhalla and announce that now everything is accomplished and consummated, and that the divine race will soon have ceased to exist. Slumber, slumber, O race of the gods!

She makes a sign to the vassals to place on the pyre the body of Siegfried, first taking off the Ring, and putting it on her finger. This fatal Ring, of which she again takes possession, she bequeaths to the Daughters of the Rhine; let them come and look for it presently among her ashes, when fire shall have purified it from the malediction which has weighed so heavily upon all who have owned it. She approaches the pyre where the body of the hero is already resting, and, brandishing a torch, she again tells the ravens to go and tell Wotan what has happened here; then to fly to the rock where she slept, and order Loge, who is still there, to betake himself to Walhalla and to wrap the royal abode of the gods in flames, — for the eternal twilight is beginning for them, and the fire, which is soon going to consume herself, will extend as far as the inaccessible retreat of the Master of the World.

She flings the brand upon the pyre, which immediately ignites. Then, turning for the last time to the assembled people, she bequeaths to them the treasure of her divine knowledge : the race of the gods is extinct ; the universe is without a master ; but there still remains to it a boon which is more precious than all, and which it must learn to cherish, more than gold, more than glory and greatness : this is Love, which alone can issue victorious from all trials and give perfect happiness.

Brünnhilde receives her horse, Grane, from two youths; she strips off all his harness, unbridles him, and shows him the pyre on which his master reposes. Then, quickly mounting the noble animal, she springs with him into the flames, which leap up, crackling and filling the whole stage. The people disperse in terror, and

PARSIFAL

CHARACTERS in the order of their first entrance.	ACT I. Tableau I.	ACT I. Tabl. II.	ACT II. Tabl. I.	ACT II. Tabl. II.	ACT III. Tabl. I.	ACT III. Tabl. II.
Gurnemanz (bass). Old Knight of the Grail, having served under the reign of Titurel and Amfortas.	■·········	·····■	····	····	■····	····□
2d Knight (bass).	··■					
3d Esquire (cont.). ⎫ The Knights and Esquires of the Grail are the	····■					
1st Esquire (sopr.). ⎬ guardians and servants of the sacred Lance and the holy vessel containing the blood of the	·····■					
1st Knight (tenor). ⎭ Saviour.	········■					
Kundry (sopr.). A double character: sometimes servant of the Grail, and inclined to good; sometimes Klingsor's slave, and inclined to evil. She was Herodias in a former existence.	··········■·······•	·········	··■	··■	··■··	····□
Amfortas (baryt.). Priest-King of the Grail, son of the old Titurel: fell before Kundry's seductions, and has thus become incapable of celebrating the sacrament without frightful sufferings.	·•········■·······	·····■	····	····	········	··■
3d Esquire (tenor). Servant of the Grail.	···········■					
4th Esquire (tenor). Servant of the Grail.	·············■					
Parsifal (tenor). Son of Gamuret and Herzeleide; becomes Priest-King of the Grail after having cured Amfortas's wound.	···············■	·····□	····	··■	···■	····■
The Brotherhood of the **Knights of the Grail** (*Chorus:* ten., bass.).	···············■	■···	····	····	·······■	
Youths (*Chorus:* cont., ten.). Half-way up the dome.	···············■	(invisible) ··■···	····	····	······	····■
Young Boys (*Chorus:* sopr., contr.). At the top of the dome.	···············■	(invisible) ···■··	····	····	······	····■
Voice of **Titurel** (bass). Dying knight, into whose care an angel formerly confided the Holy Grail and the Lance, and who thus became Priest-King. Father of Amfortas.	···············■	(invisible.) ·····■				
Klingsor (bass). Wicked Knight, who, not being allowed to become a servant of the Grail, becomes a magician and the bitter enemy of the holy institution.	···············	·······	■···	··■		
Flower-Maidens (*Chorus:* sopr., cont.). Fantastic and seductive beings, created by Klingsor's spells to ruin the Knights of the Grail.	···············	·····•·	····	■		

then the pyre sinks down, casting up a dense column of smoke. Soon the clouds are dissipated, and the waters of the Rhine are seen to be overflowing their banks and rising to the threshold of the palace, bringing the three Undines in their waves.

Hagen, who has watched all the foregoing scene with anxiety and dread, now casts himself, with a last great cry of covetousness, into the midst of the waters to seek the Ring; but he is seized and dragged down into the depths by Wellgunde and Woglinde, while Flosshilde appears on the crest of the waves, exultantly holding up the Ring, which is regained at last!

The distant sky is in flames : the conflagration enfolds the whole horizon, and the vassals, silent with awe, watch the sinister and impressive spectacle of the annihilation of the palace of the gods as it is engulfed in the stupendous horror of an ocean of fire.

With this impressive cataclysm the fourth and last day of *Der Ring des Nibelungen* comes to an end.

PARSIFAL.

On Montsalvat, a remote peak in the Pyrenees, stands a castle, built by Titurel as a sanctuary inviolable and inaccessible to the profane, where the sacred cup out of which Christ drank at his last meal with his disciples may be preserved. This sacred cup, the Grail, containing the blood which flowed from the divine wounds of the Saviour on the cross, as well as the Lance which caused those wounds, has been confided by celestial messengers to the pure knight in days of Infidel warfare when the enemies of the faith threatened to profane these precious relics.

Titurel, after having built this magnificent sanctuary

for these treasures, has gathered around him for their protection a body of knights whose pure hearts have rendered them worthy of this high mission. The Grail rewards these noble servants for their pious fidelity by imparting to them a power and miraculous valour which enable them to undertake, for the upholding of the faith, labours from which they could not issue victorious without divine help; and every year a dove, descending from the celestial regions, comes to renew the powers of the Holy Grail and its Knights.

An inhabitant of the country near Montsalvat, Klingsor, wishing, for the remission of his sins, to be enrolled in the pious order, has vainly sought to root out of his heart the tendencies to sin; and, not succeeding, he has destroyed his animal instincts by laying violent hands on himself; his unworthy action having closed the doors of the sacred castle against him forever, he has listened to the Evil Spirit, and received from him unhallowed instructions in the art of magic. Being then full of hatred against those who have rejected him as a brother, he has used his fatal power in transforming the arid land into a garden of delights, where grow, half flowers, half women, fantastic beings of irresistible beauty, who exert their seductive charms to bring about the ruin of such of the Knights of the Grail as are weak enough to fall into their snares.

Many had already been led astray when Amfortas, to whom his father, the venerable Titurel, bowed down with years, had yielded the crown, wished to put an end to these fatal enchantments, and came himself, seconded by the divine aid, to this haunt of guilty pleasure; but, alas! he was no stronger than those who had preceded him, and succumbed, as they had. What a climax of shame and defeat! His enemy gained possession of the sacred Lance, the precious relic confided to his care, and, turning it against its very defender, gave Amfortas a deep wound in his side, which no remedy can ever heal.

The unfortunate king, however, returned to Mont-salvat, bearing with him the sully of his sin mingled with eternal remorse, which is even more agonizing than the incurable wound which bleeds in his side.

From this time, the august brotherhood of knights is plunged into shame and sadness, each one of them shar-ing in the humiliation and grief of the fallen king. The latter, vainly seeking a remedy for his physical and moral sufferings, feels them more intensely every time he is forced as priest-king to celebrate the holy mys-teries, and he shrinks with terror from performing them every time they recur. It is in vain that he demands from the sacred lake, which the forest shelters, the benefi-cent alleviation of its fresh waters; in vain do his knights bring him precious balms from the most distant lands.

One day, when prostrate before the tabernacle, he was imploring the Saviour's pity, he heard a celestial voice prophesying the healing of his wound and the redemption of his sins by a being full of purity and pity, a Guileless Fool, who should come to restore the Grail to its immaculate condition, and, having regained the profanated lance from the criminal hands of Klingsor, should bring it to the sanctuary, where one touch of it should heal the wound which it formerly inflicted on the prince who was forgetful of his mission.

This Guileless Fool, the hero, full of compassion for the sorrows of others, will be Parsifal, the predestined being whom the designs of Providence will bring by mysterious ways to Montsalvat, by starting him in pur-

suit of a sacred swan; having been present at the holy
sacrifice, and having witnessed the physical and moral
distress of Amfortas, he will feel his heart illumined with
celestial light, will understand the high and regenerative
task reserved for him, and will conceive such a holy
horror of sin as will preserve him from the infernal
snares which will be set for him also by Klingsor, aided
by his faithful follower and slave, Kundry, whom he
has made the servile agent of his criminal wishes.

This strange figure of Kundry, entirely a being of
Wagner's own creation, appears in turn as the devotedly
attached servant of the Grail when she is left to her
own nature, and as their bitter enemy, the instrument
of their undoing, when dominated in spite of herself by
the magic ascendency of Klingsor, she transforms herself into a woman of "terrible beauty" and becomes
the most irresistible means of seduction in the enchanted
gardens. The pious knights are ignorant of this double
nature and regard her only as a strange invalid and un-
tamable being, whose frequent and long absences, which
are preceded by a deep sleep, always correspond with a
fresh misfortune which overtakes them; but it is she
who has seduced and ruined Amfortas, and it is on her
that the sorcerer relies to undermine the virtue of the
Guileless Fool. The unfortunate woman revolts against
these terrible missions; and therefore she is melancholy
and in anguish every time she feels weighing upon her
eyelids the heavy hypnotic sleep into which Klingsor
plunges her when he wants to subject her to his hated
power. She thus expiates the crime of a former existence, when, as Herodias, she followed Christ on his
way to Golgotha with devilish and cruel laughter. This
savage laughter is again one of her characteristics in her
new incarnation when under the evil spell of the enchanter:

then, becoming his worthy servant, she equals him in wickedness. But when free from the sorcery, she aspires, as far as her savage and ignorant nature will allow, to goodness and to atone for the sins of the enchantress, of which she preserves a vague, half-conscious memory. This is why she so ardently seeks the balms which may heal Amfortas's wound, which she helped to inflict, desiring no thanks as a reward for her trouble, and it is also this aspiration for repentance and redemption, which finally, by the help of the divine grace triumphing over Klingsor's black magic and sorceries, will permit her regeneration in the holy water of baptism, poured on her head by Parsifal, who, by the accomplishment of his sacred mission, will have become priest and prince of the Grail in place of Amfortas.

These preliminary explanations are absolutely necessary for the comprehension of the brief analysis which follows.

ACT I.

FIRST TABLEAU. — The first scene takes place in a glade in the forest which surrounds the castle of Montsalvat. On the left, a road rises towards the castle on the height. At the back, on the right, the road suddenly dips to a lake, which is felt, rather than seen, in the background.

Day is just breaking. Gurnemanz, one of the oldest Knights of the Grail, and two young squires are sleeping under a tree. At the sound of trumpets, which are heard in the direction of the castle giving forth their solemn notes, Gurnemanz awakes and invites the youths, whom he awakes in turn, to join him in the morning prayer. They all three kneel down; then, when they have concluded their devotions, Gurnemanz orders his companions to occupy themselves with the bath in which

Amfortas is about to seek some alleviation of his suffering. He asks two knights who are approaching, coming down from the castle, how the prince is, and if the new remedy which has been applied to his wound has afforded him any relief. Upon their reply in the negative, the old knight, discouraged but not surprised, sadly lets his head sink in his breast. At this moment, one of the young squires signals the approach of a new character, whom he, as well as his companions, designate with such names as Devil's Mare and Wild Amazon, and there appears a woman of strange physiognomy, with swarthy complexion, piercing eyes, and a savage glance, wearing long, floating, black tresses, and clothed in strange garb; it is Kundry. She comes in hastily, looking exhausted by a long journey, and hands to Gurnemanz a crystal phial containing a balm which she has been to seek in the most remote regions of Arabia, to alleviate the pain of the unfortunate Amfortas; then, giving way to fatigue, she lies down on the ground to rest while the arrival of the train of knights and squires accompanying the king's litter calls away the attention of those present from her.

The unfortunate prince, ceaselessly tortured by his sufferings, implores Heaven for death or for the coming of the Fool, full of compassion, who is to bring his martyrdom to an end; he, however, accepts from Gurnemanz's hands the balm which Kundry has brought, and wishes to thank the strange creature for it; but the latter, in agitation and distress, takes little notice of the king's gratitude. Amfortas orders his attendants to carry his litter to the sacred lake, and the train departs, while the worthy knight sadly gazes after it.

The squires then attack Kundry with malicious speeches, calling her a sorceress, and reproaching her

with supplying the king with hurtful drugs; but Gurnemanz defends her and reminds them of what devotion,
on the contrary, she gives proof every time she has a
chance to render any service to the Knights of the Grail,
and in going, with lightning speed, to carry messages to
those whose duties keep them in distant countries.

For many years she has been known at Montsalvat, for
when Titurel consecrated the castle, he found her asleep
in the forest. There she is always discovered after her
long unexplained absences, which, however, fatally coincide with every fresh misfortune which falls upon the servants of the Grail. During the last one of these absences
occurred the unlucky combat which was so fatal to
Amfortas. Where was she wandering at that time, and
why did not she, who was usually so devoted, come to the
aid of the unfortunate prince ? Kundry remains silent
at this question, and Gurnemanz, again occupied with
his sorrowful thoughts, describes all the details of the
humiliating defeat to his youthful companions.

His hearers next ask him to tell them about the origin
of the Grail : he narrates it at great length, in the course
of which Kundry, still lying on the ground, manifests
violent agitation, and he ends by telling them of the
consolatory promise which came from on high and alone
sustains the courage of the greatly-tried prince.

Scarcely has he finished his story, when cries are heard
in the direction of the lake : they come from some
knights who have seen a wild swan, a visitant respected
in the district and loved by the king, which has just
been wounded by an unknown hand. The bird, beating its wings, falls expiring on the ground while some
squires, having discovered the murderer, bring him to
Gurnemanz, who questions him concerning his wanton
cruelty and sorrowfully reproaches him with it.

The criminal, Parsifal, is a youth who seems totally
unconscious of the act he has just committed.   He cannot tell his own name, nor in what country he was born;
he remembers only that his mother was named Herzeleide (Broken Heart), and that he lived with her in the
forests and barren plains.   These particulars, which he
so imperfectly gives, are supplemented by Kundry,
who has been attentively observing the young innocent:
he was born after the death of his father, Gamuret, who
was slain in a combat; and his mother, hoping to shield
him from the same fate, has brought him up far from
human beings and their broils.   Parsifal then remembers
that one day, having seen brilliantly armed men mounted
on noble animals pass by, he vainly sought to join them,
and then, that in his pursuit, having lost his way, he
was forced to defend himself against wild animals and
savage men ; but in his innocence he had no knowledge
of their evil intentions with regard to him.   Kundry
then tells him that in one of her chance wanderings she
met Herzeleide succumbing to' the grief which the
disappearance of her son caused her, and that she saw
her die.   Parsifal, losing all control of himself at this
news, springs upon Kundry and would strangle her but
for the intervention of Gurnemanz, who releases the
unfortunate woman.   The half-witted youth then seems
to regret his violence ; he trembles all over and is about
to fall into a fit, but Kundry has already hastened to a
neighbouring spring, and, bringing fresh water in a horn,
she tends and revives him.

Gurnemanz praises this charitable and forgiving act;
but the strange creature sadly repulses his approbation ; she
only asks to be allowed to rest from the great weariness
which she feels coming over her, and while the worthy
knight is busy with the youth, she drags herself towards a

neighbouring thicket to seek sleep there.   Suddenly the idea of this irresistible, agonizing sleep which always precedes the odious enchantment, revolts her; she struggles and tries to cast off its influence: but the mysterious power prevails over her resistance, and she falls inanimate behind the bushes, where she remains inert and invisible.

In the meantime, towards the lake, the knights and squires are seen accompanying Amfortas on his return to the castle after his bath.   Gurnemanz, supporting Parsifal's still tottering steps, prepares to lead him to the sacred castle, where he will have him present at the mystic repast of the servants of the Grail.   Who knows if this innocent, providentially guided along the inaccessible roads of Montsalvat, may not be that Guileless Fool, the elect, destined for the rehabilitation of the Grail?

The knight and Parsifal apparently walk on, but, in reality, the scenery behind them moves; and, after a long passage among the rocks, they pass through a door leading to vast subterranean galleries, which they seem to traverse, continually ascending.

Second Tableau. — The sound of bells and trumpets is heard constantly growing nearer; at last they find themselves in an immense hall surmounted by a luminous dome.   The sound of the bells seems to come from the top of this dome.   Parsifal appears to be fascinated by the grandeur of the sight which meets his eyes, and Gurnemanz attentively watches him, to gather from his manner the first signs of the desired revelation.

To right and left, at the back of the hall, two doors open, admitting two long files of knights who gravely and deliberately enter and range themselves around tables on which cups are set.   They are preparing to celebrate the spiritual love-feast as it was instituted by the Saviour.

After them comes the train of the king, lying on his litter and surrounded by ministering brothers and squires. Two pages, who precede him, carry, carefully veiled, a shrine which they set down on a raised altar near which is placed as a throne the couch on which Amfortas is lying. Behind this couch and on a lower level is a dark chapel, whence issues the grave voice of Titurel, telling the unfortunate prince to celebrate the sacred mysteries without delay. Amfortas, who knows what sufferings are inseparable from the sacred act for him, wishes to put it off; he begs his father to officiate in his place; but the old man, in whom there is scarcely a spark of life left, refuses, and summons his son to fulfil his duty without delay. Amfortas, in extreme agony, invokes the pity of all present, supplicates the Creator to put an end to his physical pain and his moral sufferings, which are a thousand times more intense; he undergoes all the tortures that the Saviour endured on the cross; like him, he sees all his blood welling from the wound which nothing can stanch, and his heart is corroded with shame and remorse on seeing himself — he who is so unworthy — inflexibly appointed to accomplish the divine sacrifice.

But he supplicates in vain: Titurel's voice is again heard, ordering the Grail to be uncovered. The pages unveil the shrine and take out the chalice, placing it before the officiating prince. Amfortas, bowing before the holy cup, is lost in ardent prayer; he celebrates the Eucharist, the mystic Supper of Montsalvat; the hall is filled with a thick cloud, and a ray of celestial light, falling from the dome, casts a glowing and purple light around the sacred chalice. Amfortas then, transfigured

by faith, elevates the Grail before all present, who are
piously kneeling.   Slowly the shadows vanish, the bril-
liancy of the chalice pales, and when the king has placed
it upon the table, and the daylight has returned little by
little, all the cups are seen full of wine, and a piece of
bread is at the side of each.   The knights take their
places around the table, while youthful voices are heard
extolling the praises of the Most High in a song of
thanksgiving.

Gurnemanz invites Parsifal to sit beside him; but the
latter, absorbed in ecstasy, does not understand his in-
vitation; since his arrival he has been standing motionless with his back to the spectators as though stupefied.

The knights, after having communicated in both kinds,
give each other the fraternal embrace.   Meanwhile,
Amfortas, who has somewhat recovered from his state
of ecstasy, shows by his actions the pain he is again
suffering from the wound from which the blood is gush-
ing.   All throng round him, his squires replace him on
his litter and the train is formed again, in the same order
as it arrived, around the king and the precious shrine.
Day is gradually fading, and the bells are again heard.

Parsifal, who, although motionless, during the service
had seemed to be himself experiencing the terrible sufferings of Amfortas, — like him, holding his hands to his
side in agony, — is still in that species of dream which
separates him from the rest of the world.   Gurnemanz,
taking no notice of what is passing in the youth's mind,
and disappointed in his attempt, takes him brusquely by
the arm and turns him out of the place, banishing him
with harsh words from the sacred dwelling, where he
thinks him unworthy to remain.

Act II.

First Tableau. — The stage represents the retreat of the magician Klingsor, situated in a roofless tower. Steps descend into the depths of the tower, and numerous instruments, used in the cabalistic art, magic mirrors, etc., are scattered about the hall, which is plunged in almost total darkness.

By means of his sorceries, Klingsor is drawing Parsifal in his direction, after Gurnemanz, who is imprudent and ignorant of what is passing in that simple soul, has cast him out of Montsalvat. The more clear-sighted magician, recognizing in the pure youth the elect who is to save and regenerate the Grail, is going to try to ruin him as he did Amfortas, and for this purpose he calls to his aid Kundry, whose renewed servitude he has prepared by casting her into her heavy magnetic sleep.

He sets himself to his incantations and burns herbs, whose thick smoke fills the stage. From these violet and baleful fumes emerges confusedly at the back of the hall the vague and apparently fluidic form of Kundry. Awaking from her lethargy, she answers him who has her in his spells with a cry of agony which ends in a long moaning. He begins to mock her for her attachment to the Knights of the Grail, to whom she returns immediately she is delivered from his magic power, and sneeringly reminds her of what priceless assistance she nevertheless rendered him when it was necessary to destroy the purity and virtue of Amfortas. The wretched woman, trying to recover her speech, struggles against these hateful memories and curses them with a harsh and broken voice. But the pitiless Klingsor continues by reminding her that for to-day he has reserved for her a still more brilliant victory, for she has to deal with a being protected from the weakness of the flesh by the rampart of innocence.   Kundry, in the wildest agony, vainly refuses to obey : the outcast reminds her that he is her master, the sole one who could never be affected by the magic power of her beauty.   Kundry, then giving vent to a burst of strident laughter, in her turn mocks at him for his forced chastity ; the sorcerer, enraged by this allusion, tells her that he is not to be insulted with impunity : how dearly have Titurel and his race had to pay for the contempt they showed him when he wanted to be enrolled in their pious body !

But here comes the young hero whom the sorcerer, mounted on the wall of the tower, sees from afar : no more resistance, she must prepare to conquer him. Kundry still struggles, but vainly : the transforming spell is beginning to operate, she is seized with the sinister laugh which suddenly changes to a cry of pain ; then she quickly disappears to go to perform her cursed mission and with her vanishes the violet light which enveloped her.   In the meantime, from his post of observation, Klingsor sees the lost troop of knights which he has captured from the Grail dash at Parsifal, who quickly overcomes them, and then the sorcerer disappears, as well as his tower, which sinks into the earth, leaving in its place enchanted gardens full of luxuriant vegetation, tropical plants, and fantastic flowers.   At the back rises a castle in the Oriental style, approached by several terraces.

SECOND TABLEAU. — Parsifal standing on the wall, which alone remains of the preceding scene, looks around him in astonishment.   Suddenly, from the castle and groves, issues a disordered group of Flower-Maidens, the young and lovely enchantresses created by Klingsor for the ruin of the Knights of the Grail, who run about bewailing the disastrous result of the combat between their companions and the young hero. At first they call down curses on Parsifal; but when they realize that he wishes them no harm, they try the effect of their charms upon him and seek to allure him, forgetting for his sake the gallants whom they have already brought into subjection and damnation.

They disappear in turn into the clumps of foliage to deck themselves with costumes which make them look like lovely blooming flowers, and, surrounding the youth, they dispute with one another for his possession, trying to gain him with bold and wanton behaviour; but all in vain, for he resolutely repulses and tries to escape them. Then a voice is heard from a neighbouring clump softly calling: " Parsifal ! " The innocent, suddenly remembering that his mother called him thus, stops in emotion, while the Flower-Maidens regretfully leave him in obedience to the unknown voice; and he slowly turns towards the clump, which has opened and reveals lying upon a bed of flowers a maiden of exquisite beauty, who smiles upon him and invites him to approach.

It is Kundry, who, transformed by the arts of the magician and now entirely subject to his domination, is about to carry out his iniquitous plans.

The more easily to gain the chaste youth, who is protected by his simplicity, she first arouses in him the sentiment of filial love, the sole affection which has ever touched his pure heart; she tells him of Herzeleide's tenderness for the feeble being to whom she gave birth in the solitude of the woods, her solicitude for him every moment of the day, her innumerable alarms, afterwards the despair caused her by the flight of the ungrateful child, and finally, her solitary and cruel death when she

had lost all hopes of ever seeing her beloved son again.
At these words, Parsifal is greatly distressed and vehemently reproaches himself for thus having forgotten the
gentlest of mothers; the enchantress then pretends to
wish to console him; she tenderly puts her arms round
him and tries to persuade him that love alone will cure
his remorse. The youth, in tears, does not think of
resisting, but when, becoming more pressing, she imprints
a long and burning kiss on his lips, he suddenly starts up
in unspeakable terror, and lays his hand on his heart,
where he seems to feel an intense pain. Suddenly he is
struck with the remembrance of Amfortas; he again sees
the cruel wound which nothing can heal, the shame, the
humiliation, the agony, and the remorse caused by his
irremediable transgression; he again sees the terrible
Eucharist which he was made to witness at Montsalvat;
he recalls the lamentations of the unfortunate man who
had failed in his divine mission; he even hears his cries
to that God of goodness and mercy whose sanctuary
has been sullied and betrayed, cries which echoed in the
deepest recesses of his heart and illumined him with a
mystic prescience. This terrible vision will preserve
him from the magic snares prepared for his ruin; and,
although the temptress with her infernal kisses has
kindled in his veins a fire which tortures and consumes
him, he violently repulses her as Amfortas should have
done when she displayed to him the fatal seductions of
her devilish beauty. In vain Kundry, now caught in
her own snare, beseeches him for some response to the
love which she feels burning within her, in vain she
seeks to excite his pity by telling him of the sufferings
she has endured since the insult she once offered to
the Saviour, pursuing him with her cruel and impious
laughter, and in vain she begs him to regenerate and

redeem her by sharing her passion : Parsifal does not allow himself to be overcome, a divine ray has filled his heart with light, and illuminated his way. If the sinner will follow him in the road of renunciation and sacrifice, he will purify her perverse spirit, he will wash away and efface her criminal past in the fountain of life and truth ; there alone is salvation for her, as for all those who have sinned ; but to merit this unhoped-for grace she must aid him whose ruin she has attempted by facilitating the accomplishment of his sacred mission, and she must help him to find again the mysterious and inaccessible ways which will lead him to Amfortas.

At the sound of this name, Kundry bursts out into her infernal and cursed laughter, and then, intoxicated with love and anger, she alternately threatens and entreats the hero, promising, if he will yield to her seductions, to guide him along the roads he desires, or, if he resists her, to give him cause to fear the same Lance which formerly overcame and wounded him whose defender he wishes to constitute himself.

She again proffers her caresses, but Parsifal repulses her with horror ; she falls back, uttering the most terrible imprecations, and cursing every effort he shall henceforth make to find Montsalvat again.

Klingsor, running at the sound of Kundry's cries, brandishes and casts with great force the sacred Lance with which he desires to wound Parsifal ; but the weapon remains miraculously suspended above the head of the hero, who grasps it and with it solemnly traces in the air a large sign of the cross. At this sign, the enchantments woven by Klingsor are suddenly broken ; the magic castle crumbles away, the gardens wither and become as arid as a desert, the Flower-Maidens lie on the ground like withered plants, and Parsifal, standing on the wall before departing, addresses Kundry, who is stretched on the earth exhausted with the struggle, and reminds her that he awaits her yonder at the radiant fountains of life, mercy, and pardon.

ACT III.

FIRST TABLEAU. — The third act brings us back to the sacred grounds of Montsalvat, but not on the same side as in the first act. The stage shows a spring landscape; at the back, a flower-enamelled meadow gently sloping upwards; to the right, the skirts of a wood with a spring in the foreground; on the left, a rock against which leans a poor hut inhabited by Gurnemanz. The good knight, who has now reached a great age, lives as a hermit in the forest, always bewailing the distressful days of the Grail which nothing comes to succour.

As the curtain rises it is scarcely broad daylight; but the hermit comes out of his dwelling, attracted by a plaintive moaning which issues from a thick copse. He approaches and discovers the inanimate body of Kundry, whose sleep seems to be troubled by dreadful dreams. How long has the unfortunate woman been among the brushwood? He draws her forward, lays her on the sward, and tries to reanimate her by a vigorous rubbing. At last she is partly restored, and, after looking around her in stupefaction, she gazes long at the hermit. She smooths away some of the disorder of her dress and hair; her appearance is the same, although less wild and savage than when she used to serve the knights. Her complexion is paler, and the expression of her eyes has somehow become gentler, and more submissive. She begins to busy herself as usual with domestic duties without speaking a word, to the great astonishment of the old man, who is surprised at receiving no thanks for his

solicitude. He speaks to her about it, and Kundry answers in a harsh and broken voice with the single word
" Service." But alas ! there is no longer any need for
her eager devotion, no more messages to carry to distant
places, the servants of the Grail stay in their own domain,
in mourning and gloom !

Kundry, who has evidently returned to her humble
office of servant to the knights, having found an empty
pitcher in the hut goes to the spring to fill it ; from there
she perceives through the forest a new arrival, whom she
points out to Gurnemanz.

A knight in black armour, with closed visor, issues
from the wood, walking with slow and hesitating step ;
it is Parsifal who has long been wandering in search of
the roads to the Grail, from which he has been excluded
by the malediction of the enchantress. He sits down on
a mound, exhausted, and only makes signs with his head
to the kind and friendly questions which the pious hermit
puts, without recognizing him. The old man asks him
to take off his armour, as it is not proper to wear it in
the sacred domain : he must not march here armed,
with closed visor, especially on this anniversary of the
Saviour's divine expiation for our sins. Parsifal, with
a gesture, makes him understand that he did not know
it was Good Friday, and then, rising, he strikes into the
ground the Lance he holds in his hand, he lays aside his
sword and buckler, as well as his casque, and, falling on
his knees, prays long and fervently. Gurnemanz, who,
as well as Kundry, has followed the movements of the
knight in astonishment, then recognizes him ; the sight
of him fills him with emotion ; Kundry is also agitated
at the presence of Parsifal, and turns away her head.

The pure hero, having ceased his meditations, rises,
and, at last, addressing the old knight, tells him the

happiness he feels at finding him again after so many efforts in this domain of the Grail which he has sought so long in vain : the terrible malediction which weighed upon him ceaselessly led him astray just when he thought to reach the goal, raising up innumerable foes, from whom he received many wounds, for he could not fight with the sacred Lance, regained at last by the divine aid, as he wished to bring it back intact and absolutely unsullied to the sanctuary where it shall henceforth shine with an immaculate splendour. Gurnemanz is intensely moved at the sight of the sacred weapon which he has so long desired again to see, and the return of which will change the sad fortunes of the Grail to a new era of glory and joyfulness.

He tells Parsifal of the great disasters of the noble and holy brotherhood, the constantly increasing sufferings of the unfortunate but cowardly king, who, in order to put an end to his tortures and call death to his aid more quickly, has resolved no longer to distribute to them the celestial nourishment, and leaves them to feed on gross food which no longer sustains their failing strength. Finally, the greatest misfortune of all, the old and noble Titurel, deprived in common with all the rest of the comforting and sacred vision of the Grail, has not been able to survive his misery, and has just died, the victim of the transgression of his own son.

On hearing of these misfortunes, Parsifal shows the most profound sorrow ; he accuses himself of all the evils which have fallen upon the Grail, and, overcome by grief, he almost falls into a faint. The hermit supports him and Kundry hastens to revive him with the water which she brings in a basin ; but the old man sends her away, and brings the knight to the sacred spring to bathe his limbs, which are weary with his long

journey and soiled by the dust of the wayside. His body
must be as pure as his soul, for, doubtless, this very day
he will be called to accomplish a great and solemn
mission.

While Gurnemanz takes off the hero's cuirass and
Kundry bathes his feet, in a faint voice he again expresses
the desire to be conducted to Amfortas without delay.
The old knight acquiesces : to-day he will lead him to
the sanctuary where Titurel's obsequies are to be held,
during which his unfortunate son, who is responsible for
the death of that great man, has promised once more to
uncover the Grail and to officiate, however great his
sufferings may be. But henceforth he must resign these
sacred duties, which he is no longer worthy to perform,
leaving them to him who has come victoriously through the
dangerous trials. To Parsifal must revert the titles and
rights of the prince and pontiff of the Grail. He feels
this as well as Gurnemanz ; and therefore he asks the
noble servant of God to pour upon his head the purifying water of baptism. While the old man sprinkles the
bowed head of the neophyte, Kundry, a new Magdalen,
piously kneeling before her lord, anoints his feet, which
she afterwards wipes with her own thick tresses, with
the precious perfume of a golden vial, which she has taken
from her bosom. Parsifal, taking this vial from her
hands, then asks Gurnemanz to complete the work of
sanctification and invest him with the double glory of
pontiff and king.

The old knight, whose whole life has been a long example of purity and austerity, is worthy to accomplish
this great act : he hails Parsifal as the elect of the Lord,
the Guileless Fool, whose compassion for the sufferings
of others has gained for him the power of performing
the heroic action which is going to restore to the Grail

its vigour and lost splendour. Then, pouring upon his head the contents of the golden vial, he creates him Prince and King of the Grail: he anoints him Priest, calling down upon him in solemn words the grace and benediction of the Most High.

Scarcely is he invested with these functions, when Parsifal, remembering that here is a sinner longing for pardon and anxiously awaiting the redemption of her soul, dips some of the water out of the spring with his hands, without being perceived, and pronounces above the head of the still kneeling Kundry, the words of redemption which will efface the sins of the accursed past. The poor creature, at last feeling herself under divine clemency and protection, bows herself to the earth, and gives free course to her emotion and her tears.

Then, raising his eyes to the brilliant landscape around him, Parsifal admires the beauty of the woods and meadows, their calm blossoming and the purity of the foliage of this blessed region, contrasting them with the flowers of evil which he once saw. But he is surprised at Nature's serenity on this anniversary of grief and mourning, when everything that lives and breathes should lament and despair. No, says Gurnemanz, on the contrary, Nature, fertilized by the tears and repentance of the sinner, rises revivified by this beneficent dew; all creatures, feeling the divine pardon hovering over them, break out in a hymn of gratitude to the divine Redeemer; man, purified by the sublime sacrifice, addresses a long song of love to his Saviour; joy and happiness animate all creation, and this is what is expressed by the flowers that bloom in the meadows when they show themselves so brilliantly on this blessed day; it is the Spell of Good Friday!

Kundry, coming out of her ecstasy, raises her eyes

full of tears in a calm and profound glance which seems to implore Parsifal's pardon. He gently kisses her on the brow and thinks of the companions of the sinner, who have not been able to shed tears of repentance and forgiveness. But bells are heard in the distance: it is Montsalvat calling together its servants for the funeral ceremony.

Gurnemanz respectfully clothes him whom he has just anointed King with the armour and the long mantle of the Knights of the Grail which he has fetched from his hut. He leads the way, followed by the elect, who solemnly bears the Lance, and by the humbly repentant Kundry. The country rolls by, as in the first act, but inversely, for now we are on the other slope of Mont-salvat: the forest disappears, and, after having passed the doors in the rock, the three travellers penetrate into the galleries, where are visible long lines of knights in mourning robes. The sound of the bells comes nearer, till at last they enter the great hall of the castle, which is denuded of its tables and has a gloomy appearance. The side doors open to admit the knights, who on one side escort the coffin of Titurel, and on the other accompany the litter of Amfortas, which is preceded by the veiled shrine of the Grail.

SECOND TABLEAU. — A catafalque occupies the centre of the stage, and behind it, under a dais, is the throne of Amfortas.

The two processions, singing an antiphonal chant, relate the lamentable death of the aged Titurel when deprived of the comforting sight of the sacred chalice, and announce the last celebration of the holy mysteries by the guilty prince whose sin has been the cause of all these great misfortunes. They place the coffin upon the catafalque, and Amfortas upon his couch, and call

upon him to fulfil his office once more. But he, in
terror, rising on his couch, and calling upon his father,
the valiant and pure hero, begs his forgiveness, prays
him to take pity on his eternal martyrdom, and not to
prolong his tortures by obliging him to look again on
the sacred cup, the sight of which will only bring an
added capacity for greater sufferings. He calls death to
his aid : that liberator, whose kindly shades he already
feels about him, is coming, and shall he make a new
compact with a life of endless agony ? No, no, nothing shall force him to live : let his knights complete the
work of destruction, let them plunge their swords into
the gaping wound, let them deliver the unhappy man
from his horrible torment, and of itself the Grail will
regain its brilliance and its untarnished splendour! In
a paroxysm of exaltation and agony, Amfortas tears his
robe and exposes his frightful wound; all start back in
affright. Parsifal, who, accompanied by Gurnemanz
and Kundry, has come in without being noticed, advances, brandishing the sacred Lance, and with it
touches the side of the unfortunate man; Amfortas,
feeling his pain eased and understanding that his prayers
have at last been answered, is overcome with religious
emotion; he totters and falls into Gurnemanz's arms.
Parsifal then pronounces words of benediction and peace
over him and presents to the astonished and delighted
servants of the Grail, the sacred Lance, which has at
last been reconquered by him, the Guileless Fool, whom
the Most High, in his compassion for human suffering,
has endowed with the necessary power to accomplish
this act of heroism and redemption. Then, declaring
himself henceforth the servant and pontiff of the Grail,
he orders the shrine to be unveiled, and, taking out the
holy cup, he prostrates himself before the sacred relic

and fervently adores it.   In his turn he celebrates the Eucharist.   The chalice glows and illumines the whole assembly with its radiance.   Titurel, momentarily reviving, rises and blesses all present, while a white dove descends from the dome and hovers above the elect, who takes the Grail and with it makes a large and solemn sign of the cross above the adoring crowd.   Kundry falls at the feet of Parsifal, before whom Amfortas and Gurnemanz bow in silent admiration, whilst the assembly of knights, pages, and squires, who are stationed throughout the building to the top of the dome, from every part of the church with subdued voice sing a great psalm of love and thanksgiving.

CHAPTER IV

ANALYSIS OF THE MUSIC

> " The musician reveals to us the hid-
> den spirit of the world, he makes
> himself the interpreter of the pro-
> foundest wisdom, whilst speaking a
> language which reason does not un-
> derstand." — SCHOPENHAUER.

THIS chapter is the complement of the preceding
and was originally intended to form a part of it.
Just as in studying the poems it was impossible for me
entirely to avoid speaking of the music, so also it will
happen here that I shall sometimes be compelled to refer
to the dramatic action in order to show more clearly the
exact force of the musical action. This is of little importance if only it makes it clearer.

And first I would remind the reader that the special
mission of music, as conceived by Wagner, is to place
the spectator in direct communication with the very
spirit of the characters, to reveal their most secret
thoughts, and to render them transparent, so to speak,
to their hearers, who will thus often come to know them
better than they know themselves.

The music, then, may often contradict the words, but
not the action ; if, for example, we are in the presence
of a shrewd, false, or subtle person, it reveals his deceit
and permits us to grasp the real motive of his actions,
unknown to himself.

Let us add that, by an inevitable stage convention, the actors are supposed not to hear the perpetual orchestral commentary.

Now let us enter the musical domain and examine separately each of its constituent elements.

It is advisable first to study the WAGNERIAN MELODY, and to form a clear idea of what it consists.

The poverty of the French language is such that this word *melody*, infallibly causes us to think of melody of Italian origin, the *cantilena*, based on the regular rhythmical return of musical phrases, the sentiment of the key, and the invariable close with a perfect cadence, as has been practised not only in Italy, but also in France, from Monsigny to Félicien David, and in Germany also by Mozart and Haydn.

Now this rhythmical and purely tonal form, which, moreover, is perfectly logical, is neither unknown to nor scorned by Wagner, since he often uses it, notably in the Romance of the Evening Star and the March in *Tannhäuser*, in the Chorus of Spinners in the *Flying Dutchman*, in the Nuptial March, religious March, and Bridal Chorus in *Lohengrin*, in the Prize Song and *motiv* of *The Crown* in *Meistersinger*, and on many other occasions down to his very last works.

But this is only one conception of melody, and it is necessary to give a wider interpretation to the word in order to understand how it is viewed by Wagner, who has declared that, according to his idea, " in music all is melody."

Pure melody, melody in its essence, the sole kind to which this name should really be applied, is that which is complete in itself and does not need any harmonic co-operation ; in scientific musical language this is called,

rather, *homophony*. The word matters little; *homophony*
and *melopœia* are purely melodic forms. The Hymns of
the early Christians, as we see from the Catholic Plain-
Song given without accompaniment, that is to say in its
native purity, were also of a purely melodic character;
in these, however, we do not find any trace of symmetrical phrases, and the sentiment of the key was understood quite differently than at the present day. It is the
same with Oriental music even now, and with many
popular airs of all countries which have been created
without accompaniments, and to which none could be
adapted without destroying their character more or less.
The Lutheran Chorale, of more recent creation, possesses
both the polyphonic form and modern tonality, but all
idea of regular rhythm is absent from it; the pointing
alone is indicated by cadences followed by holds; no
one, however, would think of denying that this chant
constitutes a true melody. In the time of Palestrina
the air was placed most frequently in the lowest part of
the harmony, the bass. There was a time when the
cantus firmus was given to the tenor (*discantus*); to-day
we are accustomed to place it in the highest part.
There have thus been various acceptations of the same
term.

It must not be forgotten that, etymologically, *melody*
comes from the Greek *melos* (which signifies *number*,
rhythm, *verse*, *phrase*), and *ode* (*song*, *ode*); that is to say,
properly speaking, the song of a phrase or verse. By
the word *melos* the ancients understood also the sweetness of the articulate voice, words sung, and the music
of speech.

This being settled, in order thoroughly to establish
that *melody* may be understood in different ways, it is important to know that the Wagnerian melody is not sub-

ject to the laws of regular symmetrical construction, nor forced to move within the limits of one tonality, nor yet to end with a perfect cadence. Wagner's melody is free and infinite in the sense of not being finished, that is to say, never ending and always linking itself to another melody, thus admitting of all possible modulations. It is, if you prefer, an uninterrupted sequence of melodic contours, of broken bits of melody having more or less of a vocal character. The example of such interrupted melodies is given by Beethoven in his symphonic development, where it is not at all striking; but it was left for Wagner to transport the symphony to the stage, and make of it the living commentary on the action and the powerful auxiliary to the words.

Most frequently, then, this continuous melody devolves upon the orchestra, leaving the singer every liberty in his musical declamation, to the great advantage of the diction. These two points, the absolute sincerity of dramatic accent and its intimate union in every case with the symphonic tissue, may be considered as characteristic of the Wagnerian style in its highest development.

In that species of entertainment which has been much in vogue in France for several years, and which is called musical recitation, an honourable derivation from the ancient melodrama, we see an elocutionist, tragedian or comedian, reciting verses, the sentiment of which the orchestra, or sometimes, alas! the piano, endeavours to intensify.

This combination, although hybrid, may attain a considerable power;[1] but how difficult must be the execution, and also how complicated for the listener if he wants to be equally interested in the music and in the

[1] Meyerbeer, one of the first to employ it, has given an example in one of the last scenes in *Struensee*.

poetry recited! The musician and the declaimer, having nothing in common, either time or intonation, have no means of establishing perfect relations with each other, nor of keeping strictly together; they have to be content with a compromise.

If for declamation, properly so-called, lyrical declamation is substituted, if the verses are scanned and the intonation regulated according to musical notation, whilst leaving to the orchestra its own rôle both melodic and symphonic, then one part of the Wagnerian method will have been realized, that is the intimate union of the sung words with the orchestral web, both converging to the same end, forcible and clear dramatic accent, and both preserving their most energetic means of expression side by side with their own liberty of action.

But another element enters into the composition of the endless melodic tissue as Wagner understands it. This is the LEIT-MOTIV.[1] — To describe its nature I will make use of a comparison. When we read a novel in which the characters or localities are vigorously drawn, as in Walter Scott, Victor Hugo, George Sand, Balzac, or Zola, these characters or localities, although often purely fanciful and creations of the novelist's imagination, are engraved in our mind in a certain form, silhouette, or perspective, which is henceforth unchangeable. When, ten years later, we again read the same novel, these same images and no others will be outlined in our thoughts with the same attitudes, the same features, and the same details as when we first read of them, so strongly and vividly that we seem to be renewing old acquaintances, or to be travelling in a country we have already visited; but if, on the second reading, we have

[1] Type-*motiv*, leading-*motiv*.

an illustrated edition, no matter how talented the artist, we are often shocked at not recognizing our old friends, or at not seeing our ideal landscape drawn as we had imagined it.

When, therefore, we are greatly struck by the description of any character, we instinctively give it an *image* which remains proper to it (whilst being at the same time personal to ourselves), — it assumes a fixed and definite form. Our mind cannot afterwards picture it otherwise; the mere thought of the personage calls up his *image*, and, inversely, if the *image* first presents itself to our memory it brings back the personage with all the details of his character as we first learnt to know him.

The name of the hero himself is indissolubly connected with the *type* under which we have represented him to ourselves.

It is the same with any described locality, or an interior, or any stirring action, a murder, a tourney, a scene of torture, or a supernatural apparition. We first picture it to ourselves under the influence of the writer, and it thus remains definitely fixed in our mind.

This impression is not effaced with time; it may be modified in certain details by reflection, or by extended knowledge, as by reading other works in which the same characters, or the same facts are presented under another aspect, or in a fresh light; but the main outlines endure.

Every one has experienced this.

Now let it be admitted, which is not difficult, that Wagner *thought in music*, that is to say, that every objective, or subjective idea with him assumed a musical form, a melodic contour, which thenceforth clung to it, and I think the best elementary notion of what a *Leit-motiv* is will be gained.

It is, so to speak, the musical embodiment of an idea, and Wagner is neither the first nor the only one who has thus thought in music and given to a character, a fact, or a particular impression, a form which is clearly recognizable and perceptible to the hearing.

Musical language, notwithstanding its lack of precision, or perhaps for that very reason, constitutes the highest, purest, and most sincere expression of human thought, the one furthest removed from materialism and conventionalism. Whoever comes to think in music as he would think in the language he is accustomed to use, thereby finds the horizon of his ideas strangely widens. This faculty in its full power is reserved for the elect, but there is not a single true musician who has not felt something of it.

This is the origin of the *Leit-motiv*. Embryonic traces of *type-motive* may be already gathered in Gluck, Mozart, and Beethoven; [1] they become more frequent in Weber, and still more marked in Meyerbeer and Berlioz, the latter, Wagner's contemporaries. It may be said that the faculty of giving to an intellectual conception, or a state of mind, a musical contour which becomes its quasi-hieroglyphic representation, has existed in a latent state with all composers at all times; but no one had thought of raising it to a principle and making it one of the fundamental features of a system. It was an isolated, though expressive, fact, and it escaped the attention of the superficial hearer.

Wagner himself, in his first works, to *Rienzi*, does not

[1] In his purely symphonic works, Beethoven had no reason to attach the idea of a character to a *motiv*, but most certainly every *motiv* he selected for working out is associated with some philosophical thought which stands prominently out and thus becomes in the symphony the absolute equivalent of what the *Leit-motiv* is in the musical drama.

seem to pay much attention to it.   It is in *Der Fliegende Holländer* that we find his first and extremely modest application of it; three characteristic forms are found united in Senta's Ballade, as well as in the overture : a call, a figure of accompaniment, and a purely melodic contour are the subjects of frequent recurrence.   In *Tannhäuser* we already find five *type-motive*, clearly characterized, and nine at least in *Lohengrin;* but their employment is intermittent and episodical, being limited to certain important scenes to which they are intended forcibly to call attention; if they do not yet constitute the essential part of the symphonic development, they are, however, already employed with greater insistence and sagacity than ever before.

It was from this moment that Wagner began to understand the extraordinary power of this new machinery, and in all the following works which constitute his last manner, in *Tristan*, in *Die Meistersinger*, in the Tetralogy, and in *Parsifal*, we see it henceforth systematically used with conscious purpose and reason.

The Wagnerian *Leit-motiv* is always short, simple. and easy to recognize and remember.   It is almost always presented for the first time in its entirety with the words determining the meaning attached to it, or at a moment when the scenic action does not permit any misunderstanding as to its signification.   Afterwards it may be represented with infinite modifications, either in rhythm, or the details of its melodic contour, or in its harmonization, or instrumentation, broken into fragments, changed in character, ennobled or made ridiculous by *augmentation*, *diminution*, or *inversion*,[1] it is always recognizable, and creates in even a passive listener a state of mind similar to that which accompanied its first appearance.

[1] Contrapuntal methods.

Therein lies its power; with a few notes it calls up a whole throng of ideas and without any more effort on the part of the listener than in having a well-known image passed before his eyes. It is a musical portrait, though often purely imaginary, or one that we are willing to accept.

In fact, the *Leit-motive* that have an imitative and descriptive character are in the minority; I will, however, cite a few of those which are really musical *onomatopœia*; Kundry's nervous laughter, the gallop of the horses in *The Ride of the Walkyries*, the roarings of the Dragon, the noise of the Forge, and, perhaps above all, the undulation of the waves at the beginning of *Das Rheingold*; these are addressed directly to the ear. They are sound-images.

Others, by their very character, strongly call to mind the idea of the object they are intended to represent: Walhalla is majestic and solemn; the Sword gleams; the Flames crackle; the *motiv of the Eucharist* in *Parsifal* spreads out like an immense sign of the Cross, etc. Here again it is difficult to be mistaken. Others equally typical might be quoted, notably in *Die Meistersinger*.

But this is not an indispensable character of the *Leit-motiv*, whose form, on the contrary, is, in the majority of cases, much more arbitrary and unrestrained. This doubtless accounts for the notable divergences in the names which various commentators give to the same theme; to cite only one example, there is a *motiv* in *Tristan* which is considered by one as representing Vengeance, by another, the Hero, and by a third, Fate. To tell the truth, this is not a matter of supreme importance; it is not a name that must be associated with a *Leit-motiv*, it is an idea, or still better, an assemblage of ideas, a philosophical conception: the name is only a convenience; however, in the following pages I will endeavour to call every *motiv* by the name under which it is most generally known, in order to avoid criticism.

Most frequently the *Leit-motiv* consists of a melodic figure of several notes which may be modified even in its structure, in its rhythm, in its harmony, or in its orchestration; these various transformations never deprive it of its first signification, but vary either its importance or expression for the moment; it will thus pass in turn through phases of tenderness, heroism, sadness, or joy, without ever severing its connection with its own original object; it possesses an exquisite sensibility, for example, when it has to depict the character of Walter in his knightly pride, and then sad, anxious, or, again, caricatured by his rival; it acquires a touching eloquence when it has to describe Walhalla destroyed, or in ruins, after having made us acquainted with it in its splendour; it is sometimes witty to excess; when, in *Die Walküre*, the virtuous Fricka is indignant about the incestuous love of Siegmund and Sieglinde, the indulgent orchestra excuses them, murmuring: "It is Spring-time," before Wotan has even opened his lips to reply.

In other and rarer cases, the *Leit-motiv* assumes an invariable harmonic form; then the rhythmic structure and instrumental combinations alone may be changed; I will give as examples the Harmony of the Wanderer; the Harmony of the Casque (Tarnhelm); the Harmony of Eternal Sleep in the Tetralogy; the Harmony of the Swan in *Lohengrin* and *Parsifal*; and the Harmony of the Dream in *Die Meistersinger*.

More rarely the characteristic of the motif is its persistent rhythm, as in the motif of the Forge in *Siegfried*, and again in *The Ride of the Walkyries*.

To whichever of these categories (melodic, harmonic, or rhythmic) they belong, the *Leit-motive* always present themselves to the listener without exacting any efforts of attention or research on his part; Wagner constantly places them in relief, in some way or other accentuates them, or repeats them if it is necessary, and they cannot pass by unperceived except in cases where they are of no importance. It is, then, a mistake to torture your mind by searching for them; they will come to you of themselves, even if you know ever so little about their composition, as soon as you become interested in the dramatic action. They are veritable guides, valuable conductors who explain and comment upon the situations, not allowing you to go astray in erroneous suppositions, and elucidating the *scenario* like the explanation that accompanies a plan.

Several forms of typical *motive* seemed especially to haunt Wagner and return to his mind on various occasions: such as the two chords by which he represents the Swan in *Lohengrin* as well as in *Parsifal*. And what could be more natural? Is it not always the Swan of the Grail? Before leaving the above works, we must observe that the final notes of the first entry of the trombones in the Prelude of *Lohengrin* shadow forth the *motiv* of the Lance in *Parsifal;* this again is easily explained, for the Prelude of *Lohengrin* speaks of nothing but the mysteries of Montsalvat. More involuntary, perhaps, and yet perfectly justifiable, is the likeness of a group of chords frequently repeated in the *entr'acte* of the third act of *Tannhäuser* (which are found again in Tannhäuser's recital on his return from Rome) to the theme of Faith in *Parsifal*. We may quote other analogies: between two fragments, one belonging to the Romance of the Evening Star, the other to the great

Duet between Tristan and Isolde; also between a phrase which is found in the orchestra in *Die Meistersinger* forty-four bars after the beginning of the Choral of Jordan (Act III. Scene I.), and another beautiful phrase sung by Fricka at the ninety-seventh bar in the second scene of *Das Rheingold*; here the resemblance is more harmonic than melodic; they have only a family likeness; but again in *Die Meistersinger*, twenty-one bars before the Memories of Youth (Act III. Scene II.), Walter's melodic contour reproduces exactly that of the austere goddess of marriage; now precisely at this moment, he is speaking of conjugal love; we must not regard this as a chance effect; and between Wotan's Anger and Brangäne's Hesitation. Finally, on two occasions, Wagner musically quotes himself with an admirable appropriateness: the first in intercalating two *motive* from *Tristan* (*Desire* and *Consternation*) into the third act of *Die Meistersinger* a little before the celebrated Quintet of Baptism; the second in introducing some bars from *Tannhäuser* into *Parsifal*.[1]

One rather remarkable thing is that certain of these *motive* have a marked predilection for a particular key; the Walhalla *motiv* affects keys abounding in flats; the Sword appears most often in C major; the Fire much prefers sharps; the Walkyrie sleeps in E major, etc.

Although the use of typical *motive* is not constant and exclusive, which would cause too much tension,

[1] One of the most curious resemblances may be traced between the end of the Overture to *Der Fliegende Holländer* (the first fifteen bars in $\frac{6}{4}$) and the opening of *Das Rheingold* by Woglinde's entrance. It is exactly the same harmonic method, and almost the same melodic contour.

(Although *Der Fliegende Holländer* is not included in this study, which is limited to the works which form the Bayreuth repertoire, I have thought it interesting to note this reminiscence after an interval of eleven years.)

we must recognize in them the most important materials
of the Wagnerian Symphony, from the point of view of
melody as well as harmony.

Wagner never demanded extraordinary voices. He
did not write with a view to giving such or such a singer
the opportunity to sing a note which he alone could
reach, or to make a parade of his virtuosity. He wrote
simply for soprano, contralto, tenor, or bass, mezzo-
soprano, or barytone, not demanding from any one more
than he could normally produce ; keeping each voice in
the *tessitura* which suits it, but utterly doing away with
florid ornaments, roulades, and trills, which the Italian
school considered the embellishment of vocal style, and
from which neither the German nor the French school
was entirely free in his day.

He writes above all and before all for musicians, for
people who know how to sing true and in exact time;
there is no question here of holding and dying away on
a high note ; and the orchestral conductor is not there to
follow the singer; for the very form of his melody, as
we have just described, which constantly passes from the
stage to the orchestra and from the orchestra to the
stage (remaining much the longest in the orchestra), demands a symphonic interpretation. It cannot be otherwise, and that is the secret of his power; it is instrumental and a commentary on the verse or on the action,
and this is where it differs from the Italian and French
melody which is based on symmetrical rhythmical construction and the brilliant effect of the vocal technique.

Melodic ornaments are rare in Wagner; the *gruppetto*
seems reserved for the expression of amorous or passionate
sentiments, or, at least, it conveys the idea of supreme
elegance.

But what is far from rare is the episodical employment of the most frankly Italian melodic forms. See the Love Song in *Tristan* (p. 298); Flosshilde's phrase in D-flat in the first tableau of *Das Rheingold*; then at Scene II., the second part of Fricka's phrase (already cited on p. 246), immediately taken up by Wotan a tone lower, and which has received the name of *Love's Fascination* (p. 353). It is necessary, moreover, to remember that Wagner was a great admirer, at least at one time, of the elegance and suppleness of Bellini's vocal phrases. "With Bellini that song so simply noble and beautiful which charmed us was pure melody; to believe and maintain that is certainly no sin; perhaps it is no more a sin than it is to pray to Heaven before lying down that the idea of such melodies and such a method of treating song may come to the German composers." (RICHARD WAGNER, *Bellini*.)

However momentary it may have been, this impression existed, and a trace of it has always remained. Wagner, then, was an eclectic; in every school he was able to discern what was really beautiful, and truly with Bellini it was not harmony.

Wagner's SYSTEM OF HARMONY greatly resembles that of J. S. Bach and Beethoven in his third period; that is to say, he pays more attention to the rules of counterpoint than to harmony properly so-called. Not that he ignored the latter, but the necessity of frequently combining the *Leit-motive* with each other simultaneously, forced him to give most weight to the independent progress of the parts, as is allowable in the fugal style; it was the only way to play freely with these *Leit-motive*, to make them appear sometimes in one part, sometimes in another, constantly varying their form, to make them

cross, interlace, overlap, and run after one another, exactly
as the subject and its counter-subjects do in a fugue.

It would force us to enter into considerations far too
technical, to analyze here the harmonic structure of
Wagner's works. Let us simply say that those who
think they perceive errors in certain passages are absolutely mistaken; if certain combinations of chords are
irregular according to the strict rules of harmony, they
appear irrefutably logical when they are considered from
the highest view of counterpoint, a considerably enlarged
and dramatized counterpoint, untrammelled, and enriched
with the boldness of modern harmony, together with the
very frequent employment of the chord of the augmented
fifth and its inversions (which is already found in Schumann), with an extraordinary wealth of pedal-points,
often disguised, and a very evident contempt of conventional restrictions.

Altogether, it is incontestable that this system is not
simple, but its complications are always ingenious and
appropriate to the circumstances. Besides, these complications are not continual; it is sufficient to cite the
Walhalla-motiv (*Das Rheingold*, at the beginning of Scene
II.), which is entirely constructed of perfect chords;
other examples are not rare, but nevertheless they are
exceptional.

The management of modulations, from a purely musical point of view, does not seem of much importance to
Wagner, and in this he parts company with Beethoven
and Bach; his choice of key is guided solely by the
dramatic interest and by considerations of the province
of the orchestra; the action once begun, the modulation
is perpetual, and, in many places, the most ingenious person would find it impossible to name the key at any
given moment; the result is an impression of life and

struggle of inconceivable power.   On the other hand,
at the beginning of the acts, we find him attaching an
extraordinary importance to the establishment of the
first tonality, an importance to which I shall have occasion to return.

Perfect cadence is extremely rare; this is the inevitable
consequence of the system of continuous melody; in
fact, the sense of perfect cadence is conclusion, completion; now, all Wagner's phrases being linked to each
other without constantly coming to an end, the cadence
must be reserved almost exclusively for the ends of the
acts, or sometimes of the scenes, where rest is obliga-
tory; they are indeed met with here and there in the
course of the music, but then they are attenuated, dis-
simulated, and unimportant; they are only to be found
clearly characterized, and well and prominently brought
forward, in the great finales.   No composer has so spar-
ingly employed the perfect cadence; there is, however,
one case in which he has made a very characteristic use
of it, and one which is so much the more striking because it seems to be reserved for this situation; it is
when the words assert the specially loyal and chivalrous
side of a hero's character; the following page (251)
shows three remarkable examples, taken from different
works, of this beautiful and noble form, of a solemn and
heraldic character, which is very frequent with Wagner
in this special case and which may be called the formula
of loyalty, and is only found in moments of great emotion, in the announcement of death (*Walküre*) and in the
Funeral March of Siegfried (*Die Götterdämmerung*).

Generally speaking, consonant chords are much less
frequent than dissonant chords, and, moreover, they
rarely appear in their native purity, but almost always
modified by the artifices of composition, by retards,

(LOHENGRIN — Last Scene)

LOHENGRIN

Sein Rit - ter ich bin Lohengrin ge-nannt
His Knight am I, and Lohengrin my name

(DIE WALKÜRE—Act II. Scene IV.

BRÜNNHILDE

-fängt dich hold mit hoch - -hei-ligem Gruss.
hold thee long with high greeting and love

(GOTTERDÄMMERUNG—Last Scene.)

BRÜNNHILDE

mein se - - li. ger Held
my bless- ed he -ro

appoggiaturas, and alterations, more especially many alterations, which deprive them to a great extent of their reposeful character. All that is intentional and logical. It is certain that the dissonant chord with its notes of contracted progression, and its various resolutions, is infinitely more vital and full of passion than the perfect chord, which Wagner reserves for the expression of calm and placid feelings, which are more rare in the drama.

As for the difficulties which sometimes astonish the reader of the pianoforte score, they are considerably lessened by the selection of the instruments and the variety of the timbres. They are more apparent than real; they disappear in the symphonic rendering, and at Bayreuth they are not in the least noticeable; the whole combination is admirably blended with an incomparable softness, harmoniousness, and fulness, except in rare cases, which are intended for picturesque effect.

The attention of the listener is attracted by the individual movement of the parts, by their expressive character, by the interest which they gain from the suggestive appearance of the *Leit-motive*, and by the diversity of the tones of the instruments, much more strongly than by the individuality of the chords considered by themselves. Each symphonic voice sings an independent part, having its individual meaning, replying to the others, and always appropriate to the nature and tone of the interpreting instrument, without any traces of the idiotic set forms of ordinary accompaniment, and without padding of any kind.

Formerly people said that in Wagner there was no melody; I think I am more in the right in saying that there are no accompaniments, but only melodies laid one upon the other.

For the sake of completeness let us further note the total absence of *harmonic progressions*, which almost all schools have now abandoned on account of their absurdity ; the suppression of repetitions, or of the *reprises* of a principal *motiv* announced by a *rentrée*, exactly as we notice the suppression of all repetition of verses or words ; always and everywhere something new, invention, things unexpected and ingenious, always creation, sincerity, and life, and I think we shall have touched upon the principal characteristics of what is called, a trifle too briefly, *the Wagnerian formula*, a formula which cannot be too much admired and examined, but which our composers will do well not to imitate, and this for two reasons.

The first, quite sufficient in itself, is that it is impossible : " *To continue it in the true sense of the word, a man of the same breadth and calibre is required ; and if this man exists, he will not consent to play the rôle of an imitator : he himself will wish to invent something new.*" [1]

The second is that it is necessary to belong to his country and to speak his language. Now, just as Wagner deplored the tendency of German musicians to imitate French art in the following words : " *I have recognized in the French an admirable art of giving precise and elegant forms to life and thought ; I have said, on the contrary, that the Germans when they try to attain this perfection of form seem to me to be heavy and weak,*" [2] so I say to the French, in their turn, that they must guard against that false kind of admiration which leads to plagiarism ; they must keep intact the qualities proper to our national style, which always have been and always will be, in literature as in music, clearness, elegance, and sincerity of expression.

[1] *La Musique et les Musiciens*, p. 494.
[2] R. WAGNER, *Lettre à M. Monod* (October 25, 1876).

If Wagner were here to advise them, that is certainly
what his own logic would lead him to say.

Wagner's ORCHESTRATION is richer and fuller of
colour than Beethoven's.   That certainly is largely the
result of the new instruments which he has introduced,
the cor-anglais, the bass-clarinet, the contra-bassoon,
trombones,[1] the family of tubas, and the bass trumpet;[2]
partly also it is the result of the way in which he has
completed the group of wood-wind instruments, in writing three parts to the flute, three to the oboes, and three
to the clarinets, etc. (instead of two, which were generally used up to his time, except by Meyerbeer and
Berlioz), by which he is enabled to obtain a complete
chord in the same *timbre*[3]; partly, too, he owes it to
the frequent subdivision of the stringed-instruments;
but particularly and above all to his profound knowledge
of instrumentation and to his unparalleled ingenuity,
which has led him on to prodigious discoveries.

Wagner treats every instrument with the same certainty of touch as if he had played it himself; he knows,
as no one else knows, how to avail himself of its
resources, and he demands nothing of it beyond what
is entirely within their capacity.   He is often difficult to
play, but it is never an ungrateful task, for he is never
awkward nor clumsy.

Notwithstanding the large number of performers he
requires, we never see him have recourse to complicated
methods in his orchestration; the combinations are
always clear and simple, the result of which is a sonor-

[1] Beethoven had already used the contra-bassoon and the trombones, but only in exceptional cases.

[2] The bass-trumpet only figures in the Tetralogy.

[3] Organ-tone.

ity which is at once plain and powerful. The *Leit-motive* ceaselessly move about the whole orchestra, passing from one desk to another; but, nevertheless, each one has a predilection for one instrument, or one group, which harmonizes with its character, on which it was first heard, and to which it returns to take up its abode every time it must make itself heard with preponderating importance; sometimes we recognize it from its very first note by means of this characteristic *timbre*.

I think we now clearly see how, in Wagner's musical style, everything combines, — melody, harmony, and orchestration, in accentuating and determining the dramatic action : the melody, melopœia, or measured recitative, by its fine diction and the constant care given to the excellence of its prosody; the harmony, by its bold methods and the employment of *Leit-motive*; and the orchestration, by its unparalleled richness of colour.

Before commencing to analyze each work separately, I would call the reader's attention to the purely symphonic part which constitutes the PRELUDES, to which Wagner has attached a special interest and a psychological character, of which, alas! people at the opera are entirely unconscious; for if they were aware of his intention, they probably would not take advantage of this moment to talk more loudly than usual, to blow their noses, and to slam the doors, etc., — they would do all that beforehand as at Bayreuth.

Up to and including *Tannhäuser*, Wagner followed the usual custom of writing *Overtures* to his operas.

Beginning with *Lohengrin*, we find *Preludes*, and every act has its own.[1]

---

[1] There is one single exception, the Overture to *Die Meistersinger*; but *Die Meistersinger* is itself an exception in Wagner's work.

In the Preludes, Wagner the philosopher addresses himself directly to the soul by means of music; he puts it through a kind of preparatory course and gets us into the state of mind he desires, and this without ever making these instrumental pieces of excessive length.

The essential aim of a Prelude, its *raison d'être*, is to prepare the spectator's mind and bring it into that state which the author considers most favourable for the reception in all its fulness of the impression to be produced by the coming act. This end may be attained in at least four different ways:

1. By simply calming the mind, that is to say, by freeing it from all exterior preoccupations, and endowing it with perfect repose, so that it may become malleable and easily affected by the slightest emotion;

2. By recalling to the spectator's mind the action that has gone before and which he may have lost sight of during the *entr'acte*, the recollection of which is necessary for the perfect comprehension of what follows;

3. Inversely, by drawing in advance on the coming act, so as to prepare the listener for the events which are about to take place, — in this case the action to some extent begins during the Prelude;

4. By filling the mind with a vague sense of mystery, by exciting the curiosity and captivating the attention with undecided harmonies, strange tones, and unexpected and even incoherent modulations, which give no hint of what is coming next, — this is the most affecting way, the one which best prepares the heart for poignant emotions.

Wagner uses all these forms according to circumstances; without multiplying examples, I will give one of each class, leaving to the reader the task of completing them:

First form : calm — *Das Rheingold.*

Second form : recalling *motive* — third act of *Siegfried.*

Third form : announcement of *motive* — second act of *Lohengrin.*

Fourth form : vagueness — third act of *Parsifal.*
The third form, however, and next to that the second, are by far the most frequent.

One very interesting point is the extraordinary insistence with which Wagner establishes the tonality at the beginning of many of his Preludes ; we should vainly seek analogous examples in any other composer ; it is particularly in the Tetralogy, which is of gigantic proportions throughout, that this system is found in the most striking manner.

In *Das Rheingold* the first 136 bars are built upon one single perfect chord in E-flat major ; the Prelude of the second scene for 15 bars only contains perfect chords of the fundamental tone belonging to the key of D-flat, or related keys and leading into the key of the dominant ; the second scene is linked to the third by means of a pedal of the dominant on F, first in the bass, then in the treble, which is kept up for 55 bars.

In the first act of *Die Walküre* the tonality is established by the treble pedal of the tonic, which lasts for 64 bars, after which it is still long before we leave the key of D. In the third act the predominance of the key of B-minor, contrasted with the dominant F-sharp, is accented and maintained for 34 bars till the rising of the curtain.

In the first act of *Siegfried* there is a long bass pedal of the dominant on the note F for 50 bars, which becomes a treble pedal for 33 bars more, and which is succeeded by a pedal of the tonic of 12 bars on B-flat. That is Wagner's way of thoroughly establishing the tonality.

In the third act of *Götterdämmerung* it is still more strongly marked, for the key of F is not departed from for 149 bars, including not only the Prelude, but also the Trio of the Undines which follows.

Need I still cite the Prelude to the first act of *Parsifal*, which, with the exception of a few bars, scarcely leaves the key of A-flat ?

Outside the Preludes, long and imposing holds are also sufficiently frequent; the theme of the Rainbow, almost at the end of *Das Rheingold*, has a perfect chord on G-flat, which is sustained for 20 bars in a slow movement; in *Lohengrin* the long flourish of trumpets which salutes the rising of the sun in Act II., Scene III., contains no less than 58 bars, augmented by holds on the one perfect major chord of A, to which immediately succeed (with one single transitory chord), 15 bars on the perfect chord of C major. We might multiply these interesting examples, which demonstrate that it is especially at the beginning of the acts and scenes that Wagner likes to establish thoroughly the tonality, unlike Beethoven who much preferred strongly to re-establish it at the final peroration.

The ENSEMBLES are rare, except in *Tannhäuser* and *Lohengrin*, which still partake, particularly in this feature, of the form of the opera.

From *Tristan* onwards, with the exception of *Die Meistersinger*, where they play a considerable part, they may be easily counted.

In the Duet which ends the first act of *Tristan* there is one *ensemble* of 42 bars; the great Duet of Act II., Scene II., is made up of four *ensembles*, which are all admirable, the first beginning with a dialogue, becoming more and more close, the last containing very curious dissonances, as dreadful to look at in the score as they are sweet to listen to.

In *Das Rheingold* there are the nymphs' cries of joy and the *Adoration of the Gold;* in Scene III., Wotan and Loge speak several words together; in *Die Walküre*, the vocal Octet of the *Ride of the Walkyries*, the eight parts of which are sometimes independent; in *Siegfried* the few simultaneous notes of Mime and Siegfried at the end of the first act can scarcely be considered in this light; but in the third act, at the moment of Brünnhilde's awaking, there is a true *ensemble* of a dozen bars, and then another, more developed, which ends the piece; in *Götterdämmerung* the Norns sing together for a moment, but in unison; then Siegfried and Brünnhilde end their Duet with a few exclamations in thirds and sixths; there is another *ensemble* of a few bars when Siegfried and Gunther conclude their pact, cup in hand; at the end of the second act there is a true Trio between Brünnhilde, Gunther, and Hagen; in the third act is the delightful Trio of the Rhine-Daughters, which is fully developed, and becomes a Quartet on Siegfried's arrival.

In *Parsifal* there is not a single one. In this enumeration it will be noticed that *ensembles* never occur except between characters who have analogous sentiments. Everywhere else each one speaks in his turn, as in the classic tragedy, which is far more intelligent, and without repeating the verses, which is far more natural and lifelike.

Little is known of WAGNER'S MANNER OF COMPOSING. It is certain that he first wrote his poem and did not begin to set it to music until it was completely finished, sometimes even after having let it lie untouched for several years: the poem of *Tannhäuser* was finished in 1843, and the music in 1845; the poem of *Das Rheingold* was finished in 1852, and the music in 1854.

As for the *music*, he composed it as Beethoven did, walking about and gesticulating; when it began to take form, he played it on the piano, awkwardly enough, it is said, but so as to impress the outline clearly on his memory, not till then did he begin to write it out. He wrote on two or three staves, as if for the piano or organ, sometimes also he would write on a larger number, and he did not proceed to the orchestration until he had completed the composition. *Götterdämmerung* was finished in 1872, and its orchestration in 1874; *Parsifal* was finished in 1879, and its orchestration in 1882.

Moreover, he always kept several works before him, generally two, working simultaneously on the music of one and the *scenario* of the other.

All this is very perplexing, for when we closely examine his work, everything, poem, lyrical declamation, melodic and harmonic structure, and orchestration, form only one homogeneous whole, and so perfect is the cohesion of all these parts that it seems as if the whole work must have flowed in one stream, the music blending naturally with the words and necessarily entailing the instrumental combinations which could not be other than they are, so completely do they realize the ideal of perfection. That is a mistake, however; the labour was much more complex, and the growth much slower: the first sketch of *Die Meistersinger*, which was finished in 1867, dates back to 1845 (an interval of twenty-two years); the first sketch of *Parsifal*, finished in 1882, dates from 1857 (twenty-five years); it was *The Spell of Good Friday*.

In the necessarily brief and dry ANALYSES, which follow, of each of the admirable works performed at Bayreuth, I do not pretend to *catalogue* all the *Leit-motive*.

For this there are several reasons: First, I think that no one could boast of not letting one escape him, for there are some which consist of only two notes, appearing only two or three times; besides, there is nothing to prove that Wagner himself considered them as such; they are, perhaps, simple, involuntary, and purely genial reminiscences, or similar notes unintentionally reproduced under similar circumstances.

Moreover, there already exist very complete catalogues of this nature, perhaps too complete; there are some which are very well compiled, and these I will mention.

But the principal reason is that it would have seemed to me to be going beyond the purpose of this book, which is simply a guide for the uninitiated, and I think it preferable for them to be well acquainted with a limited number of themes which they will unhesitatingly recognize, than a greater number which often occasion regrettable confusion. However, in addition to the principal themes, I shall never neglect to point out those, which, although secondary, have a real importance and are frequently repeated. Those who wish to extend their researches farther and to go deeper into a work, may always do so with the aid of the catalogues of which I have already spoken.

Applying here to the *Leit-motive* the same process which I have employed for the characters in the analysis of the poems, I place at the head of each musical analysis a table and synopsis of the various scenes in which the same *motiv* appears.

However, it is necessary to remember: First, that these tables only contain the most important *motive*;

second, that I mention only the appearances of these important *motive* that are very clearly marked; third, that the scores which are adapted to the pianoforte [1] cannot always and everywhere show all the *motive* contained in the orchestral score. Such as they are, I believe these tables will be instructive and will facilitate research.

In them one may instantaneously judge of the relative importance of the *motive*, by the frequency of their employment, the great essential *motive* running through the whole table, and the *motive* which are simply episodical, only figuring in two or three neighbouring columns; in them, too, may be seen in what scenes a given *motiv* has already appeared; what are the *motive* which form the framework of such or such a scene, etc. By comparing the various tables relating to the works of different periods, we can see to some extent the method gradually form, the employment of *Leit-motive*, purely accessory in *Tannhäuser*, becoming already considerable in *Lohengrin*, and then from *Tristan* onwards, absolutely systematic and organized.

In the analyses, as in the tables, the themes will be presented in the order of their first appearance, following the course of the drama, which will allow of their being discovered without difficulty by attentively following the score without ever having to turn back. The portions of the text between [   ] and the examples

---

[1] The most complete and faithful arrangements of *Tristan*, *Die Meistersinger*, the Tetralogy, and *Parsifal* are those of Klindworth, whose work is only for *virtuosi*; amateurs will be more at their ease with the sometimes incorrect adaptation of Kleinmichel. It is from the latter edition that we have borrowed, with the authorization of the houses of Schott and Co. and Breitkopf and Härtel, the majority of the examples in this volume. MM. Durand et Fils have given me a similar permission concerning the scores of *Tannhäuser* and *Lohengrin*.

printed in small characters concern certain transformations of the *motive* which seemed to me specially interesting and worthy of notice, as I could not think of
pointing them all out.   These modifications only occur
in acts or scenes that follow ; their precise place will
always be mentioned.

Besides the *Leit-motive*, I shall also mention in several
of the works certain great phrases of an independent
character forming a complete whole of themselves, a
finished melody to which it is necessary to pay attention ;
also *Chorals* and *Songs*, sometimes foreign to the general
structure, at other times indirectly related to it, several
of which have received special names.

As far as concerns the names, which are the least
important thing, I repeat that I shall always give the
preference to those under which the typical *motive* seem
to me to be most generally known.

TANNHÄUSER

Although Wagner has called *Tannhäuser* "*Handlung*"
(action), thus showing his intention to create a new
dramatico-musical form, it is quite certain that from
its general form, with *ensembles*, *airs*, *duets*, *finales*, and
Overture, this work is still musically connected with the
methods of the old opera, and that we often find in it
the influence of Wagner's openly-professed admiration
for Weber.   Let us even say that it is an *Opera* in the
full sense of the word.   Nevertheless Wagner is already
visible here by a marked tendency to avoid the repetition
of words, by the skill with which the various parts are
bound together, by the beauty and purity of the diction,
and especially, perhaps, by the absence of all idea of
concession to public taste.   We also find here bold

flights and melodic forms which are very characteristic of Wagner.

NAMES of the principal Leit-motive in **TANNHÄUSER** in the order of their first appearance. SCENES:	Overture.	ACT I.				Prelude.	ACT II.					Prelude.	ACT III.				
		1	2	3	4		1	2	3	4	5		1	2	3	4	5
The Venusberg	●	●	· ·	· ·	·		· ·	· ·	· ·	· ·	●		· ·	· ·	· ·	●	
Pilgrims' Chorus	·	· ·	●	·		· ·	· ·	· ·	· ·	●	●						
Elizabeth	·	· ·	· ·	· ·	●		·	· ·	·	· ·	· ·		· ·	· ·	· ·	· ·	●
Song of Wolfram	·	· ·	· ·	· ·	· ·		· ·	·	· ·	· ·	●	· ·	●				
The Damnation	·	· ·	· ·	· ·	· ·		· ·	· ·	·	· ·	●		· ·	· ·	●		

The Overture is a condensed summary of the drama.

In the first place appears the famous *Pilgrims' Chorus*,[1] representing the religious element; it is first presented with an impressive gravity, and then is majestically developed in a persistent figure on the violins, and it dies away as it departs. Without transition, the *motiv* of the *Venusberg* transports us to the abode of luxury and unholy pleasures.

THE VENUSBERG

[In a style which at the same time recalls Weber when fantastic and Mendelssohn when fairy-like, this figure has the char-

---

[1] I consider it superfluous to note here the music of the themes having an independent character, which are in the memory of every one, and are in such rich abundance in *Tannhäuser*.

acter of a *Leit-motiv*, for we shall again find it in the scene of the Contest (Act II., Scene V.), each time that Tannhäuser is about to speak, thus disclosing in advance his state of mind ; then again in Act III., at the end of Scene IV., where it announces the coming of Venus.]

A little farther on, the *Hymn to Venus* bursts out like a trumpet-call, first in B major ; then, after some beautiful symphonic developments in the principal key in E major, a long pedal on the dominant brings back the *Pilgrims' Chorus*, which is soon accompanied by the strident passage on the violins, and the Overture ends with a great and brilliant finale.

Act I.

At the rising of the curtain we hear, as though framed in a *Baccanale*, which reproduces the majority of the profane *motive* of the Overture, a *Dance of the Bacchantes*, a *Chorus of Sirens*, and then the grand Duet between Tannhäuser and Venus, in which appears three times, and each time a half-tone higher (in D-flat, in D, and in E-flat), the *Hymn to Venus*, already heard in the Overture. This scene, constantly increasing in intensity, has a very striking effect.

In the second tableau a shepherd plays upon his pipe, and trills an air of archaic character, to which is immediately linked the *Pilgrims' Chorus* in the form of a choral, while the rustic strains still continue to sound in capricious arabesques.

THE PILGRIMS' CHORUS

[It will reappear in the orchestra at the beginning of the impressive phrase of the Landgrave, which appears in the finale of Act II., as again at the end of that same act.]

It is only separated by a hunting-call from the Septet, which itself is interrupted when Wolfram pronounces the name of *Elizabeth*, which Tannhäuser repeats in ecstasy.

[A similar arrangement occurs at the beginning of the finale of Act III., when the same characters evoke the memory of Elizabeth, whose funeral procession is passing.]

Finally the Septet is resumed and ends with a fine *ensemble*.

Act II.

After a short *entr'acte* the second act begins with an *Air* by Elizabeth, preceded by a recitative; here again we find a suggestion of Weber: then comes a *Duet* in the ordinary form between Tannhäuser and Elizabeth, and a recitative between the Landgrave and his niece, and then the *March* with chorus, announcing the Singing-Contest. At the beginning of this scene of the Contest, Wolfram sings of love in a beautiful but cold song which occasions a lively discussion between Tann-häuser, Walter, and Biterolf; here occurs the beautiful

Song of Wolfram, a melody of great breadth and warmth, and of a noble and pure form, which extols chaste and respectful love.

SONG OF WOLFRAM

It is not in this light that Tannhäuser regards it; he disputes it, and each of his replies, as we have already noticed, is preceded by a recurrence of the *Venusberg*.

Biterolf speaks in turn, and challenges him; before Tannhäuser's disdainful reply, the same *motiv* appears for the third time.

Finally, Tannhäuser, at the highest pitch of exaltation, for the last time sings his *Hymn to Venus*,[1] again a semitone higher than before (in E major), and the act ends with a powerful *ensemble*, full of movement and developed at great length.

ACT III.

This act is certainly the most beautiful one in the whole work. A very impressive *entr'acte*, which it would be better to call a Prelude, precedes it, containing, in the course of its development, reminiscences of the *Pilgrims' Chorus* and the announcement of the theme of *The Damnation*, which does not appear until later.

The Pilgrims, returning from Rome, gratefully sing the chorus with which the Overture has already made us acquainted; Elizabeth breathes a tender *Prayer*, and slowly mounts the hill, as if in a trance, followed by Wolfram's glance, which is sadly accented by the *motiv* of the *Song of Wolfram*, now confided to the bass-clarinet. Then the latter, after a passage of great breadth, sings the celebrated *Romance of the Star*.

Immediately, on the entrance of Tannhäuser, everything darkens, and the gloomy and terrifying theme of *The Damnation* is heard,

---

[1] These frequent repetitions of the *Hymn to Venus* make it the principal and dominating *motiv* of the work, but it never becomes a *Leit-motiv*, for it is only heard from Tannhäuser's own lips, and is always sung *in extenso*. It occurs also in the Overture, but, during the course of the work, it never gives rise to any symphonic allusion, or any insinuation, as is the mission of the *Leit-motive*.

THE DAMNATION

and, after a short dialogue with Wolfram, Tannhäuser begins the touching story of his journey to Rome, in the course of which *The Damnation* is again heard. This story, one of the most beautiful pages in the work, is stamped with the most heart-rending despair and the most poignant emotion. Suddenly the mysterious orchestra, whose tones seem to spring from the heart of the mountain, persistently repeating fragments of the *Venusberg motiv*, announces the coming of Venus, accented by an ingenious reminiscence of the *Chorus of Sirens*.

Tannhäuser is beginning to falter again and allow himself to be carried off, when in the distance are heard the voices of the Pilgrims, bearing Elizabeth's body. Tannhäuser prostrates himself upon her bier and dies. He is saved!

Then all the voices united intone a great hymn of faith and hope, a marvellous and majestic epilogue, which rises as a sort of joyous and triumphant Alleluia, reaching its splendid final development on the first bars of the religious theme of the Overture, and leaving us under the consoling influence of the great act of Redemption, which has just been accomplished before our eyes.

There are also in the score certain forms, sometimes melodic, sometimes harmonic, which may be considered as *Leit-motive* of a secondary or episodical order, as, for example, the *Song of the Sirens* in Act I.,

SONG OF THE SIRENS

which in the third act accompanies the appearance of Venus; the second phrase of the *Pilgrims' Chorus*, which is

FRAGMENT OF THE PILGRIMS' CHORUS

found again in their *Chant* in the form of a choral, and then at the 27th bar of the *entr'acte* of the third act after having already appeared in the Overture, and which Wagner will again use later in *Parsifal*; finally, the beautiful harmony,[1] *Pardon*, which runs through the whole story of the journey to Rome, and which already

MOTIV OF PARDON

possessed great importance in the preceding *entr'acte*, and perhaps others.

With regard to melodic reiteration, the following phrase by Venus in the Duet of the first act, which

Elizabeth

intentionally recurs (in the key of E–flat,) towards the middle of the *entr'acte* preceding the second act ; also the following,

Wolfram

sung by Wolfram in the Septet, shortly after the *motiv Elizabeth*, reproduced in the orchestra during the address

---

[1] This beautiful harmony, by its impressive solemnity, is very similar in character to certain *motive* in *Parsifal*, notably *Faith*.

which the Landgrave makes to the singers after the *March*, and, perhaps, some others.

LOHENGRIN

NAMES of the principal Leit-motive in **LOHENGRIN** in the order of their first appearance. SCENES:	Prelude	ACT I. 1	2	3	Introduction.	ACT II. 1	2	3	4	5	Introduction March.	ACT III. 1	2	3
The Grail....................	●		●	●				●					●	●
Elsa........................			●	●		●								●
Lohengrin...................			●	●				●		●			●	●
Glory.......................			●	●										●
The Judgment of God.........			●	●					●				●	●
Harmony of the Swan.........				●									●	●
The Mystery of the Name.....				●		●							●	●
The Dark Plots.............					●	●	●			●			●	
The Doubt..................					●	●	●			●			●	●

The Prelude of *Lohengrin* takes us into the sacred regions of Montsalvat. One single *motiv*, wonderfully developed, bears the whole burden; it symbolizes *The Grail*.

THE GRAIL

In fact, as Wagner has himself told us, this introduction is intended to describe the return of the Holy Grail to the mountain of the pious knights, in the midst of a band of angels.

This mysterious *motiv* first appears in the upper regions of the divided violins, then passes to the woodwind, thence to the violas, violoncellos, clarinets, horns, and bassoons, bursts forth on the trumpets and trombones, and then, after this prodigious crescendo, gradually fades away and dies in the glow of the muted violins, leaving behind a glimpse of supernatural radiance, which is like a foretaste of *Parsifal.*[1]

Act I.

The trumpets and the Herald proclaim *The King's Call.* After a noble recitative by the King, broken by several replies by the chorus, comes Frederick's denunciation of Elsa.

There is a fresh call by the Herald, and then *Elsa*

[1] We must not be at all surprised thus to come across germs in *Tannhäuser* and *Lohengrin* which, after being cultivated, developed many years later into *Parsifal, the wonder of wonders.* It was in this way that Wagner formed his own language ; he always embodied a philosophical thought either in a melodic figure or in a harmonic or rhythmic form, the expression of which, given identical cases, continues throughout all his works ; and by studying him many analogous facts may be noticed.

18

enters; at this moment in the orchestra is heard the
following *motiv*,

ELSA

full of hope and resignation, which will remain personally
attached to her.

[It will besides be almost immediately reproduced in a
slightly modified form in the story which Elsa relates of her
dream.]

In this same passage, which from its first entrance is
placed as if under the protection of *The Grail*, appears a

new and sparkling theme, representing *Lohengrin*, clad in
his white silver armour as she has seen him in her dream,
and as we ourselves shall soon see him.

LOHENGRIN

[This *motiv*, so characteristic, graceful, bold, and chivalrous,
will accompany the valiant knight in all heroic circumstances,
with slight transformations.

We shall find it up to the last page of the work, to the
moment when Lohengrin departs ; but there, after having been
presented in the triumphal form usual to it, it puts on mourning, it borrows the minor key.]

It is also during the recital of *Elsa's Dream* that for the first time we hear this other *motiv*, in some measure complementary to that of *Lohengrin*, whose *Glory* it seems to proclaim and whose great deeds it celebrates.

GLORY

[This will be found again in the following scene on the hero's arrival and also in the final scene of the third act.]

Frederick maintaining his calumnious accusation, the King proposes *The Judgment of God*,[1]

THE JUDGMENT OF GOD

[1] Notice the analogy with *The Treaty* in *Der Ring des Nibelungen*.

the *motiv* of which is soon followed by that of *Elsa*.
The Herald and his four trumpeters sound two successive
calls.   Elsa kneels in prayer, accompanied by a chorus
of women, and her prayer ends with a touching reminiscence of her own *motiv*.   It is then that Lohengrin
appears in the distance in a boat drawn by a swan ; the
orchestra sounds the *motive* of *Lohengrin* and *Glory*, which
have assumed a character of special pomp and impres-
siveness.   A fine vocal *ensemble* hails his arrival.

Hardly has he landed, when he blesses and takes leave
of his *Swan*,

THE SWAN

which is preceded by *The Grail* again.   The latter is
repeated, when, after having saluted the King, he
addresses Elsa and informs her that he cannot undertake
her defence except on the express condition that she
shall never know his name and shall not even seek to
know it.

Here follows the theme, at once strange and impressive, *The Mystery of the Name*, which forms a part of the
fine entrance recitative of Lohengrin and which he twice
repeats with insistence, the second time in a higher key,
which gives it more force.

The *ensemble* is heard again, and then follows the
superb scene of the combat, the laws of which are first

THE MYSTERY OF THE NAME

proclaimed by the Herald, which brings back *The Judg-ment of God*; next comes a fine *ensemble* passage: the *King's Prayer* and *Quintet* with chorus. The combat begins; at each attack of either adversary the theme of *The Judgment of God*, treated in canon, makes a fresh *entrée*; the *motiv* of *Lohengrin*, however, takes its place when he is about to strike the decisive blow.

A beautiful enthusiastic phrase by Elsa hails his victory; this same phrase is next taken up by the chorus, but with a new development drawn from the *motiv* of *Glory*. This grand and powerful *ensemble*, greatly extended, brilliantly crowns the act; then, at the moment when the curtain is about to fall, the orchestra again sounds the *motiv* of *Lohengrin*.

Act II.

The second act will only reveal two new typical *motive*, both contained in the dark phrase which mutters on the violoncellos at the beginning of the Prelude. First, *Ortrude's Dark Plots*, represented thus :

THE DARK PLOTS

[This *motiv* will reappear, particularly in the course of the dialogue between Ortrude and Frederick, which opens the act.]

The second, characterizing *The Doubt* with which Ortrude wants to fill Elsa's mind, the doubt which will be her ruin, is given in the same dialogue by the violoncellos, ten bars after its commencement.

THE DOUBT

[And here it is again as we find it a few pages farther on in the same long dialogue, mingled with significant reminiscences of *The Mystery of the Name*.]

It is impossible to tell more clearly in music that Ortrude intends perfidiously to fill Elsa's heart with doubts regarding the purity and origin of her knight, and wants to inspire her with the curiosity to penetrate the mystery in which he insists on shrouding his name.

When we understand its inner meaning, this sombre and dark episode constitutes one of the most beautiful pages of the work. It ends with a terrible phrase of imprecation, sung in octaves by the two voices, which seals their odious pact of revenge.

Elsa appears and sings a sweet melody; in the second part of her duet with Ortrude we recognize in the orchestra the *motiv* of *The Doubt*, immediately followed by *The Mystery of the Name;* the dark plots are being accomplished; the venom has been instilled and will perform its work.

The day breaks. Long trumpet-calls are heard answering in turn on the chord D, F-sharp, A; then, when suddenly the key of C succeeds it, we hear *The King's Call.* Immediately afterwards the key of D reappears, — a daring proceeding, with a most striking effect. In this scene, as in those which follow : Elsa going to the church, Ortrude's scandalous interference, and the arrival of the King and Lohengrin, there is no use made of *Leitmotive* until Scene V., which opens with *The King's Call,* immediately followed by the *motiv Lohengrin ;* then, when Frederick tries to attribute the victory of his adversary to trickery or magic, notice a reappearance of *The Judgment of God,* which he dares to question.

Finally there reappear in the orchestra in succession, *The Doubt, The Mystery of the Name,* and *The Dark Plots ;* then, at the moment when the King is about to cross the threshold of the church with Elsa and Lohengrin, we again hear *The King's Call,* immediately followed by *The Mystery of the Name,* and the curtain falls.

Act III.

The third act adds nothing to the list of typical *motive,* but all the former ones are freely used in it, though not at the beginning.

First, as an introduction, we find the splendid *Wedding March,* as joyous as it is pompous, followed from

the first rising of the curtain by a charming Chorus, a
graceful epithalamium; then comes the Duet between
Elsa and Lohengrin; in this, shortly after a fine phrase
by Lohengrin and just as Elsa manifests her culpable
curiosity, *The Mystery of the Name* is twice repeated;
the *motiv* of *The Doubt* comes into play, always more
and more insistent; then a short allusion to the *Swan*,
which Elsa thinks she sees, or pretends she thinks so;
finally, when she has put the fatal question, *The Mystery
of the Name* furiously breaks out; when Lohengrin has
just killed Frederick *The Doubt* still exists; the body is
carried out to the strains of *The Judgment of God*; Lohengrin announces to Elsa that he is going to declare
who he is before everybody, and again sounds *The
Mystery of the Name*, this time followed by *The Grail!*
Is this sufficiently explicit?

And when, in the last tableau, Elsa appears before the
King, the Nobles, and the Warriors, it is again by *The
Mystery of the Name*, which she has violated, that she
is announced; this time it is rendered gloomy, and is
directly joined to the fatal *Doubt*; the *motiv* of *Elsa* is
the third to appear and ends in the minor; it seems
to be as humiliated as herself. When the remains of
Frederick are brought before the King, *The Judgment of
God* reminds us that it is God who has struck him; when
Lohengrin, in a most touching recital, relates the splendours of Montsalvat, *The Grail* reveals its mysteries;
and finally, when he pronounces his own name, *Lohengrin* is again proclaimed by the most startling trumpet
notes, and immediately the orchestra sobers down.

The rest is short. Lohengrin is about to depart;
notwithstanding the supplications of Elsa, the King, and
the Lords, he is inflexible: it must be. *The Swan*
reappears, with its sweet and calm harmony; the Knight

bids a tender farewell to Elsa, gives her his horn, his sword, and his ring, kisses her brow, and sets foot in the boat: here there are no *Leit-motive*. But in the last pages, after Ortrude's odious malediction, when the white dove comes to hover above the head of the hero, we hear, more solemnly than ever, the theme of *The Grail*, then also with great breadth that of *Lohengrin* united with *Glory;* Lohengrin having disappeared, the same theme occurs in the minor; and, finally, the work ends, as it began, with the sacred harmony of *The Grail*.

TRISTAN UND ISOLDE

The Prelude to the first act of *Tristan und Isolde* is almost built up of the seven most important *motive*, making us feel from the first the predominance of the chromatic manner which will prevail through the greater part of this work, and which *motive* are thus presented from the very beginning. First comes *The Confession of Love*,

CONFESSION OF LOVE

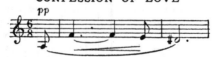

[which will be found again in Scene V. (at the moment when Isolde drinks to Tristan), under the following form :]

TRISTAN UND ISOLDE

NAMES of the principal *Leit-motive* in **TRISTAN UND ISOLDE** in the order of their first appearance. SCENES:	Prelude.	ACT I.					Introduction.	ACT II.			Prelude.	ACT III.		
		1	2	3	4	5		1	2	3		1	2	3
The Confession of Love	●	··	··	··	··	●	··	··	∴	●	··	··	●	●
Desire	●	●	●	●	●	●	●	●	●	●	··	●	●	●
The Glance	●	●	●	●	●	●	··	··	●	··	··	●	●	
The Love Philtre	●	··	··	●	··	●	··	··	··	··	··	●	●	
The Death Potion	●	··	··	●	●	●	··	●	●	··	··	●	●	
The Magic Casket	●	··	··	●	··	●								
The Deliverance by Death	●	··	··	●	··	●	··	··	··	··	··	··	●	
The Sea	··	●	●	··	··	●	●							
Anger	··	●	●	●	●	●	··	··	●	●				
Death	··	··	●	●	●	●	··	●	●	··	●	●	●	
Glory to Tristan	··	··	●	●	●	●	··	··	●	··	··	●		
Tristan Wounded	··	··	··	●	●	●	··	··	··	··	··	●	●	
Tristan the Hero	··	··	··	··	··	●								
Day	··	··	··	··	··	··	●	··	●	●	··	●		
Impatience	··	··	··	··	··	··	●	●	··	●				
Ardour	··	··	··	··	··	··	●	●	●	··	··	●	●	
Passionate Transport	··	··	··	··	··	··	··	●	●	··	··	··	··	●
Song of Love	··	··	··	··	··	··	··	●	●	··	●	●	●	
Invocation to Night	··	··	··	··	··	··	··	●	●	●	··	●	●	
Death the Liberator	··	··	··	··	··	··	··	··	●	●	··	●	●	
Felicity	··	··	··	··	··	··	··	●	●	··	··	●	●	
Song of Death	··	··	··	··	··	··	··	●	●	●	··	··	●	●
Mark's Grief	··	··	··	··	··	··	··	··	··	●				
Consternation	··	··	··	··	··	··	··	··	··	●	··	··	··	●
Solitude	··	··	··	··	··	··	··	··	··	··	●	●	●	
Sadness	··	··	··	··	··	··	··	··	··	··	··	●		
Kurwenal's Joy	··	··	··	··	··	··	··	··	··	··	··	●	··	●
Karéol	··	··	··	··	··	··	··	··	··	··	··	●	●	
Joy	··	··	··	··	··	··	··	··	··	··	··	●	··	●

but which in the Prelude is constantly followed by this other *motiv, Desire,*[1] which completes its harmonic sense

DESIRE

and gives us the impression of a sad and painful note of interrogation, four times repeated with long and affecting rests.

[Frequent employment of this *motiv* occurs in the course of this work under the most varied forms.]

espressivo

Immediately afterwards appears a new theme eloquently expressing that the mutual passion of Tristan and Isolde has had as its first cause and origin the meeting of their eyes; this is *The Glance.*

THE GLANCE

[1] Observe a certain analogy with the *motiv* of *Fate* in *Der Ring des Nibelungen.*

[Moreover, this theme of *The Glance* will often be met with, more or less modified, in the course of the work; I have given below an interesting form of it which is found at the 133rd bar of Scene III. (Kleinmichel's edition, p. 32, 2nd bar).]

Continuing the analysis of the Prelude, in which this *motiv* of *The Glance* is the subject of numerous and important developments, so that at certain times it even assumes the preponderance, we shall meet in the space of four bars with two very expressive phrases, characterizing the two philtres of love and of death, the substitution of which is, as it were, the nucleus of the action : *The Love Philtre* and *The Death Potion*, the first full of poetry

THE LOVE PHILTRE

THE DEATH POTION

and passion, the second forming a sinister and gloomy contrast, which the instrumentation still further emphasizes by confiding it sometimes to the big brass and sometimes to the bass-clarinet and oboes.

[The latter will again appear at the end of Scene III. at the moment when Brangäne is looking for the flasks in the casket.]

Now comes the *motiv* which may be considered as derived from that of *The Glance*, to which is attached the idea of this precious casket of relief, *The Magic Casket* :

THE MAGIC CASKET

[a *motiv* which will necessarily find its use when recourse is had to the casket (in Scene III.), or when any allusion is made to it].

Then, following a superb crescendo which is constructed principally of the *motiv* of *The Glance*, is introduced the theme of *The Deliverance by Death*, the last of those introduced to us in the Prelude, which finally ends with new combinations of the *Leit-motive* already mentioned.

THE DELIVERANCE BY DEATH

[On the subject of the *motiv* of *The Deliverance*, let us observe that it often undergoes radical changes; thus, when we find it at the beginning of Act III., Scene II., it has assumed the following form :]

Tristan

ACT I.

SCENE I. — The song of the young sailor perched on the mast is not in itself a *Leit-motiv*; but his third phrase, *The Sea*, does constitute one, which will be fre-

THE SEA

A young sailor

quently employed and will undergo the most curious transformations. Here, almost at the beginning of Scene I., is Isolde in disgust at having to make this voyage

across *The Sea*, the object of which is not pleasing to her; some pages further on (when the key of F arrives), it represents the phlegm and indifference of the sailors during a long and uneventful passage; it is the calm of *The Sea*:

[At Scene IV. they are joyfully approaching land, and it is still the *motiv* of *The Sea* which is changed to tell us of it: else-

where we meet with it under many other forms, which we cannot quote here.]

The *motiv* of *Anger* is expressive and easily recognizable.

ANGER

SCENE II. — So also with that which so gloomily predicts *The Death* of Tristan and the sorrows of Isolde.

DEATH

[If it is not always repeated in its entirety, it is frequently represented by one half of it or the other, the first more particularly calling up the idea of Tristan, the second that of Isolde, and numerous allusions to them occur in the course of the work.]

After various returns (occasioned by what passes on
the stage), of several important themes, notably *The
Glance*, *Desire*, *The Sea*, under the calm form which I
pointed out in the third example, *The Love Philtre*, etc.,
the scene ends by Kurwenal's mocking song of a popular character, the refrain of which, a joyous salutation,
Glory to Tristan, is taken up as a chorus by the sailors,

GLORY TO TRISTAN

but a third higher, by an amusing caprice of the
composer.

SCENE III. — The third scene only introduces us to
one fresh *motiv* of any great importance, the one which
shows us the wounded Tristan when he was cared for
and saved by Isolde, *Tristan Wounded*.

TRISTAN WOUNDED

This *motiv*, of which considerable use will be made in the remainder of the drama, as a general thing suffers very few modifications in its melodic form, but the figures of accompaniment which appear with it in different circumstances are varied with admirable and inexhaustible fertility of invention. Here are some examples:

The remainder of the scene is woven together of *motive* we already know, which appear practically in the following order: *Glory to Tristan, Desire, The Glance, Anger, The Magic Casket, The Deliverance, The Love Philtre,* and *The Death Potion,* while Isolde is relating Tristan's treason to Brangäne, and reveals her sinister designs.

SCENE IV. — After an appearance of the *motiv* of *The Sea* in its gay form, those of *Tristan Wounded, Death, Desire, The Death Potion,* and, finally, *Anger* successively reappear. This scene offers no new *Leit-motive.*

Scene V. — The first chords of Scene V. show us *Tristan the Hero* coming respectfully to salute his queen.

Then, while the supreme action of the drama, the substitution of the philtre, is taking place, all the *motive* of the first act pass in procession, ending with the acclamations of the people, and a new form of *The Sea motiv*.

Act II.

Scene I. — Almost the whole of the first scene is a development of the following new *motiv*, which is of considerable importance, and one of those which Wagner has taken pleasure in presenting under the most varied and unexpected aspects, after having given it its most simple form at the beginning of the Prelude.

This is *Day*, the enemy of the loves of Tristan and Isolde.

[This is the way we shall find it in Scene II. in the *ensemble* in A-flat in 3-time :

and earlier in the same Duet, by diminution :

Here is another form, which appears very frequently in the same piece :

and, finally, here it is again, this time by augmentation, as it is presented by Brangäne protecting the loves of Tristan and Isolde :

[One thing to be observed is that the interval between the first two notes of this *motiv* is sometimes a fourth and sometimes a fifth ; in the first case it has a very marked resemblance to the *Glory to Tristan*, of which, strictly speaking, it is only a transposition in the minor.

It also undergoes many other transformations, all of which I cannot note here, but which will afford pleasure to those who search for them in the score.]

The *motiv* of *Impatience* is sketched at the ninth bar of the Prelude, but it does not assume its definite form till the twenty-first bar.

IMPATIENCE

p *tranquillo*

[Its principal employment will occur when Isolde, after having given Tristan the appointed signal, is anxiously awaiting him.]

But a few bars farther, this *motiv*, very slightly modified, happily combines with that of *Ardour* (also called " Love's Call "), which is of considerable importance throughout this act;

ARDOUR

p *dolcissimo*

here it is under another form,

which completely changes its character. In general it does not undergo any transformations as is the case with the following, *Passionate Transport*,

PASSIONATE TRANSPORT

[which, however, we shall find again augmented and partly syncopated in Scene II., a little before *The Invocation to Night*:

It will again appear at the end of the work to serve as an accompaniment to Isolde's last words].

The *Song of Love*, which forms the orchestral web of the entire portion of this scene preceding the extinction of the torch, and the entirely Italian character of which never fails to surprise those who have not yet noticed how frequently this Italian character occurs in Wagner.

Isolde   SONG OF LOVE

This very frequently appears in the remainder of the second act.

Among the themes already known to us, those which especially contribute to the musical structure of this first scene are: *Desire*, *The Death Potion*, *Death*, and *Impatience*, and they appear almost in the above-mentioned order.

SCENE II. — This scene is only a long love-duet (Brangäne, indeed, speaks a few words, but she is invisible on the tower); during the first *ensemble* the symphonic part presents the most beautiful interweavings of the *motive* of *Passionate Transport* and *Ardour*; farther on reappears the theme of *Day*, and those of *Glory to Tristan*, the *Song of Love*, and *The Death Potion*; then appears, first in this provisional form, and almost directly afterwards in its definitive form, the *Invocation to Night*, a broad and suave melody,

Tristan   INVOCATION TO NIGHT

which gives rise to a second and important *ensemble* of striking beauty.

In the course of this same *ensemble*, which is constantly sustained by a syncopated rhythm full of life and passion, in which a few notes of the *Day* appear, the phrase undergoes numerous and great modifications; in particular, it assumes this entirely novel aspect, resulting from the introduction of passing notes, with a structure quite alien to its harmonic form, which is sometimes called "Night the Revealer."

[Now, it should be noticed that when this phrase with its passing notes, but with a contrary inverted movement, is heard in the last act, its signification will be quite different and will convey the idea of *Suspicion*.]

SUSPICION

Towards the end appears the *motiv* of *Death the Liber-ator*, with its strange dissonances,

DEATH THE LIBERATOR

[which will often reappear in the course of the drama, some-times in the voices, sometimes in the orchestra, rarely modified in its melodic contour but frequently with harmonic, or rhythmic, variants].

Immediately on the close of this *ensemble*, Brangäne
from the summit of the tower sings the *motiv* of *Day*
in the form given on p. 296; then comes this delightful
motiv,

FELICITY

which possesses an exquisite charm and an ideal sweetness, so well expressing calm happiness and *Felicity*,

[which will never be reproduced in its integrity ; but, besides partial repetitions, numerous allusions will be made to it, and it will have frequent transformations ; I will quote here one of its most curious forms in 5-time and in the bass (Act III., Scene II.)].

Now comes the superb *Song of Death* under the two aspects which it assumes in this scene,

SONG OF DEATH

Tristan

where it furnishes a third and marvellous *ensemble*.

[In the final scene of the drama, slightly modified, it will serve as the basis of Isolde's song, until the moment when the latter, growing more and more excited, finds her support in the *motiv* of *Passionate Transport*.]

Isolde

After several repetitions of *Felicity*, *Death the Liberator*, the *Death Potion* and *Day*, the scene ends with the sudden arrival of King Mark.

20

SCENE III. — Immediately the *motive* of *Impatience*,
the *Song of Death*, and *Day* reappear, and then two other
themes, which are not used anywhere but in this scene
of the act; first, the following, very prominent in the
orchestra, accents the deep grief which King Mark feels
at the evidence of Tristan's treachery: it is *Mark's
Grief*.

MARK'S GRIEF

(The dominant feeling in the good King Mark's mind
is not anger, nor jealousy, nor the desire for vengeance,
nor hatred: it is a sharp affliction, a profound grief:

how well it is expressed!). Then, shortly afterwards, comes another which expresses his *Consternation*, and, perhaps, Tristan's also:

CONSTERNATION

Lento moderato, come primo

p espressivo e dolce.

The end of this scene is largely built up of these two new *motive*, with frequent reminiscences of *Anger*, *The Confession of Love*, *Desire*, *Felicity*, *Death the Liberator*, and the *Invocation to Night*.

ACT III.

SCENE I. — The Prelude immediately takes us to Tristan's estate, by means of a *motiv*, admirably expressing its *Solitude*, which will only be used at the opening of this last act, but whose first notes are not without a certain likeness to the *motiv* already known as *Desire*.

Analyzing it in detail, we find in these first notes the feeling of despair caused by fatality, to which succeeds, in the ascent in thirds and augmented fourths, the image of solitude, and of the infinity of the ocean; a new figure expresses the condition of distress and isolation in which we find Tristan (see p. 312); after a triple organ-point, the same figures recur, followed this time (in *ff.*) by the last notes of *Death*, then the ascent in thirds comes in a third time and forms the connection with the first scene.

The whole of this Prelude, which is profoundly melancholy, prepares the mind for the climax of the drama.

SOLITUDE

Lento moderato

Just as the curtain rises, behind the scenes is heard an affecting solo on the *cor anglais*, without any accompaniment, which is very expressive and is most curiously developed.

SADNESS

[At the beginning of the first act, a young sailor was singing on the mast of the ship, and a fragment of his song furnished the *motiv* of *The Sea ;* here, it is a shepherd who plays on his pipe a sad and plaintive air, which will serve in the orchestra as an accompaniment to a good part of Tristan's delirious talk, after which the shepherd will play it a second time.]

This next *motiv* is peculiar to the character of *Kurwenal*, whose joy it picturesquely describes when Tristan first opens his eyes, as it also does later when he thinks that Isolde can effectually cure him.

KURWENAL'S JOY

Kurwenal

[It will appear again at the moment Kurwenal dashes at the followers of King Mark to meet his death at the end of the third scene.]

The calm and peaceful *motiv* of *Karéol*, forming a smiling contrast to the agony of the action, only appears on two occasions in the orchestra, and these rather close together, to recall to Tristan's memory the happy period of his youth.

KARÉOL

Kurwenal

After this, all the principal *Leit-motive* appear in such a tangle that their enumeration would be tedious; besides, they have been met with often enough to render them easily recognizable to the eye or ear. Among the most frequent, however, we may call attention to *Glory to Tristan*, *Solitude*, and then, after a return of *Karéol*, the *Invocation to Night*, and *Death the Liberator*.

Only one new *motiv* remains to be mentioned; this also depicts *Joy*, but it is not like the other *Joy*, specially attached to one single character; it relates to the joy of Tristan, as well as that of Kurwenal: when Tristan, in his fever, thinks he sees Isolde coming; and Kurwenal, when he at last can avenge his master by mortally wounding the traitor, Melot.

JOY

Scenes II. and III. do not supply any new *motive;* the old ones of which they are composed appear in the following order:

Scene II. — *Invocation to Night, The Song of Love, Deliverance, Felicity, Ardour, Death, Desire, Confession of Love, The Glance, Death the Liberator, Song of Death, Tristan Wounded, Death Potion,* etc.

Scene III. — *Joy, Karéol, Song of Death, Confession of Love, Desire, Passionate Transport,* etc., and the curtain falls upon a last transformation of *Desire.*

Besides these principal themes, there are several of secondary importance, and yet of rather frequent occurrence, such as the *motiv* of *Exaltation,* appearing in the first act,

EXALTATION

and again in Act II. at the moment of Tristan's arrival.
Several times it is used in the development of the *motiv*
Anger.

In the Prelude of the third act only, we meet with the
very expressive *Tristan's Distress*.

TRISTAN'S DISTRESS

The *Annihilation* only appears twice, in two distinct
forms : in Scene I. after the second appearance of *Karéol*,

ANNIHILATION

and quite at the end, almost at Isolde's last words.

The following also occurs in Scene I. coming very shortly after the above:

UNALTERABLE LOVE

Another, at Scene II., preceding by several pages a charming reminiscence of *Felicity*:

MALEDICTION OF THE LOVE PHILTRE
Tristan

Finally, the following, immediately after Tristan's death :

COMPANIONSHIP IN DEATH
Isolde

Many others might certainly be mentioned, but these seem to me sufficient for the comprehension of the work ; besides, once having entered on this path, it is not easy to know exactly where to stop, and one would finally end by finding *Leit-motive* where there only exist lyrical declamation and characteristic forms of Wagner's musical language. The essential matter is that the reader should know that there remain many *motive* for him to discover, which are not the less interesting because they are of secondary importance.

DIE MEISTERSINGER VON NÜRNBERG

NAMES of the principal *Leit-motive* in **DIE MEISTERSINGER** in the order of their first appearance. SCENES:	Overture.	ACT I.			Prelude.	ACT II.							Prelude.	ACT III. Tableau I.				Tabl. II.
		1	2	3		1	2	3	4	5	6	7		1	2	3	4	5
The Meistersinger	●	●		●							●	●					●	●
Waking Love	●	●	●	●				●						●	●			●
The Banner	●	●	●										●					
Love confessed	●	●							●					●				●
Impatient Ardour	●	●	●	●				●		●				●				●
David		●	●										●					
Saint Crispin			●	●		●	●	●		●						●		●
The Crown			●	●		●												
The Assembly				●														●
Saint John				●		●	●							●			●	●
Walter				●						●					●		●	
Quarrelsome Beckmesser				●						●						●		●
Sachs's Good Nature				●														
Patronal *motiv* of Nuremberg							●							●	●	●	●	
Eva								●									●	
Peace of the Summer Night									●	●	●		●					
The Serenade										●	●		●		●			
The Beating										●	●		●		●			
Sachs's Profound Emotion													●	●	●	●	●	●
Nuremberg *en fête*														●	●		●	
Harmony of the Dream														●				
Story of the Dream (Prize Song)														●	●	●	●	
Eva's Anxiety																	●	

DIE MEISTERSINGER

Overture

Although the Overture to *Die Meistersinger* constitutes a superb portal to the work and a symphonic piece
apparently independent and complete in itself, it can only
be comprehended and admired as it deserves by those
who have already gained a thorough knowledge of the
entire work, that is to say on a second reading, or hearing.
It is built upon five themes selected from the most important ones of the work, showing the dramatic material
reduced to its greatest simplicity.   Two of these themes
exhibit the learned and pretentious Corporation of the
Meistersinger; and the three others depict the various
phases of the loves of Eva and the knight Walter von
Stolzing.

First come heavy and pompous chords, with a movement at once noble and pedantic, affecting a march
rhythm,

THE MEISTERSINGER

Moderato, sempre largamente e pesante

ff vigoroso e tenuto

vividly portraying the character of the Meistersinger, men
of profound convictions and resolute principles, in the
main worthy of respect, but often carrying their zeal
to the verge of absurdity ; however, they are gay and
lively.

Immediately is heard as a gentle contrast *Waking Love*, light, discreet, and always tender: the blossoming of unconscious love:

WAKING LOVE

[We shall find this *motiv* constantly occurring throughout the work, sometimes only indicated by a few initial notes.]

This episode is short: fourteen bars; soon appears a second characteristic *motiv* of the Meistersinger.

This is *The Banner*:

THE BANNER

This is less *bourgeois*, and I will even say more heraldic than the *motiv* of *The Meistersinger*, properly so-called; you see the banner floating on the breeze, the beautiful banner which depicts King David playing the harp, the visible and glorious sign of the dignity of the Corporation, the emblem of its science, of its fidelity to rules, and of its pride.

[Just as a banner is carried at the head of any self-respecting society, or guild, when it takes part in any *fête*, or public rejoicing, we shall see the *motiv* of *The Banner* escorting that of *The Meistersinger* on all important occasions.]

This *motiv* is greatly extended, being continued by beautiful developments which exhibit under new aspects the *motiv* of *The Meistersinger*, which terminates with a majestic cadence. After a short episode of eight bars (which has been called " Love's Question "), there appears a new theme of capital importance, *Love Confessed*,

LOVE CONFESSED

[which will run through the whole work, and will find its highest expression and its final form in the last act, in the song for the Mastership, and again when the people join in the triumph of Walter and his love].

A last *motiv*, this time connected solely with the character of Walter, also forms part of the fabric of the Overture. It is called *Impatient Ardour*.]

IMPATIENT ARDOUR

[We shall see it specially haunting the worthy Sachs, notably towards the end of Act II. Scene III.]

The Overture is next developed by alternations of these various *motive* till the moment when three of them *The Meistersinger*, *The Banner*, and *Love Confessed*, are simultaneously combined in a most ingenious way, and make us feel what will be the *dénoûment* of the drama itself: the alliance and fusion of the erudite but slavish Art of the old Masters with a new and more spontaneous Art, that of Walter, which is inspired by love.

The Overture, then, is entirely symbolic; it summarizes the action, whilst neglecting the characters and burlesque incidents, and clearly presents its philosophic conception with all the weight of a thesis.

ACT I.

SCENE I. — At the rising of the curtain and during the holds of the *Choral of Baptism* (p. 337), Walter first reveals his flame with expressive gestures, which, as well as his conversation with Eva, are very naturally accompanied by the *motive* of *Waking Love*, *Impatient Ardour*, and *Love Confessed*. Next, in the preparations for the meeting of the Meistersinger, we see David for the first time, with his gay and tripping *motiv*, having the characteristics of a good fellow.

DAVID

Further on we find frequent borrowings from *The Meistersinger*, and *The Banner*, as well as the *motive* of love already mentioned.

SCENE II. — The second scene makes us acquainted with two new themes; that of *Saint Crispin*, the patron of the shoemakers, personifying Hans Sachs in the prosaic exercise of his manual labour,

SAINT CRISPIN, or HANS SACHS, THE SHOEMAKER

which appears here once in the orchestra, as David, while attending to his duties, tries to instruct Walter in the pedantic rules of tablature; and that of *The Crown*, the beautiful crown of flowers, in the form of a popular refrain, which David sings first, and which the joyous and frolicsome Apprentices take up in chorus.

THE CROWN

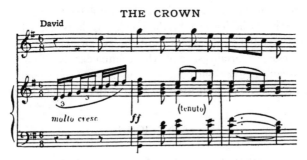

[At each of its appearances it will preserve its characteristics of the childlike joy of the Apprentices, who often sing it while dancing in a mad circle.]

Before these two themes appear, *David*, *Waking Love*, *The Banner*, and *Impatient Ardour* are often recalled.

Scene III.—Accompanying the entrance of Pogner and Beckmesser, we hear the theme of *The Assembly*.

THE ASSEMBLY

This represents the Meistersinger, no longer in their outward functions, their business, but in their private and to some extent administrative occupations, their examinations for admission, in which they preserve the same solemn forms and ritual, and the same feeling of their own importance. Less puffed up with pride than *The Meistersinger*, less blatant than *The Banner*, this *motiv* is impressed with an unctuous dignity which

21

borders on fatuity, and deliciously completes the musical
portrait of the learned brotherhood.   It lasts the whole
time that the twelve apostles of the art are making their
successive entrances, and then, immediately after the
roll-call, Pogner introduces to us a very serene *motiv*,
Saint John, which in itself expresses the joy and happi-

SAINT JOHN

ness of the festival which will be celebrated on the
morrow, but which for the moment is inseparable in the
worthy goldsmith's mind from the satisfaction which he
feels that his daughter, Eva, with her fortune, will be
the prize of the contest, that it will make her very
happy, and will considerably enhance the prestige of the
learned corporation.

   After his speech, *Saint John* is combined with *The
Assembly* and *The Meistersinger;* and *The Crown* makes
two brief appearances.   The discussion becomes heated,
and everybody speaks at once.   It is then that Pogner
presents the knight Walter von Stolzing to the Meistersinger, and the following *motiv* accompanies this presentation, depicting in a few notes his elegant and supple
figure and distinguished appearance.

WALTER

[This proud *motiv*, which never refers to any one but Walter, will run through all the rest of the work.]

It is very amusing to see how it is demeaned, in the course of the same scene, ten pages, or so, later; then it is Walter as he appears to Beckmesser through the morose eyes of his jealousy.

Almost immediately Walter sings his delightful song, *The Song to Walter's Masters* (see p. 338).

Kothner, in a strange and archaic kind of psalmody, gives a lecture on the unchangeable rules of tablature; Beckmesser utters his hoarse: " Begin ! " and Walter, seizing his words on the wing, improvises his *Hymn to Spring* (see p. 339), which is very ill received, more especially, as was to be expected, by *Beckmesser*, whose crabbed, quarrelsome, sullen and cavilling nature is well depicted in the following jerky and domineering *motiv*, full of dissonances which the orchestra takes pleasure in intensifying.

QUARRELSOME BECKMESSER

A kind of struggle goes on in the orchestra between Beckmesser's and Walter's *motive*, in sympathy with the scene between the two characters, until Hans Sachs begins to speak.   Pursued by *Impatient Ardour*, he speaks with a gentle and calm expressiveness which is in happy contrast with the preceding tumult.   Here is the theme which is called *Sachs's Good Nature*.

SACHS'S GOOD NATURE

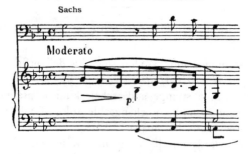

[So far he can only feel sympathy for Walter, but when later we find this *motiv* in Act III., Scene II., it will be considerably expanded ; it will not then be simply sympathy that it expresses, but the most devoted affection.]

Sachs

During the rest of the scene the quarrel becomes more and more embittered between all the *motive*, and at last the poor Sachs is defeated by the hateful Beckmesser and by a malicious recall of *Saint Crispin*.

Walter is turned out. The Apprentices amuse themselves to the air of *The Crown*; but the pedantic Meistersinger triumph, and when the curtain falls, a revengeful bassoon turns into ridicule the *motiv* of *The Meistersinger*.

Act II.

Scene I. — The Prelude of the second act recalls the *motiv* of *Saint John*. On the rising of the curtain, it alternates with *The Crown*, which is sung and danced by the Apprentices.

Scene II. — During the dialogue between Pogner and his daughter, is heard for the first time in the orchestra *The Patronal Motiv of Nuremberg*, which well represents the fine old German citizen of the 16th century, and his pleasure at the popular festival and at this interval of rest, which is at once joyful and ceremonial, and which flatters his vanity as an easy-going citizen, — a *motiv* calm, without noise or clatter, and of a placid and somewhat ponderous gaiety.

PATRONAL MOTIV OF NUREMBERG

Saint Crispin and Waking Love, faintly indicated, are the only other motive in this scene.

SCENE III. — After new allusions to Saint Crispin, the motiv of Impatient Ardour assumes great importance during the monologue of Sachs, who grows more and more excited.

SCENE IV. — Here, with Eva, appears her characteristic theme, full of grace and charm. It is indeed the type of the pretty German maiden, who is gracious without being coquettish, simple, naïve, and full of sentiment, and, moreover, intelligent.

It is thus that she must appear in the eyes of Walter with his poet's enthusiasm, and of Sachs with his almost paternal tenderness. She treats Sachs coaxingly to induce him to tell her what has happened and what is likely to happen.

The *motive* of *Saint Crispin*, *Walter*, and *Quarrelsome Beckmesser* constantly underlie the dialogue, as a commentary on the animated conversation.

SCENE V. — *Walter* appears, accompanied by his typical *motiv*; he meets Eva (*Impatient Ardour motiv*); they converse of Pogner's decision (*Meistersinger motiv*); then the Night-Watchman sounds his burlesque horn, and immediately there arrives a new *motiv* of love, impersonal this time, the harmony of which is exquisitely

PEACE OF THE SUMMER NIGHT

charming and seems to spread its soothing influence over all nature. The Watchman chants his mediæval melopœia, announcing the tranquillity of the little town, and in the distance sounds the last note on his horn; and then begins, to last to the end of the act, a series of humorous scenes in which music plays the most witty, but indescribable part.

SCENE VI. — Beckmesser comes in to croak his Serenade under his charmer's window; he comically tunes his lute, and Sachs interrupts him with a *Biblical Song* (p. 340). He, however, manages to sing in some way or other, with many contortions; but the malicious Sachs energetically scores each one of his mistakes with a loud stroke of his hammer on his cobbler's last.

The Serenade itself is perfectly grotesque, as well by its music and prosody as by the absurdity of its words, — a regular masterpiece of silliness, of German buffoonery, rather heavy, rather coarse, but, at the same time, rather amusing; the lute which accompanies it is played by one of the musicians; it is a kind of rude harp, the strings of which are like thick iron wires; the sounds which it produces are as horrible and strange as the voice of the town-clerk.

THE SERENADE

The *motiv* of *The Serenade*, according to Beckmesser's ideas, as we can feel, is correctly squared according to the regular rules, and embellished with the most ridiculous ornaments.   It is a triumph of pedantry.

SCENE VII. — All this noise stirs up first the neighbours, and then the district and the whole town ; everybody is quarrelling and fighting; from the *motiv* of *The Serenade*, which originated with the tuning of the lute, *The Beating* is derived :

THE BEATING

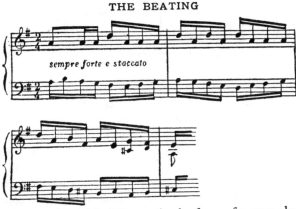

Both are treated by Wagner in the form of a very clever fugue in which every one has his part, Sachs, Walter, the Meistersinger, the Apprentices, the neighbours, and their wives ; the violins grind with rage, the brass bellows,

the tumult increases, and all this admirable uproar is
made only with a few fragments of the lute and the unfortunate *Serenade ;* it is Beckmesser baited with his own
motive.

A note on the horn of the placid Watchman puts every
one to flight, and when he enters, every one has disappeared into his own house.

The *Peace of the Summer Night* alone reigns, and is
delightfully refreshing after all this amusing uproar.

Act III.

Scene I. — The Prelude is woven out of three new
motive : Sachs's Profound Emotion

SACHS'S PROFOUND EMOTION

serves as an opening and a conclusion; *Sachs's Choral*
(p. 337) and his *Biblical Song* (p. 340) form the middle
part.   The former, grave and sad, which has also been
called the theme of Human Wisdom, has already made
a brief appearance, almost unnoticed in fact, in Act II.,
Scene III.   It is now about to become very important.

At the rising of the curtain it combines with the gay
motiv David, forming a curious contrast.   Then come
memories of the Lute, of *The Serenade* and *The Beating ;*
shortly afterwards David sings *The Choral of the Jordan*
(p. 337); a recall of *Sachs's Profound Emotion* mingling
with *Waking Love ;* the *Patronal motiv of Nuremberg* re-

appears, accompanied by a new form which seems to characterize Nuremberg in holiday attire, the town *en fête.*

NUREMBERG EN FÊTE

The Peace of the Summer Night presents itself to Sachs's mind with fresh reminiscences of *The Serenade* and *The Beating*; *Saint John* is mingled with *Waking Love.* All these *motive* enable us to penetrate into Sachs's inner thoughts, they all relate to the subject of his preoccupation, and his emotion keeps increasing in proportion as he sees the moment approach when he will be able to complete his work by making two people happy.

Scene II. — A prolonged arpeggio announces Walter's arrival, greeted by the *Profound Emotion*, which is again mingled with *Waking Love.*

Walter relates that he has had a wonderful dream; and immediately in the orchestra is heard the *Harmony of the Dream.*

HARMONY OF THE DREAM

[which will only be given in its entirety in Scene IV.,

when the question arises of naming the melody which is the result of this dream, that is to say, some bars before the Quintet of Baptism.]

It is in this scene that the theme of *Sachs's Profound Emotion* reaches its fullest expression, while Sachs is

giving Walter one of the most beautiful and elevated
lessons in composition.   Incidentally there reappear,
every now and then, annotating the lecture, *Love Confessed*, *Walter*, and *Nuremberg en Fête*, in company with
the *Patronal Motiv*.

It is also in the course of this lesson that Sachs sings
the beautiful melody of *Memories of Youth* (p. 341), and
Walter sketches his graceful and poetic *Story of the
Dream*

STORY OF THE DREAM (PRIZE SONG)

Walter

[which later, when developed and polished according to the
advice of the worthy Master, becomes the *Prize Song*].

Note that the beginning of the third Strophe is none
other than the *motiv* of *Love Confessed*, which has been
familiar to us since the Overture, and here finds its
proper use.

Walter

SCENE III. — Various fragments of the Lute, *The Serenade*, and still more *The Beating*, accompany Beckmesser's entrance, not without jostling the *Profound Emotion*, *Saint Crispin*, *The Story of the Dream*, *Nuremberg*, *The Quarrelsome Beckmesser*, etc., but there is no new *motiv* in this scene.

SCENE IV. — Shortly after Eva's arrival, we must notice a pretty melodic figure of a delightful flexibility, which wonderfully aids in depicting her *Anxiety* in all the phases through which she is successively to pass, including hope, fear, and uncertainty.

EVA'S ANXIETY

The majority of the other *motive* follow it in procession, especially that of Walter, who now repeats the *Story of the Dream* in its entirety, followed by a new outbreak of *Sachs's Profound Emotion*, which comes in very appropriately.

Here occurs a musical fact which has no parallel in all Wagner's work, and which is full of witty appropriateness: Sachs, having to say that he knows the history of Tristan and Isolde, and that he has no intention of being a second King Mark, the orchestra illustrates his words by borrowing from the very score of *Tristan und Isolde*.   And how happily they are chosen!

The love of Tristan and Isolde is represented by the *motiv* of *Desire*, and King Mark by that of *Consternation* (see pp. 285 and 307).

Next, the *Choral of Baptism* (Act I., Scene I.) is cleverly recalled several times, the *Harmony of the Dream* here receives its full expansion, then comes the delightful vocal *ensemble* which has received the name of *The Baptism Quintet*, and which departs strangely from Wagnerian methods. We shall speak of it again (p. 342).

A kind of orchestral interlude, formed in particular of the *motive Nuremberg*, *Saint John*, and *The Meistersinger*, broken into by calls on the horns and trumpets, while the scene is changing, serves as a bond of union with the next tableau, which is formed entirely of a single scene.

SCENE V. — This last scene of the work does not contain a single new *motiv*.

The Corporations defile past: the Shoemakers are escorted by *Saint Crispin*; the Tailors and Bakers are preceded by their respective flourishes of trumpets; the Apprentices dance a rustic waltz full of animation; and then the entrance of the Meistersinger occurs to the tones of their own typical *motiv*, which, as would naturally happen in view of the solemnity, is escorted by *The Banner*, hailed by all the people, who spontaneously sing *Sachs's Choral* (p. 337), which redoubles the *Profound Emotion* of that worthy man.

He makes a short but heartfelt speech, accompanied by the figure of *The Assembly*, and the *motive* of *The Meistersinger* and *Saint John*. Then the Contest begins.

Beckmesser opens the ball. He stammers out Walter's verses, disfigured and deprived of all sense, to a melody (?) of the same kind as his *Serenade*, accompanying himself on his indescribable instrument; he

breaks down, he makes a fool of himself, he is hooted
by the crowd, and still more by the orchestra; he gets
into a rage ; *Quarrelsome Beckmesser* reappears.

After this return to the coarse buffoonery of the
second act, it is Walter's turn to sing ; for the last time
he sings his *Story of the Dream*, which has reached its
complete development, and now takes the name of the
Prize-Song.

The people applaud him, the Meistersinger themselves are gained over, all the love-*motive* cross and re-
cross in the orchestra, and Eva awards him the crown,
which she places upon his brow herself, to the first
phrase of the third strophe of the *Prize-Song*.

It is needless to say that all the *motive* have had
occasion to appear in the most joyful manner during
this *ensemble* scene.

Sachs steps forward to address the victor, takes his
hand, and then we hear, as at the conclusion of the
Overture, *Love Confessed* (the third Strophe of the
Prize-Song), associated with the theme of *The Meistersinger*, which, of course, the pompous *Banner* hastens
to join.

It is on these last *motive*, that is to say, those of the
Overture, that the work ends, in a riot of brilliant
trumpets.

Chorals.

The score of *Die Meistersinger von Nürnberg*, which
takes us back into the first years of Lutheran Reform,
contains three Chorals which are very important for us
to know.

The first is heard in the old church of Saint Katharine at the rising of the curtain, and is harmonized in
the austere and classic manner of J. S. Bach.

CHORAL OF BAPTISM

The second is sung by David almost at the end of the third act (Scene I.), under the melodic form.

CHORAL OF THE JORDAN

The third, which Wagner attributes to Sachs himself, appears in the Prelude of the third act sufficiently for us to recognize it again when the people give him a flattering ovation in the last scene.

CHORAL OF SACHS

INDEPENDENT MOTIVE.

We must also mention in addition, although they do not constitute *Leit-motive*, a few absolutely independent great and beautiful melodic forms, which are complete in themselves. They must be regarded as a species of *Lieder*, which produce a sense of repose in the midst of the contrapuntal net of the continuous melody, with which they, however, are often connected, either by the amusing details of their harmonic structure, or by the melodic figures which are designedly introduced into the accompaniments. The principal ones are:

The *motiv* of *Walter's Masters*, which is unfolded in two strophes and an envoy (Act I. Scene II.);

WALTER'S MASTERS

The Hymn to Spring, also of two strophes, but unlike each other, is delightful poetry of exquisite freshness; the accompaniment of which is almost entirely made up of fragments of *Impatient Ardour* (Act I., Scene, III.);

HYMN TO SPRING

The Melopœia of the Night-Watchman, which appears twice (Act II. Scene V. and Act II. end of Scene VII.), each time preceded and followed by a comical call on the horn, which always sounds horribly out of tune;

MELOPŒIA OF THE NIGHT WATCHMAN

The Biblical Song, which is at once archaic in form and full of genial humour, is formed of three regular couplets (Act II. Scene VI.). It is recalled in the Prelude to the third act;

BIBLICAL SONG

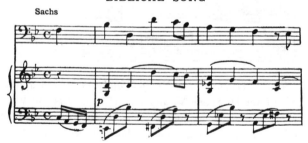

The *Memories of Youth* (Act III. Scene II.), and the

MEMORIES OF YOUTH

delicious *ensemble* of the *Quintet of Baptism*, which ends the fourth scene of the third act in the most graceful and poetic manner. The presence of a

THE PROPHETIC DREAM (Quintet of Baptism)

Quintet, a regularly-developed *ensemble* piece, is a matter of surprise in a work of the period of Wagner's full maturity.

We may, however, explain it by the consideration that the five characters on the stage at this moment are in perfect communion of ideas, and this relieves it from being in any way illogical.

However, it is probable that this piece was written long before the rest of the score, and was one of the first sketches (see p. 46), dating from the period of *Tannhäuser*.

THE TETRALOGY OF DER RING DES NIBELUNGEN.

NAMES of the Principal Leit-motive in the Tetralogy of the **RING DES NIBELUNGEN** in the order of their first appearance.	DAS RHEINGOLD	DIE WALKÜRE	SIEGFRIED	GÖTTERDÄMMERUNG

The Rhine
The Rhine-Daughters
Bondage
The Gold
The Adoration of the Gold
The Power of the Ring
The Renunciation of Love
The Ring
Walhalla
Hail to Walhalla
The Treaty
Love's Fascination
Frela
Flight
The Giants
Treaty with the Giants
The Golden Apples
Loge
The Flames' Spell
Love's Regret
The Forge
The Power of the Helm
Reflection
Alberich's Power
The Amassing of the Treasure
The Nibelung's Cry of Triumph
The Dragon
The Nibelungs' Work of Destruction
Curse of the Ring
The Norns
The Fall of the Gods
Incantation of Thunder
The Rainbow
The Sword

The Tempest
Siegmund's Fatigue
Compassion
Love
The Race of the Wälsungs
Hunding
The Heroism of the Wälsungs
Hymn to Spring
Delight
The Ride of the Walkyries
The Shout of the Walkyries
Wotan's Rage
The Distress of the Gods
Pursuit
Fate
Death
Siegfried, Guardian of the Sword
The Redemption by Love
Eternal Sleep
Brünnhilde's Sleep
The Announcement of a New Life
Wotan's Song of Farewell

Call of the Son of the Woods
The Love of Life
Filial Love
Desire to Travel
Wotan the Wanderer
Divine Power
Grovelling Mime
The Casting of the Steel
Fafner
Revenge
The Bird
The Heritage of the World
Hail to the World
Hail to Love
The Enthusiasm of Love
Peace
Siegfried, Treasure of the World
The Decision to Love

Brünnhilde
Heroic Love
Hagen's Perfidious Friendship
Treachery by Magic
Gutrune's Welcome
The Justice of Expiation
Murder
Call to the Marriage

DER RING DES NIBELUNGEN

DAS RHEINGOLD

PRELUDE. — The prelude of *Das Rheingold* consists exclusively of that colossal hold of a single chord, the chord of E-flat, of which we have already spoken (p. 257). This sustained note is in itself a *Leit-motiv* of the most expressive, descriptive, and philosophical character. It symbolizes the primitive element, water, in a state of repose; the water from which, according to the teaching of mythology, life springs complete with all its struggles and passions. During this long sustained note we hear the beginnings of life; but those are things which are outside the province of words, and which music alone, speaking without an intermediary to the intelligence, can hope to make us comprehend.

First, we hear a single mysterious note, very grave and greatly protracted: this is Nature asleep; to this fundamental, single, and primitive tone is then added its fifth; and, after a long interval, the octave; then, one by one, all the other harmonics in the same order in which Nature produces them; then, passing notes, more and more frequent; then appear rhythms, at first rudimentary, which mingle and assume complicated forms; organization has already commenced; at long intervals new instruments are added; a kind of regular and cadenced undulation is established, giving the feeling of water in movement; the sound gradually swells out and invades the orchestra like a torrent; the movement of the waves is accentuated, a trembling arises and increases, bringing the prescience of life; and, when the curtain rises, we are not in the least surprised to

find ourselves at the bottom of a large flowing river, full
to the banks; our mind had already pictured what the
scenery reveals.

[This prodigious *motiv*, which is often called the *motiv* of the
Primeval Element, throughout the whole Tetralogy is destined
to personify the Rhine, and yet its recurrences will not be very
frequent. Outside the Prologue which is constructed upon it,
we shall only find it again incidentally and hastily sketched in
the first scene of *Siegfried*, simply because the latter in his
imaginative talk speaks of the fishes which swim ; it resumes its
greatest importance in *Götterdämmerung* every time there is a
question of restoring the treasure to the Rhine, which is considered here as the representative of the primordial element,
water.

But its chief importance dominates the entire work and manifests itself in the fact that the majority of the most essential
motive are formed out of its constituent elements ; that is to say
from the *natural harmonic tones* (the perfect major chord),
grouped in various ways and more or less ornamented with pass-
ing-notes, which any musician will be able to recognize. Chief
among those which are most unquestionably derived from it in
this way, and which we shall meet in the following pages, I
will cite : *The Rhine-Daughters*, *The Rhine-gold*, *The Golden
Apples*, *The Norns*, *The Fall of the Gods*, *The Incantation of
the Thunder*, *The Rainbow*, *The Sword*, *The Ride of the
Walkyries*, and *Brünnhilde's Sleep*, etc., the signification of
which, whether material, psychological, or metaphysical, always
allows some relation or other to be established between them
and the idea of the primeval element.]

Here, then, is this important *motiv* under some of the
principal forms which it successively assumes from the
beginning of the Prelude, which Prelude it wholly fills,
constantly flooding and increasing in volume without
ever leaving the single chord of E-flat major.

It is a marvel of boldness and genius.

THE RHINE

SCENE I. — As soon as a new chord appears, life itself is manifested by the presence and the seductively innocent song of the charming *Rhine-Daughters*, gracefully swimming around their Gold.

THE RHINE-DAUGHTERS

This beguiling and flexible *motiv*, mingled with *The Rhine*, dominates the whole of the *ensemble* in Scene I., interrupted, however, by certain harsh and clashing rhythms, one on the entrance of Alberich (G minor), and the other in ²-time, both undoubtedly depicting the ungraceful gait and repulsive advances of the hateful gnome.

[The second will be recognized at the beginning of Scene III.]

When Alberich has met with the successive refusals of the three Undines, he vents his rage in a kind of miserable cry, twice repeated, formed of only two notes in the descending minor second, which vividly expresses the despair caused by his impotence.

BONDAGE

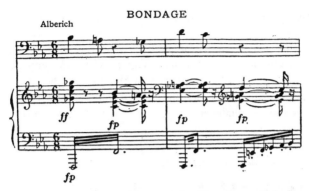

[This brief formula throughout the Tetralogy will be connected with the ideas of *Bondage,* servitude, or subjugation, and its use will be very frequent, not to say perpetual.

If it is difficult to recognize it on account of its brevity, yet the painful character of its accents will always attract attention.]

At the moment when the Gold shines forth, it is saluted by a brilliant flourish of trumpets, which is repeated several times and will remain its characteristic

GOLD

motiv, visibly derived from *The Rhine,* as it logically should be, since it is the Gold of the Rhine.

In the brilliant *ensemble* of the three voices which follows this vision of the Gold, the latter is glorified by a kind of cry of joy from the Nymphs; it assumes two different forms, which may be presented separately or in combination without losing any of its signification thereby; this cry is not afterwards attached to the Nymphs personally, except in so far as is necessary to convey the

idea of joy.   It is the *Adoration of the Gold*, nothing
more.

The first form is generally twice repeated. (We
must also notice that when Wagner wishes to impress
a *Leit-motiv* upon the attention of the listener, he never
fears insisting upon it, and that is one of the things
which never render it necessary for us to hunt for them ;
it is sufficient to listen.)

In its second form we must note its vocal accent, its
characteristic inflection and instrumental design, glittering like polished metal ; each will be employed separately

while still meaning the same thing; it is always *The Adoration of the Gold*.

It is then that one of the Nymphs commits the fatal indiscretion of revealing to the gnome the omnipotence with which a Ring will be endowed if forged from this Gold, and she does this by means of the following new *motiv*, which, it will be remarked, offers many resemblances to that of the *Ring*, which does not appear till later.

THE POWER OF THE RING

Wellgunde

To tell the truth, the action of the entire drama hinges on this; without the thoughtless chatter of the Nixies, Alberich would not have thought of stealing the Gold which is to cause so many misfortunes.

THE RENUNCIATION OF LOVE

Woglinde

But, in order to possess this Gold, another Daughter of the Rhine informs him, it is necessary to renounce love.

Alberich does not hesitate for long; seeing the impossibility of gaining and embracing the agile Nymphs, he turns his ambitious thoughts in the direction of wealth and power; the orchestra, echoing his thoughts, darkly murmurs the theme of *The Power of the Ring*, followed by the formula of *Renunciation*, and immediately afterwards, springing eagerly upon the rock, mounting, or rather scaling it, he succeeds in seizing the coveted Gold.

At the very end of Scene I. there appears for the first time the theme which is especially attached to the *Ring*.

THE RING

[This, be it understood, will run through the entire work.]

SCENE II. — By a method frequent with Wagner,
but which here finds one of its most beautiful applica-
tions, the above *motiv*, by a series of transformations,
is insensibly merged into that of *Walhalla*, which is
absolutely different in character, majestically depicting
the sumptuous Palace of the Gods. This *motiv* placidly
reveals its splendour in the calm and sweet key of D-
flat major.

WALHALLA

[It will be subject to many transformations. In *Siegfried*,
Act III. Scene I., we see it triumphant in 4-time associated
with the theme of *The Sword* :

in the second act of *Götterdämmerung*, at the end of the first
scene, where Alberich is prompting Hagen to reconquer their
power, it appears dismantled, in ruins, and contemptible.

Alberich

It has already been seen in this condition in Act II. Scene II. of *Die Walküre*, when Wotan foresees the approaching end of the gods.

Finally, it is often represented by its last notes alone, forming a conclusion of great splendour, in which we may recognize a kind of majestic *Hail to Walhalla*, found in *Rheingold*, Scene II., three bars before the suppression of the flats.]

HAIL TO WALHALLA

Three bars farther on appears the theme called *The Treaty*, representing in a general way the idea of any treaty, of a pact, or a bargain struck, which is first energetically expressed by its first two notes (which are the same as *Bondage*), followed by a descent by steps which are as deliberate, heavy, and implacable as destiny, giving the idea of a duty to be fulfilled.

THE TREATY

Forty-two bars later we find the pretty theme of *Love's Fascination*, which first forms the second half of a beautiful phrase sung by Fricka (in F), and which Wotan takes up shortly afterwards (in E-flat), thus :

LOVE'S FASCINATION

At the moment when Freïa comes flying on to the stage, this *motiv* is heard for the first time in the double

FREÏA FLIGHT

form, the two parts of which have two distinct sig-
nifications; the first belongs to Freïa, the goddess of
love, and will remain personal to her; the second represents *Flight*, and will henceforth express the act of
flight, whosoever the flying personage may be. In the
present case it represents Freïa in full flight from her
persecutors.

Almost immediately afterwards *The Giants* appear with

THE GIANTS

their ponderous, heavy, and massive *motiv*, which seems
as if it might remove rocks; this theme will undergo a
curious transformation in *Siegfried*, when it has to represent one of the Giants changed to a Dragon (p. 400).

When it is no longer a question of designating any
pact or treaty whatsoever, but only *that treaty concluded
with the Giants for the construction of Walhalla*, Wagner
has recourse to a fresh form which is not without some
affinity to the *motiv* of *The Treaty*, and which is generally treated in canon.

TREATY WITH THE GIANTS

Fasolt

It is in this scene, 37 bars after the signature of the key in A-flat, that this *motiv* is heard for the first time.

About two pages farther on, a graceful contrast is afforded by the elegant figure of *The Golden Apples,*— those apples which supply the gods with eternal youth, and which Freïa alone can cultivate, which Fafner exhibits to us on the most cavernous notes of his deep bass voice, and which, by the contrast, gives a rather curious effect.

THE GOLDEN APPLES

Fafner

The typical *motiv* which corresponds to the personality of the god Loge is as changing and variable as himself. The example given below, which accompanies his first

entrance, groups together and unites many essentially
chromatic figures, which seem to be writhing and hiss-
ing, and by which he is always represented; these same
figures are frequently inverted, and descend, or are
truncated and modified, but they are always easily recognizable, as no other *Leit-motiv* has this leaping motion
and malicious behaviour.

Closely related to the latter is the scintillating *motiv* of *The Flames*, which appears here immediately after it

THE FLAMES' SPELL

[and will guard Brünnhilde's slumber in the third act of *Die Walküre*].

The last new *motiv* which this scene presents is the following, which may be readily found when the signature of the key of D in ¾ appears: it is called *Love's Regret*.

LOVE'S REGRET

During the changing of the scene, there is a kind of interlude, which is purely musical, picturing the descent of Wotan and Loge into dark Nibelheim, to Alberich's subterranean forge.   This interlude is principally built up on the *motiv* of *Loge*, with some recollections of Lamentation, *Bondage*, *Gold*, and *Flight*, of the significa- tion of which there is no doubt ; gradually in the orches- tra the rhythm of the *motiv* of *The Forge* appears, which is taken up with an ever-increasing vigour by anvils in tune behind the scenes.

THE FORGE

Finally there is a double return of *Bondage* and *The Ring*, and we reach

Scene III., in which, almost at the beginning, as Al- berich is desirous of testing the power of the *Magic Helm* (*The Tarnhelm*) which he has made Mime forge for him, the orchestra introduces to us the mysterious harmony by which it is to be musically designated.   These chords, which are sometimes given to horns stationed in the wings, produce the most strange effect.   The German word *Tarnhelm* has been variously translated : The En- chanted Helm, The Charm of the Helm, or, again,

THE POWER OF THE HELM

After a loud repetition of the rhythm of *The Forge* there comes a strange series of disjunct thirds, which seem to represent reflection or profound meditation, applicable to various characters.

REFLECTION

Considerably farther on in the same scene when Alberich, in the fulness of his pride, fondles his Ring and waves it in a threatening manner, is heard for the first time the *motiv* characteristic of his power and the vanity which arises from it. It is very interesting closely to study this somewhat complex *motiv*, which in the following example is given to the orchestra, and in which,

ALBERICH'S POWER

though somewhat modified by the use of chromatics and of the minor, we may trace the two forms of *The Adoration of the Gold* (p. 348), followed by the first notes of *The Amassing of the Treasure*, given below.

THE AMASSING OF THE TREASURE

(The first form of *The Adoration of the Gold* is here combined with *Bondage*.)

A little farther appears the *motiv* of *The Amassing of the Treasure*, which sheds a passing glory upon the dwarf.

[It will be found curiously associated with *Bondage* and *The Forge*, when the captured dwarf is forced to give up his treasure to Wotan.]

A curiously constructed *motiv* is that which has been called *The Nibelung's Cry of Triumph*. It is composed

THE NIBELUNG'S CRY OF TRIUMPH

of one bar taken from *Walhalla*, and another assuming
the form peculiar to *Loge*, thus showing that Alberich
already considers himself, by means of fire, the master
of the world, and this is why he exults.

Much more simple, but exceedingly descriptive, is the
roaring *motiv* of *The Dragon*, which naturally occurs
when, at the request of his visitors, the proud dwarf assumes this form by the aid of his helm.

THE DRAGON

Having captured the dwarf, the gods return to the
surface of the earth with their prisoner, which gives rise
to a fresh change of scenery and a new symphonic interlude. The latter begins with a reminiscence, which is
most certainly ironical, of *The Nibelung's Cry of Triumph*,
in which the element of fire, *Loge*, displays an unusual
development; *The Ring* appears joyously and ends with
The Lamentation; then reappear the sounds of *The Forge*,
but gradually dying away; the feeling is given that we
are going over the same road in the contrary direction.
After a return of *Flight*, the *motiv* of *The Giants* is

faintly heard, as if to remind us that they are not far off;
it is combined with *Walhalla*, then with *Bondage*, and is
connected with the succeeding scene by means of a
pedal on the dominant, above which is heard *The Adoration of the Gold.*

SCENE IV. — At the very beginning of the scene
in the 9th bar, an amusing little leaping figure represents
the god Loge, joyfully dancing and snapping his fingers
around the bound dwarf.   Without having the character
of a *Leit-motiv*, it is repeated two pages later.   Note
also the imitative manner in which the orchestra renders
the noise of the rubbing together of the cords as Loge
gradually frees the Nibelung from his bonds.

Immediately he is free, the following menacing rhythm
darkly mutters in the depths of the " mystic abyss,"

THE NIBELUNGS' WORK OF DESTRUCTION

expressing the continuous labour by which the vindictive
gnomes will henceforth ceaselessly undermine the divine
abode, sapping at its base until it is completely ruined.

[This easily recognizable rhythm will not reappear in *Die
Walküre,* but it will be found very frequently in *Siegfried* and
in *Götterdämmerung.*]

Alberich, in a phrase of demoniacal expression, immediately hurls his anathema at the *Ring, which he curses,*
and which henceforth shall bring misfortune on all its
possessors.

CURSE OF THE RING

This malevolent *motiv* is nearly always acccompanied by the rhythm of *Destruction*, and, towards the end of the curse, by *Alberich's Power*, which is immediately qualified with *Bondage*.

The action proceeds without the necessity of any new *motive* being introduced till the moment of the appearance of Erda, who in sinister tones announces the theme of *The Norns*, her daughters, the Fates of Scandinavian

THE NORNS

mythology. This *motiv* reproduces, in the minor and in 4-time, the principal form of *The Rhine*, the original element.

In the same way by contrary motion the *Fall of the Gods*[1] is derived from it; this, as well as *The Ring*, appears with the last words of Erda's prophecy, which has been accompanied by *The Norns* and *The Work of Destruction*.

THE FALL OF THE GODS

The numerous *Leit-motive* which have been already created suffice for Wagner until the formidable *Incantation of the Thunder*, which stormily echoes on the blaring brass.

INCANTATION OF THE THUNDER

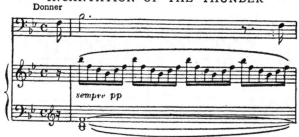

---

[1] The classic term adopted is *The Dusk of the Gods* (*Götterdämmerung*); I employ the word *Fall* here for the purpose of avoiding in the rest of this analysis any confusion between this *Leit-motiv* and the *Götterdämmerung* Day of the Tetralogy.

[This theme will only reappear once, in the Prelude of
Die Walküre.]

After the passage of a brief storm, there quickly
appears the radiant and serene theme of *The Rainbow*,
tracing its beautiful span beneath a measured and sparkling trill of the violins, flutes, and all the shrill
instruments.

THE RAINBOW

[This *motiv* will not reappear in any of the other divisions.]

The *motiv* of *Walhalla* accompanies the passage of
the gods across the celestial bridge. We feel that

Wotan's brain is busy with the idea of the *Ring* which he has had to gain, and then relinquish in payment for his palace; also *The Rhine*, from which it was originally stolen, and the necessity for creating an invincible means for his defence, thence springs, like a flash of lightning, the thought of *The Sword of the Gods*, the last new *Leit-motiv* found in the Prologue.

THE SWORD

The Rhine-Daughters are heard bewailing their stolen gold, and the entry into Walhalla takes place with a pompous *reprise* of the theme of *The Rainbow*.

DIE WALKÜRE.

SCENE I. — The Prelude represents a storm violently raging; with roaring blasts, lightning and thunder and torrents of rain, several times *The Incantation of the Thunder*, combined with the theme of *The Tempest* itself, is heard; it is one of the most beautiful storms that exist, either on the stage, or in symphonic composition.

THE TEMPEST

As the curtain rises, the tempest abates.

Then the six descending notes (B, A, G, F, E, D) of
The Tempest motiv, by a slight rhythmical modification,
become characteristic of *Siegmund's Fatigue* (a fatigue
partly caused by the tempest), as he staggers in, buffeted
and pursued by the storm.

SIEGMUND'S FATIGUE

[This fact bears a certain analogy with that which we have
already noticed in the transition of the first to the second tableau
in *Rheingold*, where the theme of *Walhalla* seems to arise from
that of *The Ring* which paid for it.   Other examples of the
same nature, all of which we cannot mention, are fairly numerous in this work, and this fusion of *motive* always logically
springs from an association of ideas.]

This first *motiv* almost immediately (shortly after Sieglinde's entrance) is united with another which we shall
find very often associated with it; the latter personifies
Sieglinde's tender sympathy for Siegmund, and has been
called *Compassion* :

COMPASSION

At the conclusion of a fine unaccompanied violoncello passage, which is taken from *Siegfried's Fatigue*, reappears the *motiv* of *Flight* which we have already seen in *Rheingold*, where it has quite another rhythm and was combined with *Freïa*. Here it is united with a new theme, *Love*, which may be thus explained : it is *Flight* which has brought Siegmund under Sieglinde's roof, and which consequently is primarily responsible for their *Love*.

FLIGHT   **LOVE**

[Some pages farther on, the theme of *Love* will precede *Flight ;* it will then signify that *Love* in its turn is the cause of the *Flight* of the twins.]

At the moment when Siegmund, somewhat refreshed and already about to depart, at Sieglinde's instance decides to remain under her roof, we hear for the first time one of the themes which are stamped with noble sadness which will henceforth represent the race which, although of divine origin, is so profoundly unhappy and persecuted, *The Wälsungs*.

THE RACE OF THE WÄLSUNGS

Associated with *Compassion*, and then followed by *Love*, this beautiful theme is heard twice almost consecutively before *Hunding's* arrival.

SCENE II.—The theme of the latter, although of noble character, by its violence, its harsh rhythm and rude orchestration, forms a startling contrast with the preceding one, and from this moment the characters of

HUNDING

the two men are clearly defined; in proportion as Siegmund is dignified and resigned in suffering, Hunding appears violent, implacable, and brutal. The whole dialogue between the enemies is illustrated by these two *motive* alternating, with some short appearances of *Love* and *Compassion*, corresponding to a word, or even a gesture, of Sieglinde's, also *The Treaty*, *The Storm*, and even *Walhalla*, according to the former events to which the poem alludes. It is only when the Wälsung ends the story of his misfortunes, that to the first theme of *The*

Race of the Wälsungs there immediately follows and is joined a second theme of a similar sentiment but particularly characterizing *The Heroism* of that race in the sufferings which pursue it.

THE HEROISM OF THE WÄLSUNGS

Before the close of the scene, when Sieglinde tries to direct her guest's attention to the weapon which is imbedded in the ash, we twice hear the *motiv* of *The Sword*, immediately followed by the menace of *Hunding*.

SCENE III. — This scene, one of the most affecting of the noble work, passes with the aid of the *motive* we already know, to which, towards the end of Sieglinde's story, is added a startling trumpet passage and a rich passage for the violins, which remind us of Weber, and are often repeated, but only in this scene. Then after a gust of wind which is represented by arpeggios on the harps, a gust at which the massive door suddenly opens, there appears the radiant and delicious *Hymn to Spring*,

HYMN TO SPRING

which, although constituting an independent figure, may
also be considered as a *Leit-motiv*, since it will be the subject of many suggestive references in the following act.

Shortly afterwards, in company with the *motive* of
Love, *Freia*, goddess of Love, and *Spring*, appears *Delight*,

DELIGHT

a caressing and intoxicating *motiv* which we shall meet with again in the Prelude to Scene III. in Act II. Siegmund is about to tear out the sword; then appear the *motive* of *The Wälsungs*, *Heroism*, *The Treaty*, *The Sword*, and the terrible formula of *The Renunciation of Love*, and on a powerful development of the latter the Sword of the Gods is in Siegmund's grasp; at this precise moment the theme of *The Sword* reaches its greatest splendour, and the act ends with symphonic combinations of former *motive*, the most important of which are *Love*, *Spring*, and *Flight*, and, finally, in the last two chords, *Bondage*.

ACT II.

PRELUDE. — This Prelude is composed of the most curious mixture of themes which are harsh, or made harsh by circumstances, which from the very beginning gives us a premonition of *The Ride of the Walkyries*, which, however, does not appear till the end.

In the opening bar we recognize *The Sword*, although quite changed in rhythm and key; then follow *Flight*, which in the same manner is merged into *The Shout of the Walkyries*, *Delight*, and then the final burst, *The Ride of the Walkyries*.

THE RIDE OF THE WALKYRIES

SCENE I. — The strident *Shout of the Walkyries*, with which Brünnhilde makes her first appearance, presents us with the peculiarity, which is perhaps unique in Wagner's work, of a phrase of 18 bars, complete in itself, ending with a cadence and twice repeated almost immediately afterwards without the least change of melody, harmony, or orchestration.

THE SHOUT OF THE WALKYRIES

The entrance of Fricka, which immediately follows, is announced by the two notes of *Bondage;* her discussion with Wotan affords opportunity for repetitions of *Hunding, Love, Spring, The Sword, Flight, The Treaty, The Ring, The Treaty with the Giants,* which subjects often rise to the surface, either in their speech, or in their minds.

When Wotan finds himself conquered by the arguments and persistence of the virtuous but peevish goddess, the orchestra introduces us to a new figure which represents Wotan in anger, *Wotan's Rage,*

WOTAN'S RAGE

It should be remarked that this very significant form, which will be very frequently used, is often reduced to its first two notes, resembling those of *Bondage,* which is easily explicable, but in that case it almost always preserves the *gruppetto* which so energetically accents the first note, and gives it the character of a kind of rumble.

Brünnhilde's return brings back *The Ride*, accompanied by *The Shout*; after which Fricka celebrates the victory which she has just gained over her husband with a highly expressive phrase, which is as though sealed as a pact by *The Treaty*, followed, immediately Fricka has disappeared, by *The Curse of the Ring*, and *Wotan's Rage*, which links it with the next scene.

SCENE II. — This long scene, in which Wotan is forced to confess his crimes and errors to his daughter as well as the circumstances which led him to commit them, cannot fail to bring them to our mind by means of the *Leit-motive*; we find *Love*, *The Treaty*, *Love's Regret*, *The Power of the Ring*, *Walhalla*, *The Norns*, *The Ride*, *The Ring*, and *The Treaty with the Giants*. Only one new figure appears, that which characterizes *The Distress of the Gods*; then return *The Curse of the Ring*, *The Sword*,

THE DISTRESS OF THE GODS

and *The Nibelungs' Work of Destruction*; here also we find that strange transformation of *Walhalla* (mentioned on p. 351), which reveals the edifice in ruins, crumbling away, and appears twice at an interval of 20 bars, announcing the fall and annihilation of the race of the Gods. However, the dominating *motiv*, especially at the beginning, is that of *Wotan's Rage*. When we have succeeded in overcoming the painful impression caused by the situation, this scene, notwithstanding its length, stands out as one of the finest in the work; but it is also one of the most difficult to grasp on the first reading or hearing.

At the moment when Brünnhilde, being left alone, gathers up her arms, we should note the theme of *The Ride*, dulled and saddened; immediately afterwards her thoughts carry her away to *The Race of the Wälsungs*, and then settle on *Wotan's Rage* and *The Distress of the Gods*. All this is wonderfully expressed.

SCENE III. — Siegmund and Sieglinde come in flying before the pursuing Hunding; the *motiv* of *Flight*, presented in a thousand ways, each one more ingenious than the other, does all the work of the scene for ten pages or so, sometimes accompanied by *Love*, sometimes by *Delight*. After a recall of the *Heroism of the Wälsungs* and *The Sword*, *Hunding* is announced by the rhythm of his *motiv*, given to the drums, immediately followed by *Pursuit* and the hoarse cry of his hounds.

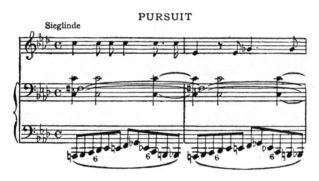

PURSUIT

When Sieglinde falls fainting in Siegmund's arms, *Love* returns with the memory of *Flight*.

SCENE IV. — Here we find one of the most important scenes. Brünnhilde comes to announce to the hero that he must die. The orchestra informs us that *Fate* has decided the *Death* of Siegmund, and that he is to go to *Walhalla*.

The two following *motive*, which are intimately connected, should be closely examined : first comes *Fate*,

FATE

the harmonization of which is almost invariable, and the formula of which, generally twice repeated, separated by rests, rises like an enigmatical and gloomy note of interrogation ; *Death* is evidently derived from it, since by suppressing the first three notes we find ourselves in the presence of the double formula of *Fate*.

DEATH

These new *motive*, mingled with those of *Walhalla*, of *Freïa*, of *The Ride*, of *Love* with *Flight*, of *Wotan's Rage*, and of *Love's Regret* suffice as commentary on the action while Brünnhilde describes to Siegmund, who is not willing to leave Sieglinde, the splendours and delights of the celestial abode ; but at the moment when the desperate Wälsung raises his blade above his sleeping wife, we hear for the first time, though in a still vague form, the theme of *Siegfried Guardian of the Sword* (Act

III. Scene I.), which informs us of the existence of the
child in its mother's frame. It is then that Brünnhilde, touched with tender emotion by this act of heroism, decides to transgress the divine commands, and take
Siegmund's part, a decision which is to be her ruin; it
is then that, with a marvellous stroke of genius, Wagner
suddenly transforms the *motiv* of *Death* from the minor
to the major, changing its character and introducing into
it the rhythm of *Flight;* it is now no longer Siegmund's
death which is decreed, but Hunding's.   From this moment this is how the *motiv* of *Death* is transfigured:

Brünnhilde having departed, the question of *Fate* is
again asked, combined with *Wotan's Rage* and joined
with *Love.*

SCENE V. — Scene V. contains no new *motive*.

Although very short, it may be considered as divided into four parts: 1, Siegmund's farewell to the sleeping Sieglinde as he departs for the combat; 2, the hostile pursuit during Sieglinde's dream; 3, the combat, with the double intervention of Brünnhilde and Wotan; 4, the malediction which Wotan launches at the Walkyrie. During the first part, the tender *motive* of *Love* and *Freïa* rule, disturbed by those of *Fate* and *Pursuit*. In the second, *Hunding's* savage shout, *The Sword* and *Pursuit*, which become more and more insistent. (Here and there occur flashes of lightning similar to those which were seen in the first Prelude.) — In the third, the combat; in a few seconds we hear the gallop of Brünnhilde's horse as she comes to encourage Siegmund in the fight, *The Ride*; then comes Wotan, who, forced by *The Treaty*, shatters *The Sword*; the death of Siegmund is accompanied by four sorrowful recalls of *Bondage*, followed by *The Heroism of the Wälsungs*, *Fate*, and *Wotan's Rage*; finally, Brünnhilde lifts the unfortunate Sieglinde upon her horse, whence we have a return of *The Ride*, and then *Fate* again and again. All this passes extremely quickly, in less time than it takes to tell. — In the fourth part of the scene, Wotan, while striking Hunding dead with a lightning glance, reflects that he has loyally fulfilled his promise to Fricka, which is told to us by means of *The Treaty*, which, it will be remembered, applies to every pact and contract of any kind whatsoever; besides, far from being appeased, the *Rage* immediately reappears, and Wotan, breaking out into sudden fury, curses the disobedient Walkyrie and devotes her to a cruel vengeance. The curtain quickly falls while the orchestra recalls to us *The Distress of the Gods*, as well as various episodes of the act, the flashes of lightning which illuminated it, and *Pursuit*, which appears here for the last time.

ACT III.

PRELUDE. — The Prelude of the third act needs no comment. It is *The Ride* in its complete development, with its sonorous neighings and prancings, its wild and exultant cries, its indefatigable activity, its shouts and savage laughter.

SCENE I. — Throughout the first part of this scene while the key of G minor and the rhythm of $\frac{9}{8}$ reign, it is all borrowed from *The Ride*, of which, to tell the truth, it is only the continuation, with the exception of a brief allusion to *Walhalla*, when Rossweisse asks if it is time to go there, twenty-three bars before the $\frac{3}{4}$ in C minor, which announces Brünnhilde's arrival. There, although its rhythm is changed, we recognize the figure in the bass of *The Distress of the Gods;* shortly afterwards in D minor it is the song of *Death* and then *Flight*. No other rhythm appears with such importance until the words of Schwertleite describing the *Dragon* keeping watch over the Ring.

In the $\frac{6}{8}$ by Brünnhilde appears in all its grandeur the splendid theme of *Siegfried Guardian of the Sword*,

SIEGFRIED GUARDIAN OF THE SWORD
Brünnhilde

of which we only gained a glimpse in the fourth scene of the preceding act, immediately followed by *The Sword*; then, when Sieglinde speaks, there appears the enthusiastic and sublime *motiv* of *The Redemption by Love*.

THE REDEMPTION BY LOVE

[The latter will only appear again in the last scene of *Götterdämmerung*, where it will acquire a preponderating importance, and will furnish the touching crown of the entire work.]

Immediately afterwards *The Storm* reappears with *Bondage*, and then a very brief *ensemble* of the eight Walkyries brings the scene to a conclusion.

SCENE II. — The second scene (Wotan's reprimands of Brünnhilde in the presence of her sisters, who at first try to conceal her, and then to defend her), is dramatically impressive enough in itself to dispense with *Leit-motive*; however, after a time, we find, frequently renewed, *Wotan's Rage*, then *Death*, superbly developed, *The Treaty*, and, finally, at the moment of the departure of the Walkyries, *The Ride*, which here resembles a rout, and from which a broad phrase detaches itself and stands out, bearing some analogy with *Death*.

SCENE III. — The beginning of the scene for some considerable time makes use of only two typical *motive*, one of which is *The Rage*, which we know. The other, which first appears in the fourth bar in a figure on the violoncello, here represents poor Brünnhilde's submissive resignation to the paternal will, which is about to impose on her a new life, a human existence :

it is repeated in the same way seven bars later, and then it is modified in the 102d bar, this time on the violins :

It must be regarded as a preparatory form, a sort of leading up to a very important *motiv* which will shortly appear on the arrival of the key of E major, *The Announcement of a New Life*,

THE ANNOUNCEMENT OF A NEW LIFE

but will only attain its fullest expansion in the symphonic part which precedes Wotan's farewell, this time in $\frac{4}{4}$, almost at the end of the act.

From this moment *Leit-motive* occur more frequently: *Love's Regret*, *The Curse of the Ring*, *Fate*, *The Treaty*, *Love*, *The Heroism of the Wälsungs*, *Siegfried Guardian of the Sword*, then· *The Sword*; finally, when Wotan utters his inflexible doom, we hear for the first time the mysterious harmony of *Eternal Sleep*

ETERNAL SLEEP

[which will frequently reappear at the end of this work and in the following ones without being applied to one character more than another, and sometimes accompanied by a figure borrowed from *The Flames*].

Here we hear it repeated twice in succession separated by a brief reminiscence of *Walhalla*.

Almost immediately we have several premonitions, at first in the minor,

of the striking *motiv* which is soon to become *The Sleep of the Walkyrie*:

BRÜNNHILDE'S SLEEP

The latter now assumes more and more importance and brings to a conclusion the second division of the Tetralogy, accompanied by the leaping of the flames of Loge:

But first occurs the affecting scene of Wotan's Farewell and the Fire Incantation. We may consider it as beginning exactly at that place of which we have already spoken when the *motiv* of *The Announcement of a New Life* in E major and $\frac{4}{4}$ time again appears in its most magnificent and dazzling aspect, rising in a splendid crescendo, and majestically bursting forth on a chord of the fourth and sixth in the theme of *Brünnhilde's Sleep*.

Then *Sleep* deepens, the minor key reappears, and, in a beautiful passage (at the eighteenth bar of the minor), we hear the phrase which is properly called *Wotan's Song of Farewell*, full of tenderness and emotion, which will never again be separated from the figure of *Sleep*.

WOTAN'S SONG OF FAREWELL

Next comes *Fate*, *The Renunciation of Love*, then, at
the moment when his words cease, *Eternal Sleep*, during
which the Walkyrie falls asleep in the arms of the god.
And while he lays her upon the rock, places her weapons
by her side, and covers her with her shield, the orchestra
repeats to us in its complete development that touching
phrase of the *Farewell Song*, with the caressing interweavings of *Sleep*.

Then comes the Fire Incantation. Immediately the
motive change. First comes *The Treaty*, then the
chromatic figure of *Loge* · and again *The Treaty*, this
time followed by *The Flames' Spell*. These two *motive*
(*Loge* and *The Flames' Spell*) never cease to pursue each
other while the rock is being surrounded by flames, and
serve as an accompaniment to whatever others are introduced until the fall of the curtain. Then once more
appears *Eternal Sleep*, in the arpeggio form which we
have above noticed on p. (386), and then, this time to
last until the end, *Brünnhilde's Sleep*, becoming increas-
ingly placid and spell-bound.

No words could express Wotan's last words; they
reproduce in its entirety and majestically amplified, the
beautiful *motiv* of *Siegfried Guardian of the Sword*, which
is immediately repeated by the orchestra, which concludes it with the solemn phrase of *Wotan's Farewell*.

Ten bars before the end, during Wotan's last look at his sleeping daughter, without any interruption either of *Sleep*, or of the leaping of the *Flames*, the sinister menace of *Fate* heavily mutters; then there is a great peace, and the curtain slowly falls.

SIEGFRIED

ACT I.

PRELUDE. — If we regard the Tetralogy in its entirety as a kind of immense symphony conceived in gigantic proportions, one movement of which answers to each day, *Siegfried* appears as its Scherzo, its impetuous Intermezzo.

Everything in it is gay, agile, and alert, like the youthful hero himself; even the comic element has its place here, and frequently appears in the rôle of Mime. The majority of the new *motive* present rhythms which are vigorous and gay, or are stamped with a youthful ardour which is very contagious. Here also musicians will find the most novel harmonies, — the most daring, if the reader prefers, — which are sometimes difficult to explain, and among them the most amusing combinations of *Leit-motive*. The *Siegfried* Day is one of repose and freshness, from which the tragic element is almost entirely excluded, to the great relief of the mind and imagination, only to reappear in a still more poignant form on the morrow.

The Prelude is constructed on themes already known: first *Reflection*, then *The Amassing of the Treasure*, interrupted by a brief allusion to *Wotan's Rage*, which is quickly transformed into *Bondage*, *The Forge*, *The Nibelung's Cry of Triumph*, *The Ring*, *The Sword*, *The Dragon*, with a modified rhythm, in fact, all that are necessary to let us know beforehand that we are in the rude Forge in which the crafty Mime labours, scheming to gain in his turn the treasure which will assure to him the dominion of the world.

SCENE I. — The same *motive*, or others equally well-known, supply the first scene until the arrival of Siegfried, which is joyously announced by his *Call of the Son of the Woods*, the hunting-call of the young and intrepid hero, breathing forth freedom, boldness, and good humour.

CALL OF THE SON OF THE WOODS

[We shall find it in this same ⅜ time, but greatly developed in the key of F, in Scene II., for it is with this that Siegfried defies the Dragon ; and again, at the beginning of the third act of *Götterdämmerung*.]

[Note that this same *motiv*, transformed and in 4-time, will appear on other occasions in the *Götterdämmerung*, where it will assume a specially heroic character, and lose all its joyousness.]

[Note also the curious combination of this *motiv* with those of *The Flames* and *Eternal Sleep* which is found in the third Act of *Siegfried*, when the hero is about to pass the circle of fire in which the Walkyrie is sleeping.]

The Flames' Spell

Son of the Woods

Eternal Sleep

Immediately Siegfried, at two successive repetitions of *The Guardian of the Sword*, has made the sword which Mime has forged fly into splinters, a new *motiv* appears which is full of animation; this is *The Love of Life*, which will dominate a great part of the scene; it must rather be regarded as the exuberance of life, the joy of living, a joy which is almost childlike:

THE LOVE OF LIFE

Siegfried

It is scarcely interrupted except by the Whining Complaint of Mime (¾, F minor), who begins again his story to Siegfried for the tenth time, without any greater success in convincing him of the benefits of the education which he has given him, and tries to appeal to his affection by his false solicitude. Siegfried is not in the least impressed, and prefers to speak of the love of children for their mother, which he himself has noticed, first in the birds, and then in the beasts, which leads him to imperiously desire to know the name of his mother.

The whole of this portion flows by on a sweet and caressing melody which characterizes the ingenuous feeling of *Filial Love* as he conceives it,

FILIAL LOVE

which is frequently broken into by tempestuous returns of the complaint of his education, as also by allusions to various *motive* of *The Wälsungs*, *The Forge*, and *The Sword*, the appropriateness of which is always most striking : he speaks of having seen his image reflected in the water (*Siegfried Guardian of the Sword*) ; what water was this ? (*The Rhine*) ; the story of his birth is accompanied by *The Race of the Wälsungs*, *Compassion*, and *Love* ; the whole surrounded by *The Love of Life*.

When at last he knows his origin, an intense desire arises in his heart to leave forever the tutelage of the obnoxious dwarf, which is marvellously expressed in an independent phrase in $\frac{3}{4}$, towards the end of which we meet with the following three bars, which various commentators call by the name of Wandering Siegfried, Travel Song, and *Desire to Travel*. We shall make use of the last name.

DESIRE TO TRAVEL

[This same *motiv* will be found expressing the same feeling in the Prologue to *Götterdämmerung*, when Siegfried is about to leave Brünnhilde to seek new adventures, then again in Act I. Scene II. in the dialogue with Gunther.]

The Ring, *The Forge*, *Reflection*, *The Dragon*, and *Love's Regret* connect this scene with the following one.

SCENE II. — Coinciding with the entrance of Wotan under the form of The Wanderer, there appears the powerful and mysterious harmony of *Wotan the*

Wanderer, or Wotan's Journey, which is divided into
two parts, one strange and chromatic, the other entirely
diatonic and of a placid solemnity, which will be subsequently used separately, but only in *Siegfried*.

WOTAN THE WANDERER

The way in which the music of this curious scene, so
curious from all points of view, is managed, is worthy
of close attention and examination.

At first it is with the theme of *The Treaty* that the
god forces the gnome to accept the singular wager, the
stake of which is the head of one of them ; and, after
malicious *Reflection*, it is with the same *motiv* that the
dwarf accepts the challenge ; we feel that he means to
be tricky in his turn, and carry it off bravely.

Then, every time Mime is searching his mind for questions to put, his search is accompanied by sounds of *The Forge* and of the *motiv* of *Reflection*, to which are joined, but only the first time, *The Treaty*, which binds him, and *The Ring*, the object of his covetousness.

His first question refers to "the race which lives in the bowels of the earth." Wotan's reply is annotated by all the *motive* of the *Nibelungs*, *The Forge*, *The Ring*, *Alberich's Power*, *Adoration of the Gold*, *The Nibelung's Cry of Triumph*, *Amassing of the Treasure*, and finally *The Treaty*.

His second question deals with " that other race which lives on the surface of the earth." Immediately, with reply appear the *motive* of *The Giants*, *The Power of the Ring*, *The Dragon*, and still *The Treaty*.

His third question concerns " the race which hovers above the peaks, among the clouds." Then *Walhalla* is unfolded in all its splendour, followed by an allusion to the defeated *Alberich* and *The Ring*. However, in the course of this victorious reply of the wandering god, there appears a new theme of majestic character, —

[which, considerably modified and enlarged, will assume great importance in the *Götterdämmerung* Day :]

it is that of *Divine Power*, only the first half of which I give here,

The Wanderer   **DIVINE POWER**

and which ends, as may be seen in the score, with a long descending scale which has nothing triumphant left in it.

Wotan the Wanderer has fulfilled his part of *The Treaty* which was concluded; the orchestra joins him in so stating. It is now his turn to question, and Mime must reply. Immediately there is a cringing and humble figure, which throughout this second half of the scene, the counterpart of the first, depicts the piteous attitude of the malicious Nibelung, now that it is Wotan's turn to ask him questions.

[It only appears afterwards in Act II. Scene III., shortly before Mime's death.]

Here is one of its forms. Let us call it *Grovelling Mime*, as it does not apply to any other character.

GROVELLING MIME

Before his cross-questioning begins, Mime seeks a pretext to evade it; he says he has dwelt apart so long in his *Forge* that he no longer knows anything at all: for he has recognized Wotan in The Wanderer, as we learn from a brief reminiscence of *Walhalla*; however, he has to bow his head beneath *Bondage*, and therefore he will reply.

In the first place, Wotan asks him what he knows about " the heroic race to whom he appears to be cruel." Mime's reply is accompanied by all the *motive* of the *Wälsungs*, their *Race*, their *Heroism*, and even *Siegfried Guardian of the Sword*.

Secondly, he wishes to know " what steel must the youth brandish to conquer the Ring by overthrowing the Dragon." Here the sole *motiv* which mingles with those of *Grovelling Mime* and *The Forge*, is *The Sword*, the sword of the gods.

Thirdly and finally, he must tell " who will be able to forge again the shattered blade." It is then that Mime is lost, for he does not know that Siegfried is the one; but the orchestra makes us know it by the persistent return of the *Love of Life*, which leaves no possible doubt as to the personality of the hero.

Wotan is about to depart. The strange and solemn harmony which introduced him, *Wotan the Wanderer*, reappears, soon to give way to *The Sword*, *The Treaty*, and *The Dragon*, when the victorious god devotes the head of the vanquished to him who has never known fear, to him who shall slay the Dragon, otherwise called *Siegfried Guardian of the Sword*.

The mocking hisses of *Loge* are heard beneath Wotan's last words, and continue during a considerable part of the succeeding scene.

SCENE III. — Although greatly developed and of absorbing interest, this may be quickly analyzed.

Mime, being left alone, is at first terrified by the crackling of the flames of *Loge;* Siegfried returns, and with him the gay *motive* of *Desire to Travel* and *Love of Life;* and then, accompanying in the most witty manner every phrase and almost every word of the dialogue, we successively recognize *The Dragon*, *The Sword*, *Bondage*,

Wotan the Wanderer, *The Guardian of the Sword*, *Love of Life*, *The Race of the Wälsungs*, *Loge*, *The Flames' Spell*, *Eternal Sleep*, *Brünnhilde's Sleep*, and *Call of the Son of the Woods*. In the meanwhile, Siegfried thinks of nothing but of forging for himself a sword with the fragments which Mime has given him. He sets to work and, while filing the steel and blowing up the fire, he gaily sings a joyous song of three couplets, the third with graceful variations, the accompaniment of which imitates the blowing of the bellows of the forge, just as before we heard the scraping of the file: let us call it The Song of the Bellows to distinguish it from another which closely follows it. (Mime, in one corner, is surreptitiously preparing a poisoned draught with which he purposes to plunge Siegfried into *Eternal Sleep*, and which will allow him basely to seize the sword which has been so valiantly restored, after Siegfried shall have conquered the *Gold* and *The Ring* to Mime's profit). Shortly after Siegfried has tempered the metal by plunging it in a tank of water, which gives occasion for a curious effect of imitative sound, appears the sole new theme of this scene, which is generally called *The Casting of the Steel*, which mingles

THE CASTING OF THE STEEL

with a kind of *reprise* of The Song of the Bellows in the major.

Here we find a new song, The Song of the Forge, the rhythm of which is accented by blows of the hammer on the anvil, forming a marvellously faithful imitation; it has only two couplets, which are separated by a reply of Mime's, who is still engaged in his iniquitous operations.

The second couplet is scarcely finished when Siegfried again plunges the still glowing blade into the water and amuses himself with the noise that it makes as it cools.

Lastly, while he finishes the work, fixes it in its hilt, and hammers it for the last time, we recognize the *motive* of *The Forge, Grovelling Mime, The Casting of the Steel,* and *The Sword,* with curious rhythms of two or three bars, and finally, when Siegfried cleaves the anvil while trying the temper of his sword, there breaks out the *motiv* of *The Son of the Woods,* which joyously ends the act.

ACT II.

SCENE I. — The Prelude, which is intimately connected with the first scene, first makes us hear the hoarse growling of *Fafner,* the survivor of the two Giants of the Prologue, who is changed into a Dragon and jealously

watches over his treasure and his *Ring* (I would remind
the reader that this *motiv* of *Fafner* is none other than a
transformation of that of *The Giants*, the lowest note of
which is now half a tone lower).

FAFNER

Towards the middle breaks out *The Curse of the Ring*,
which is closely followed by the rhythm of *The Nibelungs' Work of Destruction* and *The Nibelung's Cry of
Triumph*.   Alberich is present.

To these *motive* are added, shortly after the rising of
the curtain, a figure of *The Ride of the Walkyries*, and
the theme of *The Distress of the Gods*, announcing the
arrival of the wandering god, who is saluted by *Walhalla*.

The malicious gnome's attitude of mind towards the
god, whose not very gentle dealings he has not forgotten,
is manifested by a new *motiv*, *Revenge*, which is only of
secondary importance.

REVENGE

[It will, however, reappear in *Götterdämmerung*, Act II. Scenes IV. and V., under a more striking form.]

Farther on we find the themes of *Wotan the Wanderer*, *Wotan's Rage*, *The Treaty with the Giants*, *Loge*, *The Curse of the Ring*, and others which are easily recognized. *Fafner's* few words to Wotan are accented by his own theme, with which is curiously united, for a moment, *The Sword*, which seems to menace *The Ring*. Then we recognize *The Norns* and *The Desire to Travel*; and, at the moment of Wotan's departure, *The Ride* reappears with a memory of *Wotan's Song of Farewell*, immediately followed by *The Curse of the Ring*, twice repeated, with the rhythm of *Destruction*, and the scene ends as it began, with the *motiv* of *Fafner*, sinister and menacing.

SCENE II. — Siegfried, conducted by Mime, arrives; *The Love of Life* and the joyous beginning of the varied strophe of the Bellows Song escorts them with some rhythms of *The Forge* and a slight reminiscence of *Brünnhilde's Sleep*. Mime, being desirous of inspiring his pupil with fear, borrows some chromatic features from *Loge* ; we hear *Fafner* roar, to which Siegfried answers with *The Heroism of the Wälsungs* ; then *The Love of Life* is also briefly recalled.

Mime having gone away, or rather hidden himself, Siegfried remains alone on the stage. Then begins, properly speaking, with figures of semiquavers ($\frac{6}{8}$, in E major), the delightful idyl called *The Murmurs of the*

Forest, which has already been announced in the preceding pages.

Through these sweet and gentle sounds we perceive
the ideas which are thronging into the soul of the young
hero ; he first thinks of *The Race of the Wälsungs*, then
of his mother, as we learn from *Filial Love*, which leads
him to understand the beauty of *Love*, here represented
by the theme of *Freïa*. But his attention is soon
attracted by the song of a bird, which is hopping and
warbling in the branches above him ; here are some
fragments of this delightful song of *The Bird*.

THE BIRD

[It is well to know that each
of the above fragments will hereafter have a precise signification.
To give only one example, the
third, by which the bird will reveal to Siegfried the existence of
the sleeping Walkyrie, is identical
with *Brünnhilde's Sleep*, which

The Bird.

Sleep.

The Rhine-Daughters.

itself is only a transposition, with certain rhythmical modifications,
of the *Rhine-Daughters*.]

[From this time on, we shall find perpetual allusions to and quotations from this *Song of the Bird,* some of considerable extent and forcibly commanding the attention, others consisting only of a few notes ; an example of the latter will be found in the instrumental interlude while Siegfried is passing through the flames (Act III. at the end of Scene II.). Here four *motive* are in conjunction.]

Now, Siegfried, having listened to the Bird, first tries to imitate it by means of a rustic pipe, which he has cut with his *Sword;* this furnishes an amusing incident. Not being successful, he puts his horn to his lips and sounds his joyous call, *The Call of the Son of the Woods,* to which he adds, as if to make himself better known, *Siegfried Guardian of the Sword.*

He receives his answer from the frightful jaws of *The Dragon*; it is *Fafner* who is coming out of his cave to give battle to his challenger. The combat takes place; *The Sword* reaches his heart; *Fafner* is dying. But, before dying, he retraces his history, on which the orchestra comments by means of several appropriate *Leit-motive*: *The Work of Destruction*, *The Curse of the Ring*, *The Guardian of the Sword*, his conqueror, *The Giants*, *The Ring*, *The Dragon*, *The Son of the Woods*, and, finally, *Fafner* dies, on a stroke of the drum, at the second beat of the bar.

A brilliant flourish of *The Son of the Woods* celebrates this first victory, and then there immediately rise again *The Murmurs of the Forest*. But this time the language of *The Bird* has become intelligible to the young warrior, because he has tasted the blood of the Dragon (?); and also to us, but for another reason: because it is given to the soprano.

Scene III. — The third scene, notwithstanding its great development and complexity, does not introduce us to any new *motiv*; we have therefore only to look for those which we already know. To make it clearer, let us consider it as if it were divided into four parts.

In the first (the dialogue between Mime and Alberich), the sole *motive*, lightly sketched, are: *The Power of the Helm*, *The Forge*, and *The Nibelung's Cry of Triumph*.

In the second (as Siegfried issues from the cavern) appear: *The Ring*, *The Adoration of the Gold*, *The Gold*, and then again *The Murmurs of the Forest*, which is soon associated with *The Race of the Wälsungs*.

In the third (when Mime obsequiously approaches Siegfried), first come *The Bird* and *The Casting of the Steel*; then, farther on, the Whining Complaint, whose deceitful tone belies the words; at the moment of Mime's death, note the singular succession of descending and discordant thirds, borrowed from *Reflection*, which, joined with Alberich's mocking laughter (*The Forge*), forms a funeral oration which is somewhat pitiful, but, at the same time, quite good enough for him.

In the fourth part (which extends from there to the end of the scene) reappear *The Curse of the Ring*, *The Forge*, when Siegfried casts Mime's corpse into the cave; *Fafner*, when he rolls the *Dragon's* body into it; then *The Ring*, and, followed by a recall of *The Bird*, comes the song of *Filial Love*, which, with certain reminiscences of *The Forge*, leads us to a final return of *The Murmurs of the Forest*. This time *The Bird* proposes to Siegfried to lead him to the Walkyrie who is asleep in the heart of a circle of flames (p. 402); thus the last *motive* of this act are: *The Flames' Spell*, *Siegfried Guardian of the Sword*, *Brünnhilde's Sleep*, and, dominating them all, the warbling of *The Bird*, which does not cease until the final chord.

Act III.

PRELUDE. — A persistent rhythm of *The Ride* forewarns us of the approach of Wotan. At the same time appears an imposing ascending figure from the bass, in which we recognize *The Norns*, or *The Distress of the Gods*, or again, as it passes into the major, *The Rhine*, which are all closely related, both in their contexture and symbolic meaning, and the presence of any one of which in this place is equally explicable. *Wotan's Rage*, *The Fall of the Gods*, and *Alberich's Power*, appear here and there, and the Prelude is merged into

SCENE I. by the mysterious and solemn music of *Eternal Sleep*, to which succeed without interruption

Fate, *The Treaty*, and, just before the Wanderer's first
words, *The Announcement of a New Life.*

The same *motive* accompany Wotan's monologue and
evocation of Erda, with a recall of *Wotan the Wanderer*;
they also chiefly rule in Erda's reply and dialogue with
Wotan, during which in addition there reappear *The
Ring*, *Love's Regret*, *Walhalla*, *The Nibelungs' Work of
Destruction*, *Wotan's Song of Farewell*, and several other
motive which are merely indicated.

It is only at the end of this scene, which is one of the
most admirable of the whole Tetralogy, that a new theme
appears, *The Heritage of the World*, that world over which

THE HERITAGE OF THE WORLD

Wotan, foreseeing and desiring the end of the gods, does
not mean to reign any longer, and which he bequeaths
to his son, the triumphant Wälsung, therefore this *motiv*,
which appears several times before Erda vanishes, is escorted by all those which most closely relate to the young
hero : *Siegfried Guardian of the Sword*, *The Sword*, *Walhalla*, *The Power of the Ring*, *Flight*, and *Love*; when Erda
sinks into the earth four beautiful chords tell us that she
has again fallen into her *Eternal Sleep.*

SCENE II. — Guided by *The Bird*, Siegfried approaches,
Sword in hand.   Wotan bars his way and forces him to
tell him the purpose of the journey, as well as the reasons
which led him to undertake it.

Hence arise frequent orchestral allusions to *The Bird* which has guided him, to *Fafner* whose blood has given him the power of comprehending the song of birds; to *The Forge* where he was reared; to *The Race of the Wälsungs* from which he sprang; and to *The Love of Life* which animates him; The Wanderer's words, on the contrary, are supported by *Wotan the Wanderer*, *Walhalla*, *Wotan's Rage*, and later *The Treaty*, by chromatic figures of *Loge*, by *The Flames' Spell*, *The Ride*, and *Eternal Sleep*, when he declares himself the guardian of the rock where sleeps the Walkyrie; to these *motive* Siegfried, constantly inspired by the remembrance of *The Bird*, opposes his own, *The Guardian of the Sword*, and *The Race of the Wälsungs*, and then, at last, with a single stroke, the *Sword* shatters the god's lance.   Then gloomily appear *The Treaty*, *The Fall of the Gods*, and *Love's Regret*, constantly mingled with the joyous warblings of *The Bird*, and Siegfried springs through the flames, accompanied by the marvellous combination of typical themes which we have already mentioned (p. 403), and in which we find simultaneously *The Call of the Son of the Woods*, *The Flames' Spell*, *Siegfried Guardian of the Sword*, *The Adoration of the Gold*, *The Bird*, *Loge*, and, several bars farther on, *Eternal Sleep*, and *Brünnhilde's Sleep*.   All this procession of *Leitmotive* takes place while a curtain of flame and fiery vapours hides from view the changing of the scenery.

SCENE III. — The vapours dissipate while the *motive* of *Brünnhilde's Sleep* and *Fate* are passing, followed by a brilliant figure on the violins alone, in which we plainly recognize the features of *Freïa*, the goddess of love. Then *Fate*, *The Adoration of the Gold*, and *The Bird*.

Whilst Siegfried is contemplating the motionless Walkyrie, we hear, at first very faintly, the *motiv* of

Love's Fascination, which we have not had to mention since the second scene of *Rheingold*, and which therefore renders its employment particularly expressive. We find Brünnhilde again as though still encircled with the *motive* in the midst of which we left her, *The Ride* and *Wotan's Song of Farewell*, which is given in its entirety; with several gentle strokes of his *Sword*, Siegfried cuts the thongs of her cuirass; *Love's Fascination* gathers importance. The memory of *The Race of the Wälsungs* is evoked, and necessarily *Brünnhilde's Sleep* often reappears, accompanied by the seductive form of *Freïa*, which is interrupted in a sinister manner by the question of *Fate*, but the delicate interlacings of which graciously announce the awakening of the fallen divinity.

This awakening occurs upon the clear and luminous chords of *Hail to the World*, which gloriously glitters, twice repeated, and each time followed by sonorous arpeggios, and then brilliant scintillations on the harps,

HAIL TO THE WORLD

developing into a broad phrase in which a long passage
of thirds and a prolonged trill give it quite an Italian
character.   It is on this salutation that Brünnhilde pronounces her first words ; but when she comes to ask the
name of the hero who has awakened her she betrays her
inmost thought and her desire, for her declamation borrows the very notes with which Wotan left her, after
having put her to sleep upon her rock in the third act
of *Die Walküre*, which are none other than those of
Siegfried Guardian of the Sword.

Siegfried, in his turn, radiantly sings his *Hail to Love*,
which is full of youthful ardour and enthusiasm, ending,
like Brünnhilde's *Hail to the World*, with the phrase in
thirds above mentioned, which appears still more Italian
now that it is sung as a Duet by the two voices.

HAIL TO LOVE

Immediately after the two holds and the trill which end this portion, the basses vigorously attack the theme of *The Race of the Wälsungs*, which is joyously answered by the new *motiv* of *The Enthusiasm of Love*, which

THE ENTHUSIASM OF LOVE

again is composed of a succession of thirds and sixths, an occurrence sufficiently rare in Wagner to deserve special notice.

The Heritage of the World next appears, several times in different keys, but now in ¾, which slightly relieves its solemnity.

Mingling with it, according to the course of the dialogue, we shall recognize in particular *The Enthusiasm of Love*, *Hail to Love*, *The Announcement of a New Life*, a reminiscence of *Wotan's Rage*, and *The Ride*, and then *The Curse of the Ring*, and *Bondage;* when the key of

E major arrives, we are introduced to two themes which
are almost one, the second being the complement of the
first. First it is *Peace*, a *motiv* of sweet and placid seren-

PEACE

ity, which is employed only in this scene into which it
introduces an element of calmness and freshness ; then,
20 bars farther on, equally tender, but more passionate
comes *Siegfried Treasure of the World*, which we shall
find twice again in *Götterdämmerung*.

The peaceful *motive* during the rest of the love-duet
which forms this scene are next associated with most of
the *motive* we have already mentioned, to which must be

SIEGFRIED TREASURE OF THE WORLD

added *Fate, Brünnhilde's Sleep, The Dragon, The Ride,*
which makes only brief appearances, then *Siegfried
Guardian of the Sword*, this time given even by the hero's
own lips in the paroxysm of passion; *The Bird, The
Shout of the Walkyries*, after which a last return of *The
Enthusiasm of Love* carries us on to a kind of *stretto* by
the two voices which has received the name of *The Decision to Love.*[1]

---

[1] The three last mentioned *motive, Peace, Siegfried Treasure of
the World*, and *The Decision to Love*, together with *Sleep*, are those
with which Wagner formed the delightful symphonic piece, *The
Siegfried Idyl* (see p. 51).

THE DECISION TO LOVE

In this enchanting finale is again interwoven Siegfried's *Hail to Love*; here, again, the two voices unite in frequent thirds and sixths, and the final cadence presents an unusual *brio*. The last chords of the orchestra reproduce the *motive* of *The Guardian of the Sword* and *The Enthusiasm of Love*.

GÖTTERDÄMMERUNG

Götterdämmerung differs from the two preceding divisions in its general form by the addition of a greatly developed Prologue, which takes the place of a Prelude to the first act, to which it is joined without any break. This Prologue may perhaps be considered as divided in two parts; the first is the fine sombre scene of The Norns weaving the cord of destiny of gods as well as men; the second shows us Brünnhilde's farewell to Siegfried who is setting out for fresh conquests.

PROLOGUE. — From the very first chords, we recognize Brünnhilde's *Hail to the World*, immediately fol-

lowed by the undulatory movement of the primordial
element, *The Rhine*, which changes (at the moment
when the first Norn is about to speak) into *The Distress
of the Gods*; four bars later comes *The Flames' Spell*. As
the three Sisters in their conversation pass in review all
the events which we have seen happen during the preceding days of the *Tetralogy*, it is natural that the orchestra should also make the *motive* that correspond to
the various phases of the drama defile before us; consequently we frequently find *Walhalla, Hail to Walhalla,
Death, The Power of the Gods, The Treaty, The Fall of
the Gods, Fate, Loge, The Flames' Spell, Eternal Sleep,
The Ring, Love's Regret, The Adoration of the Gold, The
Nibelung's Cry of Triumph, The Sword, The Call of the
Son of the Woods*, and *The Curse of the Ring*, which are
introduced here in the above order, which will allow
them to be found easily in the score; the scene of The
Norns ends with the *motiv* of *Fate*, twice repeated.

During the interlude which accompanies the rising of
the sun, *The Call of the Son of the Woods*, transformed
into an heroic character in $\frac{4}{4}$, as we have already noticed
(on p. 390), is happily combined with a new theme, which
personifies Brünnhilde in her human love, in her love as
a wife, the beauty of which is marked by an expressive
gruppetto. Four bars before Brünnhilde begins to speak,
let us draw attention to a short recall of *The Ride*, en-

BRÜNNHILDE

Brünnhilde

circling *The Son of the Woods*, for it is he and not she,
who shall henceforth ride Grane.   Fourteen bars later
appears another *motiv* belonging specially to Brünnhilde,
characterizing her *Heroic Love* :

[The latter will be little used beyond the last two scenes of
Act II.]

These last *motive* are the dominating ones in the harmonic tissue of this second half of the Prologue, and are
associated with some others, which I give, as usual, in
the order of their appearance : *Hail to Love, Loge, Siegfried Guardian of the Sword, Fate, The Heritage of the
World, The Ring, The Ride, The Rhine-Daughters'* cry
of joy, *The Gold, The Ride, Love, Desire to Travel*, and
The Sword; again we have the *motiv* of *Brünnhilde*, as
she gazes after the departing hero, at the beginning of
several pages which separate the Prologue from the first
act ; then when he is no longer visible we hear in the
distance his joyous hunting call, *The Call of the Son of the
Woods* in its original form ; in this *entr'acte* we recognize
also *The Decision to Love, Love's Regret, Adoration of the
Gold, The Gold, The Rhine, The Power of the Ring*, and
finally *The Nibelung's Cry of Triumph*, only a few bars
before the rising of the curtain.

As will be seen, the majority of the preceding *Leit-motive* are suggestive reminders to the hearer of this vast Prologue, which is a kind of recapitulation and *résumé* of the preceding days, and which predisposes the mind in a marvellous way to the violent emotions aroused in this final drama.

ACT I.

SCENE I. — I purposely pass over several *motive* of secondary importance, relating to the tribe of the Gibichs and the uncongenial character of Hagen, which appear in the very first notes of the act; although very clearly characterized (so that any intelligent reader can find them for himself), their employment is entirely episodical; for this reason I will neglect them in this necessarily brief review, and give my whole attention to the great type-*motive* which dominate the entire work and are necessary to its complete comprehension. Note, however, that the *motiv* of the Gibichs (6th bar in Scene I.) does not let us forget that we are on the banks of *The Rhine*.

Hagen takes the lead in this scene; to further his dark schemes he wants Gunther to marry Brünnhilde and Gutrune to become Siegfried's wife. He tries to awake love in their hearts (*Freia*); to Gunther he describes Brünnhilde on her rock (*The Ride*, *The Flames' Spell*, even *The Bird*); to Gutrune he portrays Siegfried (*Heroism of the Wälsungs*, *Call of the Son of the Woods*, *The Ring*, the victory over *Fafner*); he explains to them the source of his power (*Power of the Ring*, *Love's Regret*, *The Gold*, *Alberich's Cry of Triumph*); and finally he tells them by what magic means he intends to bring about this double marriage, without, however, letting them know that in his inmost heart his sole purpose is to make use of them to gain the Ring and the power with which it is

endowed.   This situation causes the employment of two
new *motive* : one expresses *Hagen's Perfidious Friendship*
for Siegfried, whose death he desires; and the other

HAGEN'S PERFIDIOUS FRIENDSHIP

Gutrune

Treachery by means of *Magic,* which is often preceded
by several notes of *The Power of the Helm*, which informs

TREACHERY BY MAGIC

Hagen

us that the enchanted helm, The Tarnhelm, is one means
of which he intends to make use.

These two new *motive* appear not far apart, a little
past the middle of the scene, at the sign *meno mosso* ; first
comes *Treachery*, then two bars of *The Power of the Helm*,

27

and, seventeen bars later, *Perfidious Friendship*; they are accompanied by rare recurrences of *The Sword*, *Freïa*, and *The Curse of the Ring*, after which Siegfried announces his coming by his favourite air, *The Call of the Son of the Woods*, which first sounds in the distance and then nearer; this immediately arouses *The Adoration of the Gold*, which in turn starts the flowing of the waves of *The Rhine*, and *The Ring*, and at the moment when Siegfried sets his foot on shore,

Scene II., *The Curse of the Ring* make its terrible anathema resound anew.

The first courteous words are exchanged whilst the orchestra is saluting *Siegfried Guardian of the Sword*; the hero immediately begs that the greatest care may be taken of Grane, which gives occasion again for *The Ride*, to which is immediately joined a tender memory of *Brünnhilde*. In the conversation which follows, allusions are made to *Hagen's Perfidious Friendship*, *The Heroism of the Wälsungs*, *The Sword*, the forging of which Siegfried narrates, and consequently *The Forge*, *The Dragon* which he has killed, *Bondage*, *The Power of the Helm*, the knowledge of which Hagen imparts to Siegfried, *The Ring*, etc.

GUTRUNE'S WELCOME

Now comes the act of treachery. At Hagen's instigation his sister graciously comes forward, and, with friendly words, which are accented by the theme of *Gutrune's Welcome*, offers him the enchanted cup from which he is to imbibe forgetfulness ; before drinking the magic potion, Siegfried, still faithful to his love, sends a tender memory to Brünnhilde ; it is to her he drinks, as is attested by the themes *Hail to Love*, *The Heritage of the World*, and the termination in thirds which we have already pointed out in the Duet of the third act of *Siegfried*.

[This characteristic type-form will make its last appearance in Act III. Scene II., when Siegfried recovers the full possession of his memory.]

At the very moment when he is drinking the fatal philtre (in the key of G major, after a prolonged trill), the sombre theme of *Treachery by Magic* heavily rumbles, followed by *Gutrune's Welcome*; the philtre immediately operates, the pure hero loses his memory, the past becomes a blank, and he burns with an ardent love for Gutrune only. A few very fugitive reminiscences of *The Enthusiasm of Love*, *The Flames' Spell*, and *The Bird* show us the unsuccessful efforts he makes to recover the memories that have taken flight; henceforth he is under the spell of the traitor Hagen, whose hidden will he must passively fulfil. And

therefore for the remainder of the scene the *motive* of
Treachery (also called The Magic Imposture) and *Gutrune*
have considerable importance.

The infamous compact which is imposed on him is
entered into on the themes of *Treachery*, *Loge*, whose
flames he must again pass through, *The Ride*, *The Sword*,
The Curse of the Ring, and is frequently sealed by significant recurrences of *The Treaty*.

Having exchanged the solemn oath, the two brothers-
in-arms unite their voices in a brief *ensemble* in which
appears the *Desire to Travel* in the form of a dialogue,
as well as a new *motiv*, which each sings in turn, and
which has received the name of *The Justice of Expiation*
(according to others, The Right of Expiation):

THE JUSTICE OF EXPIATION

This is a sort of penalty of the oath: he who breaks it
shall pay for his treason with his life.

After several brief episodes, during which are heard
The Treaty, *The Welcome*, *The Ring*, *The Golden Apples*,
curiously associated with *The Forge* (the divine origin of
the hero and of his education by the dwarf), *Love's Regret*, and *The Ride* combined with *Loge* (Grane crossing
the flames), the two knights start on their journey without any further delay.

Gutrune's thoughts follow them with her *motiv* of *Welcome*, and, shortly afterwards Hagen's ambitious hopes are clearly set forth in a series of typical *motive* revealing a train of ideas, the signification of which we cannot mistake ; *The Nibelungs' Work of Destruction*, *The Nibelung's Cry of Triumph*, *Siegfried Guardian of the Sword*, *The Ride*, *Love's Regret*, *The Gold*, *The Ring* (the object he covets), *The Call of the Son of the Woods*, and *Bondage* ; he also is following the warriors with his thoughts. Borne on the wings of the symphonic music, we go on before them ; in the course of the same orchestral interlude, we are already brought into *Brünnhilde's* presence, first by her own *motiv*, and then by her *Hail to the World*, mingled with the menacing tones of *The Curse*, *The Work of Destruction* and *The Ring*, which is still in her possession.

Scene III. — In fact, when the curtain again rises to the strains of *Treachery by Magic*, we find her in rapt contemplation of *The Ring* ; her state of mind is immediately revealed to us by the memory of *Siegfried Treasure of the World*, which is quickly followed by vague sounds of *The Ride*. This is Waltraute who comes to visit her exiled sister and tell her of the distress of the gods, and to beseech her to restore the fatal Ring to the Rhine to save them. Hence we have an eloquent succession of *motive* : *The Shout of the Walkyries*, with neighings and prancings, *The Announcement of a New Life*, the *Hail to the World*, and *Hail to Love*, which testify to Brünnhilde's unconquerable fidelity to *Siegfried Guardian of the Sword* ; then follows a memory of the terrible *Wotan's Rage* ; *The Distress of the Gods*, the splendours of *Walhalla*, *The Treaty*, *Divine Power*, so sadly shaken, *Fate*, and *The Golden Apples*, which Wotan no longer touches ; here again *Walhalla* is represented in a state of ruin; then come *Bondage*, *The Adoration of the Gold*, the cause of all the evil, a touching recall of *Wotan's Song of Farewell*, *The Ring*, *The Curse*, *Love's Regret*, *The Nibelung's Cry of Triumph*, who is about to seize his prey, the two cruel notes of *Bondage*, in short, all those *motive* which are adapted to the subjects on which the two sisters converse; but Brünnhilde will not yield, she will keep her betrothal ring, all her love-themes crowd in again anew to affirm her constancy the more strongly, and Waltraute precipitately departs in a tumultuous *reprise* of *The Ride*.

Being left alone, Brünnhilde sees *The Flames' Spell* renewed, the rock is again encircled with fire; she feels Siegfried returning, his *Call of the Son of the Woods* is already sounding; she runs to meet him! Suddenly, like a knell, *The Power of the Helm* is heard: Siegfried, wearing the Tarnhelm, has assumed Gunther's form; she cannot recognize him.

The second part of this scene is one of the most painful that I know in any play, and the best thing to do is to take refuge in the purely musical interest in order to support the odious spectacle of the pure and heroic Siegfried having become a traitor to honour and to love (although by a magic subterfuge), and the sight of the violence of which he is guilty in this irresponsible condition towards the unfortunate and ever-loving Walkyrie. Happily this does not last long.

On the arrival of Siegfried-Gunther, *The Power of the Helm* asserts itself, immediately followed by *Treachery by Magic*; inexorable *Fate* follows, but Siegfried's voice is accompanied by the *motiv* of the Gibichs! The subterranean rhythm of *The Nibelungs' Work of Destruction* is heard muttering; Brünnhilde vainly tries to resist the brutal invader with *The Ring*; he opposes it with *The*

Curse of the Ring, struggles with her, overthrows her, and forces her to fall exhausted in his arms to a touching recall of *Siegfried Treasure of the World*, whom she so greatly loves and who no longer recognizes her, a terrible situation, which is accented by a simultaneous repetition of *The Power of the Helm* and of the human love of *Brünnhilde*, which serves to make only more explicit if possible a return of the infamous *Treachery*.

It is finished; she is conquered and broken: the themes which now return (*The Work of Destruction*, *Brünnhilde*, and even *Fate*) can tell us nothing more; but we must notice, although they have not the absolute character of a *Leit-motiv*, the energetic notes of the orchestra to which Siegfried, strong in the conviction of having acted as a loyal and valiant knight, unsheathes his sword, to protect his unhappy victim.

[We shall find them in Act II. and again in Act III. in the affecting final scene where their signification can be thoroughly comprehended only by remembering this poignant situation.]

Following this come *The Sword* (in this case called the protector), with *The Treaty*, next *Gutrune's Welcome*, which now alone haunts the hero's mind, *The Treachery by Magic* and its plaything *The Helm*, and the love of *Brünnhilde*, which he despises. The last *motiv* announced by the orchestra is *The Power of the Helm*, which, in truth, has played the most terrifying *rôle* in the whole act.

ACT II.

PRELUDE AND SCENE I. — The persistent rhythm of *The Work of Destruction*, *The Nibelungs' Cry of Triumph*, and lastly *The Ring*, alone form the framework of this Prelude, which is directly connected with Scene I.

This scene passes in profound darkness, only illuminated by the wan light of the heavily-veiled moon, between the Nibelung Alberich, who has risen from the depths of the Rhine, and his son Hagen, who is in a trance-like sleep ; the *motive* of hatred and ambition are necessarily the ruling ones ; first come those mentioned in the Prelude, which form the ground-work, and then *The Power of the Ring*, *Love's Regret*, and a new terribly expressive theme, *Murder*, inciting to murder

[which will be used again in Scenes IV. and V. of this act] ;

and, as if more clearly to indicate him against whom this menace is directed, here come *The Sword* with which Siegfried killed Fafner, *The Ring* which is in his *Power*, and *The Call of the Son of the Woods*, his characteristic flourish.

Farther on, in the same scene, there are allusions to Brünnhilde, who is represented by the *Announcement of a New Life*, and to *The Rhine-Daughters*, as well as the ruined *Walhalla*, the destruction of which is the ultimate aim; but these *motive* pass rapidly, leaving almost a clear field for others of sombre tints which depict the vindictive and saturnine characters of the father and son, *Murder*, *The Curse of the Ring*, and *Bondage*.

SCENE II. — The sunrise is here represented by a supple figure treated in canon on a rather long pedal of the tonic (B flat), which is somewhat remotely related to *The Rhine motiv*; it is sunrise on the banks of the Rhine.

Siegfried's arrival is announced by *The Power of the Helm*, which he still wears, and the lively *Call of the Son of the Woods*. He tells Hagen, and Gutrune, who afterwards arrives, of the success of his voyage, his passage through the flames, whence arise the scintillating theme of *Loge*, *Gutrune's Welcome*, and *Treachery by Magic*, besides the three great orchestral notes in octaves without any accompanying harmony, which we have already mentioned (p. 423), followed by *The Sword*; a combination which indicates the loyal and chaste manner in which his mission has been accomplished.

SCENE III. — Hagen's cry calling together Gunther's vassals reproduces the notes of *Bondage*; whilst the figure in the bass, which proceeds with great bounds of a ponderously jovial character, seems to characterize Hagen's gaiety. At the second bar we find a new theme, *Call to the Marriage*, which greatly resembles *Gutrune's Welcome*, of which it is merely a transformation :

CALL TO THE MARRIAGE

The vassals immediately come in, which gives occasion for a highly developed chorus of men during which the sounding of the call is frequently heard, alternating with Hagen's voice giving orders for the sacrifices to the gods.

SCENE IV. — This chorus lasts till the beginning of Scene IV., when Gunther enters leading Brünnhilde.

The entrance of the latter is accented by several sad recalls of *The Ride*, followed by *The Call to the Marriage*; when she recognizes Siegfried and during the moment of stupor which follows it, there is in the orchestra an almost uninterrupted and eloquent succession of *The Call of the Son of the Woods*, *Revenge*, *Fate*, *The Power of the Helm*, *Treachery by Magic*, *The Call to the Marriage*, *Brünnhilde*, *The Ring*, *The Curse of the Ring*, *The Work of Destruction*, *The Gold*, *The Dragon*, *The Adoration of the Gold*, *Fafner*, *Siegfried Guardian of the Sword*, and then *Bondage*, which force us to pass through all the rapid phases of thought in the mind of the unhappy fallen Walkyrie. At the moment when she invokes the gods, it is *Walhalla* that sounds, followed by *Revenge* and *Destruction*.

The rest of the scene follows its course with the aid of the above *motive*; we find in addition, but less frequently, *Love's Regret*, *Heroic Love*, *The Justice of*

Expiation, and the three sword-strokes which symbolize the loyalty with which Siegfried is conscious of having accomplished his undertaking ; the oath taken by Siegfried, and repeated by Brünnhilde in her turn, towards the middle of the scene covers the underlying *motiv* of *Murder*, to which Siegfried condemns himself without knowing it. Then we again meet with *Bondage*, *Loge*, *The Power of the Helm*, *The Ring*, and *The Call to the Marriage*, at which Brünnhilde falls into profound meditation while the page is being played by the orchestra which separates this scene from the succeeding one, after Siegfried's departure with Gutrune.

SCENE V. — Being left alone with Gunther and Hagen, her sad thoughts have full rein, the *motiv* of *The Work of Destruction* takes possession of her, *The Justice of Expiation* and *Bondage* overwhelm her, and she seems to have a presentiment of the *Murder ; Fate*, however, one of whose agents she has been, particularly haunts her, *The Heritage of the World* and *Heroic Love* return with sharp memories ; two of these *motive* in particular, *Murder* and *Bondage*, simultaneously combine, as though to foretell the fatal catastrophe ; tender memories again bring back *Siegfried Guardian of the Sword*, and the *Enthusiasm of Love*, with its successions of thirds and sixths ; but the sombre themes always predominate. It is to the persistent rhythm of *The Nibelungs' Work of Destruction* that Brünnhilde reveals to Hagen that Siegfried is vulnerable in the back, and that the assassin's blade may thus reach him, which decides his fate. *Love's Regret* appears several times with *Revenge* and *Bondage ;* the idea of *Murder* increases in intensity.

Hagen, supported by the *motive* of *Revenge* and *Destruction*, proposes the death of Siegfried.

Gunther, moved for a moment at the thought of

the grief which it will cause his sister, hesitates, whence recur *Gutrune's Welcome* and *Freïa*. " He will have been killed by a boar," Hagen suggests ; and Gunther weakly yields.

As for Brünnhilde, assisted by the *motiv* of *Murder*, and regarding Siegfried as a recreant who has betrayed her, she is the first to desire his death.

The three characters on the stage are moved by this single thought, here, therefore, occurs a Trio, in which Siegfried's death is decided.

The double nuptial train is formed to the strains of *The Call to the Marriage* and *Gutrune's Welcome*; but at the moment the curtain falls, the idea of *Revenge*, and still more that of *Bondage*, dominate the festal sounds.

Act III.

PRELUDE AND SCENE I. — After the violent emotions of the two preceding acts, we feel an inexpressible craving for freshness and tranquillity.

The delightful scene of Siegfried and the Rhine-Daughters comes most happily as a refreshing diversion to relax our over-excited nerves, and so render them more sensitive to the tragic events which are to terminate the drama.

From the first notes of the Prelude we again hear, joyous and full of life, *The Call of the Son of the Woods*, to which in the distance the horns of Gunther and Hagen reply (the *motiv* of Gunther's hunting is none other than *The Call to the Marriage*, which itself is derived, as will be remembered, from *Gutrune's Welcome*). The groaning of *Bondage*, twice recalled, is the only sombre note in this scene, which is otherwise so full of youth and charm.

First, we meet with *The Rhine*, which (with the exception of an almost imperceptible allusion in *Siegfried*),
we have not heard since the *Rheingold* Day; *The Adoration of the Gold* escorts it with *The Gold*, whereupon the
hunting-calls are renewed. Next the orchestra presents to us the graceful melody which is about to
become a new Trio of the seductive Undines, who this
time are sporting on the surface of the water, accompanied by the incessant murmur of the waves of *The
Rhine*, with memories of the lost *Gold*.

The Trio becomes a Quartet on the arrival of Siegfried, who has wandered from the hunt in pursuit
of a bear. The nymphs allure and captivate him with
their grace and joyous singing; they ask him to give
them his Ring (*Adoration of the Gold* and *The Ring*),
which he gained by killing the savage *Dragon*; he
refuses, and they taunt him with his avarice and annoy
him with their mocking laughter; then, just as he is
going to yield, they become serious again and tell him
of the curse attached to *The Ring* (this phrase ends
with *Love's Regret*); they announce his death unless he
restores to them the cursed Ring (*Power of the Ring,
Curse of the Ring, Bondage, Adoration of the Gold*, etc.).
He would have yielded to their charms, but he will not
yield before a threat; from the moment when the Ring
becomes a danger to its possessor (*The Treaty, The
Ring, Fafner*), he will keep it (*The Nibelung's Cry of
Triumph*.) The Nixies are greatly agitated as they see
their Gold once more escaping them; they try to persuade the daring mortal of his madness, but, seeing that
they must renounce the hope of regaining *The Ring*,
they quietly resume their sporting and disappear in the
brilliant *ensemble* with which the act opens.

Being left alone, Siegfried hears the hunting-calls of

Gunther and Hagen approaching, accompanied by *The Curse of the Ring* and *Bondage*, and answers them with his *Call of the Son of the Woods*.

SCENE II. — While Gunther and Hagen are approaching, followed by men carrying the spoils of the chase which they heap at the foot of a tree, the orchestra makes use of the *motive* of hunting, occasionally giving forth figures borrowed from the Trio of the Rhine-Daughters, who still occupy Siegfried's mind, and to these as soon as the dialogue begins are added *Hagen's Perfidious Friendship*, *Bondage*, *Revenge*, and some notes of *The Bird*; a little farther on come *Heroic Love* and *The Justice of Expiation*, in combination with *Loge* (the snare), *Treachery by Magic*, which is following its course, and then, when Siegfried at Hagen's request is about to tell of his infancy and youth, *The Forge*, and again *The Bird*.

The story which follows and which brings us directly to the scene of assassination, is so wonderfully annotated by the orchestra that we might follow its windings without the help of words.

First comes *The Forge* where he was reared in a state of *Bondage*, in the hope that one day he should kill *The Dragon*; there is Mime's whining complaint; there is *The Casting of the Sword* and the victory over *The Dragon*; next reappear *The Murmurs of the Forest*, in which Siegfried now sings the part of *The Bird*; Mime's death occasions a last return of *The Forge*. At this moment, Hagen, pursuing his evil machinations, prepares a new philtre which will restore his memory, and presents it to him under the deceitful strains of *Perfidious Friendship*; Siegfried empties the cup at one draught, while there mysteriously glides into the orchestra the theme of *Treachery by Magic*, solemnly preceded

by *The Power of the Helm*, and immediately followed
by *Heroic Love* and the human love of *Brünnhilde*.
Memory has returned, he resumes his story; with it
return *The Murmurs of the Forest*, *The Bird*, *The Flames'
Spell*, *Freïa* (beauty), *Brünnhilde's Sleep*, *The Heritage of
the World*, *Hail to the World* , and the termination in
thirds of the Love-duet, the memory of his first ecstasies.
It is then that the traitor Hagen, pointing out to Siegfried Wotan's two ravens which are flying past croak-
ing, induces him to turn his back and plunges his spear
between the shoulders of the hero. *The Curse of the
Ring* thunders out, and, then, like a solemn knell, *Siegfried Guardian of the Sword*, which is followed at a short
interval by *Fate* and *The Justice of the Expiation*, amid
general stupefaction. Siegfried is wounded unto death,
but he is not dead. In his agony and in a state of
ecstasy, he continues his story, which the fatal blow has
only interrupted. *Hail to the World* recurs in its complete development; *Fate*, *The Guardian of the Sword*,
Hail to Love, the *Enthusiasm of Love* follow, and then,
with a last recall of *Fate*, he falls dead.

Here commences (in the key of C minor), the
admirable symphonic page which it is the custom to
call the *Siegfried Funeral March*, but which we must
regard as the most touching and most eloquent of
funeral orations rather than as a march : a funeral
oration which is without words, and for that very
reason so much the more impressive and solemn, for
we have arrived at that degree of tension where, words
having become powerless, music alone can minister to
an emotion which is almost superhuman.

Here the whole life of the hero is retraced. All the
heroic *motive* that we know pass before us, not in their
accustomed dress, but gloomily veiled in mourning,

broken with sobs, inspiring terror, and forming in the atmosphere surrounding the dead hero an invisible and impalpable train, the mystic train of living thoughts. First, grave and solemn, comes *The Heroism of the Wälsungs*, which we remember having heard the first time when Siegmund, at the opening of *Die Walküre*, sadly tells of his misfortunes; next comes *Compassion*, representing the unhappy Sieglinde, and Love, the *Love* of Siegmund and Sieglinde which was to give birth to Siegfried: does it not seem that the tender souls of his father and mother, whom he loved so dearly without having known them, are hovering above him and have come to be chief mourners? Then, we have *The Race of the Wälsungs* in its entirety, which, in a superb movement of the basses, joins the funeral *cortège* in the same way as the weapons of the deceased are laid upon the coffin: *The Sword*, the proud sword, is there, still glittering and flaming, having become heraldic in the luminous glow of C major, which only appears for this single moment; finally comes the one *motiv* above all others of the hero, *Siegfried Guardian of the Sword*, twice repeated in an ascending progression, the second time with its frank and loyal ending, and followed by *The Son of the Woods* in its heroic form, again singularly extended, which occasions a sacred memory of *Brünnhilde*, his only love. Could anything more affecting be imagined? At the last notes of the *Funeral March*, which only ends with

Scene III., are heard two gloomy chords which have in them as much of *Bondage* as of *The Nibelung's Cry of Triumph*, just as in the following bars another figure, which *The Curse of the Ring* underlies, may be regarded at will either as a bitter memory of *Gutrune's Welcome*, or of *The Call to Marriage*, two *motive* which equally relate to the idea of treachery.

Many a time the listener, deceived like Gutrune, thinks he hears the accustomed *Call of the Son of the Woods*; but the flourish is not completed; it is always broken and seems to stagger; we hear Grane wildly neighing with several notes of *The Ride;* Gutrune anxiously tries to find *Brünnhilde;* she is possessed by the idea of *Fate,* with which is joined *The Nibelung's Cry of Triumph.* Suddenly reappears the *motiv* of *Revenge,* accompanying Hagen's hoarse cry, which is borrowed from *Bondage.* From here the orchestra moves onwards to Gunther's death with a small number of *motive*: *The Call of the Son of the Woods,* which is changed to the minor, and *Love's Regret;* on the arrival of the body, *Siegfried Guardian of the Sword,* which is only given by its first notes, *Murder, The Justice of Expiation, The Ring, The Curse,* and *Fate.* It is on the last *motiv* that Gunther receives his death-blow.

Hagen immediately tries to get possession of the Ring, whereupon the dead Siegfried's arm is raised in a menacing manner, clenching the Ring in his closed fingers with a terrifying clash of *The Sword,* which protects the hero even in death.

Then, to an extended figure formed of *The Fall of the Gods, The Norns,* and *The Rhine,* and tragically ending with *Fate,* Brünnhilde appears. At the close of her first phrase, the development of *Fate* shows us the song of *Death.* She dismisses Gutrune, reminding her of her perfidious *Welcome,* and, with the theme of *The Heritage of the World,* proclaims herself the sole true spouse of the dead hero; to a last recall of *Treachery by Magic,* Gutrune curses Hagen whom she has obeyed, and retires in shame and desolation.

From now on, the character of Brünnhilde will alone fill this never-to-be-forgotten scene of terrible majesty and splendour, so splendid and emotionally stirring that no words can describe it.

While Brünnhilde orders a pyre to be raised and her horse to be fetched, the ruling *motive* are : *Divine Power*, *The Flames' Spell*, *Siegfried Guardian of the Sword*, and *The Ride*; next tender memories return, with *Hail to Love*, and a repetition of *The Sword* (which we now hear for the last time); these touching notes are brusquely broken into by the three significant orchestral strokes which we found for the first time in the terrible Duet of Act I. Scene III.; in the hero's actions while under the power of a spell they signified what chivalrous loyalty meant to him ; here to Brünnhilde they stand for cold and incomprehensible treachery. After a recall of *Fate* she addresses herself to the gods; then we have *Walhalla* and the *Announcement of a New Life*, which reappears more expressive than ever; and to *Bondage*, *The Curse of the Ring*, and the *Distress of the Gods*, succeeds like a farewell, sad and yet radiant, a last *Hail to Walhalla*.

Divine Power reappears for an instant, followed by *The Fall of the Gods* and *The Rhine*, three closely-related *motive* ; she is talking to the *Rhine-Daughters* now, and of *The Gold* which she is going to restore to them under the form of *The Ring* which the flames of the pyre will at last purify from *The Curse* weighing upon it.

To the brutally energetic accents of *The Treaty*, succeed the leaping figures of *The Flames' Spell*, *Loge*, *The Fall of the Gods*, and *The Norns*. Brünnhilde has seized a torch, and, after having fired the pyre, she has cast a burning brand against *Walhalla*.

The Ride reappears, wild and furious; she is now speaking to her faithful Grane, he shall carry her alive into the pyre, and shall die there heroically with her. Then appears in its wondrous splendour the magnificent *motiv* of *Redemption by Love*, which the great composer, after having given us only a glimpse of it in the third act of *Die Walküre* (Scene I., during Sieglinde's rôle), has kept in reserve for use here as the radiating aureole of the pure and intrepid heroine. This *motiv* will keep ceaselessly rising and increasing, lovingly entwining with that of *Siegfried Guardian of the Sword*, as Brünnhilde's exaltation, already excited by the incessant crackling of *The Flames*, attains a paroxysm of intensity; suddenly, with a thrilling utterance of her old *Walkyrie Shout*, she urges her noble horse into a gallop, and both plunge into the flaming pyre!

The fire leaps up, the flames hiss, the *motive* of *Loge* and *The Flames* rage, *Eternal Sleep* greatly expands, *The Rhine* rises and invades the stage; *The Curse of the Ring* is heard again once more, though broken and incomplete; the tenacious Hagen dashes into the waves to seize the Ring, which the joyous *Rhine-Daughters* at last have regained.

The drama is ended, but there still remains to be heard a prodigious epilogue which is purely instrumental, during which our emotion, which seems already at its height, will nevertheless be increased, and this by the sole power of the music and the harmonic combinations of the *Leit-motive*.

While *The Rhine*, gradually becoming calm, carries away with it the jubilant *Rhine-Daughters* sporting with their golden Ring, while *Walhalla*, lost forever, finally doomed, but still solemn and splendid, is illumined with the first flames which will devour and annihilate it, there comes floating above everything, like the penetrating and sweet perfume exhaled by Brünnhilde's pure soul, or the blossoming of her infinite tenderness, the radiant song of *Redemption by Love*, which every moment becomes more and more ethereal. All these *motive* run side by side as in a prophetic and luminous dream, without any confusion, each one preserving immutably its own character, whether majestic, happy, or ecstatic, and the result is a complex, indefinable, and profoundly affecting impression, which, after all these scenes of a mythological nature, plunges the deeply moved soul into a state of almost divine contemplation and Christian ideality.

In the four following pages I give a kind of sketch showing the curious way in which this prodigious combination has been effected, indicating, as nearly as possible, the marvellous orchestration.

What first attracts attention is the majestic theme of *Walhalla*, which is given to the family of Tubas and to the Bass Trumpet (the Wagnerian brass), solemnly swelling out in the $\frac{3}{2}$ bar; when this *motiv* ceases for a moment, the Tubas are replaced by the Trombones, without being confounded with them. — In the meantime on the Violoncellos, the Violas and Harps, appears the undulatory movement of the waves of *The Rhine*, with its usual rhythm in $\frac{6}{8}$. — The Oboes and Clarinets, to which the English Horn and the third Flute are afterwards added, recall the supple movements of the swimming *Rhine-Daughters*. It is only at the last that there appears on the first and second Violins, reinforced by two Flutes, the theme, glowing in splendour like a marvellous apotheosis, *The Redemption by Love*, in a very extended bar of $\frac{2}{2}$ of such grandeur and such sublimity in this supreme transformation, that we feel ourselves transported into the realms of the unknown.

We next find *Divine Power* which sinks down abruptly into the bass; we are in the presence of the conflagration and fall of the Palace of the gods, for the last time the

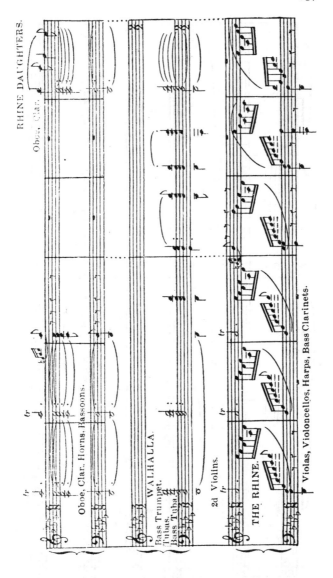

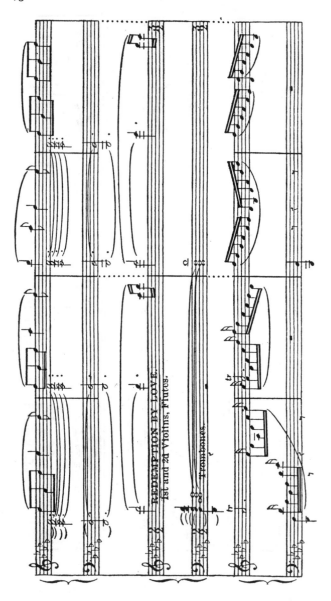

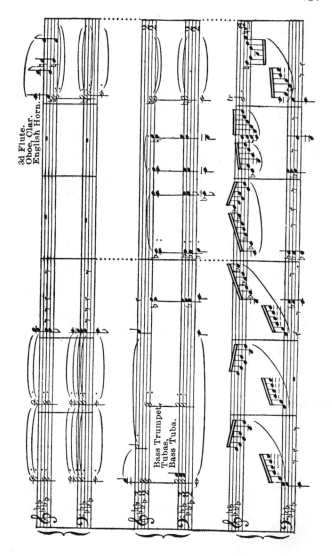

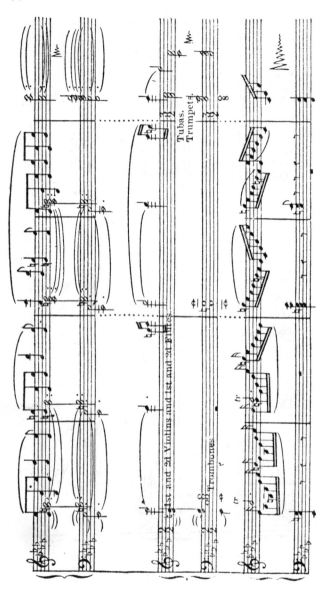

valiant notes of *The Guardian of the Sword* sound, while still higher in the celestial regions hovers, like a last and supreme benediction, the consolatory phrase which is so sweet and so nobly serene, in which the whole drama is summed up: *The Redemption by Love*.

It is of a most marvellous completeness, and it all moves with such ease that the hearer does not for an instant receive the impression of the actual complication of what he hears. All the *motive* stand out from one another clearly, and the dissonances which are sometimes formed among them disappear, thanks to the clearly defined diversity of the *timbre*. There is no confusion, no harshness; we float blissfully in an ocean of luminous waves of harmony, and we would like to be able indefinitely to prolong this delicious sensation, and, however slowly the curtain may fall, we are torn from this lovely dream to return to the reality of life all too soon.

And the lesson which we learn from it is this: "It has passed like a breath, this race of the gods; the treasure of my sacred knowledge I leave to the world: it is no longer goods, gold, or sacred pomp, houses, courts, lordly magnificence, nor the deceitful ties of dark treaties, nor the harsh law of hypocritical manners, but only one single thing which in good as in evil days makes us happy: Love!" (R. WAGNER.)

PARSIFAL

PRELUDE. — By the very Prelude we are initiated into all the great symbolic *motive* of the Holy Grail.

The first sound which issues from the depths of the " mystic abyss," a simple, low A-flat on the G string of the thirty-two violins, in a slow syncopated movement, this sound, bewildering inasmuch as it seems to rise from

PARSIFAL

NAMES of the principal *Leit-motive* in PARSIFAL in the order of their first appearance. SCENES:[1]	Prelude	ACT I.			Prelude	ACT II.			Prelude	ACT III.	
		1	2	3		1	2	3		1	2
The Eucharist	●	●	●	●	..	..	..	●	..	●	●
The Grail	●	●	●	●	..	●	..	●	●	●	●
Faith	●	●	●	●	..	..	..	●	●	●	●
The Lance	●	●	●	●	..	●	..	●	●	●	●
Suffering	..	●	●	..	..	●	..	●	..	●	●
The Promise	..	●	..	●	..	●	..	●	●	●	●
The Gallop	..	●	●	..	..	●	..	●			
Kundry	..	●	●	●	●	●	..	●	●	●	●
The Balm	..	●	..	..	..	..	..	..	..	●	
The Breeze	..	●	●	..	..	..	..	●	..	●	
Magic	..	●	●	●	●	●	..	●	●	●	
Klingsor	..	●	●	..	●	●	..	●	..	●	
The Flower-Maidens	..	●	..	..	..	..	●				
Parsifal	..	..	●	●	..	●	●	●	..	●	●
The Swan	..	..	●	●							
Herzeleide	..	..	●	..	..	..	..	●			
The Cry to the Saviour	..	..	●	●	●	●	..	●	..	●	●
Plaint of the Flower-Maidens	..	..	..	..	..	..	●	●	●	●	
Herzeleide's Grief	..	..	..	..	..	..	..	●			
Good Friday	..	..	..	..	..	..	..	●	..	●	●
The Desert	..	..	..	..	..	..	..	..	●	●	●
Expiation	..	..	..	..	..	..	..	..	..	●	
The Second Form of the Desert	..	..	..	..	..	..	..	..	..	●	●
The Spell of Good Friday	..	..	..	..	..	..	..	..	..	●	

[1] In *Parsifal* the division of scenes is entirely arbitrary, but agrees with the analysis which follows.

all parts of the hall at the same time, is the initial note
of the mysterious *motiv* of the Eucharist: a *motiv* of ex-

THE EUCHARIST

treme breadth in its calm and majestic simplicity; at first
presented bare, without any kind of accompaniment, it is
immediately repeated, harmonized with arpeggio envelop-
ments, to which the harp lends its priestly character.

After a long silence, the same *motiv* returns, this time
in the minor, which gives it an extraordinary impression
of suffering, which becomes still more painful when it is
emphasized by being harmonized.

Another long rest! These solemn silences are wonderfully eloquent and expressive; we feel that there is
food for much meditation on the single theme which has
just been presented, and so we meditate.

More detailed analyses will show how this first *motiv*
may be subdivided into several fragments, each one of
which has a special mystical signification.

The second theme to appear is *The Grail*, which musi-

THE GRAIL

cally represents the sacred vessel, and, by extension, the temple in which it is piously preserved.

Thirdly, still without leaving the key of A-flat, we have the austere *motiv* of *Faith*, which is developed with

FAITH

great length and pomp, momentarily intersected by a return of *The Grail*, and then expanding magnificently.

A mysterious roll of the drums, succeeded by a prolonged *tremolo* of the strings, announces and accompanies the reappearance of *The Eucharist* with new and curious harmonies, from which stands forth a *motiv* formed of four of its notes, typifying *The Lance*, which will con-

THE LANCE

stantly reappear in all portions of the work, except in the Prelude of the second act and in the scene of the Flower-Maidens. Although very short, it is easily recognized, being frequently orchestrated in a striking and incisive manner which at once attracts attention.

[These four *motive*, *The Eucharist*, *The Grail*, *Faith*, and *The Lance*, together with a fifth which will soon appear (*The Promise*), constitute the religious and to some extent liturgical

element which predominates in the first and third acts. Of
these important *motive*, *Faith* is the only one which undergoes
harmonic and rhythmic transformations which might prevent our
recognizing it at first sight, of which it is well to be warned;
this is why I give it below under the various aspects it assumes
from the beginning of the first act (in bars 34, 134, 404, and
486), always in the rôle of Gurnemanz, the knight of robust
faith, whose favourite theme it naturally is.]

After a short development of *The Lance*, the *motiv* of *The Eucharist* forms a connecting link between the Prelude and the first act.

ACT I.

As *Parsifal* is not divided into scenes, for the sake of facilitating the analysis we must establish arbitrary demarcations between the various parts of the continuous acts.

Let us divide the first act into three parts: 1, from the beginning to Parsifal's arrival; 2, from Parsifal's arrival to the change of scene; 3, the scene in the temple.

The *motive* of *The Eucharist*, *The Grail*, *Faith*, and again *The Eucharist* give the signal for waking and the morning prayer. The dialogue begins between Gurnemanz and two of his youthful companions, two Esquires of the Grail; here the orchestra presents *Faith* under the first transformation given above (in B major), and, four bars farther on, a grievous bass figure tells us of the physical *Suffering* of the King, Amfortas, who comes down, borne on a litter, to take the bath which alone can afford him momentary relief:

At the 65th bar of the act, the orchestra expressively, but slightly as yet, indicates the *motiv* of *The Promise*, which will be more fully given two pages later. (See p. 449).

A rustling of leaves which gives us the sensation of a wild ride is heard, followed by the harsh and excited rhythm of *The Gallop*, which, after having continued for

THE GALLOP

several bars, growing louder and nearer, ends in a sort of convulsive laughter, which almost always accompanies the appearance of the strange character of *Kundry*.

The painful *motiv* of the King's corporeal *Suffering* and the violent *motive* of *The Gallop* and *Kundry's* savage laughter, coming after the grave and solemn harmonies of the Prelude, produce an effect of striking contrast.

One of less importance, accompanying Kundry's few rude and broken words, is associated with the idea of *The Balm* which she has been to fetch from the wilds of Arabia without any orders from her superior.

THE BALM

Amfortas's train is approaching; we recognize in the orchestra *Suffering*, *Faith*, in a second transformation (p. 444 in D flat), and a fragment of *The Eucharist*. *Suffering* returns, but it seems lessened by the coming of the charming *motiv* of *The Breeze*, the invigorating

THE BREEZE

breeze, which for a moment alleviates the pain of the unfortunate Amfortas, and ends with the last notes of *The Eucharist.*

[The *motiv* of *The Breeze*, will be found slightly indicated in the third act, shortly after Parsifal's arrival at Gurnemanz's hut, but its form is changed into E major and $\frac{3}{4}$.]

Parsifal

Some notes of the King's recital introduce us to the prophetic theme of *The Promise*, on the faith of which

Amfortas   THE PROMISE

he awaits a saviour, who can be none but a " Guileless
Fool, whose own heart alone instructs him ! "

The flask which Gurnemanz gives him recalls the
motiv of *The Balm*, with that of *The Gallop* and *Kundry's* sinister laughter; while the latter, in her wild way,
rejects the King's thanks, mysterious and tortuous
figures bristling with chromatic notes reveal to us somewhat of her strange nature; they end with a still more
violent recurrence of the nervous laugh.   The train
having resumed its march, to the groanings of the cruel
Suffering, which however is tempered by *The Breeze*,
the conversation again becomes affectionate and confi-
dential between the knight Gurnemanz and the young
esquires who are eager for instruction.   What can be
the subject of conversation?   The *Holy Grail*, the
subject of every thought of the pious Knights; *Kundry's*
strange and enigmatical ways and her still recent *Gallop;*
The Eucharist, which forms the symbolic base of the
worship of the Grail; *The Promise* of a new Redeemer,
who will come to deliver the King from his torture;
The Magic, which with its evil spells and machinations
opposes the purity of the holy religion of the *Grail*, *The
Lance* and *Faith*, which are summed up in one word,
The Eucharist.

MAGIC

Gurnemanz

[The theme of *Magic*, as well as *Klingsor*, which follows, will appear in their full development in the second act; they only figure here as episodes, for the purpose of annotating the story.]

A brief return of *Suffering*, lightened by *The Breeze*, occurs at the moment when two of the Esquires, returning from the lake, as they pass by give news of the King; then the good Gurnemanz continues to instruct his pupils, this time with fresh explanations of *Faith*, *The Grail*, *The Eucharist*, and *The Lance* (all these *motive* coming in the order named), he tells them who *Klingsor* is.

KLINGSOR

He speaks of his infamy, the seductions with which he tries to corrupt the holy Knights, the use he makes of *Magic* (here in the orchestra rapidly pass the *motive*

of *Kundry*, and the *Flower-Maidens*, Klingsor's tools),
and, finally, how the wretched Amfortas, in his attempt
to fight him, became his victim, losing at once his
chastity and the sacred *Lance*, in addition to receiving the
terrible wound "which nothing can close," except, as
has been prophetically revealed, by the intervention of
the "pure and simple," the subject of *The Promise*.
Marvelling and saddened at the story, the Esquires are
repeating in chorus the *motiv* of *The Promise*, when a
startling flourish, this time restricted to its first three
notes, but which will later be recognized as the personal
motiv of *Parsifal*, followed by shouts and cries of terror,
puts an end to the conversation.

PARSIFAL

[When *Parsifal* reappears in his black armour, at the beginning of Act III., this *motiv* is in B-flat minor; and when, at

the last, having in his turn become Priest-King and Master of
the Grail, he performs the miracle of healing the King's wound,
it assumes this particularly triumphal form :]

Here begins the second part of the act. Parsifal, ignorant of the law of The Grail, which requires that animal life shall be held sacred within its domains, has just killed a swan; the profanation is the cause of all the outcry. The dying swan is brought to the good Gurnemanz, who questions and severely reprimands the unconscious offender. At the first notes of his reply, his character is revealed to us in all its simplicity.

To the themes of *The Eucharist* (scarcely indicated), *Faith*, which always accompanies Gurnemanz's words, and the healing *Breeze*, there is here added a new theme, consisting of two chords only, which in Wagner's mind is clearly associated with the idea of *The Swan*, since he has already made use of it in *Lohengrin :*

THE SWAN

Affected by the paternal reproaches of the good Knight, Parsifal breaks his bow and casts away his arrows. Gurnemanz, continuing his inquiries, can get nothing out of him, unless, indeed, he remembers his mother, which is doubtless intended by the sad and gentle *motiv* of *Herzeleide :*

HERZELEIDE

(The Grieving Heart, or the Unhappy Woman, according to the commentators.) The *motiv* of *The Swan* reappears in between, in the few touching and solemn bars which it is customary to call " The Funeral March of the Swan."

When *Kundry*, a little later, helping him to gather together his recollections, informs him of his mother's death, we find *The Gallop*, several gleams of *Parsifal*, and then *Herzeleide*; when he flies at the throat of the wild woman, there is a strong but dissonant crash of the *motiv* of *Parsifal*, succeeded by a sad memory of *Herzeleide*; when Parsifal faints and Kundry runs to fetch him some water, *The Gallop* returns, followed by the fatal

laughter; when she offers him this water, this restora-
tive, she is inspired by *The Grail* and the idea of *The
Balm* intervenes; it is the ministering Kundry, but she
is soon surrounded by the Satanic *motive*, *Magic* and its
practices and *Klingsor* who is already calling her: she
shudders, tries to stand erect, falls down in convulsions,
and sinks into a heavy sleep.

Then the moving scenery gives us the impression that
we are accompanying Gurnemanz and Parsifal in the
ascent of Montsalvat; in these almost exclusively symphonic pages the principal *motiv* of which announces
the chiming of *Bells* of the Grail, we necessarily find all
the themes of a religious character, and, in addition, the
mournful and characteristic figure of *The Cry to the
Saviour* :

THE CRY TO THE SAVIOUR

Towards the end of this interlude, the *motiv* of *The Eucharist*, at which we are about to be present, assumes a
predominating importance, till the moment when *The*

Bells (see p. 472), ringing out in full peal, introduce us into the sanctuary itself. Throughout this third part of the act, Parsifal will remain motionless, as though petrified with astonishment, with his back to the audience, silently contemplating the impressive and touching scene of the Office of the Holy Grail.

To a marked rhythm which keeps time to the ringing of *The Bells*, the Knights, answering the call of *The Grail*, come in and solemnly range themselves around the tables; to the same rhythm, but doubling the pace, young Esquires, more alert, enter in their turn and take their place. Voices of Youths, forming a three-part chorus, placed half-way up the dome, give forth *The Cry to the Saviour*, which is accompanied in the orchestra by some notes of *The Lance*, followed by the harmony of *The Grail*. Another four-part chorus of Children stationed at the top of the dome, in turn sings the theme of *Faith*, treated as a choral. (This curious superposition of three choruses at different heights, the men on the floor of the temple, the youths half-way up, and the children at the top, which produces a most striking effect, had been tried by Wagner long before, in 1843, in the Church of Our Lady at Dresden, in his *Das Liebesmahl der Apostel.*)

Titurel's voice, issuing from the depths of a kind of crypt, commands his son to perform the holy sacrifice; Amfortas, to the *motiv* of *The Cry to the Saviour*, begs to be relieved of the task; but Titurel, supported by two sacred recalls of *The Grail*, orders the sacred vessel to be uncovered. Then begin the terrible agonies of the unhappy fallen Priest-King, tortures far more moral than physical, which bring back sharp memories of *Kundry*, mingled with the sacred themes of *The Grail*, *The Eucharist*, *The Cry to the Saviour*, and *The Lance*,

with which the Satanic *motiv* of *Magic* is at war, while
he describes to us the cruel sufferings he endures every
time he is forced to exercise his priestly functions.
From the choir of the Youths mysteriously falls a memory of *The Promise*; the Knights insist that the unfortunate man shall fulfil his duty, and Titurel's voice more
imperatively commands *The Grail* to be uncovered.

Then *The Eucharist* is heard in all its majesty, almost
in the same orchestral arrangement as at the beginning
of the Prelude, except that the violins are supplanted by
the Children's voices, which seem to come from the sky
with the words of Consecration.   In the meantime the
miracle is accomplished.

The Bells are again heard ; then the three choirs, first
the Children, next the Youths, and lastly the Knights,
sing a psalm of thanksgiving.   Then, by an inverse
arrangement, first the Knights, then the Youths, and finally
the Children raise their voices in a sort of formula of
faith, hope, and charity, which is harmonized by the
theme of *The Grail*, and is lost in the heights of the
dome.

The King's train withdraws, and then the Knights,
and the troops of Youths again marching with a more
active step, escorted by the same *motive* which accompanied their entrance and the chime of *The Bells of the
Grail*.

Gurnemanz and Parsifal being left alone, the orchestra, in a singularly expressive combination, recalls the
motive of *The Promise*, *The Cry to the Saviour*, *Parsifal*, and
The Swan ; and when Gurnemanz, after having turned
Parsifal out, has himself retired and the stage is deserted,
a prophetical voice is heard in a repetition of *The Promise*,
to which the voices of the dome reply, like a celestial
echo, with *The Grail* and *The Lance*.

Act II.

Following our methods in the first act, we shall divide the present one into the three parts which naturally present themselves: 1, the evocation of Kundry; 2, the Flower-Maidens; 3, the scene between Kundry and Parsifal, and the latter's victory over Klingsor.

The Prelude is entirely one with the scene; if it were not for *The Cry to the Saviour*, which is not immediately explicable, it would be entirely made up of the diabolical *motive* of *Klingsor*, *Magic*, and *Kundry:* the evocation occurs to *Magic* and *Klingsor*, but Kundry's appearance brings back *The Cry to the Saviour*, the sole and supreme aspiration of the unhappy victim of the curse; desperately she clings to it, seeking by this ardent prayer to free herself from the influence of the magician. Each of these useless efforts is accented by a wild cry of *Kundry*, the wild woman whose terrible destiny it is to be alternately subject to the infernal powers and to the sweet influences of the holy temple.

Klingsor reminds her of their numerous victories, among others, *The Lance*, which, thanks to her, he has succeeded in capturing, and tells her of the fresh victim whom he has in store for her for to-day: " A Guileless Fool," personified by the *motiv* of *The Promise*. The remainder of this scene, during which Kundry does not cease to maintain a useless struggle against the dominating will of the magician, gives rise to frequent returns of the preceding *motive*, mingled with memories of the *Suffering* of Amfortas, over which the odious enchanter gloats; of *The Grail*, the power of which he hopes to gain; and then *Parsifal's* theme is heard. Klingsor, climbing up to the battlements of his tower, joyfully watches him overthrow all the defenders of his castle, whom he excites to the combat, while Parsifal continues to advance, accompanied sometimes by his own theme, *Parsifal*, and sometimes by that which symbolizes his character and his unconscious mission, *The Promise*. Meanwhile, *Kundry*, finally brought to submission, has disappeared to prepare for her rôle of seduction.

Second Tableau: the Flower-Maidens. To the above dark and sinister scene, by one of those violent contrasts which Wagner is always fond of, there instantaneously follows the picture of the Enchanted Gardens, seductive, if not by its scenery, at least by its action and music, a place of perdition especially created by Klingsor for the Knights of the Grail. There, seductive and perfidious creatures, half-women, half-flowers, are about to put our chaste hero to various proofs for which he is not in the least prepared. After his arrival, in terror, they utter their *Plaint* in a very close dialogue, in which this characteristic figure frequently occurs:

PLAINT OF THE FLOWER-MAIDENS

their only thought is to bewail the aggression which has just spread destruction among their lovers, Klingsor's slaves; but, immediately *Parsifal* appears, their conduct changes, and they no longer think of anything but allurement;

the *Plaint* gradually dies away and gives place to *motive* full of grace and charm, among which several pervading forms, such as the following, intertwine in the most voluptuous and brilliant manner. Half singing and half dancing (posturing), *The Flower-Maidens* many times renew the attack, which is always repulsed by *Parsifal* with a gentleness which is not free from a certain curiosity, quite excusable in view of such provoking entice-

THE FLOWER-MAIDENS

Flower-Maidens

ments ; whence arise frequent interweavings of the typical *motiv* of the chaste hero and those, so full of teasing playfulness, of the seductive beauties :

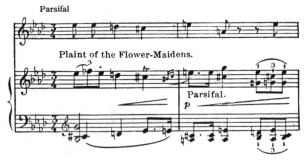

It is then that Kundry takes a hand; now, also, the name of Parsifal is pronounced for the first time, and the notes to which it is spoken are none other than those of *The Promise*. The perfidious enchantress begins by softening his heart with a long conversation about his mother, *Herzeleide*, after having sent away the sportive band, whose *Plaint* we again recognize.

The great scene of seduction, highly developed and of extreme importance in the work, makes use of several of those themes we already know, and introduces us to two new ones; the order in which they occur is mainly as follows: *The Promise*, which personifies the chaste and pure character of the hero; *The Lance*, which he has found again; *Magic*, which seeks to enfold him; *Herzeleide* and *Herzeleide's Grief* (which is often called *Herzeleide's Second Motiv*).

HERZELEIDE'S GRIEF

Next appears the *motiv* proper to *Kundry*; her kiss belongs to *Magic*; but Parsifal immediately remembers *The Eucharist*, at which he was present, and *The Cry to the Saviour*, and he understands Kundry's odious rôle; Amfortas's *Suffering* comes into his mind with *The Grail* and *The Lance*. All these *motive*, powerfully developed, struggle with those of *Magic* and *Kundry*, whom he recognizes as the one who has ruined the King. She herself reveals her psychical nature to him, the curse which weighs upon her, and the sin by which she has deserved this chastisement: that she saw the Saviour (*The Eucharist*) on the day of his crucifixion (*Good Friday*) [1], that she laughed

(*Kundry*), that she is the cause of the agony of Amfortas (*Suffering*), and that she acts under the compulsion of the spells of a magician (*Klingsor* and *Magic*). Parsifal promises *Kundry* that she shall be redeemed (*The Promise* and *Faith*); she, becoming more and more passionate, again displays all her seductive wiles, she begs him (*Plaint of the Flower-Maidens*), she threatens him, pursues him (*The Gallop*), and tries to take him in her arms by force (*Kundry*). Suddenly Klingsor appears, brandishing *The*

---

[1] We must be very careful not to confound this *motiv* with the Spell of Good Friday (see p. 468), which is of an entirely different character.

Lance and menacing Parsifal with it; but the weapon remains suspended motionless above the head of the latter, who seizes it and traces the sign of the cross (*The Grail*).[1] At this sign the Gardens crumble away, the magic flowers wither, and *Klingsor* falls dead.

We see with what wonderful art the *Leit-motive* are manipulated in this great scene, the moving incidents of which, thanks to them, we can follow step by step, even if we are ignorant of the language or cannot distinguish the words.

ACT III.

This last act is of itself divided into two tableaux: 1, the hut of the old knight, Gurnemanz, in the domains of The Grail; 2, the scene in the Temple.

This Prelude, which is also intimately connected with the action, from the very beginning shows us one of the aspects, at once smiling and forbidding, of the district around the castle of Montsalvat, that of *The Desert*,

THE DESERT

[1] At the very moment when Klingsor throws the sacred weapon at Parsifal, a curious orchestral effect must be pointed out to the attentive listener: to produce the impression of the *whizzing* of The Lance through the air, Wagner employs a long *glissando* on the harps, two octaves in extent, which is singularly descriptive.

where the pious servant of *The Grail* has established his retreat, as well as the subjects of his constant meditation, the enigmatical *Kundry*, *The Promise* of a new redeemer, the enchantments of *Magic*, *The Lance* which only a "Guileless Fool" can regain, the Satanic rôle of the *Flower-Maidens* (represented by their Plaint) and of the sorcerer *Klingsor*. Gurnemanz's attention is attracted by groans which seem to come from a bush, and which his piety leads him to regard in the light of *Expiation*:

EXPIATION

in fact, beneath the brambles, he discovers the motionless body of Kundry, still under the influence of *Magic*. He succeeds in restoring her to animation, and as she awakes from her hypnotic sleep with a memory of the *Plaint*, although henceforth under the influence of The Grail, she utters a loud cry, which carries out in a sinister manner the fantastic figure of the laughter of *Kundry*; a recurrence of *The Balm* clearly shows that we are now in the presence of the beneficent and repentant Kundry. Gurnemanz, however, remarks a change in her conduct, which he attributes to the sanctity of this day, consecrated above all others to *The Grail*, *Good Friday*. While busying herself with occupations which seem quite customary to her, she warns Gurnemanz with a sign that a stranger is approaching from the forest. The orchestra immediately informs us who the stranger is: it is *Parsi-*

fal, clad in his black armour, with his vizor lowered, so that Gurnemanz does not recognize him. He, however, kindly welcomes him with the salutation of *The Grail*, and informs him that on this day of *Good Friday* people must not walk armed within the sacred domain. Parsifal then takes off his armour and arranges it as a kind of trophy, piously kneeling before it. Then both Gurnemanz and Kundry recognize him, which necessarily brings back the sacred *motive* of *The Eucharist*, *The Lance*, on which Gurnemanz gazes with fervent emotion, *The Promise*, *The Cry to the Saviour*, *Good Friday*, and, the moment Parsifal concludes his prayer, *The Grail*.

Here, under certain words of the old Knight, appears a short melodic figure which will return somewhat frequently, and which may be considered as a new aspect of the surrounding country, *The Second Form of The Desert*: eight bars farther on, notice a sweet and delight-

THE SECOND FORM OF THE DESERT

ful return of *The Breeze*. All the *motive* which are interwoven during the rest of the scene are now too well known to the reader to need being mentioned; also during the essentially Biblical or rather evangelical scene, when Kundry washes Parsifal's feet and Gurnemanz consecrates and anoints him King of the Grail, we necessarily find all the sacred themes, with a few rare allusions to those of a demoniac nature, such as that of the *Plaint of*

the Flower-Maidens, which now becomes the Plaint of
Kundry.   When Parsifal in his turn baptizes the sinner,
Faith is the dominant theme; the sinister fit of nervous
laughter is silenced and will never appear again.

Immediately after the baptism, a delightful phrase, a
pervading figure, full of the most divine sweetness and
grace, gently forces itself upon our attention (it has
been already announced in a vague way and with a syncopated rhythm in the key of A-flat, as I reproduce it
here, shortly after the opening of the act, on Parsifal's

arrival, when Kundry tells Gurnemanz that a stranger is
approaching); without absolutely constituting a *Leit-
motiv*, for only one allusion will be subsequently made to
it, it is of very great importance in this scene, over which
it spreads an intense feeling of calm and sweet reflection;
it is called *The Spell* (or *The Enchantment*) *of Good Friday.*[1]

In the course of this suave and placid episode, while
Gurnemanz is explaining to his new King how this day,

---

[1] It is also sometimes called *The Flowering Meadow.*   It was
written long before the rest of the score.

THE SPELL OF GOOD FRIDAY

which most people consider as fatal and cursed, is at
Montsalvat, on the contrary, regarded as the day of supreme blessing, we find again in the orchestral web:
Expiation many times repeated, *The Eucharist, Good
Friday, The Cry to the Saviour, The Grail, The Plaint of
the Flower-Maidens* (Kundry's Plaint), and finally *The
Promise.* But what is particularly interesting is that we
here find that employment so characteristic of the Wagnerian style of the harmonic and melodic progression
which is found in the two Choruses of Pilgrims in *Tannhäuser*, to which I have already called attention (p. 270).

We must not regard this either as a fortuitous resemblance or a simple reminiscence; when we have identical

sentiments it is rational to employ an identical mode of
expression, and that is what the composer has unhesitatingly done:

The Bells of Montsalvat are calling us to the holy
place.   As in the first act, moving scenery conducts us
there.   We arrive even in advance of the characters.

There, with the same scenery as in the first act, we
first see two processions, — one bearing Titurel's coffin,
the other Amfortas's litter; and again the latter is called
upon by all the Knights once more to fulfil his priestly
functions, but neither *The Cry to the Saviour*, nor *Faith*,
nor *The Eucharist* and *Good Friday* can induce him to
perform them; the *Suffering* he has to endure fills him
with terror.

It is then that *Parsifal* appears followed by Gurnemanz and Kundry, and with a still better escort in the
sacred *motive* of *The Grail* and of *The Lance* which he
holds in his hand.   With the point of the sacred weapon
he touches the dreadful wound, and *Suffering* vanishes in
the theme of *The Promise*, which is now fulfilled.

The *motiv* of *Parsifal* then sounds triumphantly, followed by *Faith* and *The Lance*, and, in his turn, he commands: " Let the Holy Grail be uncovered."   Then in
his hands the miracle is repeated; amid sparkling arpeg-

gios are heard the themes of *The Grail, The Eucharist,
Faith*, and the choir of three stages, now united, chant in
a mighty Alleluia : " Salvation to (Parsifal), the Saviour."

Then come the *motive* of *Faith*, and lastly *The
Eucharist*, majestically terminating the symphonic epi-
logue, " *Strong is Desire ; but still stronger is Resistance.*"
(R. WAGNER.)

In the course of the work we may still gather a certain number of secondary themes, which have more or
less the character of *Leit-motive*, but which it is not indispensable for us to know in order to understand the
work, because they occur merely as episodes. I here
offer a few only, with the sole aim of facilitating research, only repeating that, having once begun, here, as
elsewhere, a much greater number of them may be discovered :

Ardour, which only appears in the second part of the
Duet between Kundry and Parsifal, in the second act :

Resignation, which is merely outlined a few pages
farther on, but which we find, in the exact form given
below, in the first scene of the third act, where Kundry
is bringing some water to the fainting Parsifal :

RESIGNATION

Benediction, which immediately succeeds the preceding *motiv* :

BENEDICTION

Gurnemanz's *Lamentations* over Titurel's death, which are only separated from *The Benediction* by 26 bars, and will be found at the first words of the chorus of Knights (in the last tableau) :

LAMENTATIONS

The Bells of Montsalvat, whose grave and solemn ringing almost always accompanies the religious ceremonies, which, by an entirely natural transformation, becomes the march rhythm to which the Knights of the Holy Grail defile past, etc.

THE BELLS OF MONTSALVAT

8ᵗᵃ bassa............

In ending this brief analysis of the style which Wagner created with the ringing of the bells of Montsalvat, I cannot help drawing attention here (which will strengthen what has already been said on pp. 239, 244, 245, 250, 251, 271, 273, 344 and others, and which will now be better understood) to what may be called *the roots* of the Wagnerian musical language.

If we compare certain very characteristic *motive* with each other :

 The Bells of Montsalvat . . . . .
which serves as a march for the Knights,
 Waking Love . . . .
of *The Meistersinger*,
 The Beating . . . .
of the second act of the same work,
 The Waltz of the Apprentices . . .
of the third act,
 The Love of Life . . . .
in *Siegfried*,
 and *The Decision to Love* . . . . .

also in *Siegfried*, third act, we are struck by the analogy of the structure which they present with their regular descents by successive fourths, and by the similar sentiments they express : there is always the feeling of intention and decision, of a resolution formed.

It is therefore indisputable that this particular and energetic form naturally presented itself to Wagner's mind every time he desired to express the idea of voluntary action, and free and unconstrained movement, and that he thus employed it. Whether this is intentional or involuntary, it matters little, — it is a fact.

And this remark becomes still more interesting when we state that Beethoven, who is most certainly one of the spiritual ancestors of Wagner, his forerunner most indisputably before all others, had already employed an identically similar formula for the purpose of expressing an act of laborious decision :

DER SCHWER GEFASSTE ENTSCHLUSS

That is a *root*. — There are others, there are many others, some of which it has only been possible to indicate by inference in the course of this chapter. — It is a whole unexplored mine to be exploited by the learned musicographers who wish to go more deeply into the mysteries of the Wagnerian philosophy, where everything has not yet been discovered.

---

[1] " Must it be ? It must be ! " Beethoven, the motto of the Quartet in F major, op. 135.

CHAPTER V

THE INTERPRETATION

> " Suit the action to the word, the word
> to the action ; with this special ob-
> servance, that you o'erstep not the
> modesty of nature: for anything so
> overdone is from the purpose of
> playing, whose end, both at the first
> and now, was and is, to hold, as
> 't were, the mirror up to nature."
> SHAKESPEARE.

WE have seen in the life of Wagner how exces-
sively repugnant to him was the mere thought
of *following Art for money*. Money, however, was necessary to him, and even indispensable for the realization
of his vast conceptions; but he never considered it as
anything but a *means*, not as an *end*.

This noble way of looking at the cultivation of Art
has become in some measure the device of the courageous band from which the Festival-Theatre is recruited,
every time it is opened for a series of performances; the
characteristic of every Wagnerian artist-interpreter, as we
find him at Bayreuth (and there only), is complete dis-
interestedness, the abnegation of his own personality, as
well as his own interests; according to the example set by
the Master, he comes there with no other motive than
the pure desire of producing *Art for Art's sake*. Therefore no one, neither the singers nor the members of the
chorus, the musicians in the orchestra nor the scene-
shifters, the instructors nor the leaders of the orchestra,

receive anything in the nature of money or reward; they all receive a simple indemnity which scarcely covers their living expenses; sometimes even they have refused that; their travelling-expenses are paid, and they are lodged with an inhabitant at the charge of the administration; when the performances come to an end, they depart, without having realized any pecuniary profit, for they have not come for that. The happiness of co-operating in the great work, of participating in a magnificent display of the beautiful, is sufficient for them; they are Priests of Art, *artists* in the purest and highest sense of the word, and, with rare exceptions, they are religious artists, convinced of the greatness of their mission.

For the singer who is heard in Paris, Munich, Brussels, or elsewhere, the greatest composer will always be the one who has afforded him the greatest number of successes; the best work that in which the best rôle is allotted to him; he thinks more of the business side than of the art, seeking above all to please the public and have himself intrusted with an important and sympathetic rôle, so as to be able afterwards to look forward to a more advantageous engagement, and finally to get rich. But on the day when he comes to Bayreuth, all idea of lucre is dismissed in advance: it is a pilgrimage that he is performing, and from that moment his whole will and intelligence are directed solely to a reverential interpretation of the work, putting aside the sordid considerations and jealousies of the green-room. His sole aim henceforth is to render as faithfully as possible the part which is assigned to him, without attempting to introduce into it any other effects than those which are contained in it, respectfully conforming to the exact letter and to the tradition which is still alive in the minds and memories of the surviving collaborators of the revered Master.

We can understand, aside from the individual value of each assistant, what cohesion and truth the execution and interpretation may gain when the actor is inspired with such feelings, when he regards his functions like an accomplished priest with happiness and pride, and when he feels around him comrades who are impregnated with the same respect for the dignity of Art.

It is not, therefore, the perfection or personal virtuosity of this or that singer to which the exceptionally striking and captivating character of the Bayreuth performances must be attributed, but to that intimate solidarity, to that boundless devotion to the common cause, which allows an artist, who is everywhere else accustomed to play the leading parts, to accept here, without feeling any loss of dignity, the very slightest character, in which he will acquit himself with as much zeal and conscientiousness as if he were the hero. These same singers may be seen on other boards but they will never be as they are here, because they have not the same inspiration.

The interpreter who intends to attack the Wagnerian *répertoire* must be endowed with rare and manifold qualities. Before all, he must possess naturally the artistic sense, he must be an excellent musician, a musician who cannot be baffled by any difficulty of intonation : — for Wagner, by the very essence of his style, as we have shown, treats the voice as a chromatic instrument, or rather as a keyboard,[1] with a low and high compass, and

---

[1] In a work which I esteem very highly (Ernst, *Richard Wagner and Contemporary Drama*), I have seen this same subject treated in terms which at first sight seem contradictory to mine ; it is not so, however, it is merely a question of words. I call the way in which Mozart has treated the voice *vocal style*, not entirely neglecting the side of virtuosity, and, in comparison, the way in which Beethoven employs the voice I consider more *instrumental*. When I say that

various registers, but he neither takes, nor should take, account of the effort required to pass from one note to another, or constantly to change the key, or to bridge difficult intervals; he does not try either to be easy or to favour a singer's showy effects or virtuosity; dramatic accent and declamation, sung and intoned, stand for him above every other consideration, and it is by this means that he obtains truth of language, absolute cohesion between the poem and the measured recitative which the singers have to give forth on the stage, while the symphonic web is being unwound in the orchestra, two elements of equal importance. — The Wagnerian interpreter must also have the true qualities of a tragedian; for there is as much action and by-play as singing, and the least fault, the least stage awkwardness, here becomes the equivalent of a false note; it is a discord.

But what is indispensable above all else is absolute docility and submission to the gentle and urbane directions of those in charge of the instruction, including Julius Kniese, who for many years has fulfilled the duties of chief of the singing, and, more especially, Frau Wagner, who watches with maternal care over the treasures committed to her keeping, takes an active part in all the rehearsals and performances, and possesses the precious traditions in a higher degree than any one else, and *does not intend them to fall into decay;* and in this she is perfectly right.

Every rôle has been minutely mapped out to the smallest detail by Wagner; effects are not to be *sought after,* those

Wagner treats the voice as an instrument, I mean as a *special instrument,* the *vocal declamatory instrument,* if you like, and I no more say that he writes for the voice as for the violins, than that he writes the flute parts like those of the trombone, which would be a simple absurdity.

that are *intended* are simply to be observed. The best interpreter is therefore the one who is most faithful and sincere. And, above all, let it not be thought that this docile and respectful manner of interpretation lessens in the smallest degree the singer's prestige; on the contrary, it shows that he is possessed of the purest and most exquisite artistic feeling.

Moreover, this is how Wagner, speaking of the celebrated tenor Schnorr, the marvellous creator of Tristan, expresses himself on this subject:

"Schnorr was a born poet and musician: like myself he passed from a general classical education to the particular study of music; it is very probable that he *would soon have followed in the same direction* as myself if he had not developed those inexhaustible vocal powers that were to help to realize my highest ideals, and consequently to make him directly associated with my career, by complementing my own labours. In this new vocation our modern civilization offered him no other expedient than that of accepting engagements on the stage, of becoming a tenor, very much as Liszt, in a similar case became a pianist."

In saying this, he ranked the genius of interpretation with that of creation, and showed in what esteem he himself held the artist who was capable of assimilating the author's inmost thoughts and faithfully portraying them.

As for the rest, Bayreuth should not be visited for the sake of hearing the actor, but for seeing the work, considering ourselves happy if we have the good fortune to chance upon an interpretation of absolute genius, which sometimes happens, but this is *not necessary* for the understanding of the work.

From its origin to 1892, the Festival-Theatre was entirely dependent, so far as its singers were concerned, on the great theatres of Germany; at present the school of dramatic singing, of the creation of which Wagner had long dreamed, which, to tell the truth, only yet exists in a rudimentary form, and which is often called the Conservatoire of Bayreuth, is beginning to bear fruit.

There, under the direction of Julius Kniese and the strong impulse of Mme. Wagner, young people of vocal talent learn what is necessary for the interpretation of the Wagnerian works; they are first made thorough musicians and elocutionists, their voices are developed, their musical and dramatic intelligence is elevated, opportunity is afforded for them to rehearse in scenes of secondary and sometimes of higher importance, and then they make their first attempts at the Festival-Theatre as simple members of the chorus. Thus in 1894 five pupils of the Bayreuth School were found in the choruses, three women and two men, Breuer and Burgstaller; both the latter were at the same time entrusted with rôles which form mere episodes in *Lohengrin*, *Parsifal*, and *Tannhäuser*. In 1896, Breuer made an excellent Mime, whilst Burgstaller interpreted the important character of Siegfried in a more than satisfactory manner.

These are the first productions of the youthful School of Bayreuth, from which we may hope to see a race of *musician-singers* arise, a species of extreme rarity, and one almost unknown, alas! under our skies.

The theatre of Bayreuth has been opened eleven times since its erection to 1896.

In 1896 the Tetralogy of *Der Ring des Nibelungen* was given three times . . . . . 12 performances.
In 1882, *Parsifal* . . . . . 16 "
In 1883, *Parsifal* . . . . . 12 "
In 1884, *Parsifal* . . . . . 10 "

In 1886, *Parsifal* . . . . . 9 performances.
    and *Tristan und Isolde* . . 8   "
In 1888, *Parsifal* 9   "
    and *Die Meistersinger* . . 8   "
In 1889, *Parsifal* : 9   "
    Tristan und Isolde . . 4   "
    and *Die Meistersinger* . . 5   "
In 1891, *Parsifal* 10   "
    Tristan und Isolde . . 3   "
    and *Tannhäuser* 7   "
In 1892, *Parsifal* 8   "
    Tristan und Isolde . . 4   "
    Tannhäuser 4   "
    and *Die Meistersinger* . . 4   "
In 1894, *Parsifal* 9   "
    Lohengrin 6   "
    and *Tannhäuser* 5   "
In 1896 five performances of the
    Tetralogy of the *Ring* made 20   "

which makes a total of 182 representations,

    32 of The Tetralogy (each division 8 times),
    92 of *Parsifal,*
    19 of *Tristan,*
    17 of *Die Meistersinger,*
    16 of *Tannhäuser,*
  and 6 of *Lohengrin.*

Below, also, we give the distribution of the rôles, as well as the persons directing each of these series of performances; I think that much interesting information on various points may be gained from these lists, which have never been published, but the perfect authenticity of which I guarantee.

DER RING DES NIBELUNGEN
IN 1876 AND 1896

	1876 [1]	1896
CONDUCTOR:	Hans Richter.	Hans Richter. Felix Mottl. Siegfried Wagner.
STAGE-MANAGER:	Karl Brandt.	Julius Kniese.
INSTRUCTORS and assistant-musicians on the stage.	Anton Seidl. Franz Fischer. Hermann Zimmer. Demetrius Lallas. Joseph Rubinstein. Felix Mottl.	Michael Balling. Frantz Beidler. Willibald Kähler. Oscar Merz. Carl Pohlig. Edouard Risler.

RHEINGOLD

Wotan.	Franz Betz.	Hermann Bachmann. Carl Perron.
Donner.	Eugen Gura.	Hermann Bachmann.
Froh.	Georg Unger.	Alois Burgstaller.
Loge.	Heinrich Vogl.	Heinrich Vogl.
Alberich.	Carl Hill.	Fried. Friedrichs.
Mime.	Carl Schlosser.	Hans Breuer.
Fasolt.	Albert Eilers.	Ernst Wachter.
Fafner.	Franz von Reichenberg.	Johannes Elmblad.
Fricka.	Friederike Grün.	Marie Brema.
Freia.	Marie Haupt.	Marion Weed.
Erda.	Luise Jaïde.	E. Schumann-Heink.
Rhine-Daughters.	Lilli Lehmann. Marie Lehmann. Minna Lammert.	Joséphine v. Artner. Katharina Rösing. Olive Fremstad.

DIE WALKÜRE

Siegmund.	Albert Niemann.	Emil Gerhäuser. Heinrich Vogl.[2]
Hunding.	Joseph Niering.	Ernst Wachter.
Wotan.	Franz Betz.	Hermann Bachmann. Carl Perron.
Sieglinde	Joséphine Schefzky.	Rosa Sucher.
Brünnhilde.	Amalie Materna.	Ellen Gulbranson. Lilli Lehmann-Kalisch.
Fricka.	Friederike Grün.	Marie Brema.
Gerhilde.	Marie Haupt.	Joséphine v. Artner.

[1] The names of the *Creators* of the Tetralogy are engraved on a marble slab in the peristyle of the theatre.

[2] Vogl's name was not on the programmes.

Helmwige.	Lilli Lehmann.	Auguste Meyer.
Ortlinde.	Marie Lehmann.	Marion Weed.
Waltraute.	Luise Jaïde.	E. Schumann-Heink.
Siegrune.	Antonie Amann.	Johanna Neumayer.
Rossweisse.	Minna Lammert.	Luise Reuss-Belce.
Grimgerde.	Hedwig Reicher-Kindermann.	Katharina Rösing.
Schwertleite	Johanna Jachmann-Wagner.	Olive Fremstad

SIEGFRIED

Siegfried.	Georg Unger.	Alois Burgstaller. Wilhelm Grüning. Gustav Seidel.[1]
Mime.	Carl Schlosser.	Hans Breuer.
The Wanderer.	Franz Betz.	Hermann Bachmann. Carl Perron.
Alberich.	Carl Hill.	Fried. Friedrichs.
Fafner.	Franz von Reichenberg.	Johannes Elmblad.
Erda.	Luise Jaïde.	E. Schumann-Heink.
Brünnhilde.	Amalie Materna.	Ellen Gulbranson. Lilli Lehmann-Kalisch.
The Bird	Marie Haupt.	Joséphine v. Artner.

DIE GÖTTERDÄMMERUNG

Siegfried.	Georg Unger.	Alois Burgstaller. Wilhelm Grüning. Gustav Seidel.
Gunther.	Eugen Gura.	Carl Gross.
Hagen.	Gustav Siehr.	Johannes Elmblad. Carl Grengg.
Alberich.	Carl Hill.	Fried. Friedrichs.
Brünnhilde.	Amalie Materna.	Ellen Gulbranson. Lilli Lehmann-Kalisch.
Gutrune.	Mathilde Weckerlin.	Luise Reuss-Belce.
Waltraute.	Luise Jaïde.	E. Schumann-Heink.
The Norns.	Johanna Jachmann-Wagner. Joséphine Schefzky. Friederike Grün.	Marie Lehmann. Luise Reuss-Belce. E. Schumann-Heink.
The Rhine-Daughters	Lilli Lehmann. Marie Lehmann. Minna Lammert.	Joséphine v. Artner. Katharina Rösing. Olive Fremstad.
	Chorus of 28 men and 9 women.	Chorus of 30 men and 12 women.

[1] Seidel's name was on the programmes, but he was not called upon to fill the part.

TANNHÄUSER

In 1891, 1892, and 1894.

	1891	1892	1894
CONDUCTORS:	Hermann Levi. Felix Mottl.	Julius Kniese. Hermann Levi. Felix Mottl. Carl Mück. Hans Richter.	Julius Kniese. Hermann Levi. Felix Mottl. Hans Richter. Richard Strauss.
CHORUS-MASTERS:	Julius Kniese. Heinrich Porges.		
REHEARSERS and musician-assistants on the stage.	Carl Armbruster. Albert Gorter. Engelbert Humperdinck. Otto Lohse. Oscar Merz. Paumgartner. Hugo Röhr. Hans Steiner. Richard Strauss.	Carl Armbruster (director of music on the stage). Kurt. Hösel. Engelbert Humperdinck. Oscar Merz. Carl Pohlig. Heinrich Porges (chorus-master). Max Schilling. Siegfried Wagner.	Carl Armbruster. Eng. Humperdinck. Oscar Jünger. Franz Mikoren. Carl Pohlig. Heinrich Porges. Anton Schlosser. Siegfried Wagner.
The Landgrave Hermann.	Georg Döring. Heinr. Wiegand.	Georg Döring.	Georg Döring.
Tannhäuser.	Max Alvary. Herm. Winkelmann. Heinr. Zeller.	Wilhelm Grüning.	Wilhelm Grüning.
Wolfram.	Theodor Reichmann. Carl Scheidemantel.	J. Kaschmann. Carl Scheidemantel.	G. Kaschmann. Theodor Reichmann.
Walter.	Wilhelm Grüning.	Emil Gerhäuser.	Emil Gerhäuser.
Biterolf.	Emil Liepe.	Emil Liepe.	Michael Takats.
Henry.	Heinrich Zeller.	Heinrich Zeller.	Alois Burgstaller.
Reinmar.	Franz Schlosser.	Carl Bucha.	Carl Bucha.
Elizabeth.	Pauline de Anna. Elisa Wiborg.	Adolphine Welschke. Elisa Wiborg.	Pauline de Anna. Elisa Wiborg.
Venus.	Pauline Mailhac. Rosa Sucher.	Pauline Mailhac.	Pauline Mailhac.
A young shepherd.	Emilie Herzog. Luise Mulder.	Luise Mulder. Ida Pfund.	Marie Deppe. Luise Mulder.
	Chorus of 53 men and 46 women.	Chorus of 61 men and 42 women.	Chorus of 65 men and 52 women.

Dancing under the direction of Mme. Virginia Zucchi; invariably 30 males and 34 females.

LOHENGRIN

1894

CONDUCTORS:	Julius Kniese. Hermann Levi. Felix Mottl. Hans Richter. Richard Strauss.
REHEARSERS and musician-assistants on the stage :	Carl Armbruster. Eng. Humperdinck. Oscar Jünger. Franz Mikoren. Carl Pohlig. Heinrich Porges. Anton Schlosser. Siegfried Wagner.
King Henry.	Carl Grengg. — Max Mosel.
Lohengrin.	Ernest van Dyck.
Frederick.	Demeter Popovici.
The Herald.	Hermann Bachmann.
4 nobles.	Hans Breuer, Carl Bucha, Joseph Cianda, Heinr. Scheuten.
Elsa.	Lilian Nordica.
Ortrude.	Marie Brema. — Pauline Mailhac.

Chorus of 65 men and 52 women.

The composition of the orchestra is almost fixed and invariable ; it can hardly be increased on account of the impossibility of enlarging the space allotted to it, but certain works necessitate the presence of a greater or smaller number of instrumentalists on the stage.

Here is the exact number of which the orchestra has been composed on the various occasions :

In	1876	1886	1888	1889	1891	1892	1894	1896
Violins	32	32	31	32	32	32	32	33
Violas	12	12	13	12	12	12	12	13
Violoncellos	12	12	12	12	12	12	12	13
Double-Basses	8	8	8	8	8	8	8	8
Flutes	4	4	5	5	5	5	5	5
Oboes	4	4	4	4	4	4	4	4
Cor Anglais	1	1	1	1	1	1	1	1
Clarinets	4	5	4	4	4	4	4	4
Bass-Clarinets	1	1	1	1	1	1	1	1
Bassoons	4	4	4	4	4	4	4	4
Contrabassoons	1	1	1	1	1	1	1	1
Horns	7	9	7	9	11	11	10	10
Trumpets	4	4	4	4	4	4	4	4
Bass Trumpets	1							1
Trombones	4	4	4	4	4	4	4	4
Trombones — contrabass	1							1
Tubas — tenor	2							2
Tubas — bass	2	1	1	1	1	1	1	2
Tuba — contrabass	1							1
Kettledrums	3	2	2	2	2	2	2	3
Harps	8	4	4	4	4	4	4	8

As will be seen, the String Quartet has suffered only the slightest modifications; the most curious are in the Horns, which have varied from seven to eleven; the Bass Trumpet and the Tuba Contrabass only appear when *The Ring* is played; the latter also requires a third Drum and four additional Harps.

The largest orchestra was that of 1896, containing 125 musicians, nine more than in 1876.

Like the singers, the orchestra is recruited from every direction, more particularly in Germany, as is natural, but also largely abroad. It is incontestably a body of experts, and it is not rare to find in it artists who elsewhere fulfil the duties and bear the title of Leader of the Orchestra, Kapellmeister, and Director of the Court Music. But here, under the admirable direction of the great artists, Hans Richter, Hermann Levi, and Felix

Mottl, they receive at the same time a technical instruction and an artistic impulse which they might seek for in
vain elsewhere.

HANS RICHTER.

There is no need of severity to obtain exactitude and
obedience from them; they all come with goodwill to
range themselves under the great and noble banner; the
orchestra is a united family, and the undisputed authority

of the chief is marked with a good humour which is quite
fatherly.   At a recent rehearsal of *Siegfried*, one of the
drums had been struck a little before the right moment.

HERMANN LEVI.

" Sir," said Richter gently, " I would have you observe
that Fafner does not die till the second beat," — which
was duly noted.

During the performances, if he darts an angry glance
at a culprit (which sometimes happens there as else-

where), he never fails to bestow a smile of satisfaction
and encouragement on the soloist who has just distinguished himself by an exact interpretation of his rôle; I

FELIX MOTTL.

say rôle, for, there is no mistake about it, all the rôles are
not upon the stage; there are many, and not the least
important, which are confided exclusively to the orchestra,
and each musician, by the instruction gained at rehearsal,

knows, at any moment, the meaning of what he is doing, whether he is simply contributing to an *ensemble* effect, or whether the musical phrase in his charge possesses any particular signification which must be accentuated, and to what degree; he is not one of those who know better than all the commentators the force of the *Leit-motive*, often without knowing their names, which are always conventional and often variable, but, what is better, he understands their spirit and inner meaning. Thence results a symphonic execution which, even if it sometimes sins on the side of individual virtuosity, is characterized by exceptional intelligence; it is not always perfection, but right intention is always perceptible and it never becomes meaningless.

At Bayreuth the orchestra, although so large, is never noisy. If any fault is to be found with it, it is rather that of being sometimes too subdued; it never drowns the voice of the singer, and every syllable is distinctly audible; this may arise partly from the utterance of the actors, which is exceedingly clear in general, and from the numerous consonants of the German language; but it is certain that the underground situation of the orchestra, like an inverted amphitheatre and partly covered with screens, has much to do with it; the fusion of brasses and strings in the depths sometimes produces an organ-tone which can only be heard there.

Moreover, there is nothing more curious than the appearance of the orchestra during a performance; unfortunately no one, without a single exception, is allowed to go into it; the entrance is strictly guarded. The carefully shaded incandescent lights illuminate the stands before which the musicians are seated, the majority of them in their shirt-sleeves, for it is warm in July, and they give their whole heart to the work; people are fond of telling how "bocks" accumulate beside them, which, of course, are not touched till there are a certain number of bars' rest, but this is absolutely false. The truth is that when their part gives them a rest, the neglected ones of the orchestra, the Trombones and Tubas, who dwell in the depths of the cave, surreptitiously creep, gliding among the music-stands, to try to get a glimpse, if only for a moment, of a corner of the stage, a happiness which is reserved alone for those of the first and second violins who are placed above in the first row.

The conductor above (who, like the others, takes off his jacket and cravat), has his face lighted up by two lamps whose powerful reflectors are turned upon him, so that no one, on the stage or in the orchestra, may lose any of his gestures or facial expressions; it is not his score that is illuminated, he knows that by heart and rarely glances at it; it is himself, the absolute master, the sole one on whom the whole responsibility of the entire interpretation falls.

Notwithstanding the talent and conscientiousness of each of the participants and the profound experience and conviction of the chiefs, it is only after infinite and laborious study that works so complex as those which form the Bayreuth *répertoire* are finally produced. The singers arrive, already knowing their parts by heart, and the majority of musicians have already had opportunities in other German theatres (except in the case of *Parsifal*, which has never been performed elsewhere); but it still remains for them to acquire that marvellous cohesion, and that feeling of respect for the work which particularly characterizes and gives a colour of its own to the model-interpretation at the Festival-Theatre.

It seems to me therefore that it will be interesting to give the reader as an example the Table of Rehearsals of the *Tetralogy* of *The Ring of the Nibelung* in 1896.

This preparatory work, arranged and settled in advance, lasted from June 15th to July 18th without intermission except for three days of rest wisely provided for towards the close of the studies.

It follows in detail :

RHEINGOLD

June 15	9	to 11 o'clock	. . .	Wind instruments.[1]
	11	to 1 "	. . .	Strings.
	10	"	. . .	Stage with piano.
	3.30	to 5.30 "	. . .	Full orchestra.
	5.30	to 8 "	. . .	Stage with piano.
June 16	9	to 11 "	. . .	Full orchestra.
	11	to 1 "	. . .	Stage with piano.
	3	to 7 "	. . .	" " "
June 17	10	to 1 "	. . .	Stage with orchestra.
	4	to 7 "	. . .	Orchestra.

DIE WALKÜRE

Act I.

June 18	9	to 11 o'clock	. . .	Wind instruments.
	11	to 1 "	. . .	Strings.
	10	"	. . .	Stage with piano.
	3	to 5 "	. . .	Full orchestra.
	5	"	. . .	Stage with piano.

Act II.

June 19	9	to 11 o'clock	. . .	Wind instruments.
	11	to 1 "	. . .	Strings.
	10	to 1 "	. . .	Stage with piano.
	3	to 5 "	. . .	Full orchestra.
	5	to 8 "	. . .	Stage with piano.

[1] The partial rehearsals of the orchestra take place in the Restaurant-Brasserie, to the left of the theatre as you face it. The conductor bravely mounts a table with his chair and stand and the musicians group themselves around him. It is very home-like and picturesque.

ACT III.

June 20
9	to 11 o'clock	. . .	Wind instruments.
11	to 1 "	. . .	Strings.
10	to 1 "	. . .	Stage with piano.
3	to 5 "	. . .	Full orchestra.
5	"	. . .	Stage with piano.

ACTS I. AND II.

June 21

9.30 to 1 o'clock . . . Stage with orchestra.

ACT III.

5 o'clock . . . . . . Stage with orchestra.

SIEGFRIED

ACT I.

June 22
9	to 11 o'clock	. . .	Wind instruments.
11	to 1 "	. . .	Strings.
10	"	. . .	Stage with piano.
3	to 5 "	. . .	Full orchestra.
5	"	. . .	Stage with piano.

ACT II.

June 23
9	to 11 o'clock	. . .	Wind instruments.
11	to 1 "	. . .	Strings.
10	to 1 "	. . .	Stage with piano.
3	to 5 "	. . .	Full orchestra.
5	to 8 "	. . .	Stage with piano.

ACT III.

June 24
9	to 11 o'clock	. . .	Wind instruments.
11	to 1 "	. . .	Strings.
10	to 1 "	. . .	Stage with piano.
3	to 5 "	. . .	Full orchestra.
5	"	. . .	Stage with piano.

ACTS I. AND II.

June 25

9.30 to 1 o'clock . . . Stage with orchestra.

ACT III.

5 o'clock . . . . . . Stage with orchestra.

DIE GÖTTERDÄMMERUNG

Prologue

June 26
- 9   to 11 o'clock . . . Wind instruments.
- 11   to 1   "   . . . Strings.
- 10   "   . . . Stage with piano.
- 3   to 5   "   . . . Full orchestra.
- 5   "   . . . Stage with piano.

Act I.

June 27
- 9   to 11 o'clock . . . Wind instruments.
- 11   to 1   "   . . . Strings.
- 10   "   . . . Stage with piano.
- 3   to 5   "   . . . Full orchestra.
- 5   "   . . . Stage with piano.

Act II

June 28
- 9   to 11 o'clock . . . Wind instruments.
- 11   to 1   "   . . . Strings.
- 10   "   . . . Stage with piano.
- 3   to 5   "   . . . Full orchestra.
- 5   "   . . . Stage with piano.

Act III.

June 29
- 9   to 11 o'clock . . . Wind instruments.
- 11   to 1   "   . . . Strings.
- 10   "   . . . Stage with piano.
- 3   'to 5   "   . . . Full orchestra.
- 5   "   . . . Stage with piano.

Prologue and Act I.

June 30
- 9.30 to 1 o'clock . . . Stage with orchestra.

Acts II. and III.

- 5 o'clock . . . . . . Stage with orchestra.

July	1	Das Rheingold.	
"	2	"	
"	3	Die Walküre.	Full rehearsals with orchestra.
"	4	"	
"	5	Siegfried.	
"	6	"	

July	7	Die Götterdämmerung.	} Full rehearsals with
"	8	"	} orchestra.
"	9	"	}
"	10	(Rest).	
"	11		Reunion.
"	12	Das Rheingold.	Full rehearsal.
"	13	Die Walküre.	
"	14	(Rest).	
"	15	Siegfried.	Full rehearsal.
"	16	Die Götterdämmerung.	" "
"	17		Reunion.
"	18	(Rest).	

On the following day, the 19th, the performances began.

The studies had been conducted otherwise and at greater length at the time of the inauguration.

The four weeks of July, 1875, were given up to rehearsals with the piano: first week, *Das Rheingold*; second, *Die Walküre*; third, *Siegfried*, and fourth, *Die Götterdämmerung*. From the 1st to the 15th of August of the same year, the same works were rehearsed with the orchestra, in the third week of August the stage part was studied.

These rehearsals, however, were only preparatory, for, in 1876, from June 3rd, the rehearsals were recommenced, sometimes with the piano, sometimes with the orchestra, and afterwards the stage; from August 6th to August 9th the full rehearsals were held, and on Sunday, the 13th, at 7 p. m., the first performance began, with *Das Rheingold*.

So that in 1875 and 1876 there were about three months of rehearsing.

From this we see that the life of the members of the orchestra during the preparatory studies is not an idle one.

But the authorities know how to make it pleasant for them. Mme. Wagner is there and loves to receive them, to give them a hearty welcome, to *fête* them and encourage them in their work. They are welcome guests at Wahnfried.

Generally they take their meals in common, in groups, according to their hours of rehearsal, in one of the large restaurants near the theatre, where they are very well served at an exceedingly reasonable price.

Certainly they work very hard and tire themselves; but above their fatigue hovers the inspiriting thought of the great performance to be realized, of the end to be attained; and so no one complains, all rejoice in their mutual efforts and aid and encourage each other.

Immediately under the orders of the conductor are placed the *assistant-musicians* of the stage, generally eight in number, sometimes six, and rarely nine. Their duties are very numerous and include those of chief of the singing and chorus, prompter, rehearser, and accompanist in charge of those studying their rôles; they are constantly about the stage, some at certain fixed points on the right or left of the curtain, others following the singers, score in hand, whilst keeping out of sight behind the wings and portions of the scenery, constantly guiding the actors, giving them the key, beating time to help them *attack*, seeing that the shifting of the scenery exactly agrees with the musical text, giving the signal for the effects of light, etc., etc. They are the leader's staff officers. Besides this, it falls within their province to play those instruments which are only rarely used, — the large organ in *Lohengrin* and the *Meistersinger*, another, very small (having only four pipes), placed in a corner of the orchestra and serving notably to reinforce the E flat at the beginning of *Das Rheingold*, the Glockenspiel (the Bells), Beckmesser's lute, the thunder, etc., etc. It is needless to say that these important functions, which are so full of responsibility, can only be fulfilled by musicians whose certainty of touch is absolute, and who are entirely calm, collected, and capable of independent initiative. In 1876, Mottl was one of these assistants; later we frequently

SIEGFRIED WAGNER.

find among them the names of Humperdinck, Carl Armbruster, a London organist, Heinrich Porges, and finally, in 1892 and 1894, Siegfried Wagner served his apprenticeship here before assuming the conductorship.

I regret not being able to give the names of all these

great musicians hailing from all parts of Germany, Austria, England, Switzerland, and Russia. In 1876, France was represented in the orchestra by a M. Laurent, at that time a violinist at Montbéliard; in 1896 two Frenchmen took part in the performance, one as first violin, the other as rehearser of rôles and stage assistant; these are: MM. Gustave Fridrich, who was long a first violin at the Opéra and at the Société des Concerts; and Édouard Risler, the young and already great pianist, one of the brightest blossoms of our Conservatoire de Paris, who accompanied on the piano the majority of the stage rehearsals.

These two artists, whose extreme value and devotion Mme. Wagner fully appreciates, have several times been called upon, in company with the greatest singers, to charm her audience of distinguished guests at the Wahnfried *soirées* during the Festival season.

Wagner attached a very great importance to the scenery which he planned himself and which was executed under his orders and after his minute directions by the artist-decorators. The smallest detail did not escape him.

It is easy to understand that in an entirely darkened hall, where the eyes of the spectator are neither dazzled by the footlights nor attracted by any trifling or passing incidents, the expressive force of the scenery is singularly increased. The curtain itself is expressive. It does not rise, as everywhere else; it parts in the middle gracefully, rising towards the top corners with a suddenness or a deliberate majesty according to circumstances, regulated, like everything else, by the scrupulously careful Master who left nothing to run the risks of interpretation. For example, after the terrifying scene with which *Götterdämmerung* ends, the curtain closes as if regretfully, letting us gaze long on the affecting flames of the pyre and the conflagration of Walhalla; whilst it brusquely shuts out the riotous buffoonery in the scenes of the second Act of *Die Meistersinger*, by falling at a single blow as the theatre is flooded with light amidst the joyous laughter of the spectators.

If the Wagnerian scenery is not always of extraordinary richness, if it is more sober than that of the Opéra de Paris, or of the Châtelet, it is, on the other hand, more harmonious, and by this I mean that it harmonizes better with the work, and, so to speak, is incorporated with it; with rare exceptions it succeeds in producing the desired illusion.

Among those that seem to me defective, I will particularly mention that of the Flower-Maidens with its loud and brutal tones and monstrous and improbable blooms, which rather remind one of the hotel wall-decorations of small provincial towns than of flowers of magic and sorcery; the Rainbow of the last scene of *Das Rheingold*, which seems to be made of wood; the tableau of the Venusberg, which has never been a success on any stage, and which, perhaps, it is impossible to realize; the God Loge may be reproached for his extreme parsimony in the matter of the flames which should surround the sleeping Walkyrie on all sides; the Ride may be considered childish. But these are very small details, to which we attach no importance whatever when we are captivated by the subject.

What we may regard with unbounded admiration are the superb pictures of the first and third acts of *Lohengrin*, the Ship and Karéol in *Tristan und Isolde*, almost all the scenery of *Die Meistersinger*, and that one (which perhaps is the most striking of all in its austere sincerity) of the first and third acts of *Parsifal*; in the Tetralogy of *The Ring of the Nibelung*, the first scene of the Prologue,

32

the depths of the Rhine, Alberich's cavern, the Rock of the Walkyries, the Forge, the forest scene by the Rhine, and the two views, interior and exterior, of Gunther's abode with the river in the background. All these are, in truth, splendid, and add not a little to the emotion roused by the music.

Despite all that has been said about it, the machinery is not at all extraordinary; it is that of every well-organized theatre; sometimes, however, it is very ingenious, but always with simple means; thus the scenery in *Parsifal*, which passes first from left to right and then from right to left, giving the spectator the impression that it is he who is moving, is managed by simply rolling up, on vertical cylinders, with varying speed, lengths of scenery placed at different distances on the stage. To avoid closing the curtains at the change of scene there is an ingenious system of jets of vapour rising from the ground and mingling with the clouds painted on gauze, cleverly concealing from the audience what is passing on the stage. The Rhine-Daughters, who seem to be really swimming in the waters, moving with surprising ease, and covering the whole height of the scene, sometimes darting to the very top as if to breathe the air at the surface of the water, are simply lying in a kind of metal case, raised by means of invisible cords by strong workmen moving freely above the stage.[1] At the first rehearsal one of the Undines fainted; however, there is no danger, for each of them is provided with six men commanded by one of the assistant stage-musicians who sees that their evolutions coincide with the music and with the impotent efforts of Alberich, who looks like a St. Bernard the Hermit chasing prawns, or sea-horses, in

[1] This device dates from 1896. The means employed in 1876 was at once more complicated and less ingenious.

an aquarium. The Dragon is the ordinary fairy-stage contrivance ; a man makes him open his jaws and roll his eyes, while the actor (Fafner), standing behind the scenery at the back, bellows and roars into an immense speaking-trumpet.

The stage business is quite different to ours. The actors play much less to the audience than to each other ; they look at each other when they speak ; they are not afraid of turning their backs on the audience when occasion demands, witness Parsifal, who stands in this attitude in the foreground without moving during half of the first act : they behave on the stage as they would do in real life, without seeming to be conscious of an audience in front of them. This is so natural to them that it does not seem at all remarkable to us ; but if one of them happens to differ and act in the conventional manner, addressing his gestures and words to the audience, we are immediately astonished and shocked. When there is a chorus, moreover, the members do not arrange themselves symmetrically in two rows, drawn up like soldiers in line, or in a half-circle, exactly facing the audience and raising their arms all together like automata at the loudest note. Each one has his individual part, he plays, sings, and acts it, and the result is a feeling of truth and life that is infinitely more satisfying.

Wagner, then, had long put in practice the system of natural stage action tried of late years at the Théâtre-Libre in Paris by a French comedian, — a system, which, most happily, tends more and more to be generally adopted.

The men's costumes are generally very beautiful ; those of the women do not lend themselves to splendour so readily as the brilliant armour of the Knights. With the exception of the martial equipment of the Walkyries, a few rich female toilettes in *Lohengrin*, and the betrothal toilettes of Eva and Isolde, Queen of Cornwall, the heroines, by their very character, are not intended to make a parade of elegance.   Let us note in passing that Freïa's adornment, in *Rheingold*, was copied in detail from one of the most graceful figures in Botticelli's *Spring*.

The expenses are very considerable ; to give only one example, the cost of staging *Der Ring des Nibelungen* in 1896 amounted to 800,000 francs ($160,000), spread over two years' work.

I would inform those who are astonished at this expense that the scenery alone (that of 1876 having been lost), cost 155,000 francs ($31,000), 35,000 francs ($7,000) of which went for the clouds alone ; and the scenery is not all ; there is its maintenance and machinery, the maintenance of the theatre itself during the off years ; the costumes, the lighting, for which a special electrical plant has been established near the theatre ; then there are the travelling and lodging expenses for all the artists, singers, soloists, members of the chorus, instrumentalists, etc.

Finally, here, as in every other theatre, there is a number of persons who are never seen by the spectator, but who are necessary for working the scenery and machinery, for lighting and dressing ; here they are· in detail :

On the stage :
- 2 head scene shifters.
- 2 assistant shifters.
- 28 working shifters (from Dresden, Carlsruhe, Darmstadt, etc.).
- 45 carpenters.
- 10 joiners.
- 10 ordinary workmen.

- 1 chief of the light effects.
- 3 assistants.

- 1 chief of the general lighting.
- 5 assistants.

At the electric plant :
{
1 chief engineer.
2 working electricians for running the dynamos.
2 ordinary workmen.
}

{
1 head tailor.
4 tailors.
5 *couturières*.
12 dressers (when *Tristan* or *Lohengrin* is played, and there are sometimes 250 people on the stage, the number of dressers is increased to 80).
1 chief hairdresser.
1 chief female hairdresser.
4 hairdressers.
}

Total :   140 to 220 persons.

Adding together the actors, dancers, and chorus who may be on the stage (sometimes 250), the orchestra with its full complement of 11 horns and 8 harps (125), and the stage assistants (220) we arrive at a grand total of 603 as the respectable effective of the little army gathered directly or indirectly under the command of the Conductor.

There is no bell to announce the end of the *entr'acte*. When the time has come, a band of trumpets and trombones furnished by the regiment in garrison at Bayreuth, but in civilian costume, comes out of the theatre and sounds a loud flourish to the four cardinal points in succession. Like all the rest, the *motive* for these calls have been regulated by Wagner himself. They are always taken from the work being played and announce one of the *motive* of the act about to commence. Here is the full list :

TANNHÄUSER   ACT I

THE HUNT

Trumpets in C

ACT II

BEGINNING OF THE MARCH

ACT III

MOTIV OF PARDON

LOHENGRIN

ACT I

THE KING'S CALL

ACT II

THE MYSTERY OF THE NAME

Act III

THE GRAIL

TRISTAN UND ISOLDE   Act I

FRAGMENT OF THE YOUNG SAILOR'S SONG

Act II

DEATH

ACT III

FRAGMENT OF SADNESS — MOTIV
OF THE SHEPHERD

DIE MEISTERSINGER   ACT I

DIE MEISTERSINGER

ACT II

THE SERENADE

ACT III

FANFARE OF THE CORPORATIONS

DIE TETRALOGIE DER RING DES NIBELUNGEN

DAS RHEINGOLD

INCANTATION OF THE THUNDER

DIE WALKÜRE   ACTS I AND II

THE SWORD

ACT III

THE SWORD

SIEGFRIED · ACT I

CALL OF THE SON OF THE WOODS

ACT II

VARIATION OF THE CALL OF THE SON OF THE WOODS

ACT III

SIEGFRIED GUARDIAN OF THE SWORD

DIE GÖTTERDÄMMERUNG · ACT I

CURSE OF THE RING

ACT II

CALL TO THE MARRIAGE

ACT III

WALHALLA

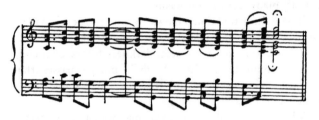

PARSIFAL

ACT I

THE EUCHARIST

ACT II

PARSIFAL

THE EUCHARIST   THE LANCE

The number of trumpeters varies in accordance with the importance of the *motiv* that serves as the call, and according to whether it is presented with or without its harmony; for the last calls of *Lohengrin* and *Götterdämmerung*, which are given with exceptional pomp, there are as many as 24 musicians.

The "three traditional blows" are not struck. When in obedience to the orders of the herald-trumpeters everyone has returned to his seat, darkness follows, bringing with it complete silence. A whole minute passes thus in profound reflection, and then the first sound issues from the orchestra.

That is dignified, solemn, and majestic, and commands respect.

We have now ended this study of the Theatre of Bayreuth and its arrangements. I hope that the reader has taken as much interest in reading it as I myself have experienced pleasure in gathering together the materials.

I have thought it necessary to enter into many details, some of which may seem idle to some people, but not to all; in my opinion, nothing is insignificant when we are dealing with an organization that is so wonderfully comprehensive and complete.

I have been able to demonstrate how easy and agreeable is the short necessary journey, and to describe the courteous and welcome reception one is sure of receiving

ANTON SEIDL.[1]

from the Bay.₍ᵤ₎th inhabitants; I have succeeded in broadly sketching the principal periods of the life of the

[1] Anton Seidl (born in Budapest, May 7, 1850), who was invited to conduct *Parsifal* in Bayreuth in 1897, ranks among the greatest of the Wagnerian conductors, not only because of his genius and

creator of all these prodigious marvels, a life so troubled and yet led in a straight line, keeping tenaciously and scholarship, but because he also possessed the correct Wagnerian traditions given to him by the composer himself. A pupil of Hans Richter, he became Wagner's musical secretary in 1872, was one of his musical stage-directors for the Festival of the *Ring* in 1876, and lived at Wahnfried for six years on the most intimate terms with Wagner. Wagner confided to him the task of arranging the greater part of the first vocal score of *Parsifal*. He conducted the *Nibelungen Ring* in Berlin in 1880, in London in 1881, and introduced this work in Königsberg, Dantzig, Brussels, Amsterdam, Karlsruhe, Darmstadt, Stuttgart, Hanover, Venice, Bologna, Rome, Turin, Trieste, Budapest, and other European cities, with the greatest success. In 1885 Mr. Seidl came to New York to become conductor of the Metropolitan Opera House. Under his direction were represented for the first time in America : *Die Meistersinger*, Jan. 4, 1886; *Tristan und Isolde*, Dec. 1, 1886 ; *Siegfried*, Nov. 9, 1887 ; *Die Götterdämmerung*, Jan. 25, 1888; and *Das Rheingold*, Jan. 4, 1889. Mr. Seidl conducted the Wagnerian operas in London in 1897, and was to have conducted two cycles of the *Nibelungen Ring* at Covent Garden in June, 1898. Almost the last words he ever wrote were the following, which he sent to me on March 26, for this book, in which he took much interest. I quote verbatim : —

"The *Parsifal* conductors of 1897 : Anton Seidl, the 1st, 5th, 6th, 7th, and 8th performances ; Felix Mottl, the 2d, 3d, and 4th performances ; Hermann Levi doesn't conduct any more ; Siegfried Wagner conducted (1897) the second and third cycles of the *Nibelungen Ring*; Hans Richter conducted only the first cycle of *The Ring of the Nibelungen* (1897). The list in 1897 of *Parsifal:* Amfortas, Carl Perron ; Titurel, Wilhelm Fenten ; Gurnemanz, Carl Grengg and Carl Wachter; Parsifal, Van Dyck and Grüning ; Klingsor, Fritz Plank ; Kundry, Marie Brema and Miss Mildenburg."

In 1890 Anton Seidl became conductor of the New York Philharmonic Society and held this post at the time of his greatly deplored death, which occurred suddenly in New York on March 28, 1898. Although Seidl's fame will rest chiefly on his Wagnerian work, it is only just to the memory of this exceptionally great musician to say that his interpretations of Bach and Beethoven would alone have placed him among the greatest conductors the world has ever produced. His insight into the score, his loyalty to the composer, his repose, and his peculiar magnetic temperament, which communicated itself alike to the orchestra and to the audience, made him unique among orchestral leaders. — E. S.

unswervingly towards the unique goal he finally attained; I have been able to furnish a twofold analysis which seems to me capable of serving as a guide to the neophyte and facilitating his comprehension of the pure Wagnerian style, at least when he hears it for the first time; I have, moreover, been able to make the reader acquainted with the details of the inner mechanism of the Festival-Theatre and its Model Performances, in which everything is combined at once by art and knowledge to minister to the delight of the ear, the eye, and the intellect; but what I must despair of expressing, because it is inexpressible, is the profound and lasting emotion which springs from the entire surroundings of an interpretation thus conceived and prepared. We may hear Wagner everywhere else under apparently satisfactory conditions with some of the same interpreters, or even with interpreters who are superior, if you will; but nowhere else do we live the lives of the characters of the drama or identify ourselves with them in the same manner, nowhere else are we bound as by a spell — and what a sweet spell! — by the dramatic and musical action.

He who has had the privilege of hearing and enjoying a fine Bayreuth performance of *Parsifal*, the Tetralogy, or *Die Meistersinger* departs with the delightful sensation of having been morally elevated.

For lack of means of comparison there is only one way to form any idea of this salutary and quasi-magnetic fascination, and that is to pay a personal visit to Bayreuth; no description, however ardent and enthusiastic, can take the place of the journey.

" *He who would understand the poet must visit the country of the poet.*" We can thoroughly understand Wagner only by going to Bayreuth, just as we can understand Raphael only by visiting the museums of Italy.

BIBLIOGRAPHY

CATALOGUE OF THE MOST IMPORTANT BOOKS PUBLISHED IN FRENCH ON RICHARD WAGNER AND HIS WORK.[1]

I head the list with Wagner's own writings. The others are classified alphabetically according to authors. The asterisk indicates those to which I have been most largely indebted.

R. WAGNER. Art et Politique. (Bruxelles. *J. Sannes*, 1868.)

R. WAGNER. Le Judaïsme dans la Musique. (Bruxelles. *J. Sannes*, 1869.)

*R. WAGNER. L'Œuvre et la Mission de ma Vie, trad. Hippeau. (*Dentu.*)

*RICHARD WAGNER. Quatre Poèmes d'opéras (Le Vaisseau Fantôme, Tannhæuser, Lohengrin, Tristan et Iseult) précédés d'une lettre sur la musique, avec notice de Charles Nuitter.
Nouvelle édition. (*A. Durand et fils* et *Calmann-Lévy*, 1893.)

BAUDELAIRE. Richard Wagner et Tannhäuser à Paris. (1861.)

*CAMILLE BENOIT. Richard Wagner, *Souvenirs*, traduits de l'allemand. (*Charpentier*, 1884.)

CAMILLE BENOIT. Les Motifs typiques des Maîtres Chanteurs. (*Schott.*)

LÉONIE BERNARDINI. Richard Wagner. (*Marpon et Flammarion.*)

*LOUIS-PILATE DE BRINN' GAUBAST et EDMOND BARTHÉLEMY. La Tétralogie de l'Anneau du Nibelung. (*E. Dentu*, 1894.)

*LOUIS-PILATE DE BRINN' GAUBAST et EDMOND BARTHÉLEMY. Les Maîtres Chanteurs de Nürnberg. (*E. Dentu*, 1896.)

*HOUSTON STEWART CHAMBERLAIN. Le Drame wagnérien. (*Léon Chailley*, 1894.)

COMTE DE CHAMBRUN et STANISLAS LEGIS. Wagner, avec une introduction et des notes, illustrations par Jacques Wagrez (2 volumes). (*Calmann-Lévy*, 1895.)

---

[1] There is a general catalogue of all the writings published on Wagner, entitled *Katalog einer Richard-Wagner-Bibliothek, Nachschlagebuch in der gesammten Wagner-Litteratur.* — 3 vols., Leipzig, 1886–1891.

CHAMPFLEURY. Richard Wagner. (1860.)
GUY DE CHARNACÉ. Wagner jugé par ses contemporains. (*Lachèze et Cie*, Angers.)
ERNEST CLOSSON. Siegfried de Richard Wagner. (Bruxelles, *Schott frères.*)
CHARLES COTARD. Tristan et Iseult. Essai d'analyse du drame et des Leitmotifs. (*Fischbacher*, 1895.)
THÉODORE DURET. Critique d'Avant-Garde. (1869.)
DWELSHAUVERS. R. Wagner. (*Bibliothèque Gilon*. Verviers, 1889.)
DWELSHAUVERS-DERY. Tannhæuser et le Tournoi des Chanteurs à la Wartbourg. (*Fischbacher*.)
*ALFRED ERNST. Richard Wagner et le Drame contemporain. (*Calmann-Lévy*.)
*ALFRED ERNST. L'Art de Richard Wagner. (*Plon, Nourrit et Cie*, 1893.) 1er volume (paru), L'œuvre poétique; 2me volume (annoncé), L'œuvre musicale.
ALFRED ERNST et POIRÉE. Tannhäuser (*Durand et fils.*)
EDMOND EVENEPOEL. Le Wagnérisme hors d'Allemagne (Bruxelles et la Belgique). (*Fischbacher*, 1891.)
FLAT (PAUL). Lettres de Bayreuth.
FUCHS (Mme). L'Opéra et le Drame musical, d'après l'œuvre de Richard Wagner. (1887.)
GASPERINI (A. DE). La Nouvelle Allemagne musicale: Richard Wagner.
*JOHN GRAND-CARTERET. Wagner en caricatures. (*Larousse*, 1891.)
MARCEL HÉBERT. Trois Moments de la pensée de Richard Wagner (*Fischbacher*, 1894.)
MARCEL HÉBERT. Le Sentiment religieux dans l'œuvre de Richard Wagner. (*Fischbacher*, 1895.)
EDMOND HIPPEAU. Parsifal et l'Opéra wagnérien. (*Fischbacher*, 1883.)
ADOLPHE JULLIEN. Mozart et Richard Wagner à l'égard des Français (1881).
*ADOLPHE JULLIEN. Richard Wagner, sa vie et ses œuvres. (1886.)
M. K. (Maurice Kufferath). Richard Wagner et la 9me symphonie de Beethoven. (*Schott*, 1875.)
M. KUFFERATH. Parsifal de Richard Wagner. (1890.)
M. KUFFERATH. L'Art de diriger l'orchestre. Richard Wagner et Hans Richter. La Neuvième Symphonie de Beethoven. (1891.)
*MAURICE KUFFERATH. Le Théâtre de R. Wagner. De Tann-hæuser à Parsifal. (*Fischbacher*, 1891.)
*MAURICE KUFFERATH. Lettres de R. Wagner à Auguste Rœckel. (*Breitkopf et Härtel*, 1894.)
PAUL LINDAU. Richard Wagner. (*Louis Westhauser*, 1885.)
CHARLES DE LORBAC. Richard Wagner. (1861.)
CATULLE MENDÈS. Richard Wagner. (1886.)

Mᵐᵉ ÉMILIE DE MORSIER. Parsifal et l'idée de la Rédemption. (*Fischbacher*, 1893.)

GEORGES NOUFFLARD. Richard Wagner d'après lui-même. (1885.)

JACQUES D'OFFOEL. L'Anneau du Nibelung et Parsifal, traduction en prose rythmée exactement adaptée au texte musical allemand. (*Fischbacher*, 1895.)

HIPPOLYTE PRÉVOST. Étude sur Richard Wagner, à propos de Rienzi. (1869.)

M. DE ROMAIN. Étude sur Parsifal. (*Lachèze et Cᶦᵉ*, Angers.)

M. DE ROMAIN. Musicien-philosophe et Musicien-poète. (*Lachèze et Cᶦᵉ*, Angers.)

ÉMILE DE SAINT-AUBAN. Un pèlerinage à Bayreuth. (*Albert Savine*, 1892.)

CAMILLE SAINT-SAENS. Harmonie et Mélodie.

*ÉDOUARD SCHURÉ. Le Drame musical. (1886.)

GEORGES SERVIÈRES. Richard Wagner jugé en France. (*Librairie illustrée.*)

ALBERT SOUBIES et CHARLES MALHERBE. L'Œuvre dramatique de Richard Wagner. (*Fischbacher*, 1885.) — Épuisé.

ALBERT SOUBIES et CHARLES MALHERBE. Mélanges sur Richard Wagner. (*Fischbacher*, 1892.)

CHARLES TARDIEU. Lettre de Bayreuth. L'Anneau du Nibelung. Représentations données en 1876. (*Schott*, 1883.)

ELIZA WILLE, née SLOMAN. Quinze Lettres de Richard Wagner, traduites de l'allemand par *Auguste Staps*. (Bruxelles, *veuve Monnom*, 1894.)

HANS DE WOLZOGEN. L'Anneau des Nibelungen, l'Or du Rhin, la Valkyrie, Siegfried, le Crépuscule des Dieux. *Guide musical.* (Paris, Delagrave.)

*LA REVUE WAGNÉRIENNE. 1ʳᵉ année, du 8 février 1885 au 8 janvier 1886; 2ᵉ année, du 8 février 1886 au 15 janvier 1887 (très rare.)

TRISTAN UND ISOLDE

In 1886, 1889, 1891, and 1892.

	1886	1889	1891	1892
CONDUCTORS:	Hermann Levi. Felix Mottl.	Hermann Levi. Felix Mottl. Hans Richter.	Hermann Levi. Felix Mottl.	Julius Kniese. Hermann Levi. Felix Mottl. Carl Mück. Hans Richter.
CHORUS-MASTERS:		Julius Kniese. Heinrich Porges.	Julius Kniese. Heinrich Porges.	
REHEARSERS and assistant stage-managers:	Heinrich Porges. Carl Franck. Felix Weingaertner. Armbruster. Oscar Merz. Albert Gorter. Wirth. C. Harder.	Carl Armbruster. Otto Gieseker. Eng. Humperdinck. Oscar Merz. Hugo Röhr. Heinrich Schwartz. Arthur Smolian. Richard Strauss.	Carl Armbruster. Albert Gorter. Eng. Humperdinck. Otto Lohse. Oscar Merz. Paumgartner. Hugo Röhr. Hans Steiner. Richard Strauss.	Carl Armbruster (director of music on the stage). Kurt. Hösel. Eng. Humperdinck. Oscar Merz. Carl Polig. Heinrich Porges (chorus-master). Max Schilling. Siegfried Wagner.
Tristan.	Heinr. Gudehus. Heinr. Vogl. Herrn. Winkelmann.	Heinrich Vogl.	Max Alvary.	Heinrich Vogl.
King Mark.	Gustav Siehr. Wiegand.	Franz Betz. Eugen Gura.	Georg Döring. Heinr. Wiegand.	Georg Döring. Eugen Gura.
Kurwenal.	Plank. Scheidemantel.	Franz Betz. Anton Fuchs.	Fritz Plank.	Fritz Plank.
Melot.	A. Grupp.	A. Grupp.	A. Grupp.	Heinr. Zeller.
A shepherd.	W. Guggenbühler.	W. Guggenbühler.	W. Guggenbühler.	W. Guggenbühler.
A young sailor.	Halper. Kellerer.	A. Dippel. Seb. Hofmüller.	Heinr. Scheuten.	Georg Anthes.
A pilot.	Schneider.	W. Gerhartz.	Rudolf Pröll.	Georg Hüpeden.
Isolde.	Thérèse Malten. Amalie Materna. Rosa Sucher.	Rosa Sucher.	Rosa Sucher.	Rosa Sucher.
Brangäne.	Gisela Staudigl. Sthamer-Andriessen.	Gisela Staudigl.	Gisela Staudigl.	Gisela Staudigl.
	Chorus of 31 men.	Chorus of 55 men.	Chorus of 53 men.	Chorus of 61 men.

DIE MEISTERSINGER

In 1888, 1889, and 1892.

	1888	1889	1892
CONDUCTORS:	Hans Richter. Felix Mottl.	Hermann Levi. Felix Mottl. Hans Richter.	Julius Kniese. Hermann Levi. Felix Mottl. Carl Mück. Hans Richter.
CHORUS-MASTERS:	Julius Kniese.	Julius Kniese. Heinrich Porges.	Julius Kniese. Heinrich Porges.
REHEARSERS and musician-assistants on the stage:	Heinrich Porges. Carl Franck. C. Armbruster. E. Humperdinck. Bopp. Oscar Merz. Singer. Max Schlosser. Alfred Steinmann. Kienzl.	Carl Armbruster. Otto Gieseker. Eng. Humperdinck. Oscar Merz. Hugo Röhr. Heinrich Schwartz. Arthur Smolian. Richard Strauss.	Carl Armbruster (director of music on the stage). Kurt. Hösel. Eng. Humperdinck. Oscar Merz. Carl Pohlig. Heinrich Porges (chorus-master). Max Schilling. Siegfried Wagner.
Hans Sachs.	Fritz Plank. Theodor Reichmann. Carl Scheidemantel.	Franz Betz. Eugen Gura. Theodor Reichmann.	Eugen Gura. Fritz Plank.
Veit Pogner.	C. Gillmeister. H. Wiegand.	Heinrich Wiegand.	Moritz Frauscher.
Sextus Beckmesser.	F. Friedrichs. B. Kürner.	F. Friedrichs.	Emil Müller. Carl Nebe.
Fritz Kothner.	Emil Hettstädt. Osc. Schneider.	Ernst Wehrle.	Hermann Bachmann.
Walter von Stolzing.	Heinr. Gudehus.	Heinr. Gudehus. Seb. Hofmüller.	Georg Anthes.
David.	C. Hedmondt. S. Hofmüller.		Max Krausse. Fritz Schrödter.
Vogelsang.	Otto Prelinger.	Franz Denninger.	Gerhard Pikaneser.
Nachtigall.	W. Gerhartz.	W. Gerhartz.	Theodor Bertram.
Zorn.	A. Grupp.	A. Grupp.	A. Grupp.
Eislinger.	J. Demuth.	A. Dippel.	F. Palm.
Moser.	W. Guggenbühler.	W. Guggenbühler.	M. Moscow.
Ortel.	Eugen Gebrath.	Eugen Gebrath.	Carl Bucha.
Schwartz.	Max Halper.	Heinrich Hobbing.	Oscar Schlemmer.
Foltz.	Carl Selzburg.	Carl Selzburg.	Adalbert Krähmer.
A night-watchman.	F. Ludwig.	F. Ludwig.	Peter Ludwig.
Eva.	Kathi Bettaque. Thérèse Malten. Rosa Sucher.	Lilli Dressler. Louise Reuss-Belce.	Alexandra Mitschiner. Luise Mulder.
Magdalene.	Gisela Staudigl.	Gisela Staudigl.	Gisela Staudigl.
	Chorus of ?? men	Chorus of ?? men	Chorus of 61 men

PARSIFAL

In 1882, 1883, 1884, 1886, 1888, 1889, 1891, 1892, 1894.

	1882	1883	1884	1886	1888	1889	1891	1892	1894
CONDUCTORS:	Hermann Levi. Franz Fischer.	Hermann Levi. Franz Fischer.	Hermann Levi. Franz Fischer.	Hermann Levi. Felix Mottl.	Felix Mottl.	Hermann Levi. Felix Mottl.	Hermann Levi. Felix Mottl.	Hermann Levi. Felix Mottl.	Hermann Levi. Felix Mottl.
CHORUS-MASTERS:	Julius Kniese.				Julius Kniese.	Julius Kniese. H. Porges.	Julius Kniese. H. Porges.		
REHEARSERS and assistant stage-managers:	Julius Kniese. H. Porges. Oscar Merz. Eng. Humperdinck. C. Franck. Otto Hieber. Stich. Franz Thoms. A. Gorter.	H. Porges. J. Kniese. O. Franck. Otto Hieber. Stich. Franz Thoms. O. Merz. A. Gorter. Eichel.	J. Kniese. H. Porges. Oscar Merz. Eng. Humperdinck. C. Franck. Otto Hieber. Stich. Franz Thoms. A. Gorter.	H. Porges. C. Franck. F. Weingaertner. Armbruster. O. Merz. A. Gorter. Wirth. C. Harder.	H. Porges. C. Franck. C. Armbruster. Eng. Humperdinck. Bopp. O. Merz. Singer. Schlosser. Steinmann. Kienzl.	C. Armbruster. Otto Gieseler. Eng. Humperdinck. O. Merz. Hugo Röhr. H. Schwartz. Art. Smolian. Rich. Strauss.	C. Armbruster. A. Gorter. Eng. Humperdinck. Otto Lohse. O. Merz. Paumgartner. Hugo Röhr. Hans Steiner. Rich. Strauss.	Armbruster (director of the music on the stage). Kurt. Hösel. Eng. Humperdinck. O. Pohlig. H. Porges, director of the chorus of Flower-Maidens. Max Schilling. Siegf. Wagner.	Armbruster. Eng. Humperdinck. Oscar Junger. Fr. Mikoren. C. Pohlig. H. Porges. Ant. Schlosser. Siegf. Wagner.
Amfortas.	Reichmann. Fuchs.	Reichmann.	Reichmann.	E. Gura. Reichmann.	Reichmann. Scheidemantel.	Carl Perron. Reichmann.	Reichmann. Scheidemantel.	J. Kaschmann. Scheidemantel.	Kaschmann. Reichmann. Takáts.
Titurel.	Kindermann.	Fuchs.	Fuchs.	Schneider.	Heinr-Hobbing. Schneider.	Lievermann.	C. Bucha. Fr. Schlosser.	C. Bucha.	Bucha. Wilhelm Fenten.
Gurnemanz.	Scaria. Siehr.	Scaria. Siehr.	Scaria. Siehr.	Siehr. Wiegand.	Gillmeister. Wiegand.	E. Blauwaert. Siehr. Wiegand.	Carl Grengg. Wiegand.	Moritz Frauscher. Carl Grengg.	Carl Grengg. Max Mosel.
Parsifal.	Gudehus. Winkelmann. Jaeger.	Gudehus. Winkelmann.	Gudehus. Winkelmann.	Gudehus. Heinr. Vogl. Winkelmann.	Ernst van Dyck. Ferd. Jäger.	Van Dyck.	Van Dyck. Grüning.	Van Dyck. Grüning.	Birrentovan. Doeme. Van Dyck. Grüning.
Klingsor.	Hill.	Pegela.	Plank.	Plank. Scheidemantel.	Plank. Scheidemantel.	Anton Fuchs. Lievermann.	Liepe. Plank.	Liepe. Plank.	Plank. Popovici.
1st Knight.	Fuchs.	Fuchs.	Kellerer.	A. Grupp.	A. Grupp.	A. Grupp.	A. Grupp.	Gerhäuser.	Gerhäuser.
2d Knight.	Stumpf.	Stumpf.	Wieden.	Schneider.	Wieden.	Wieden.	C. Bucha.	C. Bucha.	C. Bucha.
3d Esquire.	Hubbenet.	Hubbenet.	Hubbenet.	Forest.	Hofmüller.	Dippel. Hofmüller.	Zeller.	Max Wandren.	Scheuten.
4th Esquire.	Mikorey. Keil.	Mikorey. Keil.	Mikorey. Keil.	Guggenbühler. Reuss-Belce.	Guggenbühler. Kaufer.	Guggenbühler. Kaufer. Reuss-Belce.	Schusten. Kleil.	Guggenbühler. Luise Mulder.	Hans Breuer. Luise Mulder.
1st Esquire.	Keil.	Keil.	Keil.	Sieber.	Franconi.	Franconi.	Luise Mulder.	Franconi.	Deppe.
2d Esquire.	Galfy.	Galfy.	Galfy.						
Kundry.	Materna. Malten.	Materna. Malten.	Materna. Malten.	Malten. Materna. Sucher.	Malten. Materna. Sucher.	Malten. Materna.	Mallac. Malten. Materna.	Mailhac. Malten. Mohor-Ravenstein.	Brema. Malten. Sucher.
Flower-Maidens:	Horson. Meta. Keil. Andre. Belce. Galfy.	Herzog. Meta. Horson. Keil. Galfy. Belce.	Herzog. Meta. Horson. Keil. Galfy. Belce.	Fritsch. Forster. Hedinger. Dietrich. Kaufer. Reuss-Belce. Sieber.	Bettaque. Dietrich. Forster. Fritsch. Hedinger. Kaufer. Rigl.	Borchers. Lilli Dressler. Fritsch. Hedinger. Kaufer. Reuss-Belce.	de Anna. Hedinger. Herzog. Kleil. Stolzenberg. Wiborg.	Hartwig. Hedinger. Mitschiner. Mulder. Pfund. Wiborg.	de Anna. Deppe. Holldobler. Krauss. Mulder. Zerrn.
	Chorus of 46 men, 36 women, and 45 children.	Chorus of 46 men, 36 women, 45 children.	Chorus of 46 men, 36 women, and 45 children.	Chorus of 46 men, 36 women, and 45 children.	Chorus of 56 men, 41 women, and 45 children.	Chorus of 55 men, 41 women, and 45 children.	Chorus of 53 men, 46 women, and 45 children.	Chorus of 61 men, 42 women, and 40 children.	Chorus of 65 men, 52 women, and 40 children.